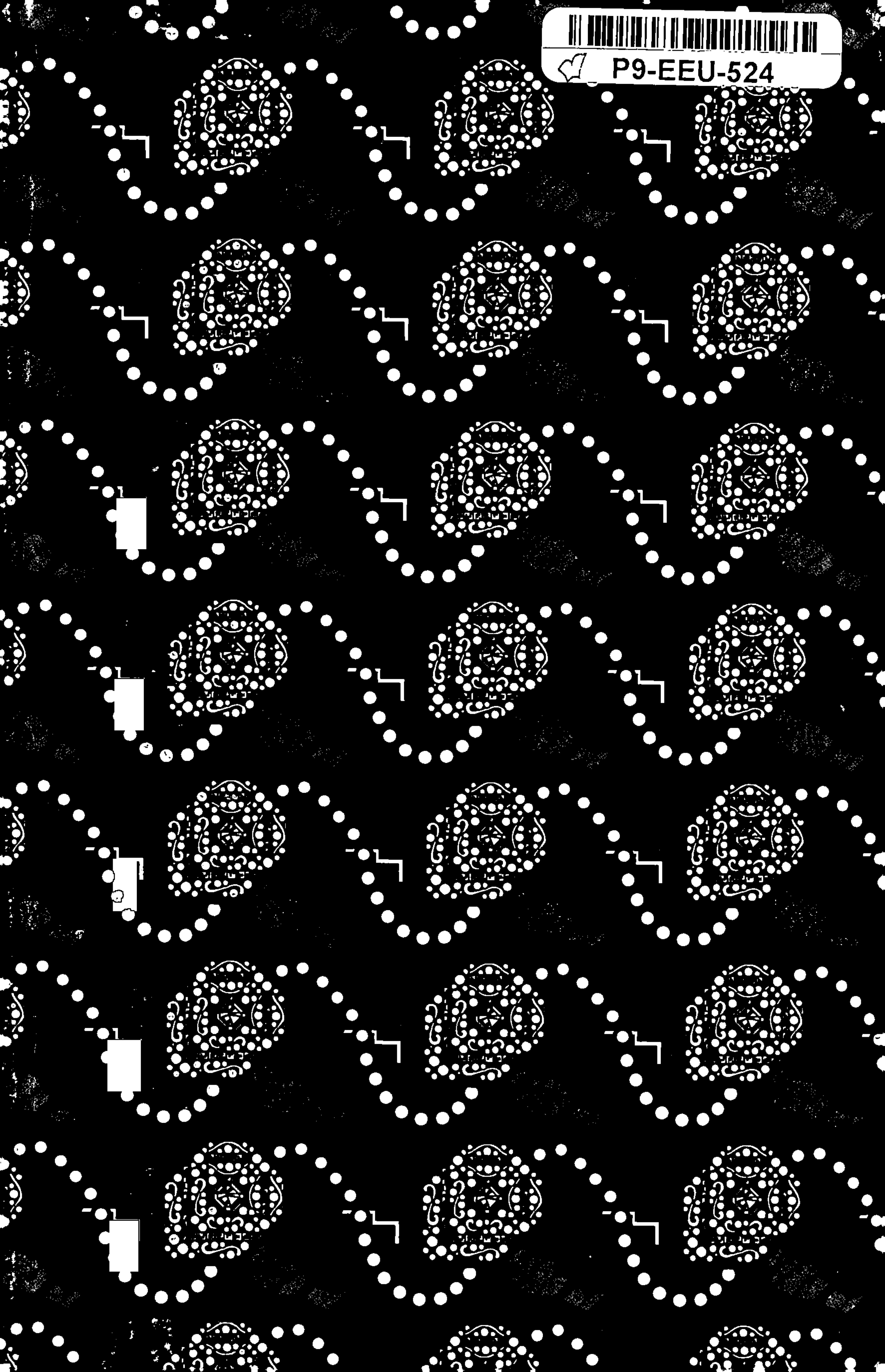
P9-EEU-524

Books by Jude Deveraux

The Velvet Promise
Highland Velvet
Velvet Song
Velvet Angel
Sweetbriar
Counterfeit Lady
Lost Lady
River Lady
Twin of Ice
Twin of Fire
The Temptress
The Raider
The Princess
The Awakening
The Maiden
The Taming
The Conquest
A Knight in Shining Armor
Wishes
Mountain Laurel
The Duchess
Eternity
Sweet Liar

Published by POCKET BOOKS

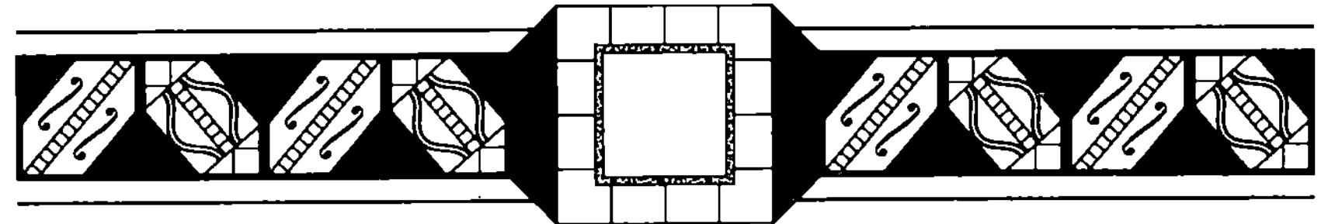

SWEET LIAR

POCKET BOOKS
New York London Toronto Sydney Tokyo Singapore

This book is a work of fiction. Names, characters, places and incidents are either products of the author's imagination or are used fictitiously. Any resemblance to actual events or locales or persons, living or dead, is entirely coincidental.

POCKET BOOKS, a division of Simon & Schuster Inc.
1230 Avenue of the Americas, New York, NY 10020

Deveraux, Jude.
Sweet liar / Jude Deveraux.
p. cm.
ISBN 0-671-68973-8
I. Title.
PS3554.E9273S93 1992
813'.54—dc20 92-8146
CIP

First Pocket Books hardcover printing September 1992

10 9 8 7 6 5 4 3 2 1

POCKET and colophon are registered trademarks of
Simon & Schuster Inc.

Design: Stanley S. Drate/Folio Graphics Co. Inc.

Printed in the U.S.A.

Prologue

Louisville, Kentucky January 1991

"Why would my father do something like this to me? I thought he loved me," Samantha Elliot said to the man who had been her father's lawyer and friend for as long as she could remember. That this soft-spoken man had colluded with her father intensified the hurt and the sense of abandonment that she was feeling.

Not that she needed anything to intensify the pain she already felt. Three hours ago she had stood by the grave of her father and watched with hot, dry eyes as they lowered his coffin into the ground. She was only twenty-eight years old, yet she had already seen more death than most people experience in a lifetime. She was the only one left now. Her parents were gone; her grandparents were gone; and Richard, her husband, might as well be dead, for she'd received the final divorce papers on the day her father died.

"Samantha," the attorney said, his voice soft and pleading. "Your father did love you. He loved you very, very much, and it's because he loved you that he made this request of you." He was watching her closely; his wife had said she was worried that Samantha had not shed a tear since her father had died. "Good," the attorney had said. "She has her father's strength."

"But her father wasn't strong, was he?" his wife had snapped in return. "It was always Samantha who had the strength. And now she's stood by and watched her father shrivel and die before her eyes, yet she's taken it all without a tear."

"Dave always said Samantha was his rock." The lawyer closed his briefcase and left the house before his wife could say anything more, for he was dreading what she was going to say when the contents of David Elliot's will became public knowledge.

Now, watching Samantha as she stood in her father's library, he could feel sweat trickling down his neck as he remembered trying to talk Dave Elliot out of this will, but he'd not been able to persuade him. By the time Dave had made this last will, he weighed ninety-two pounds and could barely speak. "I owe her a chance," Dave had whispered. "I took her life away from her and now I'm going to give it back. I owe her."

"Samantha is a young woman. An adult woman who has to make her own decisions," the lawyer had answered, but he might as well not have said anything for all the attention Dave paid him; his mind was set.

"It's just for one year. That's all I ask of her. One year. She'll love New York."

She'll hate New York, the attorney thought but didn't voice his opinion. He had known Samantha all her twenty-eight years. He'd given her piggyback rides when she was a child, and he'd seen her laugh and play like other children. He'd seen her run races and play tricks on her parents, and he'd seen her pleased with a good grade on a test and crying when she'd not done as well. He'd seen Samantha argue with her mother over the color of a dress or whether she could wear lipstick or not. Until she was twelve years old, she'd been a normal child in every way.

But looking at her now, just a few hours after Dave's funeral, he could see what she had become: She was an old woman in a young woman's body, hiding her beauty under a proper little dark suit that would have suited a woman three times her age. In fact, it seemed that she did everything she could to hide her femininity: She pulled her pretty hair back, she wore little to no cosmetics, her clothes were shapeless, too long, and nondescript. But worse than her outward appearance was the inner

Samantha; for many years now Samantha had rarely smiled, and he couldn't remember when he'd last seen her laugh.

When she did smile, he thought, she was very, very pretty. His mind slid backward, remembering a time a few years ago, before Samantha married, before she left Louisville, when she had come home after a visit to the gym. Dave was in the den on the telephone, and she hadn't known anyone else was in the house. Standing by the sliding-glass patio doors, a glass of iced tea in his hands, the attorney had been about to say hello to Samantha when she removed her wrap and started doing stretches in the living room, her shapely leg with a slim thigh and curving calf propped on the back of the couch. The attorney forgot all about her being the daughter of a friend and had stared in open-mouthed admiration at a young woman that for years he'd thought of as rather plain. Her hair had come loose from its confining band and little coils clung to her face in soft, curling tendrils of spun gold; her skin was rosy from her workout, and her eyes were thick lashed and brilliant blue. He'd never noticed that her lips were so full that they looked almost pouty or that her nose had an impudent little tilt to it. Nor had he noticed that she had a body that should have been immortalized in a magazine spread with curves where they should be and all of her tightly toned.

"They do grow up, don't they," Dave had said from behind him, startling the lawyer, who turned red from being caught gaping at a girl young enough to be his daughter. Obviously, what he had been thinking showed on his face. Embarrassed, he turned away and went outside with Dave.

It was years later, while Dave was preparing his will, that he said that he'd taken all the "juice" out of Samantha. "I've done things to her that a father shouldn't do to a child," he'd said, and the lawyer, all too vividly remembering Samantha's curvy little body in a red leotard, had quickly put away his papers and left the house. He remembered too well that afternoon when he'd felt stirrings of forbidden lust that he should not have for a friend's daughter. Even though Dave was on his deathbed, he didn't want to hear confessions of the type that Dave seemed on the verge of making. He didn't want to hear confessions of what should never happen but all too often did.

Now, the attorney wondered what Dave had done to Samantha—*if* he had done anything—but he was not going to ask, for he was not brave enough to step into a world he'd rather not hear about.

"I don't want to do this," Samantha said, looking down at her hands. "I have other plans."

"It's only for one year," the lawyer answered, repeating Dave's words. "And you'll receive a great deal of money at the end of the year."

As Samantha walked to the window, she put her hand on the brocade curtains. One of the last things she and her mother had done together was choose these curtains, and Samantha remembered looking at hundreds of samples of fabric before deciding on exactly the right color and texture. In the backyard was a tree her grandfather and she had planted when Samantha was a toddler. When she was ten, Granddad Cal had carved a big C+S on the trunk, saying that, this way, they'd be together as long as the tree lived. Turning, she looked around the room, the room that had been her father's, the place where she'd sat on her father's knee, the place she and both her parents had played and laughed together. Richard had proposed to her in this room.

Solemnly, she went to her father's big desk and picked up the rock he had used for a paperweight. On its smooth surface, painted in blue paint in a child's crude lettering, were the words *I love you, Daddy.* She had made the paperweight for him when she was in the third grade.

Two weeks before her father died, while Samantha was nursing him, at a time when she thought they had become the closest they had ever been, he had secretly sold the house and most of its contents. She hadn't thought much about herself in those weeks before her father died, but he had repeatedly asked her what she was going to do after his death. Reluctantly, Samantha had said she'd probably live in the house, take a few college courses, teach some computer classes on the side, and do what other people did who weren't working six days a week as Samantha had been doing for the last two years. Her father hadn't said a word in reply to her answer—but obviously he had not liked her answer.

Samantha put the paperweight down and looked at the attorney. "He gave no reason for selling the house?"

"He said only that he wanted you to spend one year in New York and during that time you were to look for your grandmother. I don't believe he thought she was still alive; I think he meant for you to see if you could find out where she went after she left her family. Your father had intended to search through records himself and see if he could find out what happened to her, but he . . ."

"He didn't have time to do many things he wanted to do," Samantha said, causing the lawyer to frown, for she sounded bitter. "So now I am to search for her in his place?"

The lawyer cleared his throat nervously, wondering how soon he could politely leave. "I don't think he literally meant search, I think he was afraid you'd stay here in this house alone and see no one. I think he thought that since your mother had no relatives and with Dave gone there would be no one left on his side of the family except his mother, if she's still alive, that is, so . . ." He trailed off.

Samantha looked away from the man so he couldn't see her face; she wanted to give away nothing of what she was feeling. Pain—betrayal—as deep as hers was not something she wanted anyone to see. Right now what she wanted most was to be alone. She wanted this man to leave her house, wanted him to close the front door behind him and never open it again. When the house was empty, she wanted to crawl into a warm, dark place and close her eyes and never open them again. How many terrible things could a person live through and still survive?

Pulling a ring of keys from his pocket, the attorney put them on the desk. "These are the keys to your father's apartment. Dave had everything arranged. He was going to take an early retirement and move to New York so that he could search for his mother. He rented an apartment, even furnished it. Everything was ready, but then he decided to go for a checkup and . . . and the cancer was found."

When Samantha didn't turn around, the attorney backed toward the door. "Samantha, again, I am sorry about Dave. I loved the man and I know you did too. And, however it may seem now, he loved you too. He loved you very much and he wanted the best for you, so I'm sure that whatever he did, he did for love of you." He was talking too fast and he knew it. Maybe he ought to offer her something. If nothing else, he should give her a shoulder to cry on, but the truth was he didn't want to hear about pain such as Samantha must be feeling. He felt sorry for the kid—so many deaths in such a short life, but he didn't offer her a shoulder. He wanted to go home now, home to his healthy, smiling wife, and leave this house forever. Maybe Dave was right to have sold it, maybe there were so many bad memories here that only abandonment would clear them away.

"I'm leaving the papers for the apartment on the desk," he said quickly, backing up. "The landlord will give you the keys to the outer door when you get there, and here, on the floor, I left the box of your grandmother's things."

As he put his hand on the knob of the front door, he felt rather like a runner dying for the starting gun to sound so he could get away. "If you need anything else, please let me know. Samantha?"

She nodded, but she didn't turn around when she heard him leave. Instead, she continued to look out at the leafless yard behind her father's house. But not his house anymore. Nor was it hers. When she was growing up, she'd thought that someday she'd raise children in this house, but . . . Blinking a few times to clear her vision, she realized she now had ninety days in which to vacate her childhood home.

Turning, she looked at the packet of papers on her father's desk—the desk that now belonged to someone else. She was tempted to walk away from the entire deal. She could support herself; when it came to that, she very well knew that she could support another person too, but if she didn't do what her father wanted, she would lose all the money he'd left, money from the sale of the house and the money he had saved for years as well as the money he'd inherited from his father. She knew that if she were careful, the money she'd inherit would make her financially independent for the rest of her life, and she could live where she wanted, do what she wanted to do.

But for some reason, her father had decided that before she could have the money she had to spend a year in a big, dirty city looking through musty old files in the hope of finding some trace of a woman who had walked out on her family when Samantha, her granddaughter, was eight months old. The woman had left behind a husband who adored her, a son who loved her, a daughter-in-law who missed her, and a granddaughter who would someday need her desperately.

Turning, Samantha picked up the rock paperweight and for a moment she considered throwing the rock through the window. But the impulse was short-lived, and carefully, slowly, she put the rock back on the desk. If her father wanted her to try to find his mother, then that is what Samantha would do. Hadn't she been doing exactly what he wanted for years?

She started to leave the room, but pausing at the door, she turned back, picked up the old-fashioned hatbox her father had left her, the one he had said contained all his mother's effects, and carried it upstairs with her. She felt no curiosity about the box, no desire to look inside it. In fact, Samantha was sure that, all in all, it was better not to think about anything, better not to remember. Better to do than to think, she thought, and right now she had a great deal of packing to do.

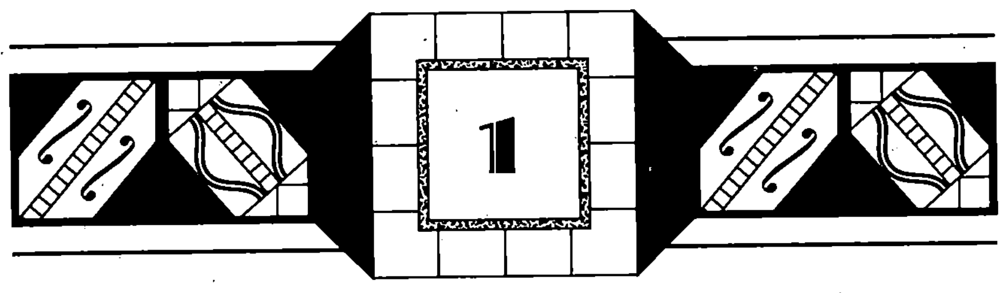

New York
April 1991

Fifteen minutes after Samantha Elliot landed in New York, her wallet was stolen. She knew it was her own fault, because she had reached inside her purse to get a tissue and forgotten to close the zipper, so all the thief had to do was slip his or her hand inside and remove her wallet. One MasterCard, one American Express gone, as well as most of her money. At least she'd had sense enough to put a hundred and fifty dollars in her carryon, so she wasn't destitute.

After she discovered the theft, she had the brand-new learning experience of canceling her credit cards. To Samantha everything that had happened was traumatic: coming to the big, bad city of New York for the first time, being welcomed by a pickpocket, and having to cancel her charge cards. To the bored young woman behind the claims counter, these were all things that happened fifty times a day. Handing Samantha forms to fill out, she pointed to a wall chart with the credit card companies' telephone numbers on them and told her to call them. While Samantha was on the telephone, the woman managed to crack her gum, polish her nails, talk to her boyfriend on the phone, and tell her colleague what she wanted for lunch, all at the same time. Samantha tried to tell the young woman about her lost wallet, tried to tell her that the wallet had belonged to her mother and had a leather lining printed with what her father had called a psychedelic design. But the woman gave Samantha a blank look and said, "Yeah, sure." If the woman hadn't just demonstrated that she had enough intelligence to do several tasks at the same time, Samantha would have thought from the blank expression in her eyes that she was terminally stupid.

By the time Samantha got away from the lost articles department, her suitcase had been locked into a glass-fronted room and she had to find a guard to open it—no mean feat, because no one she spoke to knew who had the key to the room. In fact, no one seemed to know the locked room even existed.

By the time she got her suitcase, pulling it along behind her on a wheeled cart, her carryon slung over her shoulder, she was shaking with exhaustion and frustration.

Now all she had to do was get a taxi, the first taxi she had ridden in in her life, and get into the city.

Thirty minutes later, she was inside the dirtiest automobile she had ever seen. It stunk of cigarette smoke so strongly she thought she might be sick, but when she tried to roll down the window, she found that both of the inside handles of the doors were missing. She would have spoken to the driver, but his name on the paper under the meter seemed to be spelled mostly with x's and k's, and he didn't seem to speak much English.

Looking out the dirty window of the cab, trying not to breathe, she attempted the impossible task of not thinking of anything at all, not where she was, why she was there, or how long she was going to have to stay.

The cab drove under a bridge that looked as though it should have been condemned, then down streets filled on both sides with tiny, dirty-windowed shops. When the driver asked for the address for the third time, Samantha gave it to him yet again, trying not to relay her frustration to him. The paper her father's attorney had given her said the apartment was in a brownstone, located in the East Sixties, between Park and Lexington.

When the driver slowed, looking for the address, she was on a street that seemed quieter and less cluttered than the other areas they had driven through. After the cab stopped, she paid the driver, quickly tried to calculate the tip, then removed her two bags without his help from the floor of the car.

Looking up at the building in front of her, she saw a five-story house that was only two windows wide. It was a very pretty town house, with a tall staircase leading up to a door with a fanlight over it. A wisteria vine growing up the left side of the house all the way to the roof was covered with purple buds just about to burst into bloom.

Samantha pushed the doorbell, then waited. There was no answer. Even after three rings and fifteen minutes, there still was no answer.

"Of course," she said, sitting down on her suitcase. What had she expected? That the landlord would be there to give her a key to the outside door? Just because she had written him and informed him of her arrival time didn't mean he should bother himself to be there to open the door for her. What did it matter to him that she wanted a shower and to sit down on something that wasn't moving?

As she sat on her suitcase waiting for the man, wondering if he was going to show up at all, she speculated about what she would do in a city the size of New York with no place to stay. Could she take a taxi to a hotel and spend the night there? Could she get her father's attorney to wire her more money until she could open a bank account in New York?

Several more minutes went by, but no one came, nor did any of the passersby seem to notice her. A couple of men smiled at her, but she pointedly looked away.

While Samantha was sitting at the top of the stairs, she looked to the side and noticed that at ground level was another door into the house. Maybe that was the front door of the house and she was to knock there.

Not knowing whether it was safe or not to leave her bags on the top of the stoop, she decided to leave them and pray they weren't stolen. Going down the stairs and around them to the ground floor door, she walked around a pretty wrought-iron spike-tipped fence and knocked several times, but there was no answer.

Taking a deep breath, her fists clenched, she looked back up at her suitcases sitting safely at the top of the stairs. Beside the ground floor door was a box of red geraniums, and the sight of the flowers made her smile. At least the flowers seemed happy: They were well cared for, not a dead leaf was on them, the soil was moist but not wet, and the flowers were heavy with bloom.

Still smiling, she started toward the stairs, but just as she rounded the corner, a football came whizzing so close over her head that she ducked. When the flying football was followed by what looked to be a couple hundred pounds of male clad in denim shorts and a sweat shirt with both armholes torn out to the waist, Samantha moved to slam herself flat against the wall of the stairs.

At least she tried to get out of the way of the man, but she wasn't fast enough. He caught the football as it sailed over her head, then, startled, he saw her just as he was about to land on her. At the same time that he released the ball, he reached out to catch Samantha before she fell against the spikes of the fence.

Giving a little gasp as she nearly fell, his hands caught her and pulled her to him in a protective way.

For a moment she stood encircled by his arms. He was taller than her five foot four, probably just at six feet, but the protective way he bent toward her made them almost eye level with each other. They were nearly isolated, with the tall stairs behind them, the next house's stairs not far in front of them, the fence and flower box nearby. Samantha started to say thank you to the man, but as she looked at him, she forgot what she was going to say.

He was an extraordinarily good-looking man, with black, curling hair, heavy black brows, and dark eyes with eyelashes any female would kill for, all atop a full-lipped mouth that looked as though it belonged on a sculpture by Michelangelo. He might have looked feminine if his nose hadn't been broken a couple of times and he didn't have three days' growth of black whiskers on his chin and if his finely sculpted head weren't sitting on top of a body that bulged with muscle. No, he didn't look feminine. All the eyelashes in the world couldn't make this man look less than one hundred percent male. In fact, maleness oozed from him, making Samantha feel small and helpless, as though she were wearing yards of lavender lace. He even smelled male, not the artificial smell that could be purchased in a store; this man smelled of pure male sweat, a little beer, and acres of bronzed skin warmed by sun and exercise.

But it was the man's mouth that fascinated her. He had the

most beautiful mouth she'd ever seen on a human being. It was full and sculptured, looking both hard and soft at the same time, and she couldn't take her eyes off of it. When she saw those lips moving toward her own, she didn't move away. He placed his lips on hers, softly at first, as though asking permission. Samantha, reacting to instinct and need and to something even more basic, opened her mouth slightly under his, and he pressed closer. Had her life depended on it, she couldn't have moved her lips away from his warm, sweet mouth, but when she put her hand up in half-hearted protest, she came in contact with his shoulder. It had been a long time since she had felt male skin near her own. And she had never felt a shoulder such as this one. Hard, firm muscle rounded over the top of his arm, and Samantha's hand curved over the muscle, her fingers digging into the resilient flesh.

When her hand closed over his arm, he leaned closer, his big, hard, heavy body pressing against hers, pinning her close to the wall. Samantha's hand slipped to his back, slipped under his open-sided shirt and met with the contours of the muscle on his back.

A moan escaping her lips, her body began to sink into his.

Putting one big hand behind her head, he turned her to the side and began to kiss her with all the passion she had missed in her life. He kissed her the way she had always wanted to be kissed, had dreamed of being kissed, kissed her the way fairy tales are supposed to end, the way all the books say a kiss should feel—the way no one had ever kissed her before.

As he moved one of his big, muscular thighs between her much smaller ones, Samantha's arms went fully around his neck, pulling him closer, pulling him as close as he could come to her.

Moving his mouth away from hers, he kissed her neck, kissed her ear lobe as his hands moved down her back. Cupping her buttocks in his hands, he moved her so most of her weight was on his thigh, then ran one hand down the length of her leg and lifted it, settling her ankle about his waist.

"Hey Mike, you're drawin' a crowd."

At first Samantha didn't hear the voice, didn't hear anything; she only felt.

It was the man who broke away. Pulling his lips from her

skin, he put his hand to her cheek, caressing her cheek with his thumb while looking into her eyes, smiling at her.

"Hey, Mike, this your long-lost cousin or somebody you picked up on the street?"

Leaning forward, the man gave Samantha one more soft kiss then took her ankle from his waist and held her hand.

It was when he moved away from her that Samantha began to think again. And the first emotion she felt was horror, absolute, sheer horror at what she had done. She tried to snatch her hand from the man's grasp, but he held her fast.

There were three sweaty men who looked as though they wore their cigarettes rolled up in their T-shirt sleeves and drank beer for breakfast standing in front of them, all with leers on their faces, all with smirking expressions, as though they knew something they weren't supposed to know. "You gonna introduce us or not?"

"Sure," the man said, holding onto Samantha's hand in spite of her tugs as he pulled her forward. "I'd like you to meet . . ." Turning, he looked at her in question.

Samantha looked away from him; she didn't want to look in his face again. No mirror was needed to tell her that her own face was brilliant red with embarrassment. "Samantha Elliot," she managed to whisper.

"Oh, yeah?" the man holding her hand said, then looked back at the three men, who were now nudging each other at this new knowledge that Mike didn't know the woman he had moments before been kissing as though he meant to swallow her whole.

"I'd like you to meet my tenant," the man said with a grin. "She's going to be living in my house with me." The pride and delight in his voice came through clearly.

Giving a sharp jerk on her hand, Samantha freed herself from his grip. She would have thought her mortification could not deepen, but at the realization of who this man was, it did. Horror, humiliation, panic, revulsion were all emotions that crowded into her, and she wanted to flee. Or die. Or preferably both.

"Some roommate!" Laughing in a vulgar way, one of the men looked her up and down.

"You wanta live with me, baby, just let me know," the second man said.

"With you *and* your wife," the third man said, hitting the second one in the ribs. "Honey, I'm not married. I'll take real good care of you. Better than Mike would—or could."

"Get out of here!" Mike yelled back good-naturedly, no animosity in his voice, just good humor as he picked up the football and tossed it to them.

One of the men caught the ball, and the three of them went down the street, punching each other and laughing as they walked.

The man turned to her. "I'm Mike." Putting out his hand to shake, he didn't seem to understand when Samantha only stared at him. "Michael Taggert." When she still didn't respond, he began to explain. "Your landlord. You wrote me a letter, remember?"

Not saying a word, Samantha walked past him, careful not to touch him, and went up the stairs. Her luggage was in her hands before he was beside her.

"Wait a minute while I open the door. I hope the apartment's all right for you. I had a crew come in and clean the place and put clean sheets on your bed. I'm sorry I wasn't here when you arrived, but I lost track of the time and—Hey! where are you going?"

A suitcase in each hand, Samantha had gone down the stairs and was three houses down the block by the time he got the door unlocked.

Bounding down the stairs two at a time, Mike came to a stop in front of her and reached out to take her bags, but she jerked them away from him, trying to walk around him, but he wouldn't let her pass.

"You're not mad because I was late, are you?"

Giving him a quick, hard glare, Samantha again tried to move around him. After three pivots and his blocking of every one of them, she turned and started walking in the other direction, but he blocked her that way too. Finally, she stopped and glared at him. "Would you please let me pass?"

"I don't understand," he said. "Where are you going?"

Intelligent stupid people, she thought. Was this city full of them? Still glaring at him, she said, "Mr. Taggert, I am going to find a hotel."

"A hotel? But I have your apartment ready for you. You haven't even seen it yet, so you can't dislike it. It's not me, is it? I told you I was sorry I was late. I'm not usually late, but my watch got wet last week and it's in the shop and I couldn't tell what time it was. And those bozos I was with probably couldn't tell time if they had a watch and could figure out how to buckle it on."

Giving him a look that was meant to wither him on the spot, Samantha moved around him.

He wasn't to be put off so easily as he stepped back in front of her and started walking backward. "It's the guys, isn't it? Pretty crude, aren't they? I apologize for them. I only see them when I want to toss a ball around with someone and at the gym. I mean, I don't see them socially, if that's what's worrying you. You won't have to see them in our house. I promise."

Halting for a moment, Samantha had to marvel at the man. How could he be so very beautiful and understand so very little? She forced herself to look away from him. It was his beauty that had gotten her into trouble in the first place.

When she started walking again, he was beside her. "If it's not that I was late and it's not the guys, then what's the problem?" he asked.

At the corner of the block, she stopped. Now what was she to do? she wondered. She had no idea where she was or where she was going, but she saw lots of yellow taxis driving by. In the movies people hailed taxis by standing on the curb and lifting their arms, so she hoisted her tote bag onto her shoulder and raised her arm. Within seconds a taxi came to a halt in front of her. Acting as though this was something she'd done a thousand times, she put her hand on the car door.

"Wait a minute!" Mike said as she started to open the door to the cab. "You can't leave. You've never been in the city before, and you don't know where you're going."

"I am going as far away from you as I can get," she answered, not looking at him.

Mike's face was the embodiment of surprise. "But I thought you liked me."

With a gasp of exasperation, Samantha started to get into the cab.

But Mike stopped her by taking her suitcase, then her arm, both of which he held firmly. "You're not leaving," he said; then, glancing into the cab at the driver, he said, "Beat it."

The driver took one look at Mike, at the muscles bulging on

his body, most of them exposed by the skimpy clothing he was wearing, and asked no questions, not even waiting for Mike to slam the door before he sped away.

"All right," Mike said quietly, as though talking to a skittish horse. "I don't know what's going on, but we're going to talk about it."

"Where? In your house? The house where I'm supposed to live with you?" Samantha asked angrily.

"Is that what this is all about? You're mad at me because I kissed you?" Giving her a slow, soft smile, his voice lowered significantly. "I rather thought you liked my kissing you," he said, stepping closer to her.

"Get away from me." She took a step backward. "I know this is a city that's not supposed to care, but I imagine someone will pay attention if I start screaming."

At that Mike stepped back and looked at her. She was dressed in a prim little "outfit"—that's the only word he could think of to describe what she had on—of navy blue. It was a very plain dress with a skirt that reached below her knees and a jacket with a white collar and cuffs. Somehow, that boring little dress managed to completely hide every curve of her body. If Mike hadn't just had his hands all over her and hadn't felt for himself what an incredible body she had, he would have thought she was as straight as a stick. When he'd kissed her, he'd found his hand at the small of her back, atop what seemed to be a rather deliciously curved fanny, and he'd run his hand down the length of her, over the lovely curve of her bottom, down firm, perfect thighs, down to her ankle and her slim little foot. He would have taken odds on it being impossible to hide a body like hers under any amount of clothing, but somehow she had done it.

Looking at her face, he saw that she was a cross between pretty and cute, but she wore very little makeup, as though she meant to detract from her prettiness rather than enhance it, and her hair was pulled tightly back from her face. He could tell her hair was long, and the way she wore it made it look absolutely straight, but a wisp had escaped from the band at the back and the stray strand curled along her cheek. Remembering his thumb pulling that strand loose, Mike now wished he could touch it again.

Looking at her now, it was difficult to believe that this was the woman he'd kissed, for there was no sexiness in her face or her body. Actually, in her prim little dress, her blonde hair pulled back in a neat and utterly tidy bun, he would have thought she was the mother of a couple of children and taught Sunday school. If he had passed her on the street, he wouldn't have looked twice at her. But he remembered vividly that he'd seen her looking very different a few minutes ago. The lusty, desirable, hungry beauty who had kissed him was in there somewhere.

When he had leaped around the stairs to catch the football, he had nearly trampled her, and out of instinct, he had caught her before she fell against the spikes of the railing. He had opened his mouth to ask if she was all right, but when he had looked into her eyes, he'd not been able to say a word, for she was looking at him as though she thought he was the best-looking, sexiest, most desirable man in the world. Mike had known since he was a kid that he was attractive to girls and he'd used his looks whenever possible, but no woman had looked at him as this one had.

Of course he had to concede that maybe he had been looking at her in much the same way. Her big, soft blue eyes had been filled with surprise and desire, looking at him from over a small, pert nose that was set atop a mouth so full and lush that he thought he might die from wanting it so much.

He'd kissed her, at first not sure if he should, because he didn't want to do anything to scare her away, but the moment his lips touched hers, he knew he couldn't stop himself, knew he couldn't hold back. No woman had ever kissed him as this one did. It wasn't just desire he felt coming from her, but hunger. She kissed him as though she'd been locked in a prison for the last ten years and now that she'd been released, he was the man she wanted most in the world.

Right now Mike didn't understand what was going on with her. How could she kiss him like that and ten minutes later look at him as though she detested him? For that matter how could this proper little lady be the same enchantress who'd wrapped her leg around his waist?

Mike didn't have answers, nor did he understand anything that was going on, but he knew one thing for certain: He couldn't let her get away from him. He *had* to find out what was making her want to get away from him. For his part he'd like to pick her up and carry her back to his house and keep her there, maybe forever. But if she wanted something from him first, like maybe for him to climb to the heavens, pick up a dozen or so stars, string them together, and hang them in her bedroom, he thought he would like to know so he could start tying ladders together.

"I apologize for whatever I did to offend you," he said, although he didn't mean a word of it. All he could remember was her ankle on his waist.

Samantha narrowed her eyes at him. "Is that supposed to make me believe you?" Taking a deep breath, she tried to calm down, for she was aware that they were beginning to draw the attention of the people on the street.

"Couldn't we go somewhere and talk about this?" he asked.

"Your house maybe?"

Missing the sarcasm in her voice, Mike thought that was a fine idea but didn't say so.

"There's nothing to talk about."

This time there was no missing her insinuation that she believed his house to be a den of sin. Mike took a deep breath. "We'll go back to the house, sit on the stoop—in plain sight of all of New York—and talk about whatever the problem is. Later, if you still want to leave, I'll help you find a hotel."

Samantha knew she shouldn't listen to him; she should hail another cab and find somewhere to spend the night.

"Look, you don't even know where you're going, do you? You can't get into a cab and say, 'Take me to a hotel.' Not any more. You don't know where you'll end up, so at least let me call and make a reservation for you."

Seeing her hesitation, Mike took the opportunity to start walking toward his house, hoping she'd follow her suitcase and tote bag. Not wanting to press his luck with the headway he'd made with her, he didn't say any more as he walked, moving slowly, but stopping now and then to make sure she was following him.

When he reached the town house, he carried her bags to the top of the stairs, set them down, and turned to her. "Now, you want to tell me what's wrong?"

Looking down at her hands, Samantha knew that she was very tired from the long, exhausting day. For that matter, it had been a long, exhausting year. "I think the problem is obvious," she said, trying not to look at him because he had on so very little clothing. While he stood there leaning against the rail, he reached inside the old sideless sweat shirt he wore to scratch his chest, and Samantha saw a stomach covered with washboard muscle. When he said nothing, she spoke again, this time intending to make herself very clear. "I do not plan to live in the same house with a man who will spend his time chasing me all over the place. I am in mourning for my father, I have just ended my marriage, and I do not want more complications."

Perhaps Mike shouldn't have taken offense at her words, but she made him sound like a dirty old man who couldn't keep his hands off the luscious young girl. Resisting the temptation to point out that he had by no means forced himself on her, he was also tempted to tell her that all they had shared was a kiss, nothing more, and that there was no reason to act as though he were a convicted rapist who'd just tried to molest her.

"All right," he said in a cold tone. "What are the rules?"

"I have no idea what you're talking about."

"Oh yes you do. Anybody who dresses as you do must live by rules, lots of them. Now tell me what your rules are."

At that Samantha picked up her tote bag and reached for her suitcase, but putting his hand on it, he wouldn't let her have it.

"All right," he said again, this time with a sigh of defeat. "I apologize again. Couldn't we start over?"

"No," she said. "It's not possible. Would you please release my bag so I can leave?"

Mike wasn't going to let her leave. Besides the fact that he wanted her so badly there was sweat running down his chest even though it was a cool day, there was his promise to her father. He was aware that she knew nothing about how close he had been with her father, didn't know that Dave and Mike had spent quite a bit of time together until Dave had told him Samantha was coming home. After that announcement Dave had confined their friendship to letters, which had been sent to the attorney, because for some reason, Dave hadn't wanted Mike and Samantha to meet, at least not while Dave was alive. Then, two days before Dave died, he had called Mike, although by then Dave had been too weak for Mike to hear all of what he had to say, but Mike had understood the essence of it. Dave had said he was sending Samantha to him in New York and he had asked

Mike to take care of her. At the time Mike hadn't felt he'd had any other choice, so he'd given his word that he'd protect her and watch out for her. But so far, Mike didn't think these last few minutes were what Dave had in mind.

Mike looked down at Samantha's two bags. "Which one has your overnight things in it?"

Samantha thought that was a very odd question, but then the last few minutes had been the oddest of her life.

Not waiting for her answer, he picked up her tote bag and opened the door to the house. "Five minutes, that's all I ask. Give me five minutes, then ring the bell."

"Would you please give me back my bag?"

"What time is it now?"

"Quarter after four," she answered automatically after a glance at her watch.

"Okay, at twenty after ring the bell."

Shutting the door behind him, he left Samantha standing alone on the stoop, half of her luggage missing. When she pressed the doorbell, there was no answer. She was tempted to take her large case and leave, but the fact that her remaining money was hidden in her tote bag made her sit down on her suitcase and wait.

Trying not to think of her father, trying not to ask herself why he had done this to her, and especially trying not to think of her husband—correction, ex-husband—she forced herself to look at the sidewalks and the street before her, forced herself to look at the people, at the men dressed in jeans and the women in outrageously short skirts. Even in New York, the air seemed to be full of the laziness of a Sunday afternoon.

This man, this Michael Taggert, had said he wanted to start over, she thought. If she could, she'd like to start her life over, like to start from the morning of the day her mother died, because after that day nothing in her life had ever been the same. Today, having to be here, was part of all the pain and trauma that had started that day.

Looking at her watch again, her first thought was that maybe she could pawn it, but the watch had cost only thirty dollars new, so she doubted that she could get much for it. Noticing that it was twenty-five after four, she thought that maybe, if she rang the bell now, Michael Taggert would answer and maybe he'd give her back her bag so she could find a place to stay. The sooner she got started on this year-long sentence the sooner she could get out of this dreadful city.

Taking a deep breath, smoothing her skirt, making sure her hair was tightly in place, she put her finger on the doorbell.

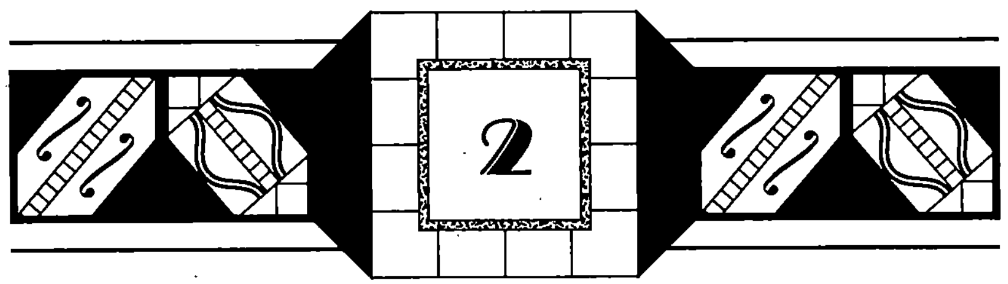

When the man opened the door promptly at Samantha's ring, she stood for a moment blinking at the change in him. He was wearing a clean blue dress shirt, partly unbuttoned but still neat, a loosened silk tie, dark blue tropical weight wool trousers, and perfectly polished loafers. His thick growth of black whiskers was gone and the black curls of his hair had been tamed into a conservative, neatly parted style. Within minutes he had gone from resembling the sexy, rather dangerous leader of a gang of hoodlums to looking like a prosperous young banker on his day off.

"Hello, you must be Miss Elliott," he said, extending his hand. "I'm Michael Taggert. Welcome to New York."

"Please give me back my bag." She ignored his outstretched hand. "I want to leave."

Smiling, acting as though she hadn't spoken, Mike stepped aside. "Won't you please come in? Your apartment is ready for you."

Samantha did not want to enter this man's house. For one

thing, she found it disconcerting that he could change his looks so quickly and so completely, that within minutes he could go from looking like a muscle-bound jock who'd never done anything more intelligent than memorize a few football plays to looking like a young professor. If she had met this man first, she wouldn't have guessed what he was really like. As it was now, she wasn't sure which man was the real one.

When Samantha saw her tote bag at the foot of the stairs, she stepped inside the house to get it, but as her hand touched the handle of the case, she heard the door close behind her. Turning toward him in anger, her lips were tight, but his glance didn't meet her eyes.

"Would you like to see the house first or just your apartment?"

She didn't want to see either, but he was standing in front of the door, blocking her exit, as big as a boulder in front of a cave entrance. "I want to get out of here. I want—"

"The house it is, then," he said cheerfully, as though she'd answered positively. "The house was built in the twenties, I don't know the exact year, but you can see that the rooms have all the original moldings."

Refusing to move away from her bag, she stood where she was.

But Mike forced her to participate, however reluctantly, as he put his hand on her elbow and began to half pull, half push her out of the foyer, propelling her toward the living room. She saw a large room, with big, comfortable-looking black leather chairs and a couch strewn about, a rough, hand-woven carpet on the floor, folk art from all over the world tastefully scattered about the room, as well as two enormous palm trees in the corners by the windows. Several masks hung on the walls, as well as Chinese tapestries and Balinese paintings. It was a man's room, with dark colors, leather, and wooden objects—the room of a man of taste and discrimination.

The room didn't look much like a bordello as she would have thought from her first impression of him. In fact, the man beside her, the one wearing the banker's clothes, looked more at home in this room than the jock she had first met.

Aware that Mike was looking at her face, she sensed that he seemed to be pleased with what he saw, because the pressure on her arm lessened. Reluctantly, but with less anger, she followed him from room to room, seeing a dining room with a large table from India and a magnificent cinnabar screen against one wall, then a powder room papered with Edwardian caricatures.

Relaxing more every minute, she was shown a library paneled in oak with floor-to-ceiling shelves filled with books. She was impressed by the sheer number of books until she saw that, as far as she could tell, all the books dealt with American gangsters: their origins, biographies, even books on the economics of being a gangster. Looking away from the books with a grimace of disgust, she saw in the corner of the room, near a big desk heaped with papers, large white cartons labeled with the names Compaq and Hewlett Packard. Surprise showing on her face, she turned to look at him.

"Your rent," he said in answer to her silent question. "A whole year's rent is in those boxes, and I have no idea what to do with the damn things."

"I could—" Samantha stopped herself, knowing she was feeling a computer aficionado's heartfelt lurch at seeing powerful computer equipment sitting unused in boxes. It must be how a doll collector would feel at seeing boxes in an attic labeled, "Great-Granny's dolls" and not being allowed to open the boxes.

"You wouldn't by chance know which end of a computer to use, would you?" he asked innocently, knowing full well that she was a whiz with computers. He'd bought what Dave Elliot, in one of his letters, had told him Samantha said he should buy.

"I know a little about them," she said vaguely, slowly turning away from the boxes.

Leading her upstairs, he showed her two bedrooms, both of them decorated with plants and art from around the world, one of them furnished with wicker chairs with pillows printed with ivy vines.

"You like it?" he asked, not attempting to control the eagerness in his voice.

Samantha smiled before she caught herself. "I do like it."

When he grinned in response to her assertion, Samantha almost felt her breath leave her. He was even better looking when he smiled like that, such a smile of pleasure, untainted by any other emotion. Feeling that it had suddenly become very, very hot in the room, she started toward the door.

"Want to see your apartment now?"

Looking away from him, looking at anything but him, she nodded.

She followed him up the stairs to the third floor. When Michael opened the door to the first room, Samantha forgot all about New York and this man who unsettled her, for she could feel her father in this room. Her father had always said that if he had to start from scratch, he would decorate his house in green and burgundy—and this living room had been made for her father. A dark green couch had been placed at an angle to a green marble fireplace, with two big, comfortable-looking green-striped chairs across from the couch, all of them set on an Oriental rug handwoven in colors of green and cream. Around the room were pieces of dark mahogany furniture, not one piece having spindly legs that would make it easy for a man to knock over.

Walking to the mantel, Samantha saw several framed photos of her family: her mother, her parents together, her paternal grandfather, and herself from infancy to one year ago. Tentatively, she picked up a silver-framed photograph of her mother and, holding it, she looked about, closing her eyes for a moment. The presence of her father was so strong in the room she almost expected to turn and see him.

Instead, when she turned, she saw a stranger standing in the doorway—and he was frowning at her.

"You don't like it," Mike said. "This room's not right for you."

"It's perfect for me," Samantha said softly. "I can feel my father here."

Mike frowned harder. "You can, can't you?" As he spoke, he looked at the apartment with new eyes, seeing that it wasn't a room for a pretty blonde female. This was a man's room. Specifically, it was David Elliot's room.

"The bedroom's through here." As Mike walked behind Samantha, he saw every corner through different eyes. His sister had decorated these rooms as well as the ones downstairs. At the time, Mike had bragged to Dave that all you had to do was tell his sister what you wanted the finished product to look like and she could do it. Dave had said he wanted his apartment to look like an English gentleman's club, and that's what it looked like. Now Samantha looked as out of place amid the dark colors as she would have in an all-male club.

In the bedroom the walls were painted dark green and the windows leading onto a balcony were hung with curtains of green-and-maroon-striped heavy cotton velvet. The bed was a four-poster with no canopy, and the linens were printed with plaids and sporting dogs. Watching, he saw Samantha lovingly run her hand over the comforter. "Did my father ever stay here?"

"No," Mike said. "He did everything by mail and telephone. He was planning to come here, but—"

"I know," she said, looking at the dog prints on the wall. Being in this room was almost as though her father weren't dead, almost as though he were still alive.

Mike showed her a wine safe next to the bedroom, then two bathrooms done in dark green marble, a sitting room with red and green plaid chairs and bookshelves filled with the biographies her father loved. On the fourth floor was a guest bedroom, and a study with a heavy oak desk and French doors opening onto a balcony. Opening the doors, she stepped out and saw the garden below.

She had not expected a garden in New York—certainly not a garden such as this one. In fact, looking at the lush green lawn, the two tall trees, the shrubs about to burst into bloom, and the beds of newly set annuals, she could almost forget she was in a city.

Turning back to look at Mike, her happiness showing on her face, she didn't notice his frown. "Who takes care of the garden?"

"I do."

"May I help? I mean, if I were to stay here, I'd like to help in the garden."

His frown gave way to a slight smile. "I would be honored," he said and should have been pleased by her words, but for the life of him he couldn't figure out what was bothering him. He wanted her to stay, but now he was almost wishing she wouldn't, and his ambivalence had something to do with the way she moved about the rooms—Dave's rooms. Something about the way she was still gripping that photo of her mother to her breast made him want to tell her to leave.

"Would you like to see the kitchen?"

When Samantha nodded, he went to the west side of the room and opened a door, exposing a narrow, dark stairway leading downward. "It's the servants' stairs," he explained. "The house hasn't been remodeled into apartments, so you and I will have to share a kitchen."

She looked at him sharply.

"You don't have to worry about me," he said, annoyed that once again he was defending himself. Maybe he should give her a police statement that swore to his clean record, swore he wasn't a rapist or a murderer or had ever had so much as a speeding ticket. "I know less about kitchens than I do about computers, so you won't be running into me in there very often. I can work a refrigerator and that's about it. Even toasters confuse me."

Saying nothing, she continued to look at him, letting him know that she was far from convinced of his good intentions.

"Look, Sam, maybe the two of us got off on the wrong foot, but I can assure you that I'm not a . . . a whatever you seem to think I am. You'll be perfectly safe here with me. Safe from me, that is. All your doors have good, sturdy locks on them, and I don't have keys to the locks. Your father had the only set. As for sharing the kitchen, if you want, we can set a schedule for use. We can arrange our whole lives around a schedule if you want, so we don't have to see each other at all. Your father paid me a year's rent in advance, so I think you should stay here. Besides, I've already spent the rent money on that pile of metal downstairs, so I wouldn't be able to refund your money."

She wasn't sure what to answer, whether to say she'd stay or not. Of course she shouldn't stay, not after the way they'd met, but right now she could feel her father's presence more strongly than she could remember this man's touches. Maybe she shouldn't stay here with him, but could she leave the second home her father had created? She had lost her home in Louisville with all those memories and all those ghosts, but here she could feel the beginning of new memories.

Reluctantly, she put the photo of her mother down and started walking down the stairs, all the way to the ground floor where the kitchen was. For all that this man said he knew nothing about cooking, someone did, for the pretty, spacious, blue and white kitchen looked to be well equipped and highly usable.

She started to ask questions, but then she looked toward the end of the kitchen across a charming little breakfast room and saw the double glass doors leading into the garden. Turning away from him, leaving the kitchen behind, she went out the doors and into the garden. As backyards go, the space wasn't very large, but it was surrounded by an eight-foot-tall solid wooden fence, so the yard was private and secluded. Upon closer inspection, she could see that the garden was prettier than it had seemed from the fourth-floor balcony, with pink climbing roses just budding, growing over the fence. They were the old-fashioned full-blown fragrant roses that she had always loved, not the modern tight scentless roses.

Turning, she smiled at Mike. "You have done a beautiful job."

"Thank you," he said, seeming to be truly pleased by her praise.

As she inhaled the fragrance of the roses and thought about the rooms upstairs—her father's rooms—she whispered, "I'll stay."

"Good. Maybe tomorrow I could show you a few places to buy furniture. I'm sure you'll want to change the rooms, since they're not exactly what a female would want. My sister is an interior designer, and I can get things wholesale through her so—"

Turning toward him, her face was stern. "Mr. Taggert, thank you so much for your offer, but I want to make myself clear from the start. I am not looking for a friend, a lover, or a tour guide. I have a job to do in this city and when it's finished I'm leaving, and between now and then I have no desire to . . . start anything. Do you understand?"

Looking at her with one eyebrow raised, he let her know he did indeed understand. "I understand perfectly. You don't want anything to do with me. Fine. Your keys are on the kitchen countertop, one for the front door, another for the deadbolts inside your apartment. Your father wanted the locks in his apartment keyed alike so he'd have only one key to bother with."

"Thank you," she said, walking past him toward the kitchen.

"Samantha," he said as she passed him. "I have a request."

She didn't turn around. "What is it?" she asked, bracing herself.

"We're going to be seeing each other now and then in passing, especially in the kitchen, and I'd like to ask you . . ." His voiced lowered. "If you should come downstairs at night or early

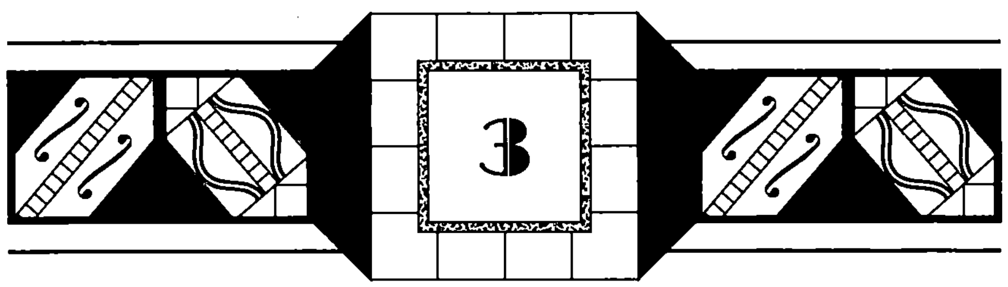

On her first night in New York, Samantha slept in a bed chosen by her father, and the trauma of the day was somewhat softened. But when she awoke, she felt worse than she had when she went to bed, because the full reality of her situation hit her. In Louisville, in her father's house, she'd been all right, but now she was in a strange place, surrounded by strangers. Never in her life had she been alone before. Not really, truly alone, for she'd had her parents, her grandfather, then her husband.

Hearing a noise outside, she got out of bed and went to the window to look out into the little graden below. The man, her landlord, was watering his plants, and the moment Samantha moved the curtain, as though he'd heard her, he turned and waved, making Samantha jump away from the window, flinging the curtain back into place.

Not only was she alone, she thought, but she was surrounded by predators. The image came to her of being lost at sea, bobbing in the ocean with a life preserver about her waist, watching an ocean liner filled with happy, laughing people who were having too good a time to hear her cries for help—and sharks were circling her. At the moment, the sharks seemed to be in the form of one Michael Taggert.

After she showered and dressed, she pulled her hair back from her face and waited until she heard the front door open and close before venturing down the stairs. Pausing at the front door of the town house, she dawdled, not wanting to go outside. In fact, she wished she didn't have to leave the house at all, but she had to buy food and open an account at a bank so she could have money transferred from Kentucky.

Quite honestly, New York terrified her. Now, peeking out the curtains, there wasn't a story she had ever read or heard about the city that didn't enter her head the moment she stepped outside. All over the world New York was used as a bogeyman for adults. When something dreadful happened in any other town in America, people said things like, "This place is getting as bad as New York," or "At least this isn't New York." Well this *was* New York and she had to go out into it all alone.

What happened when one walked alone in the city? she wondered. Through the door glass she could see women walking past the town house, some of them with dogs on leashes, some of them in long, tight black suit jackets with tiny skirts below. None of them seemed to be terrified.

Taking a deep, fortifying breath, she finally opened the door, closed and locked it behind her, then went down the stairs, walked to the end of the block, and took a left. Reading the green street sign, she saw she was now on Lexington Avenue. As she walked north along the block, she saw a grocery with outdoor bins of fruit and vegetables, a shoe store, a dry cleaners, a branch of the Bank of New York, a tiny video rental store, a delicatessen that had freshly baked breads and pastries in the window, and a bookstore.

Within two hours she had opened her account at the bank and bought groceries, fresh flowers, and a paperback novel—and she'd done it all without so much as crossing a street. She went back to the corner, took a right, and went straight back to the town house where she put her key in the front door lock, opened it, closed the door behind her, then leaned against the door, giving a great sigh of relief. She had just made a foray into the city of New York all alone and she had returned safely. She hadn't had a knife held to her throat, hadn't had her purse snatched, nor had anyone tried to sell her drugs. Right now she felt as though she'd climbed a mountain, planted a flag on top, and returned home to tell the story.

After putting the groceries away, she made herself a bowl of cereal and a pot of herbal tea, took a cranberry muffin from the bakery bag, put it all on a tray, and took it into the garden.

As she sat in the garden, lounging on one of the chaises, she stretched and wiggled her toes. Perhaps she should have felt lonely, but instead of feeling lonely, she thought how wonderful it was to have no duties or responsibilities. Sometimes it seemed to her that she had been taking care of people all her life. When she had been married, there had never been a minute to herself, for her husband was *always* needing something. If he wasn't hungry, he was asking her to help him find something, or he needed clean clothes or someone to listen to him describe how miserable his life was.

At that thought Samantha tightened her mouth. Altogether, it was better not to think about her ex-husband and his "writing."

"I see you made it to the grocery."

At the sound of the voice, Samantha nearly jumped out of her skin, then immediately went from lounging in the chair to sitting upright, her feet on the ground, her hands in her lap. She did not look up at him.

"Did you have any trouble?" Mike asked, looking down at her, annoyed that she seemed convinced that he was an ax murderer with uncontrollable sexual urges.

"No, none," she said, standing, then starting back into the house.

"You don't have to leave because I'm here." His annoyance was evident.

She didn't look at him. "No, of course I don't have to leave. I have things to do, that's all."

Frowning, Mike watched her go back into the house, knowing that she was leaving to avoid being near him.

Samantha went to the rooms her father had chosen, the rooms that reminded her of him, the rooms that made her feel safe, settled down in a dark green chair, and began to read her book. She had all day in which to do exactly what she wanted to do, in fact, she had a whole lifetime before her in which to do what she wanted to do. All she really had to do was serve her sentence in New York, then she'd be free.

For the next few weeks Samantha enjoyed her freedom with the delight that only one who has not had freedom can enjoy it. Not since her mother died had she had time to sit and read or to just be still and daydream. When she was a child, she used to take long bubble baths, but she had only had time for showers since her mother's death. Looking down the road at her future life, she saw that she'd at last have time to read all the books she'd ever wanted to read and time to take up a hobby as soon as she found one she liked. Time to do anything and everything.

Each morning she awoke and looked about her father's room and smiled, craving the feeling of his being so close and having the prospect of a long, empty day before her. She made a list of books she wanted to read. There were many biographies in her father's library, and she started on a biography of Queen Victoria that must have weighed four pounds.

She didn't leave the town house unless she had to go to the grocery, otherwise, she had everything she needed right in the house. There was a washer and dryer off the kitchen; there was the garden; she had a VCR and exercise videos; she had books; she had a television with cable; she had time. There was no reason to leave the house unless she had to.

The only disturbing element in her lovely, peaceful life was her landlord. He was true to his word in that he didn't bother her. In fact, for the first two weeks of her stay, she might have been living in the house alone, but of course Samantha went to great lengths to avoid him. She would have liked to get to know his habits so she could avoid seeing him at all, but as far as she could tell, he had no set schedule to his life. Sometimes he left the house early in the morning, sometimes he didn't leave until afternoon, and sometimes he didn't leave at all. On the days when he didn't leave, Samantha had difficulty avoiding him, for he always seemed to decide to come to the kitchen whenever she went downstairs for food, so she had to run up the stairs to keep from seeing him.

On the days when he was out, she sometimes walked through his rooms, for there was no door shutting them off from the rest of the house. She didn't touch anything of his, she just looked, reading the titles of his books about gangsters, but nothing interested her. He wasn't a very tidy person, for he seemed to leave his clothes on the floor where he took them off, but on Wednesdays a rather pretty young woman came to the house to clean. She picked up all his clothes, washed them, and put them away. On one Wednesday, Samantha heard the telephone ring then the front door slam, and she knew the young woman had left early.

Going downstairs, Samantha saw that the dryer was full of clothes and the dining room table was littered with dirty dishes. Without conscious thought of what she was doing, she began to clean the room. When the dryer buzzer went off, she folded his clothes, took them to his bedroom, and put them away, telling herself all the while that she was free and if she wanted to do this she could. Besides, her landlord would never know who had done the work.

It was at the beginning of the third week that Samantha found out about New York delivery services. As she was carrying three bags of groceries out of the store, one of the employees suggested that she have them delivered; after all, the delivery was free. All she had to do was tip the delivery boy a couple of dollars. For that matter, if she was very busy, she could call the store and tell them what she wanted, and they'd deliver her order. Samantha thought this was a marvelous idea, because now she wouldn't have to leave the apartment at all. First thing the next morning, she went to the bank and withdrew five hundred dollars in cash, knowing that the money would enable her to stay in the house for a long time.

When she returned to the town house, glad as always that it was empty, she breathed a sigh of relief and thought about what she wanted to do. Reminding herself that she was free, she knew she could do anything. With that thought, she popped herself some popcorn, went back to bed, and watched videos. But the videos her father had were all intellectual treatises on the lives of various bugs and birds, so after a while she fell asleep. How wonderful to be able to sleep in the afternoon, she thought, for surely a nap was one of life's great luxuries.

When the sound of laughter awakened her at twilight, she got out of bed, went to the window, and looked into the garden, where her landlord seemed to be having a party. He was cooking steaks on an outdoor grill—and Samantha could see he was doing it incorrectly, piercing the meat as he turned it—and drinking beer with a half dozen nicely dressed people.

As always, he seemed to sense when she was watching him, for abruptly, he turned and waved his arm, beckoning to her to come down and join them, but Samantha stepped back into the room and drew the curtain closed. Putting a CD on the player, she sat on her father's chair and picked up a book—she was now reading a five-pound biography of Catherine the Great. When the laughter from downstairs became louder, she turned up the music. All of her father's CDs were of old blues singers, music from the twenties and thirties, mournful songs sung by people like Bessie Smith and Robert Johnson. It wasn't music that Samantha would have chosen, but she was beginning to like it since it was what her father liked.

As the third week ran into the fourth, Samantha found that what she really wanted to do most was sleep. It had always seemed to her that since she was twelve and her mother had died, she had never had enough time for sleep. There had always been school and household chores and other people's needs to see to. Then, after she'd married, she'd had to prepare three meals a day and work eight to twelve hours a day six days a week. Now it seemed perfectly feasible that her tiredness would be catching up with her, and she was glad for the time to rest.

When she was in Louisville, she hadn't been able to bear giving all of her father's clothes away, so she'd boxed some of them and mailed them to New York. She found that it made her feel closer to him to wear his shirts over her jeans; she liked sleeping in his pajamas, and she especially liked his heavy flannel bathrobe.

By her fourth week in New York, Samantha was feeling very relaxed. It was amazing how much she could sleep; sometimes she didn't wake until ten in the morning, when she'd go downstairs to get a bowl of cereal, but sometimes she didn't eat anything. When she did eat, instead of cleaning up after herself, she discovered that she could leave her dirty dishes in the sink and the young woman who came on Wednesdays would clean them. Samantha was glad of that because, quite honestly, she felt too tired to do much cleaning.

Every day by noon she was feeling sleepy again, so she didn't bother to take off her father's pajamas. In fact, it began to seem like too much effort to bathe and put on clean clothes, after all, she couldn't be too dirty since she did little more than sleep. When she tried to read a book about Elizabeth I, she could hardly keep her eyes open.

Several times over the weeks she heard laughter in the garden, but she no longer got up to see what was going on. And her landlord no longer disturbed her. A few times she'd seen him in the kitchen, but she just smiled sleepily at him and went back upstairs, no longer running to get away from him.

Putting the book on the bedside table, she turned off the light. It was only seven in the evening and it was full daylight outside, but she was too sleepy to stay awake. As she fell asleep, she thought that as soon as she was rested, she'd finish the book and all the others in the apartment, but right now she wanted to sleep.

Looking across the picnic table in the back garden at Mike, Daphne Lammourche knew it didn't take a genius to see that he was upset about something. Usually Mike was cheerful, always making jokes, and usually he came close to eating his weight in meat, but tonight he was pushing his steak around on his plate as though he weren't hungry.

Daphne didn't know why he'd invited her tonight, but then maybe it was because she'd pretty much invited herself because she was "between jobs" at the moment, as people put it so politely. The last club where she'd worked had hired a new manager, a greasy little creep who thought it was Daphne's honor to be allowed to do things to his body. When Daphne had declined the honor, she'd been fired as a result. She had a bit of money saved, and she knew she'd be okay until she got another job, but until then she knew Mike was good for a meal.

"You okay?" she asked.

"Sure, fine," he said, but he was almost mumbling.

Daphne had never seen Mike like this. Usually he was the life of the party, always laughing, always ready to have a good time. With his looks, he always had women falling all over themselves for him, even though, for the most part, Mike remained unaffected by them. Daphne wondered if he had a girlfriend back home somewhere, or for all she knew, maybe he had a steady girl right here in the city. When she saw the girls from the club who worked with her fling themselves at Mike, Daphne felt like telling them to stop wasting their time, because they weren't going to get a guy like Mike.

Daphne was aware that all the girls thought she slept with Mike, and she never told them differently, but she and Mike were just friends.

Daphne had a problem that, unfortunately, she shared with too many women: She desperately wanted a man to love her, but every man who did love her she couldn't seem to care about, so she spent all her time and energy, and often her money, trying to make uncaring, screwed-up jerks love her. When they did nothing but abuse her, she cried on the shoulders of the people who did love her—usually men—that all men were scum—just as her father had been. As for Mike, she thought he was lovely to look at and he always took care of her when yet another of her boyfriends dropped her, but she didn't think of him as a man. Not an actual man, because Mike had never treated her with contempt as the men Daphne was attracted to did.

When Daphne was sober, she laughed about the long list of losers in her life, and when she was drunk, she cried about them. But drunk or sober, she basically understood that the reason she, of all the girls at the club, was invited to this rich house was because she never made a pass at Mike.

"How's your book coming?" she asked.

Mike shrugged. "All right. I haven't worked on it much lately."

Daphne had no reply to that. To her, there was something magic in putting words on paper and having them mean something, so she tried to think of something else to talk about. Feeling the need to try to cheer Mike up was something altogether new—it was usually Daphne crying while Mike laughed and told her she was better off without so and so.

"So how's your tenant?" she asked.

"I guess she's all right. I never see her." He toyed with his food. "I don't think she likes me."

Daphne laughed. "You, Mike? There's a girl on this planet who doesn't like *you?*" When Mike didn't say anything, Daphne kept laughing. "And what do you think of her?"

Mike looked up at Daphne with eyes so hot, eyes that showed such desire, that Daphne, who thought she'd seen everything a man could dish out, leaned away from him and had to take a deep drink of her cold beer before she could speak. "I don't know whether I envy her or I'm afraid for her," she whispered, holding the frosty bottle to her cheek.

Mike looked back down at his plate.

"Have you asked her out?"

"Tried to, but she runs away every time I get within ten feet of her. If she hears me coming, she hits the stairs, and except for meals, she stays in her apartment all the time, never leaves."

"What's she do all day?"

"As far as I can tell, she sleeps," Mike said in disgust.

Daphne took a bite of her steak. "Poor kid. Didn't you tell me her father just died and that she just got a divorce?"

"Yeah, but from what I heard, her husband was no great loss."

"Maybe so, but losing your guy makes you feel rotten. I remember the first time a guy walked out on me. Lord! but I was in love with that man. He was my first and I lived my whole life for him, anything he wanted, I gave it to him." She snorted in memory. "That was when I first started stripping. He said I was so good at it when I did it for him that I ought to make us some money. But even when I did what he wanted, one day I came home and he was gone. No note or nothing. Of course, looking back on it, I doubt if the bum could read and write. Brother! was I depressed after that. I didn't think I had anything to live for after he left me. I managed to drag myself to work for a few days, but after a while I even stopped doing that; just stayed in the apartment and slept. Hell, I'd probably still be sleeping if that man hadn't made me see what a creep the guy was—that he wasn't worth sleeping for."

Mike was only half listening to Daphne's story as her stories tended to depress him. He'd told her once that she could walk into a crowd of a hundred nice guys with one wife-beating scum-of-the-earth hidden among them, and she'd be able to pick out the bad guy within thirty seconds. Daphne had laughed and said that if he was bad enough, she'd have him moved into her apartment and be supporting him within three minutes.

What Mike was thinking about was Samantha. Maybe over the years he'd become spoiled with women liking him, maybe girls had been too easy for him to get. Samantha was a challenge. Since she'd come to New York, he'd tried everything to get her attention, up to and including slipping invitations under her door. He'd "accidentally" met her in the kitchen a few hundred times. He'd even hinted repeatedly that he'd like to learn how to use a computer, but she'd looked at him as though she'd never heard the word before.

For the life of him he couldn't figure her out. There was the prim little miss who hadn't wanted to stay in a house alone with a man; there was the hot tamale who'd kissed him like he'd never before been kissed; and lately there was the grubby little zombie who silently moved about the kitchen wearing her father's pajamas and robe. He rarely heard her footsteps above anymore and when he did see her, she was always yawning, even though she usually looked as though she'd just waked up.

Mike's head came up sharply. "What did you say?"

"I said I missed him so much that I wore only his clothes. I couldn't button his shirt across my chest, but that didn't matter because wearing his clothes made me feel closer to him. If that man—"

Mike came out of his seat. "What man?"

Daphne looked startled. "The man at the hospital. Haven't you been listening to what I've been telling you? I wanted to sleep forever, so I decided to do just that. I took a bottle of pills and woke up in a hospital, and that's where that man talked to me, told me I had to keep on living."

Mike stood looking down at her for a moment, but he wasn't seeing her, because he was beginning to comprehend what Daphne was saying. "Samantha's had a hard time, Mike," he could hear Samantha's father saying over the phone, his voice harsh and weak, heavy with his impending death. "She's had a hard life, and when I'm gone, I don't know what she'll do. I wish I knew my daughter better, but I don't. I don't know what goes on inside her head, but I want to leave this world knowing that she's going to be taken care of. I want you to look out for her, Mike, and I want to make up to her for some of what I did to her. Take care of her for me. There's no one else I can ask."

Mike had experienced the death of his uncle Mike, but that was all—and that was enough. He couldn't actually imagine more death in his life or losing as many people as Sam had. He definitely couldn't imagine what he'd feel like if his father died—or if, like Samantha, his last and only friend and relative died.

Looking up at Samantha's windows, he saw that, as always, the curtains were drawn. No doubt she was sleeping again. Sleeping forever, as Daphne put it.

"You're a poor guardian, Taggert," he said to himself, then turned to look at Daphne.

"Want me out of here, Mike?" she asked as she picked up her purse and started to go back through the house to leave, but at the door she turned back. "You need anything, Mikey, honey, you let me know. I owe you a few favors."

Absently, Mike nodded, but he was looking up at Samantha's windows, and his mind was wholly on his tenant. Two minutes later he was on the phone ordering a meal to be delivered from La Côte Basque.

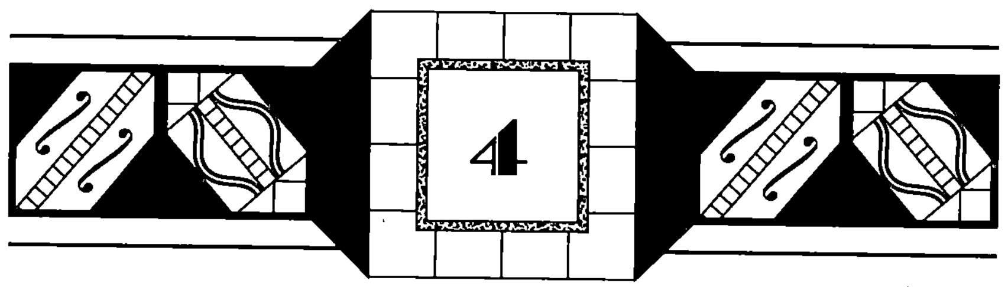

4

Standing outside Samantha's door, Mike took a deep breath, then knocked. He had no idea if what he was doing was right, but he was going to give it his best shot.

She didn't answer his knock, but then, he hadn't actually expected her to; so, balancing the tray in one hand, he took his key out of his pocket, inserted it into the lock, opened the door a crack, and saw that all the lights in the room were out. Raising his eyes skyward, he murmured as he stepped into the room, "Please don't let her be wearing white."

~

Samantha came awake slowly, reluctantly opening her eyes against the bright light and trying to focus. For a moment, she lay in bed blinking at the light, gradually coming awake enough to realize she was seeing her landlord standing over her, a tray in his hands.

"What are you doing in here?" she asked, frowning and pulling herself into a sitting position, but there was no real fear in her voice or even much interest. The truth was, she was so tired her bones ached and nothing could make her feel very much.

"I brought you something to eat," he answered, setting the tray down on the desk by the window. "It's food from one of the best restaurants in New York."

Samantha rubbed her eyes. "I don't want anything to eat." As she came awake more fully, she looked through the living room toward the closed door of her apartment. "How did you get in here?"

Smiling as though it were all a great joke, Mike held up his key.

Samantha pulled the covers up to her neck. With her wakefulness was coming anger. "You lied to me! You said you didn't have a key. You said—" Her eyes widened as she pressed herself back against the headboard. "If you come any closer, I'll scream."

At that moment, an ambulance went down Lexington Avenue, and the ear-piercing screech through the half-open window was so loud it practically made the curtains shake. "Think anyone would hear you?" Mike asked, still smiling at her.

Samantha was now, indeed, beginning to feel, and the panic rising in her showed on her face. Trying to remain calm, she folded the blanket back and started to get out of bed, but Mike caught her arm.

"Look, Sam," he said, his voice pleading. "I'm sorry I somehow gave you the impression that I'm a sex pervert. I'm not. I kissed you because—" With a boyish grin, he stopped speaking. "Maybe we better not go into that. What I want from you is more important than sex. Maybe not nearly as nice, but in the long run, more important. I came in here to talk to you about Tony Barrett. I want you to get me in to see him."

Abruptly, Samantha stopped trying to pull away and looked at him as though he were crazy. "Would you get your hand off of me?"

"Oh, sure," he said. He'd meant only to hold on to her elbow to keep her from running from the room, which she looked like she might do, but instead, he had spread his fingers and was moving his hand up her arm. She was by no means the most desirable-looking woman he had ever seen, because she looked as though she hadn't had a bath in days, her hair was greasy and tangled, there were black circles of fatigue under her eyes, and her lovely mouth had a downward turn to it. But in spite of the look of her, Mike had never in his life wanted to climb into bed with a woman as much as he wanted to with her. Maybe spring was getting to him. Maybe he needed to spend a long weekend in bed with one of Daphne's friends. Or maybe he needed Samantha.

Releasing her, he stepped back from the bed. "I think we need to talk."

When Samantha looked at the bedside clock and saw that it was ten minutes after eleven at night, she took a deep breath. "The first time I met you, you nearly attacked me. Tonight you used a key that you swore you didn't have to unlawfully, not to mention discourteously, enter my apartment in the middle of the night. Now you ask me about a man I've never heard of. And you ask why I should be upset. Mr. Taggert, have you ever heard the word *privacy?*"

"I've heard lots of words," he said, dismissing her comment as though his being in her private apartment meant nothing. Instead of considering her rights, he sat down on the edge of the bed, facing her.

Samantha again started to get out of the bed. "This is intolerable."

"I'm glad to see you're angry. At least that's better than sleeping your life away."

"What I do with my life is none of your business," she snapped as she got off the bed and grabbed her father's robe.

Turning to the tray behind him, Mike lifted the napkin that covered the basket of bread and took out a roll. He bit into the delicious bread, then with his mouth full said, "Don't put on that robe. It's too big for you. Don't you have something girly?"

Giving him a look of disbelief, she defiantly shoved her arms into the sleeves of the big flannel robe. The man really was too much to bear. "I suggest that if you want something . . . girly—what an old-fashioned word—you should go elsewhere."

Her tone, her hostility, not to mention her direct request that he leave had no effect on him as he ate the rest of the roll. "I'm an old-fashioned guy. I wouldn't do that if I were you."

Samantha had her hand on the doorknob, and when he warned her, for the first time she felt fear. With her back to him, her hand on the verge of trembling, she didn't turn to look at him.

"Ah, Sam," he said, annoyance as well as exasperation in his voice, "you don't have to be afraid of me. I wouldn't hurt you."

"Am I supposed to believe you?" she whispered, trying to be calm, trying to hide her fear, but failing. "You lied about the key."

Mike could hear the fear in her voice, and he didn't want her to be afraid of him—that was *last* thing he wanted from her. Slowly getting up from the bed—no sudden movements—he went to her, but she continued facing the door. Very gently, he put his hands on her shoulders, then frowned when she drew her body together, as though to fight off the coming blows. As gently as though she were a wounded animal, he led her to the bed, pulled the cover back, and directed her into it, smiling at her in a way that he hoped was reassuring.

"No," she whispered, her voice almost quivering with fear.

It was obvious that she thought he wanted her in bed so he could more easily attack her—or worse. Never before had any woman thought Mike was a rapist. Never had a woman been afraid of him and he didn't like it, but more importantly, he damned well didn't deserve her fear.

"Oh hell!" Mike said as he pushed her down on the bed where she landed in a tumble of bedclothes. He was sick of being thought of as some sexual deviant who regularly attacked his tenants. Walking away from the bed, he turned back to glare at her. "Okay, Sam, let's get some things straight between us. So I kissed you. Maybe according to your rules I should be hanged for that, or at the very least castrated, but we live in a permissive society. What can I say? We have people selling drugs to children, serial killers, child molesters, and me. I kiss pretty girls who look at me like they want me to kiss them. Unfortunately, the law doesn't punish sickies like me."

Crossing her arms protectively under her breasts, Samantha set her mouth in a tight line. "What's your point?"

"The point is, you and I have work to do and I'm tired of waiting for you to come up for air."

"Work? I don't know what you're talking about."

It took him a minute to realize that she was telling the truth. "Did you read your father's will?"

Anger as well as pain surged through her, but she stamped the pain down. "Of course I read it. I know its contents anyway."

"Then you *didn't* read it." His sense of frustration was building.

"I really wish you would go away."

"I'm not going away, so you can save your breath. I'm tired of seeing you skulk about, not eating, not taking an interest in anything. How long has it been since you left this house?"

"What I do or do not do is none of your business. I don't even know you."

"Maybe not, but I'm your guardian."

Samantha looked at him, opened her mouth to speak, closed it, opened it, closed it again. This man was insane. Guardians were something out of Gothic novels, not real life, and even in novels, guardians were not given to twenty-eight-year-old divorced women. If she could get him out of this room, she was going to pack a bag and leave this house forever.

It was easy for Mike to see in her eyes what she was thinking, and it made him angry. She was going to listen to him if he had to tie her to the bed. Instead of tying her up—she'd no doubt take him to court for that—he picked up the tray of food and set it on her lap. "Eat," he commanded.

Samantha wanted to refuse, but she was too afraid of him not to obey. When she hesitated, he spread something on a piece of toast and held it in front of her mouth. He had an expression on his face that made her think he was capable of holding her nose and forcing her to eat, so Samantha reluctantly opened her mouth. It was pâté de foie gras, one of the most heavenly things she had ever tasted in her life. As she chewed, she relaxed a bit and took the second piece of toast he offered from his hand.

"Now," Mike said, "I'm going to talk and you're going to listen."

"Do I have a choice?" She was on her third piece of toast. Maybe she was a bit hungry after all.

"No. No choice at all. You're not very good at listening, are you? You obviously didn't listen to your attorney when he told you to read your father's will."

"I am an excellent listener and I meant to read it." He was spreading pâté on warm toast nearly as fast as she could eat it.

"Like you meant to take a bath?" He wanted to insult her and make himself believe that she wasn't the sexiest female he'd ever seen. But even when she should have been so unappealing, he had several thoughts about what he'd like to do to her delicious—perhaps that wasn't the right word just now—little body. If she could read his mind, she really would be afraid. He'd like to see that tongue of hers on something besides the piece of pâté that had fallen to her wrist.

"If you don't want to be around me, you could always leave. You have my permission," she said. Now that she was fully awake, now that her fear of him was lessening, she was looking at him. He had on a soft, dark brown cotton shirt and jeans, and he should have looked respectable, but she could see the outline of his chest muscles under the shirt. While he was slathering pâté on bread and handing pieces to her, he was eating just as much as she was, and when he chewed, his lower lip—that beautiful full lower lip—moved. She looked away.

"I'm not going to leave until you've heard everything. When were you planning to start looking for your grandmother?"

That startled Samantha into looking back at him. How did he know about that? "I am an adult and I—"

Mike grunted. "That's what I thought. You had no intention of looking for her, did you?"

"It's not any of your business, is it?"

"It's entirely my business. Did it ever occur to you to wonder who was to check your research? Who was to approve what you'd done and say you'd done enough searching so you'd get the money your father left you?"

Samantha paused with a piece of toast on the way to her mouth and stared at him. No, not one of those questions had entered her mind.

Knowing he had at last piqued her interest, Mike got up, went to the wine safe and took out a cool bottle of white wine. He knew there were several bottles of wine in there because he had put them there in preparation for Samantha's arrival. Now, he had correctly guessed that every bottle would still be there. She may have problems, he thought as he looked in the safe and saw every bottle he'd put in there still sealed, but she was no drinker. Opening the bottle, knowing exactly where the corkscrew was, he took the wine back to her bedroom and poured two glasses full, frowning at the look on her face. "This is not a prelude to a seduction, so you can stop looking at me as though I'm a satyr. Drink it or not, your choice. I'm sure that someone as uptight as you is probably too prudish to do something so wild as drink a glass of wine."

Curling her upper lip at him in a sneer of what she hoped looked like contempt, she took the glass, drained it, then handed it back to him for a refill.

Mike laughed, "A real sailor, are you? Any tattoos?"

Samantha didn't bother to answer him, but she wished she hadn't drunk the wine. She had not eaten very much, and the wine was already going to her head, yet she desperately needed to be alert right now, not fuzzy-headed and relaxed as the wine was making her feel. "Not any tattoos I'm going to show *you,*" she heard herself say, then grimaced, for she had always been the very easiest of drunks. Half a glass of wine and she was dancing on tables—or at least thinking about dancing. It was something about her that had always disgusted Richard, but he had managed to cope with the problem. As always, he figured out a solution to all of Samantha's "problems": Because she had no head for drinking, he didn't allow her to drink.

Looking down at the tray across her legs as he lifted the cover, she saw a fat, succulent steak smothered in sauce. "I don't eat meat," she said, looking away.

"Why not? You don't like it?"

"Where have you been for the last century? Haven't you read the reports on meat? Fat content. Hardening of the arteries. Cholesterol. No fiber."

"Is that all? The air's worse for you than any steak. Eat it, Sam."

"My name is Samantha, not—" She didn't say any more because he shoved a piece of meat into her mouth. When she chewed, she found the flavor to be divine, really truly divine. Continuing to chew, she remembered that she had first given up meat as a way to cut down on their grocery bill.

"Hated that, didn't you?" he said smugly, watching her.

She ignored his comment. "I thought you wanted me to listen to you. Would you say what you have to say, then get out of here?" Cutting another bite of steak, he started to feed it to her as though she were a child or, perhaps, as though they were on far more intimate terms than they were, so she took the fork from his hand and fed herself. He didn't seem to notice the look she gave him when he picked up her salad fork and began helping himself to part of the steak. Samantha tried not to think of the scene: her sitting at the head of the bed, him sprawled across the middle, his head near her knees as they both ate from the same plate.

"Ever hear of Larry Leonard?"

"Yet another person we do not have in common," she said jauntily, pointing her fork at him. She definitely should not have drunk that glass of wine.

"Larry Leonard is—was—a writer of murder mysteries. He didn't write very many of them and they didn't sell well, but they received some critical acclaim because they were so well researched. All of them were about gangsters."

Her mouth was full of steak and she kept sipping on the second glass of wine. "The two of you should have gotten along splendidly as that's all you read about." As soon as she said it, she blushed.

Mike grinned knowingly. "Been snooping, have you? By the way, thanks for putting my clothes away the day Tammy had to leave."

Samantha looked down at her plate so he couldn't see her red face.

"Anyway," Mike continued, "Larry Leonard was actually named Michael Ransome, and he was my honorary uncle, a friend of my grandfather's, and I was named after him. Uncle Mike lived in a guesthouse on my father's land in Colorado, and I spent a lot of time with him when I was a kid. We were . . . buddies," he said softly.

Samantha stopped chewing when she heard the barely concealed pain in his voice, for she understood all too well how it felt to have people you loved die. Reaching out her hand to him, she pulled back before touching him.

Mike didn't seem to notice as he kept eating and talking. "When Uncle Mike died three years ago, he willed everything he owned to me. There wasn't any money, but there was his library of books on gangsters." He smiled at her teasingly. "The books you've seen."

"I'm sure they're your own taste in literature." She speared a cherry tomato before he could take it.

"He also left me work he'd done on a biography of a big-time gangster named Dr. Anthony Barrett."

"The man you think I know."

Raising one eyebrow in praise of her memory, Mike didn't

answer directly but made a stab at the last bite of steak, then just as he was about to eat it, offered it to her.

Samantha almost took it, but then shook her head. "I really wish you would finish this story and leave." The intimacy of this shared meal was not something she wanted to continue.

Removing the last cover from the tray, Mike revealed a deep dish of chocolate mousse. Samantha started to refuse, but it looked so rich and dark and creamy that before she knew what she was doing, she had dipped her spoon in it at the same time that Mike dipped his.

"Where was I?" he asked, leaning back, licking his spoon while Samantha watched him, wondering if he was always so at ease. "Oh yes. The biography. I read what work Uncle Mike had done and became interested in this Tony Barrett. I'd just finished the course work at school and I was at loose ends, so I thought I might continue what Uncle Mike started. So I decided to move to New York and continue researching. When I was moving Uncle Mike's books, I found the file folder."

When he said no more, Samantha looked up at him. "Is that supposed to intrigue me? Am I now supposed to ask, 'What file folder?' "

"I could stand a little interest on your part, yes. But I can see that I'm not going to get it." He filled his spoon with mousse. "The folder was simply labeled 'Maxie' and inside was a newspaper photo of you, your grandmother, and your dog."

Samantha put her spoon down with a clatter. "My grandmother ran away when I was eight months old. There *is* no photo of the two of us."

Leaning on his elbow, he looked at her intently, without blinking, as though trying to relay some message to her.

"Oh," Samantha said. "*That* picture." It had taken her a while to remember, not that she remembered the incident, but her grandfather had told her what happened. "Brownie," she said at last. "I was staying with my grandmother, and I crawled into a pipe in a ditch in the backyard."

"And you got stuck, and your grandmother called the fire department."

"And a bored newspaper reporter looking for a story happened to be at the station that day so he came with the firemen, but it was Brownie who saved me."

"Your dog crawled into the pipe, bit into your soggy diaper, and pulled you out of that pipe. The reporter took a picture of you, your grandmother, and Brownie, the wire services picked the photo and story up and sent it around to papers all over the country, where it was seen by my uncle Michael Ransome as well as the rest of the world. Uncle Mike cut the photo out and wrote *Maxie* in the margin. All through his notes a woman named Maxie is mentioned." He looked up at her, studying her. "Maxie was Barrett's mistress." When Samantha didn't jump out of her skin at this news, as he was hoping she would, he leaned back on the bed and put his hands behind his head. "I think Maxie and your grandmother are one and the same."

When Samantha didn't say anything, just kept cleaning out the dish of mousse as though he'd said nothing, he looked back at her. She was looking sleepy again. "Well?" he asked impatiently.

She put down the empty dessert bowl. "Are you finished? Have you told me what you wanted to tell me? You think my grandmother was the mistress of a gangster. Okay, you've told me, now go."

For a moment, he could only blink at her. "You don't have an opinion on this?"

"I have an opinion on you," she said softly. "You have been reading too many of those gangster books. I didn't know my grandmother, but she was a regulation grandmother, cookie baking, that sort of thing. And her name was Gertrude. She was not a gangster's moll—is that the right term?" She put her hand up when he started to interrupt her. "And besides that, what does it matter if she was? *Now* will you leave?"

Rolling over to his side, he frowned at her. "It matters because I think your grandmother was in love with Barrett and bore him a child. Tony Barrett just may be your real grandfather."

At that Samantha very slowly, very carefully, set the tray to one side, got out of bed, and walked to the door. "Out," she said as though talking to someone who didn't understand English. "Get out. In the morning I will find another place of residence."

As though she hadn't spoken, Mike rolled onto his back and stared up at the ceiling. "Your father thought Barrett was his real father."

"I don't want to hear anymore," she said louder. "I want you to leave."

"I'm not going to leave," he said without looking at her.

Samantha didn't say a word, but if he wouldn't leave, she would. Stepping out of the room, she started down the stairs.

Mike caught her in his arms before she reached the bottom of the stairs. She struggled against him, but he held her easily, his arms about her body, her back against his front, and as she struggled against him, Mike felt his desire for her growing. He could feel her body against his, her hips, her breasts, her thighs, all touching him. "Be still, Sam," he whispered, sounding desperate, which he was. "Please, please be still."

There was something odd in his tone that made Samantha stop struggling and go perfectly still in his arms.

"I'm not going to hurt you," he said, his voice ragged, his lips near her ear lobe. "You have nothing to fear from me. All of this was your father's idea, not mine. I told him he should ask you to help me find Maxie, not force you to do it." Still holding her close to him, he moved his face to touch her neck, not kissing her, but feeling her softness, smelling her skin.

With a sharp jerk, Samantha pulled away from him, then leaned back against the stair rail. Her heart was pounding in her breast, her breathing deep and irregular. When she looked at him, she saw that his heart was pounding too and his skin was flushed.

"You want to sit down somewhere and talk about this?"

"No," she answered. "I don't want to talk about anything, nor do I want to hear anything you have to say. I don't want to hear your made-up stories about my father or my grandmother or about anything else for that matter. All I want to do is leave this house and never see you again."

"No," he said, pleading, but there was something else in his eyes. "I can't allow you to leave. Your father gave me the care of you and I mean to be worthy of his trust."

Samantha blinked at him several times before she was able to speak. " 'Gave you the care of me?' You mean to be 'worthy of his trust'?" She didn't know whether to laugh or run away. "You sound like something from the past, something from the Middle Ages. I am an adult woman and I—"

Abruptly, Mike's face changed. "Oh the hell with it. You're right. Who am I to take any of this seriously? I told Dave this was a dumb idea. I told him he should give you your inheritance with no strings attached, but he insisted that this was the only way. He wanted you to find out the truth."

Mike threw up his hands, palms up in surrender. "I give up. I'm not a good jailer. First I let you stay alone in a room until, as far as I can tell, you're on the point of suicide, then I play the heavy and try to make you do what you don't want to do. You *are* an adult and you can make your own decisions. You're not interested in any of this, so go on back to bed. Put a chair in front of your door if you want—that should keep out even a dedicated pervert like me. In the morning I'll call a real estate agency and help you find somewhere else to live and I'll give you back your rent money. Why don't you take that computer equipment with you because I don't know what the hell to do with it. Good night, Miss Elliot," he said, then walked down the stairs, turned, and went into the living room.

Shaking from her wrestle with him, shaking from all of it, Samantha slowly went back up the stairs.

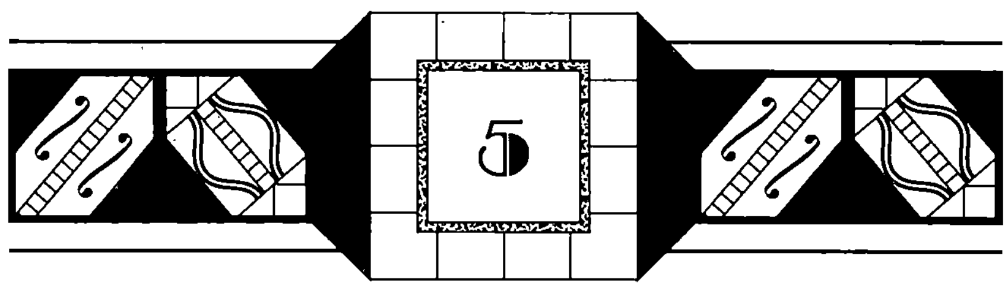

5

As Samantha entered her father's apartment, her first instinct was to pack a suitcase, but she didn't. She felt so very tired. Closing the door, she wedged a chair under the knob, removed the chair, then climbed back into bed.

She couldn't sleep. She did her best not to think about her father and his will, but it was no good. It was the old "don't think of elephants" dilemma.

At three in the morning, she got out of bed and began to search for her father's will. She had purposely not read it, for she hadn't wanted to know the details of his after-death rules, hadn't wanted to know what he had planned for her to do.

She found the will among some other papers, then sat down to read it. Her father's lawyer had told her everything that was in the will except for the single sentence that said she was to report all her findings to one Michael Taggert, and on Taggert's approval of her research, she was to receive her money—money that should have been hers unencumbered.

Samantha's first instinct was to tear the document into a

thousand pieces; but controlling herself, she smoothed it and replaced it with the other papers. Her father was dead; she had never been angry with him when he was alive, and she was not going to get angry at him now that he was gone. That he wanted someone to take care of her after he was dead was a sign that he loved her. It made no difference that Samantha didn't know this man, because her father had and he had approved of Michael Taggert—just as he'd approved of Richard Sims as her husband.

Getting up, Samantha went to the bathroom where she took a long, hot shower and washed her hair. When she emerged, she felt better. She dressed in gray cotton slacks and a long, loose pink sweater, combed her hair, tied it back from her face, and even put on makeup. It was still dark outside, but there was the feeling of dawn approaching, so she opened the doors leading onto the balcony and breathed the fragrance of the roses in the garden below.

Hearing something that she couldn't place, for a moment she stood still, listening. It was the sound of a typewriter being punched with heavy fingers. The sound made Samantha smile, for she hadn't heard a typewriter in years.

She knew she should stay in her room, knew she should pack her suitcase, but she didn't. Going to the door, she opened it and went down the stairs.

It was easy to follow the sound of the typewriter. Michael was in the library, the room dark except for a light over the desk, and he was punching away on an ancient typewriter that looked like something a war correspondent had used during World War II. He typed with his two index fingers, and he typed as though he were furious.

All at once feeling cowardly, Samantha started to leave the room.

"If you have something to say, say it," he said without turning toward her.

She blurted her words. "My granddad Cal was my father's father. He was a wonderful man and I don't believe he wasn't."

As he turned to look at her, she was surprised to see that he looked tired. Just like her, he had obviously been up all night.

"Believe what you want," he said, turning away to pull the paper out of the typewriter and insert another sheet.

"Why are you typing?" She took a step toward him.

Glancing at her over his shoulder with a look that said she'd been born without a brain, he said, "Because I want something typed."

She motioned toward the manual typewriter. "Why not just use a stone tablet and a chisel? It would be the same difference."

He didn't say a word but just kept typing. She should go back to her room and pack, she thought, or maybe take a nap, but for once, she wasn't sleepy. She wanted to ask him what he was typing, but she didn't allow herself to do so.

"I guess I'll go back to bed," she said and started toward the door, but stopped. "Are you going to release the money if I don't look for my grandmother?"

"No," he said firmly.

Samantha started to protest but didn't. After all, it was her choice as to what she did, and the money wasn't all that important to her. She would do fine without the money because she knew very well that she could support herself. If she didn't fulfill the requirements of her father's will, she could leave New York today and she could go to . . . She could go to . . .

She was unable to finish her thought, because she knew she had nowhere to go, no one to go to. Slowly, she started walking toward the stairs.

"Your grandfather Cal was sterile," Mike said loudly into the silence. "He had mumps while he was in the service—two years before he met your grandmother—and the mumps left him sterile. He couldn't father children."

Samantha sat down hard on a chair by the doorway. A full circle, she thought. She had traveled full circle. She had lost her grandmother, her mother, her father, her husband, and now she was being told that her grandfather had never been hers to begin with.

She didn't hear Mike move, but he was suddenly standing in front of her. "You want to go get something to eat and talk about this?" His voice was full of concern.

"No," she said softly. All she wanted was to go back to her rooms, rooms where she felt safe.

Grabbing her by the shoulders, Mike pulled her upright to stand in front of him, angry in his belief that her reluctance to go somewhere with him was her continuing conviction that he was half rapist, half murderer. "While you're in this house I'm responsible for you. Whatever you think of me, I rarely attack women in public places so you can at least have a meal with me."

Samantha looked surprised. "I didn't mean—" She looked away from him, not wanting to be so close to him, for she had an urge to sink into his arms, knowing that it would be good to be held by another human being. The last person who had touched her, besides this man on the day she had met him, had been her father, and in those last months he had been so very fragile. It would be nice to feel strong, healthy arms about her. But Samantha wasn't in the habit of asking for things from people. She'd never asked her husband to hold her, and she wasn't going to ask this stranger for comfort, so she jerked her shoulders away from his hands.

Not understanding her look or her actions, Mike released her, his mouth twisted with disgust. "All right, I'll keep my hands off of you, but you're going to eat."

Samantha started to repeat her no, but instead, she said she needed to get her purse.

"What for?" he asked.

"To pay for—"

Not allowing her to finish, he took her elbow and propelled her toward the front door. "I told you, I'm an old-fashioned guy. I pay. When I'm with a female, I pay. Whether she's my sister, my mother, or girlfriend, I pay. No Dutch treat. No her picking up the tab. Understand?"

Samantha didn't say a word. There were too many other things on her mind than who paid for breakfast.

As he ushered her out into the early morning light, she saw that there were a few people on Lexington Avenue, but not many, and the city had an eerie feeling, as though they were alone in it. Silently, she walked beside him, following him into an all-night coffee shop.

Smiling familiarly, the waitress brought Mike a cup of coffee. "Mike, you been at it all night again?" she asked.

He smiled back at her. "Yeah," he said then turned to Samantha. "Scrambled eggs, bagels, okay with you? And tea, right?"

She nodded, not asking how he knew that she didn't like coffee. The truth was, she didn't really care what she ate.

Leaning back in the booth, Mike sipped his coffee. "I wish

your father had told you more. I wish he hadn't left it to me to explain everything."

"My father liked to . . . manage things," she said softly.

"Your father liked to control people's lives."

That snapped her out of her lethargy. "I thought you said you liked my father!"

"I did. We had some wonderful talks and we became friends, but I'm not blind. He liked to make people do what he wanted them to do."

Samantha glared at him.

"All right," Mike said. "I get your point. No more comments about your sainted father. You want to hear his theory—his, mind you, not mine—on what happened with your grandparents?"

She did want to hear and she didn't. It was rather like paying to see a horror film that you wanted to see yet also didn't want to see.

"Your father believed that in 1928 Maxie was pregnant by Barrett, but something happened to prevent them from marrying. Maybe she told him she was pregnant and he refused to marry her, I don't know. I do know that she left New York, went to Louisville, met Cal, and married him. She stayed with him for thirty-six years, then the photo of her appeared in the paper. Your father thought Barrett probably saw it and that's how he located Maxie."

While watching her with the concentration of a snake, Mike drank more of his coffee. She was difficult to read, and he couldn't tell what she was thinking. "Two weeks before Maxie left, Dave said she was on the phone a lot and seemed upset. Just last year he was still berating himself, saying he should have asked her what was wrong, but he was fascinated with his baby daughter and had no thoughts for anyone else. Then, out of the blue, Maxie said her aunt was ill and needed her. She left, and no one in your family ever saw her again. At the time, Dave wanted to search for her, but your grandfather Cal said no—violently no. Dave believed Cal might have known that Maxie had gone back to Barrett. It was your father's guess that after Barrett had seen her picture, he probably contacted her and asked her to come back to him and she did."

Samantha took a few moments to adjust to what he had told

her. "If that's the case, why in the world would my father want to search for an adulteress? An adulteress! Scum-of-the-earth."

Mike watched her. "Interesting. Such a forceful opinion about adultery. Any personal reasons for such vehemence?"

Not answering him, she watched the waitress place the food before them.

"Your father wasn't sure what happened to his mother," Mike continued. "He thought for a while that she was a victim of foul play. Purse nabbed, then murdered, that sort of thing, but a year after she disappeared, she sent Cal a postcard from New York saying she was safe."

"How thoughtful of her," she said sarcastically.

Mike waited a moment for her to say something else, but when she was silent, he spoke again. "Maxie wrote that she was *safe.* Not that she was happy or well or send my clothes to so and so. She said she was *safe.*"

"Safe in the arms of her lover?"

"Is that bitterness I hear in your voice?"

"What I think or feel is none of your business. All I want from you is to know how much I have to do before the requirements of the will are met."

"Get me in to see Barrett and that's it. I want to meet the man. No one's seen him in twenty years. He's a recluse who lives on an estate in Connecticut with fences, dogs, and armed guards."

"Has it ever occurred to you that my grandmother—if she's still alive—might be living there with him?"

Mike grinned. "The thought had crossed my mind."

Samantha thought about the possibility of seeing her grandmother again. Her grandmother had abandoned her family, had left the people who loved her for another man, and Samantha wasn't sure she could forgive the woman. On the other hand, she thought of this man Barrett, a man she didn't know but who may actually be her grandfather.

"I might like to see him," she said, then added quickly, "but not her."

Mike's shock showed. "You can forgive a man for being a gangster, but you can't forgive a woman for adultery? Murder seems worse than sleeping with someone besides your spouse?"

She ignored his comment. "What is it you want me to do?"

"Nothing much. I'll write a letter to Barrett telling him that

Maxie's granddaughter wants to meet him. It's my guess he'll answer right away, then we go to meet him. Simple."

"What if he wants to see me alone?"

"I thought of that, actually, so I need a good, solid reason to be your escort. You wouldn't like to get married this afternoon, would you?"

"I'd rather be roasted alive," she answered sincerely.

Mike laughed. "Liked being married, did you?"

She narrowed her eyes at him. "You know, there's a *reason* for all the divorce in this country."

Dave had told him little about Samantha's marriage, saying only that he had encouraged her divorce and had helped her obtain it, but even so, Mike was startled by her hostility. Looking down at Samantha's hand on the table, he knew he shouldn't touch her because she seemed to have such an aversion to being touched—at least by him, anyway—but he couldn't seem to help himself.

Picking up her hand, he looked at it, so small in his own, then kissed the palm. "I could show you one heck of a great wedding night."

Angrily, she jerked her hand out of his grasp.

He sighed. "Is it me you hate or all men?" He was surprised at how much he wanted her to say that she didn't hate him personally.

But Samantha didn't answer his question as she looked at her eggs. "Why don't you tell him the truth?"

It took Mike a moment to remember who they'd been talking about. "You mean tell Barrett that I want to write about him?"

"I can fully understand his aversion to writers." She said the word *writers* with disgust in her voice.

"I take it that writing is another mark against me," he said with a sigh. "Want to tell me why?"

He didn't even expect her to answer. "All right, keep your secrets. Ever hear of Al Capone? Of course you have. The reason you've heard of him is not because he was the biggest gangster or even the most violent. You've heard of him because Capone loved publicity. He used to take corps of pressmen along with him when he went fishing. The man thought everything he did was worth recording. Actually, in his day in New York, Barrett was bigger than Capone, but Barrett hated publicity of any kind. Wouldn't even allow a photo to be taken of him, and never gave an interview."

"So now you think that if you wrote and told him the truth, saying that one maybe-granddaughter and one nosy writer wanted to meet him, he'd say no?"

"I'm sure of it. That's why I have to be something close and personal to you. Sure a husband is out? Okay, then how about a fiancé?"

"How about my half brother?"

"If Barrett has seen Maxie, he'd know that was a lie."

She tried to think of something else for him to pretend to be, for she didn't want the implied intimacy between them even for one afternoon.

He knew what she was thinking as clearly as though he could read her mind. "What is it you have against me anyway?"

She narrowed her eyes at him. "Do you *really* want to marry me? Settle down, have a couple of kids?"

"I hadn't planned on getting married this week," he answered.

"Then you're not in love with me? Deeply, really in love?"

"We haven't had a conversation yet that wasn't full of hostility."

"Ah . . . Then what you really want is to go to bed with me and that's all." She leaned forward. "Let me tell you something, Mr. Taggert. Just as you're an old-fashioned man, I'm an old-fashioned woman. I'm not a modern woman who debates whether or not to go to bed with a man on the first date. I'm the kind of woman who debates whether or not to *kiss* a man on the *third* date. I do not want to go to bed with you and, heaven help me, I do not, under any circumstances, want to get married again. One major mistake per life is my motto, and I've made mine and I've learned from it. Do I make myself clear?"

Leaning back in the booth, Mike stared at her, trying his best to understand where all her hostility was coming from. Nothing Dave had told him had prepared him for this animosity.

"I thought so. Now, do we have things clear between us? I want to fulfill the requirements of my father's will and get out of this city, and I'll do what's necessary but no more. Understand me?"

"A little better than I did," he said softly.

"Good. Now maybe we can proceed. You may write Barrett

and tell him I'll come with my fiancé. After the meeting I'll move out of your house and you will give me a document saying that I have fulfilled the requirements. Agreed?"

"Almost. I have a stipulation. Between the time we send the letter and when we receive a reply, probably a few days at most, I don't want you out of my sight."

"What?"

"I don't want you staying alone in your father's apartment. Until your father's will is carried out I am responsible for you."

"Of all the— Oh, I see, you said before that you thought I was near suicide. I can assure you, Mr. Taggert, that I—"

"And I can assure you, Miss Elliot, that I have made up my mind about this. We can do whatever you like, go shopping, visit the Statue of Liberty, whatever, but we do it together."

"I will not—"

He started to leave the table. "This conversation is over. Let's go back to the house and I'll help you pack."

"Pack?"

"So you can leave."

"But . . ." She knew what he meant. Either she did what he wanted in the way he wanted it done, or she left his house. He held all the cards. If she wanted the money her father had left her, she had to do what he said. "All right," she said in disgust as she stood up. "But keep your hands off of me."

He was looking at her oddly. "That husband of yours must have been one big bastard."

"Not particularly so. Show me a woman who's been married to the same man for more than two years and I'll show you a woman with a very high pain tolerance."

"I guess your pain level wasn't too high or you'd still be married to him."

She looked away. "That's where you're wrong," she said softly. "My capacity for pain seems to be limitless."

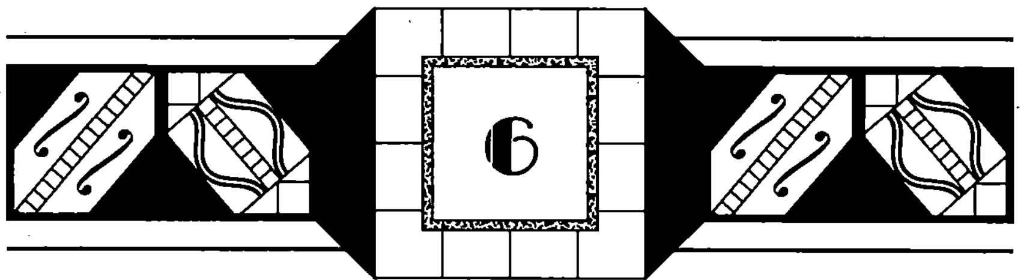

The mirror on the wall shuddered when Samantha slammed the apartment door behind her. Just who did he think he was? she thought. What right did he have to give her ultimatums? The instant she thought the words, she knew the answer. Her father had given him the right to decide whether she met the requirements of the will or not, but her father hadn't given him the right to control every minute of her day, she thought defiantly.

She opened her closet doors. Statue of Liberty, she thought with disgust, knowing how much she genuinely hated anything that could remotely be called a tourist attraction. In the four years she had lived in Santa Fe she had never visited anything that was frequented by busloads of people who were ruled by timetables prepared by someone else.

As she looked at the contents of her wardrobe, she smiled. Perhaps he could force her to do what he wanted her to do, but he couldn't make her enjoy it. Perhaps if she were disagreeable enough, he'd leave her alone. Rummaging inside two packing boxes, she found what she was looking for.

Mike wrote the letter to Barrett, called an express mail service, and sent it off, letting out his pent-up breath when the letter was gone. Now it was up to Barrett as to what he did, but Mike hoped he'd allow Samantha and him to visit. It was Mike's guess that the old man would very much want to see his granddaughter—at least Mike hoped that was the case. But who could tell what a ninety-one-year-old man was going to do?

As Mike watched the express mail truck drive away, his thoughts turned to Samantha and he smiled. For all her bristles, all her hostility, he was looking forward to spending the day with her. It wasn't just that she was the sexiest female he'd ever seen or that he wanted to take her to bed, there was something about her that intrigued him. He wondered what she was like when she wasn't angry. Now and then he caught a glimpse of her, a glimpse of what he had come to think of as the real Samantha. He'd seen the real Samantha the first day he'd met her, and last night when she'd drunk the glass of wine and had made jokes, he'd had a look inside her. These rare sights made him sure there was another Samantha under the one she presented to the world, or he thought with a smile, maybe she presented the bristle-coated side only to him.

Now, he wondered, what did one do with a young lady who looked as though she wore a hat and gloves to church on Sundays? He couldn't very well take her to his favorite New York haunts, some of which consisted of bars, nor did he think she'd appreciate visiting Daphne and her friends.

Picking up the telephone, he called his sister Jeanne, for she would know what to do to entertain someone like Samantha, he thought as he dialed his parents' telephone number in Colorado. His mother answered the phone.

"Mom, is Jeanne there?"

"No, Michael, dear, she isn't." Patricia Taggert knew the sound of each of her children's voices, and she knew when they needed something. "Can I help you?"

Feeling a little odd asking his mother such a personal question, Mike prayed she wouldn't start asking awkward questions, but he did need a woman's advice. "I met a woman—Now, wait a minute, before you start thinking orange blossoms—"

"I didn't mention orange blossoms, Michael, dear, *you* did," Pat said sweetly.

Mike cleared his throat. "Well, anyway, I met this woman. Actually, she's the daughter of a friend of mine and—"

"Is this the young woman who's living in your house with you?"

Mike grimaced. His mother was in Chandler, Colorado, over two thousand miles away, yet she knew what he was doing in New York. "I don't even want to know how you know who's rented the apartment," he said.

Pat laughed. "Tammy cleans for your cousin Raine, too. Remember?"

Mike rolled his eyes. The big mouth of one of his Montgomery cousins. He should have known. "Mom, you want to answer my question or find out every tiny detail of my life secondhand from other people?"

"I would love to hear directly from you."

"She's never been to New York, and the place terrifies her. Where can I take her to make her like the city?"

Pat's mind raced. Why was the young woman living in New York if she hated the place? To be near her son? And if she and Mike were in love, what was she like?

"I mean, Mom, should I take her to the top of the Empire State Building? Rockefeller Center? What about the Statue of Liberty? How about Ellis Island?"

Pat drew in her breath, for she knew that Mike hated tourist attractions. Unfortunately, her son was much more at home in a smoke-filled bar than in a group of gawking sightseers, but he must be serious if he was willing to brave the Statue of Liberty for her. "Is she a normal girl?"

"No," Mike said. "She has three arms, practices several bizarre religions, and talks to her black cat. What do you mean, is she a normal girl?"

"You know exactly what I mean," Pat snapped. "Is she like that stripper who visits you, or is she one of those muscle girls from your gym? Knowing you, Mike, she could be a down-on-her-luck prostitute."

Mike smiled at the phone. "And what would you say if I said she was one of those and that I was going to marry her?"

Pat didn't hesitate. "I'd ask what you wanted for a wedding gift."

Mike laughed. "Okay, she's normal. Very normal, if by that you mean prim and proper. Sam could marry a preacher."

Pat put her hand over the phone, rolled her eyes skyward, and whispered, "Thank you." "Take her shopping," Pat said with enthusiasm. "Show her the stores on Fifth. Take her to Saks. Your cousin Vicky is a buyer at Saks."

"Oh?" Mike said without much interest. He had too many relatives to remember half of them. "And which one is she?"

"You know very well that she's J.T. and Aria's youngest. If your young lady still doesn't like New York after she's seen Saks, take her walking on Madison. Start at Sixty-first, walk up to the Eighties, and look in all the store windows."

Mike was laughing. "Especially in the jewelry store windows? Maybe buy her a diamond or two? The kind of diamonds in engagement rings? Tell me, Mom, how many women have you mentally married me off to in my short life?"

"At least six," Pat said, laughing in return.

Mike's voice changed to serious. "Mom, you and Dad are happily married, aren't you?"

At the tone of his voice, Pat thought her heart skipped a beat, for something was troubling her child. "Of course we are, darling."

"Samantha—that's her name—said that any woman who has been married for longer than two years to the same man has a very high pain tolerance. *You* don't think that's true, do you?"

After a futile attempt at controlling her laughter, Pat released it. Even when Mike kept saying, "Mom! Mom!" she kept laughing. Even when she knew he put the phone down in disgust, she still couldn't stop laughing.

Mike put down the telephone, more than a little annoyed at his mother, actually, annoyed at all women. If they thought marriage to a man was so horrible, why were they all trying to get married? All of them except Samantha, that is, he thought. Or maybe her reluctance was merely an act.

Smiling, he went to the bedroom to dress. For Samantha he would put on a suit and tie. Maybe he'd even wear that Italian number his sister had picked out for him.

Forty-five minutes later, he emerged from the bedroom,

showered, shaved, and dressed, then checked the hall mirror and straightened his tie. Not bad, he thought. Not bad at all.

"Sam!" he yelled up the stairs. "You ready to go?"

He had to wait a few minutes before she came down the stairs, but when he saw her, he smiled at her and offered her his arm.

When Samantha saw the way Mike was dressed, she wanted to die. Just plain sit down and die. She'd had dreams of embarrassing him, of making him say that he wasn't going to be seen with her dressed as she was—that's what her ex-husband would have said if she had appeared wearing her workout clothes—so she'd dragged an ancient pink sweat suit, worn bare in places, discolored in others, from the closet. Across the chest of the sweat shirt was emblazoned "At first he put me on a pedestal and now he wants me to dust it."

As Samantha stood at the head of the stairs, looking down at Mike in his beautiful dark suit, she knew she had never seen a better-looking man in her life. At least this time when her father had chosen a man for her, he had picked one who looked good. She hadn't been as fortunate with Richard.

After one look at Mike's eyes, she knew he wasn't going to be embarrassed by her. In fact, she wasn't sure he was aware that what she had on was inappropriate. Smiling at her as though he was looking forward to going out with her, he held up his arm for her to take.

"I can't—" Samantha began. "I have to—"

"Samantha, it's eleven o'clock. If you take any longer to get dressed, the stores will be closed."

"Stores," she said, horror in her voice as she tried to pull away from him, but he held her firmly.

"I cannot go to a store looking like this," she said.

Mike looked her up and down and read her shirt. "You look fine to me. I like pink on you. Besides, we can buy you new clothes if you want."

Pulling at her arm didn't gain her release. "I have to change."

Giving her a look of frustration, one of those count-to-ten looks, he said with exaggerated patience, "If you didn't like what you had on, why did you wear it?"

Samantha wouldn't answer that, since she couldn't very well tell him that it had been her intention to make him refuse to be seen with her, especially not since he didn't seem to notice what she had on.

Feeling like a child who was being punished, her chin down, she followed him out of the house and into the streets. So far, her total experience of New York had been Lexington Avenue. Now she walked with Mike toward Madison Avenue, then to Fifth, and the closer they got to Fifth Avenue, the more Samantha became aware of her atrocious clothing. In magazines one saw models wearing gorgeous designer clothing, and a person in the real world of Middle America sometimes wondered who in the world *wore* those things. Most Americans wear bright-colored sportswear, looking as though they spend their lives climbing mountains or running marathons. But in New York the men and women—especially the women—looked to Samantha as though they had stepped from designer showrooms.

As she walked with Mike, her hand held firmly in his arm, Samantha was painfully aware of the women around her. They were so fantastically well groomed. Their hair looked as though they shampooed it with fairy nectar, their nails were perfectly trimmed and polished, as though they never used their hands, and their clothes were nothing less than divine.

Of course one drawback to New York women was their snobbery. Many of the women gave Samantha looks of pity when they saw the way she was dressed, and some of them even smiled at her in a way that made Samantha move closer to Mike, as though for protection. Turning, he looked down at her, patted her hand, and smiled when she moved closer to him, seeming to have no idea what was going on between the woman who clung to him and the women on the street. Samantha thought it must be wonderful to be able to be oblivious.

By the time they reached Fifth Avenue, Samantha wanted to crawl in a hole. Mike seemed to have a place he wanted to go so they hurried past store after store with beautiful clothing in the windows. They passed Tiffany's, Gucci, Christian Dior, Mark Cross. After a while Samantha stopped looking at the clothes because the more she saw, the worse she felt.

At Fiftieth Street, they came to a large store with dark blue awnings, and to her horrified amazement, Mike started toward the revolving doors. Samantha pulled away from him. In the first place, revolving doors puzzled her; she couldn't seem to get the hang of when she was to enter and when she was to exit. Once, she had gone around one of the things three times before she was able to get out. In the second place, she saw that this was Saks Fifth Avenue. She could not, absolutely could not, enter a world-renowned store dressed in a worn-out, faded pink sweat suit.

Mike went round the revolving doors, saw Samantha wasn't with him, then went round again, this time stretching out his hand and grabbing her arm. After wedging her into the pie-shaped door area with him, he pulled her out of the door into the store at the appropriate time.

When they entered the store, Samantha stood still for a moment, dazzled by what she saw before her. To anyone who had spent four years in a town like Santa Fe, Saks was heaven come to earth. Here were consumer goods that did not have howling coyotes on them. Here was clothing that was not made from Pendleton blankets. She saw saleswomen who wore something other than Mexican cotton and acres of turquoise and silver jewelry. She saw people who moved faster than sun-warmed lizards, and people were wearing shoes that in no way resembled the footwear of cowboys. Best of all, there was not one single solitary piece of leather fringe in sight.

"Like it?" Mike asked, watching her face, which showed her awe as she looked at the sparkling Judith Leiber purses in the case before her.

Samantha could only look at him, much too stunned to speak.

"Want to do a little shopping?" He was on the verge of laughing at her as he asked the rhetorical question. "I think the escalator is back there."

As Samantha came out of her trance, she became aware of the women in the store looking her over, knowing full well that she failed on every count. Maybe she could go back to the house, she thought, change her clothes, and come back here. With the money she had saved, she could afford a new dress. But the truth was, Samantha knew she didn't own a garment that was up to the fashion standards of the women she saw in this beautiful store.

"I can't go shopping wearing this," she whispered to Mike.

From the look on his face she could see that he didn't understand what she was saying. Sometimes it seemed that the language difference between men and women was as great as that between Chinese and English. How could she explain to a man that saleswomen would have nothing to do with a woman who looked as though she *needed* their goods?

"You look great," Mike said, then began pushing Samantha toward the back of the store.

There were tall, beautiful young women offering other customers samples of perfume, but they took one look at Samantha with her pulled-back hair and repulsive old sweat suit and didn't offer her the perfume. One woman after another glanced at Mike, then at Samantha, then back at Mike, with an expression that asked, How could a great-looking guy like you be seen with a frump like her?

As Mike practically pushed her into an elevator, Samantha almost hid behind him, trying to keep anyone from seeing her.

Pulling Samantha along, Mike got out on the ninth floor, then led her through the children's department.

"Where are you dragging me?" she asked, trying to pull out of his grasp, but it was like trying to break free of a tow truck.

"I'm taking you to see a friend of mine. Not really a friend, more like a cousin."

Pulling her through offices, he didn't stop until he came to one glassed enclosure. Behind a desk sat a young woman who was not beautiful exactly, but very striking. Her hair looked as though it were incapable of being out of place, and her clothes had obviously been made for her body alone. The sight of her made Samantha look about for a hiding place where she wouldn't be seen by this elegant young woman.

As soon as the woman saw Mike, she smiled and stood up, but Mike did not smile. Drawing himself into a military at-attention stance, he clicked his heels together, took her fingertips in his hand, and kissed them. "Your royal highness," he said in a voice of an official courtier.

Looking about the office at her co-workers nervously, the woman said, "Mike, stop that."

Grinning, Mike grabbed her into his arms, bent with her like something out of a Fred Astaire movie, and kissed her neck enthusiastically. "Better?" he asked as he lifted her to stand straight again.

"Much," she said, blushing, trying to act annoyed but obviously charmed by him as she moved out of his grasp.

"So how's the palace and the folks?" Mike asked, smiling as though very pleased with himself.

"Everyone is fine—as you'd know if you bothered to visit. Mike, as honored as I am by your visit, I have work to do. What can I do for you?"

"Help us shop." Pulling Samantha from the hiding place she was trying to make for herself between the door and a filing cabinet, he presented her as though she were something he wanted repaired, like a watch or, actually, more like a squirrel-eatin', rifle-totin' hillbilly.

Seeing the way the woman looked from her to Mike in question, considering the proprietary way Mike was holding her arm, Samantha tried to explain. "It's not like it looks. He's my guardian." As soon as she said it, she realized how dumb the words sounded, how she was making things worse by speaking.

"Rather like Tinkerbell," Mike said, still grinning.

"More like Captain Hook," Samantha retaliated quickly.

At that the young woman laughed and walked toward Samantha with her hand extended. "It sounds as though you understand him. My name is Victoria Montgomery and Mike and I are cousins of sorts." Looking Samantha up and down with a professional eye, she appraised her face, her figure, and the dreadful clothes. "What can I do for you?"

Giving the young woman a crooked smile, doing what she could to redeem herself, Samantha said, "Make me look like one of those women on the street."

With a smile of complete understanding, Vicky said, "I think we can manage something." She turned to Mike. "Why don't you meet us in about three hours?"

"Not on your life," Mike answered. "I'm staying through all of it. If she's left on her own, she dresses like Rebecca of Sunnybrook Farm. Can you fix her up?"

He made Samantha sound like a car whose transmission had fallen out and it was questionable whether the car was repairable or not. After one sympathetic look at Samantha's face, now the same color as her deplorable sweatsuit, Vicky turned to her cousin. "Mike, you've been using your muscles too much and your brains not enough. Mind your manners!" Her voice carried authority as well as much affection for her handsome cousin.

After a smile filled with gratitude directed toward Vicky, Samantha turned toward the elevators and started walking, feeling better already.

"How much?" Vicky whispered to Mike when Samantha was a few feet away.

"Whatever," Mike answered, shrugging.

Vicky lifted one perfectly plucked eyebrow at him. "Are we talking Christian Dior or Liz Claiborne?"

"I guess that means expensive or cheap. I want her to have both. Everything. But don't let her see the prices on the clothes and send the bill to me." He paused a moment in thought. "And I want shoes and whatever else women wear."

"What about hair?" Vicky was studying her cousin. She knew very well that he could afford what he wanted to buy, but she also knew that he didn't spend his money frivolously.

Mike was looking at Vicky with eyes that nearly begged for her help. He was so tired of seeing Samantha with her beautiful hair scraped back into a tight, ugly bun. "You know," he said wistfully, "I think her hair just may be curly when it's down."

"You don't know for sure?" Vicky asked archly, doing her best to figure out what this woman meant to him.

"Not yet," Mike said with confidence and a wink at his pretty cousin. "Not yet."

Samantha knew she had never spent such a heavenly day in her life as the one she spent at Saks with Vicky and Mike. When Samantha was a child she had often gone on shopping expeditions with her mother, and they had been an enormous amount of fun, but after her mother had died, she hadn't seemed to have much time or even the inclination to adorn herself. After she was married and had moved to Santa Fe, she had had neither money nor time nor the desire to shop.

But even when she'd been with her mother, she'd not had as good a time as she had on this day. Vicky's taste in clothing and corresponding accessories was irreproachable, and her diplomacy in guiding Samantha toward the correct garments was something that had to be experienced to be believed. At first Samantha haphazardly and hesitantly chose a few outfits from the racks and tried them on, but when she looked in the triple mirrors, she found that she looked as she always did: boring. Then Vicky very sweetly, casually, tactfully, asked if she might be allowed to choose a few things for Samantha, and of course Samantha agreed. What woman hadn't yearned for an elegant, regal-looking woman like Victoria to help her dress?

Within twenty minutes after Vicky handed Samantha the first garment, she began to see a completely different version of herself. Stepping back in the large, luxurious dressing room on the third floor, she looked at herself in the perfect-fitting suit by St. John and saw a person she did not recognize: elegant but maybe a little sexy, comfortable but refined, fashionable but classic.

"May I?" Vicky asked as she removed the rubber band from Samantha's hair and let her blonde hair float about her shoulders.

Looking at herself in the mirror, Samantha remembered that she had started pulling her hair back to get it out of her way when she was working on computers, but she'd also found that she was taken more seriously when she didn't have a couple of feet of blonde hair falling in her face.

Stepping back in the dressing room, Vicky studied Samantha, looking at her as an artist would look at a painting, first one way then the other. "Could we cut your hair? Perhaps style it and shape it so it falls properly? Would you mind?"

Mind? Samantha thought. It was as though someone was asking her if she'd mind going to heaven. "I think that would be all right," she said, trying her best not to sound as though, inside, she were jumping up and down and yelling, Yippee!

Vicky smiled graciously, pretending she couldn't see how Samantha was feeling, but her happiness was infectious. Vicky seldom got to work with a customer who was so purely delighted with things as ordinary as new clothes and a haircut. "Now you must show your suit to Mike."

Involuntarily, Samantha frowned because she didn't want to show Mike anything. In fact, she'd just as soon forget that he existed. Vicky had explained that a Saks credit card would be issued in Samantha's name and that Vicky could arrange for the cost of the clothes to be prorated over months. Samantha would receive the clothes at Vicky's cost, thereby making her able to afford an entire new wardrobe. If Samantha was paying for them, why did she have to show her clothes to this man?

Seeing Samantha's reluctance to model for Mike, Vicky didn't understand it, because when she'd first seen them together, Samantha had been clinging to Mike as though he were a life perserver. "I think he will want to see you in your new clothing," Vicky urged, feeling a little guilty at the elaborate lie she'd concocted to keep Samantha from knowing Mike was actually paying for the clothes.

Hesitantly, and with more than a little reluctance, Samantha left the dressing room, walking onto the sales floor where Mike was ensconced on a pretty pink sofa with a cup of tea someone had brought him and a newspaper. He was so comfortable that he looked as though he owned the store, looking as at home here among these women and the very feminine clothes as he had looked the first day she'd seen him, when he was wearing cutoffs and a torn shirt.

Remembering too vividly the indifference she had received from her father and her husband when it came to her clothes, Samantha didn't want to model for him. Her husband had wanted her covered up and looking neat and tidy, but past that he hadn't cared what she wore. Her father didn't notice the difference between his daughter in heels and hose and his daughter in jeans and a gardening shirt.

But Mike didn't ignore Samantha and was far from indifferent to her. When he first saw her walking toward him, he put down his paper, slowly got out of his chair, and went to her. When he reached her, he took her hand, turned her about, and studied her, looking at the fit, cut, and color of the suit. "Yes," he said after considerable thought. "It shows her off."

Samantha tried her best to control her enormous grin at his praise. It wasn't the words so much as the way he paid her the compliment, as though she were beautiful and he was judging whether the clothes were worthy of her. As she turned to follow Vicky back to the dressing room, Mike caught her shoulder.

To her consternation, he leaned forward, put his face in her neck and kissed her ear. "You ever cover up your hair again and you'll answer to me."

Samantha moved away from him, but not before goose bumps of pleasure raised on her body.

Within an hour she became used to modeling for Mike. In direct opposition to her first opinion that Mike was oblivious, she found that he was very aware of women's clothes and she soon learned to trust him. "No, the jacket's too long for you. Covers up your rear end," he said in utter seriousness.

"That is not a reason to dislike a garment," Samantha snapped, but Mike just grunted. Samantha decided to buy the jacket and wear it often, but in the dressing room, when Vicky asked if she would take it, Samantha hesitated. "No," she said at last.

Samantha soon began saying yes to what Mike liked and no to what he didn't like.

To bring Samantha garments from floors other than the designer apparel on the third floor, Vicky enlisted the services of two saleswomen, telling them what she wanted and where they were to get it. The women brought armloads of lacey underwear, nightgowns, and even shoes to Samantha, and they brought purses, gloves, hosiery, and costume jewelry from the first floor.

It was when Samantha was trying on a lovely Carolyn Roehme dress, that she realized Mike was also approving or vetoing the underwear that was being presented to her. "That color's wrong for her," she heard him say. "No, not black. I want the white nightgown," she heard him say twice. Samantha felt her face grow red as she remembered what he'd said to her on that first day: that he wouldn't be able to control himself if she wore something white and lacey.

"Do you have any *blue* nightgowns?" Samantha asked Vicky.

Vicky smiled and moments later a sedate, blue nightgown appeared. "Mike doesn't like it," Vicky said.

"Good," Samantha answered. "I'll take two of them."

Samantha bought many, many items. By four o'clock she had lost count of all the suits, shoes, dresses, and casual clothes she had said yes to, only a few of which were to be charged to her account. "This is going to cost too much," she said to Vicky. "This must be hundreds of dollars."

Vicky had her back to Samantha so Samantha couldn't see Vicky's raised eyebrows. Hundreds? Vicky thought and realized that Mike had been right. He'd said he doubted if Samantha could even conceive of a single dress costing seven thousand dollars, so all price tags had to be removed before she tried on the clothes. Removing the tags had been a great bother to Vicky and her assistants, but for what Mike was spending, they could afford the bother. And, as Samantha had an unconscious eye for quality, she had spent many thousands. If she were presented with two pairs of shoes, one costing six hundred dollars and the other pair a mere two hundred and fifty, Samantha unerringly chose the more expensive shoes.

Straightening, Vicky looked at Samantha. "They are ready for you now in the hair salon."

Nodding, Samantha wondered what Mike would have to say about her hair, hoping he wasn't one of those men who said, "Take off a quarter of an inch and no more." When it came to feminine hair, her father and her husband had thought that women should have one style: They should be able to sit on their hair.

Preparing herself for the coming disagreement, Samantha thought of arguing that she should be able to choose the way she wanted to wear her hair, but she knew before trying that it would be a useless attempt. Mike walked into the salon, not seeming to be bothered by the sheer femininity of the place—in fact, he even winked at a woman who had her hair covered with folded pieces of aluminum foil. Immediately, he began telling the hairdresser how Samantha's hair was to be cut. "I want her curls to show," Mike said. "And I don't want any style that makes her use hair spray. I can't stand the stuff, scratches a man's face."

"I will wear my hair any way I want to," Samantha said. Both the hairdresser and Mike turned to her with blank looks on their faces, as though they were surprised and totally unconcerned with her opinion. As they turned back to each other, Samantha looked in the mirror and sighed. That Mike was saying what she herself wanted to say made no difference; it was the principle that mattered.

While her nails were being manicured, the hairdresser cut inches off her hair, cutting it into layers of different lengths. With each inch that fell away, Samantha felt lighter and younger. Even before the dryer was held to her hair, she could see the curls forming about her face. When it was done, she shook her head and laughed.

Mike was beside her, looking in the mirror at her. "I didn't think you could be prettier, but you are," he said softly, making Samantha blush.

Taking her by the hand, he led her to another chair and there she got a makeup lesson and a small shopping bag full of cosmetics and skin care products. She would have been shocked to learn that the cosmetics alone were over three hundred dollars.

It was late afternoon when Samantha, dressed in a red Christian LaCroix suit, her hair short and curling about her head, her face perfectly made up, left Saks on Mike's muscled arm. They carried no bags since Vicky had said she'd have everything sent to Mike's house. This time, when they went through the cosmetics area on the first floor, many of the tall, thin young women rushed forward to offer Samantha a sample of their perfume, but she waved them all away. Mike stopped at the Lancôme counter, and in spite of Samantha's insincere protests, he chose Trésor for her, paying for it with cash.

Holding the little bag of perfume tightly in her hands, as though it were very precious, Samantha looked up at Mike. "Thank you," she whispered. "Thank you for today."

He smiled at her, a smile of pride and pleasure. "Want something to eat?"

"Yes," she said, "I'm starving."

Tucking her arm under his, he led her from the store. As they walked out together, Samantha noticed that Mike was as proud to be seen with her when she was wearing her old sweat suit as he was when she was in designer clothes. It really didn't matter to him what she was wearing.

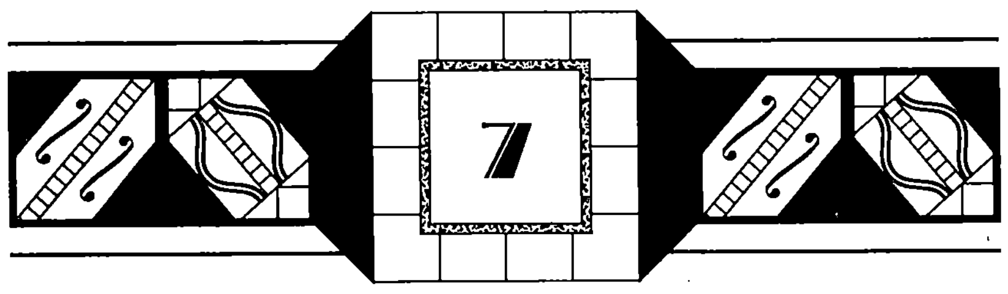

7

As they walked back to the town house, Samantha kept touching her hair, feeling the way it curled about her face.

"Like it?" Mike asked, and she nodded.

She wasn't aware of it, but she was walking straighter, taking longer strides than she had when they'd first walked down the streets. Feeling some regret that Samantha was no longer clinging to him, Mike was pleased to see her smiling and happy, and he was delighted to see her looking as good as she did.

When they neared the town house, Samantha was the first one to see the women sitting on the stoop. There were four of them, and it was easy to conclude that they were not what her mother would have referred to as "nice" girls. Their clothes were too tight, too short, too brightly colored, their faces painted with too much contrast between lips and eyes and cheeks. Three of them were smoking; two of them were sitting on the iron railing, and they made no attempt to pull their tiny skirts down over the parts of their bodies that they were exposing.

"I think you have guests." Samantha realized she was frowning, for she'd been looking forward to ordering a salad plate from a deli and sitting in the coolness of the garden with it, but now she'd have to retreat to her father's room.

Seeing her frown, Mike pulled her hand into his arm. "You'll be my hostess."

"I can't . . ." she began because she didn't want to become more involved with this man than she already was.

"It's just Daphne and some of the girls wanting a free meal. They'll be gone before full dark."

"Oh," she said softly, eyes wide. "They work at night?" She was trying to sound sophisticated, as though she weren't shocked by the dress and manner of these flamboyant women.

"They strip."

"Oh," Samantha said again, relieved, for stripping was healthier than what she'd first thought they did. As they drew nearer, Samantha felt one of the women looking at her with more interest than the other three, and she knew without a doubt that this woman was Daphne. When the woman left her perch on the rail, Samantha saw that she had to be at least six feet tall. Samantha thought that under the face paint the woman was probably quite pretty, but it was difficult judging her facial beauty because her body was so distracting: a great deal of it was cantilevered from her broad-shouldered frame. "Is she Daphne?" Samantha asked, whispering.

"Every inch of her." Mike was watching Samantha's face, hoping for a sign of jealousy.

Leaning closer to Mike, Samantha whispered, "Are parts of her . . . augmented?"

"As far as I can tell, most of Daphne is fake," Mike said with enthusiasm. "She's been augmented, supplemented, subtracted from, added to, from her face to her feet. When you touch her, all the balloons she's had inserted under her skin slide away at crazy angles." Even as closely as he was watching Samantha, he couldn't see any signs of jealousy.

"And Daphne is an . . . an exotic dancer?"

"No, she's a plain ol' garden-variety stripper, there is absolutely nothing exotic about Daphne."

Halting, Mike faced Samantha, his hands on her shoulders. "Sam, my girl, you don't have to meet these women, and I'd understand completely if you didn't want to. I can send them home, and then you and I could go out to a quiet dinner somewhere. I'll take you to La Cirque."

"What a ridiculous thing to say," she said sharply, realizing that he didn't understand that her questions were curiosity; he seemed to think she was a Puritan snob who wouldn't sit at a table with a stripper. "Of course I want to meet them. And would you *please* stop touching me?" Moving away from him, she started down the street, and the next moment she was introducing herself to the women, who looked at her with bored eyes.

Daphne came down the stairs, towering over Samantha. "You're Mike's . . . tenant?" she asked.

When she figured out what the woman was asking, Samantha realized why the women were looking at her with hooded eyes. "His tenant and nothing else," she said with emphasis. When she saw the slight smiles of relief on the faces of the women, she realized that these women considered Mike to be their property and Samantha an intruder.

Mike unlocked the door, and in the next moment the women swept inside and took over the town house. They turned on Mike's stereo, then went to the kitchen and began pulling out dishes while one woman went to the telephone to order enough food for a dozen people. One of the women said she had a new routine for the club and wanted Mike's opinion on the strip dance, but he declined her offer for a private viewing. Samantha was somewhat curious as to what a stripper really did, but she couldn't very well ask the woman to perform for her alone.

The food arrived, and before she knew what was happening, Samantha was acting as both a hostess and a maid. For the rest of the evening, she seemed to always be in the kitchen ladling food onto plates, pouring beer into tall glasses, and carrying trays into the garden. Once, Mike caught her just as she stepped into the garden and pulled her into his arms, with her back pressed against the front of him, his strong arms about her waist. He bit her earlobe.

"Release me!" she hissed. With her hands full with a heavy tray of food, she couldn't hit him in the ribs with her elbows as she wanted to do.

"I'd like to hold onto you forever," he said into her ear, nibbling on her lobe.

"You're drunk." Giving a sharp twist to get away from him, she set the tray down, then turned and gave Mike a hard look, but that didn't keep him from laughing at her. As Samantha went back into the kitchen, Daphne was standing inside the house by the glass doors, watching the two of them.

"You're not in love with him," Daphne said flatly.

Samantha looked surprised. "No, I'm not. Is that unusual?" Glancing toward the three women in the garden, she watched them taking turns dancing with Mike. "He seems to have quite enough women in love with him."

Daphne smiled. "He does. He's an easy man to love. He's sweet and generous and not at all hard to look at, and he takes care of his wounded birds."

After pausing for a moment, Samantha put potato salad in a bowl. "Wounded birds?"

"Yeah," Daphne said. "Like a boy scout, I guess, although I've not met too many of them. Mike likes to rescue people."

"And what does he do with them after he rescues them?" Samantha asked softly.

Daphne smiled. "Gets rid of them fast, as far as I can tell." She nodded toward the women in the garden, each of them looking at Mike with adoring eyes. "Look at them. Each of them thinks she's going to be the one to catch Mike. But you know what? This time next year not one of them will even be invited to this house. But look at me, I've known Mike for two years, I've seen women come and go, all of them looking at him just like they are, but not one of them, as far as I know, even went to bed with him."

"But you're still here," Samantha said.

Daphne picked up the bowl Samantha had filled. "But then I've never fallen for him, have I?" She gave Samantha a look that could only be interpreted as warning. "You watch out, honey, Mike is a heartbreaker, a real heartbreaker."

After her talk with Daphne, Samantha stayed in the kitchen by herself for a while. A heartbreaker, she thought. What she did not need in her life was her heart broken another time. In fact, she didn't think she could stand having her heart torn out of her body another time.

"You okay?" Mike asked from behind her.

Turning, she looked at him. He was so good-looking that it was sometimes difficult to think when he was around. All day long, with every word he'd spoken, she'd been aware of the way his lips moved.

Mike took a step closer to her. "You're looking at me strangely. Want me to tell them to leave?"

Samantha smiled at him coolly. "No, please don't." She turned away from him. "I'm rather tired and I think I'll go to bed."

Moving to stand beside her, Mike cocked his head to gaze inquisitively at her, then put his hand under her chin and made her look at him. "Something's bothering you. Did Daphne say anything? She didn't tell you one of her stories about men, did she? I can tell you that Daphne has a very odd outlook on life."

"No," Samantha said, lying as she moved her chin out of his hand. "It's been a long day and I want to go to bed, that's all."

Mike looked at her. Without moving, without touching her, his face changed to one of such heat, of such desire, that Samantha felt her skin grow warm. "I'd like to go to bed, too," he said softly.

Samantha took a step back from him.

Abruptly, Mike's face changed from desire to anger. "Who's turned you off sex, Samantha?" he asked, making her name sound like a synonym for priggishness.

That made Samantha laugh, and the temptation she'd felt a moment before was gone. "Men are so predictable," she said. "Whether they're a CEO or work in a filling station, they're the same. Because I don't want to go to bed with *you,* you like to think I'm frigid or a victim of incest or something else awful has happened to me. For your information, Mr. Taggert, no one has turned me off sex. But you with your constant touching of me and your vulgar little innuendos are about to. Why don't you ask one of *those* women to go to bed with you?" She nodded toward the women on the other side of the glass doors. "Or do you only want women who tell you no? Is it the challenge that intrigues you? When you're adding another notch to your bedpost, do the women who've told you no repeatedly get a star by their notch?"

Mike was looking at her in bewilderment. "What in the world have I done to make you have such a low opinion of me?"

Turning away from him, Samantha knew she wasn't being fair, for he had been so very kind to her all day. He'd taken more time with her in this one day than any other person had since her mother had died, yet here she was saying vile things to him because he was making a pass at her. But wasn't that what males were *supposed* to do: try?

Maybe his kindness and constant attention was the problem. Maybe she didn't want anyone to pay attention to her.

"I apologize," she said. "I thank you for today, for taking me to the store, for introducing me to your cousin, for—"

"I don't want your bloody thanks," Mike said angrily before turning away to stalk out the door.

Samantha stood where she was for a moment, then went up the stairs to her apartment. She undressed slowly, carefully hanging her lovely new suit up, and for a moment she leaned against the closet door. Sometimes she wished she could cry. Sometimes she wished she could just sit down and bawl like other women seemed able to do, but as much as she wanted it, Samantha knew the tears would not come.

After washing and creaming her face, she put on her nightgown and went to bed. From the lights in the garden below, she could see the outline of her father's furniture. Taking a deep breath, she gave a bit of a smile, for it was good to have her father's things around her, very good indeed.

She went to sleep and somewhere in the middle of the night she woke when a flash of lightning lit the room. Over the outside noise she heard what was becoming a familiar sound to her: Mike was typing. Feeling calmer, she went back to sleep.

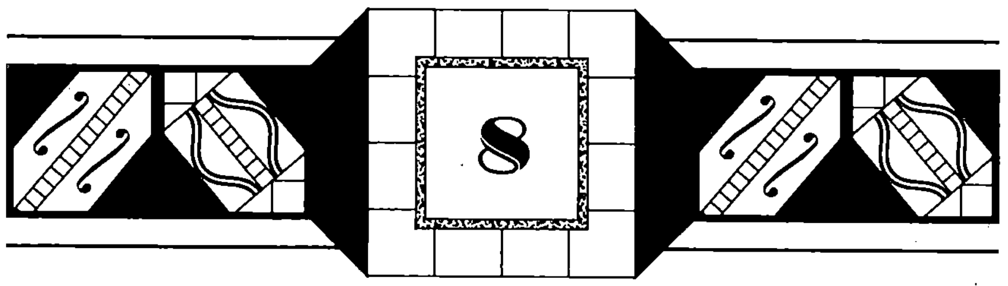

Samantha woke at seven o'clock, but the rain gently coming down outside her windows made her not want to get out of bed. Snuggling under the covers, she went back to sleep. After all, it was Saturday, so why should she get up?

Waking again at nine-thirty, her first thought was of Daphne telling her that Mike was a heartbreaker. Samantha did not want more heartbreak. After a reassuring glance about her father's room at his furnishings, smiling, she went back to sleep.

At eleven she was awakened by a brief knock then the door to her bedroom opening. Sleepily, she looked up to see Mike entering with a tray covered with white food bags. "Go away," she murmured and hid under the covers.

Of course he didn't obey, for as far as she could make out, Michael Taggert was a combination of watchdog, militant nurse, and lecher.

Putting the tray down on the edge of the bed, he sat down beside it. "I brought you food and your clothes from Saks came and Barrett has invited us to tea day after tomorrow. He's sending a car for us."

"Oh?" she said, turning over and looking at him. It was almost beginning to feel familiar to have him sitting on the edge of her bed.

"Which one interests you? The food or Barrett or the clothes?"

"Do you think that little blue jacket came? The one with the big buttons?"

He pulled a muffin from a bag. "So it's the clothes. I don't blame you for being uninterested in a man who may or may not be your relative. Relatives give me a pain too."

Slowly, yawning, Samantha sat up in bed and leaned against the headboard. "You don't know what you're talking about. You don't know how lucky you are to have relatives. Your cousin Vicky was very sweet to me—and very tolerant of you."

Handing her a muffin and a large styrofoam cup full of freshly squeezed orange juice, he said, "She's one of the few Montgomerys who's even tolerable, but then she's not one of the Montgomerys from Maine."

Mike already had his mouth full and there were crumbs on her bed, but he looked so good sprawled there. His thick, dark hair was still damp from a shower, he was freshly shaved, and he had on a soft old denim shirt that outlined every muscle in his body. It was better to keep him talking, she thought, for if he were talking, he wouldn't be touching her. She took a deep breath. "Who are the Montgomerys?"

"They're my cousins and a bigger bunch of wimps you never saw."

"Wimps?"

"Wimps. Pansies," he snapped. "Tea drinkers. There isn't one of them that wouldn't faint at the mere sight of a beer served in its very own bottle."

"And these cousins live in Maine?" she asked as she bit into a bran muffin.

"Yeah." There was hostility in his voice, and she wondered what his cousins had done to cause his antagonism. Seeing the look on her face, he began to explain. "It's a tradition in my family that the Montgomery kids spend half the summer in Colorado and the Taggerts, half in Maine. I don't know who started that tradition, but I'm sure he's roasting in hell now."

"Oh? What happened when you were in Maine?"

"My bastard cousins tried to kill us!"

"You must be kidding."

"Not in the least. They did everything they could to see that we didn't live through the summers. The lot of them live on the sea and they're half fish. My brother says they have fish scales for skin. They used to do things like row us out into the ocean, then dive off the boat and swim back to shore. They knew that not one of us could swim."

"How did you get back to shore?"

Michael smiled in a smirking way. "Rowed. We couldn't swim, but all of us have a bit of muscle."

Samantha smiled at the way he flexed his biceps when he said this. "And what happened when they came to Colorado?"

"Well, we were a bit miffed at the way they'd treated us when we were in Maine."

"Understandable."

"And, too, you have to understand the Montgomerys. They are the most annoying bunch in the world. They were always thanking my mother, and they never forgot to use their napkins at the table. And they folded their clothes."

"That bad, huh?" Sam said, hiding her smile in her cup, but Mike didn't seem to hear the sarcasm in her voice.

"We all felt we were justified in what we did. We put them on the wildest horses we could find. We used to take them into the Rocky Mountains and leave them alone at night with no food or water, without any covering."

"Wasn't that dangerous?"

"Hell, no, not to a Montgomery. As far as we could tell, they're not killable. One of my brothers took one of them out, put the son of a gun at the end of a rope, lowered the rope down a cliffside, and went off and left my cousin hanging there." Mike smiled in memory. "It was two hundred feet down."

"What did your cousin do?"

"I don't know. Somehow, she got back up the rope. She wasn't even late for dinner."

It was the "she" that made Samantha start laughing. Setting her orange juice on the bedside table, she put her hands over her stomach and laughed hard. "Mike, you're dreadful," she said, now realizing that he had been joking all along, creating the story (or, at the very least, exaggerating extravagantly) to entertain her, to make her laugh.

As Michael lay on the bed, he smiled at her, looking thoroughly pleased with himself, the cheshire cat, the cat that ate the cream. His smile made her certain his story hadn't been serious at all, that he had meant to amuse her and was glad he'd done so.

"I'm glad to see that you can laugh," he said, reaching into one of the bags and withdrawing a delicious-smelling muffin. "I got this especially for you."

As she took it from his hand, she thought, He feeds me and he makes me laugh. "What kind is it?"

"Chocolate chip."

Regretfully, she handed the muffin back to him. "Too fattening. I can't eat it."

Sprawling back on the bed, he didn't take the muffin from her. "Just as I thought."

"What does that mean?"

"Nothing. I just won a bet with myself. You don't drink any alcohol to speak of, and left on your own, you dress like an old woman. You ever eat any food that isn't good for you? I'm sure you've never even been tempted to do drugs."

She glared at him. "Hand me that pat of butter. Better yet, hand me *two* pats."

Smiling at her suggestively, he passed her the butter and a plastic knife. "If you're worried about working those calories off, I know a *great* exercise."

Samantha was too intent on her utterly delicious muffin to pay any attention to him. Chocolate chips. Soft white dough. Melted butter.

"Damn it, Samantha, stop looking at *food* like that," Mike said, genuine anger in his voice. Grabbing her hand, he pulled it toward his mouth and took a bite out of her muffin, catching one of her fingers in his soft, warm mouth and licking butter from it. As he did so, he looked at her with hot eyes.

She snatched her hand away. "Does anything, *anything at all,* discourage you?"

"No," he said without much concern, licking his fingers. Lazily, he got up off the bed and stretched.

Watching him, Samantha halted with her muffin halfway to

her mouth. He had broad shoulders, a slim waist, and heavy thighs, and the sight of Michael's body displayed that way was enough to make her forget even chocolate.

When he stopped flexing, she looked away quickly before he saw her gawking. Bending agilely, he shoved leftover food back into the bags.

"Why do you . . . I mean," she said, clearing her throat. "Why do you look as you do?"

"What do you mean?" he asked with exaggerated innocence.

Samantha knew he was trying to get a compliment from her. No doubt he wanted her to say, Why are you dripping muscle? Why do you look like a Greek god? Why do you have a body that Michelangelo would have loved to sculpt? Instead of the words he wanted to hear and the words that came to her mind, she gave him a look that said, You know very well what I mean.

"Power lifting," he said, picking up the tray and setting it on her father's desk.

"Like in the Olympics?"

Mike gave a snort of derision. "Pretty boys. That's Olympic lifting and what Schwarzenegger does is bodybuilding. I power lifted in college in competitions. Heavy stuff. Now I just do what I can to maintain."

Samantha wasn't very good at hiding a smile. "I take it that power lifting is what 'real' men do."

He smiled at her as though he had no idea she was making fun of him, but then, with lightning speed, he scooped her and a couple of blankets off the bed, and while she was demanding that he put her down, he opened the door to the terrace and carried her outside.

Samantha had her hands to her side. "Put me down," she said, doing her best not to touch him.

As though she weighed nothing at all, Mike held her over the rail, then half dropped her.

With a squeal of fright, Samantha grabbed him about the neck, holding him tightly.

"I like this," he said, nuzzling her neck, and when Samantha's grip loosened, he let his arms go slack until she again almost fell. She renewed her tight grip.

Samantha liked being in his arms, liked it very, very much. He was big and warm and so very strong. When he put his lips on her neck, for a moment she closed her eyes.

"Samantha," he whispered.

She had too much self-discipline to give into his plea or into her own desires. "Release me," she said, her voice serious.

Reluctantly, he set her down and for a moment he put his hand to her cheek. "You want to tell me what's bothering you?" he asked softly.

For a moment, Samantha opened her mouth to speak but closed it again and quickly moved away from him. "I have no idea what you're talking about. If I seem unusual to you, I'm sure it's because I have recently buried my father and gone through a divorce. I doubt if anyone is 'normal' for a long time after two such traumatic events."

"Did you write that little speech then rehearse it?" he asked, then when she started to speak, he put up his hand. "I don't want to hear anymore lies or platitudes. Why don't you get dressed and come downstairs and make that computer work? Or better yet, don't dress."

Although Samantha let out a sigh of seeming frustration, she was glad he was no longer being serious. For a happy-go-lucky guy, he could sometimes be disconcertingly perceptive, which was yet another reason for her to get out of New York and away from him.

Grinning, she tried to match his mood. "I shall wear a white lace gown and—"

"Don't!" Mike said, his eyes serious.

"I was just kidding."

Turning away, he went to the door. "I'll give you fifteen minutes, then I want you downstairs. You can't stay up here in this mausoleum." He frowned at the dark furniture and the dark curtains. "You can't stay in this shrine to your father." He left the room before Samantha could think of a reply.

Samantha spent the day with Mike. Heaven, she thought, but he was easy to be with. He was as unlike her father and husband as a person could be. Both her father and Richard had been CPAs, and perhaps that's what gave them their exaggerated sense of order, but both men had always wanted everything in its place—a place chosen by them. Richard's organization of the refrigerator had sometimes made Samantha want to scream. Her idea of doing something wild had been to put the bread in the milk spot. Once, when he was away on an overnight trip, she had taken everything out of the refrigerator and put it all back in different places. She'd even put the breads on three different shelves, something that would have sent Richard into a rage. Of course she put everything back in its correct order before he returned.

Mike wasn't like Richard or her father. Mike seemed to have no hard and fast rules about anything. He didn't eat by the clock, he ate when he was hungry. And he could feed himself! To Samantha this was a miracle. After her mother had died, Samantha had taken over the household chores, and it had been her responsibility to feed her father. She prepared meals at eight in the morning and twelve and at six-thirty, and after she had married, the schedule had stayed the same. Once, at a dinner party in Santa Fe, after she'd had two glasses of wine, someone had philosophically asked, What does it mean to be rich? Samantha was feeling too good to remember her place and control her tongue. Before anyone else spoke, she said, "A rich woman is one who, when she is in the vicinity of a man and that man says he is hungry, does not have a responsibility to feed him. The woman is *truly* rich." Everyone at the table had laughed uproariously at Samantha's comment, but Richard had been furious and after that he'd talked to her about her "tendency toward alcoholism" and had "suggested" that she stop drinking.

Mike wasn't like the two men she had known, for he didn't seem to have rules. Except maybe something on the order of, If it feels good, do it. When he saw Samantha pick up two of his shirts where he'd tossed them across a chair and without thinking about what she was doing slip them onto hangers, he snatched the third shirt out of her hands and threw it on the back of the couch. "I have a maid," he said.

Embarrassed at having performed such a wifely little chore Samantha went to the boxes in the corner of the room and opened them. Pulling the flaps back, she inhaled what has come to be a heavenly smell to modern people: new vinyl. Mike laughed at the look on her face, which made Samantha feel embarrassed again, but she'd already discovered that Mike could take teasing as well as dish it out, unlike her ex-husband who considered himself sacrosanct.

"The smell of new electronic equipment is certainly better

than the cheap perfume that you seem to prefer," she snapped at him, making him laugh.

She had an idea that he meant to sit back and watch her hook up the computer, but she told him she wanted his help. Of course he had no idea how different this was for her. Her father and Richard believed that there was woman's work and men's work and that the two of them should not mingle. In the house she shared with her husband in Santa Fe, she had been in charge of computers, and it wasn't unusual for her to come home from her second, evening job and find Richard in bed asleep, the computer left on, ready for her to save the material he had written that day and turn the machine off.

Now, it didn't take Samantha long to hook up the computer and screen and attach the laser printer. It took a little more time to install the word-processing software, make an autoexec.bat, and set up a few other batch files.

Once the computer was set up, she told Mike she was ready to teach him the basics of how to use it. In the past four years she had taught many people how to use a computer, and she'd dealt with some bizarre problems. There was the woman who had stapled floppies to her printouts and the man who had broken the plastic case off the floppy and tried to insert the thin inner membrane into the disk drive.

But not in four years had she encountered anyone as difficult to teach as Mike, for he couldn't seem to remember anything she told him. In teaching, she'd learned that patience was everything, but after two hours with him, she was losing her composure.

She found herself beginning to shout. "*F* seven, not the number seven," she said to him, but Mike once again hit the number seven key, then looked at her with wide eyes.

Ten minutes later Samantha lost it. Clutching his neck with her hands, she began to choke him. "The F seven key! Do you hear me? The F seven key!"

Laughing, Mike pulled her into his arms, and they went tumbling to the floor together. It was then that she realized he had been pretending to be stupid, and she understood that he'd wanted to know how far she'd go before she lost her composure.

As she rolled away from him, she was extremely annoyed. Why was he always trying to drive her to the point where she was angry?

"Come on, Sam," he said, "Don't give me that look. Don't turn back into little miss goody two shoes."

What she *should* do, she thought, was go upstairs and read a book. Instead, turning, she looked at him sitting there on the living room rug and, in spite of herself, she smiled. "You can really be a pain, you know that?"

Before she could move, he kissed her neck. "Why don't I give you some research cards and you type what I've written into your machine?" he asked.

"I see, I do all the work and you get the credit."

"I'll share anything I have with you," he said softly with great meaning to his words.

Samantha pushed him away. "Let me load the data base, and I'll start putting your information into the computer."

As he smiled at her complacently, she knew he had attained his objective: a secretary.

An hour later, Samantha didn't mind because what Mike was giving her to type was interesting. He had written out what looked to be a hundred pages of information on various gangsters who'd had something to do with Tony Barrett. She read the names of Nails and Hop Toad and Mad Dog and the Waiter and Half Hand Joe and Gyp the Blood with interest.

The more she read, the more she wondered about Tony Barrett, who might or might not be her biological grandfather. But there was very little information about him in the notes Mike gave her to type. When she asked Mike why there was so little on Barrett, who was to be the subject of the biography, Mike didn't really answer but gave her notes on what Samantha soon realized was the slaughter of May the twelfth, 1928.

She didn't like typing about that day in 1928. The leading gangster of New York had been afraid of Barrett's growing power and had decided to kill him and all his men. It didn't seem to matter that during his failed attempt to kill Barrett, Barrett had been in a speakeasy and that many innocent people were killed along with the gangsters in the blasts of machine gun fire.

With growing distaste, Samantha read about the bloodshed of that night. "I don't like this," she said, pushing the notes away.

Mike raised an eyebrow. "Maxie disappeared that night. Aren't you curious as to why?"

She looked at him in disbelief. "It seems simple enough to understand why she left. Even if she did love Barrett, she wouldn't want to be part of something as horrifying as that bloodbath."

Mike looked at her for a moment, then asked if she wanted something to eat. When her answer was positive, he called a deli and ordered tuna salad sandwiches. After they arrived, they took them into the garden to eat.

"How did your mother die?" Mike asked abruptly, as soon as they were seated at the picnic table.

"I killed her," Samantha said before she thought, then blushed and looked away. She was annoyed with him for making her tell things that she didn't want to tell and annoyed with herself for confiding in him. "I don't mean that, of course. It's just what I felt at the time. A child's fantasy." She tried to make light of the fear that had plagued her for most of her life.

Mike was looking at her in silence, waiting for her to continue.

"I was twelve and I'd been invited to Janie Miles's birthday party. It was a very important party because Janie was the most popular girl in school and she was going to have *boys* at her party, but Mother didn't want me to go. When she said I was too young for boys, I got very angry and said she didn't want me to grow up. Mother said I was right, that if it were up to her I'd stay twelve years old forever." Samantha tried her best to make her story sound amusing, for she didn't want Mike to know what she had felt—and still felt now—about her mother's death. Actually, she didn't want anyone to know the full extent of how her life, her world, had changed after that fateful afternoon.

Samantha took a deep breath. "Anyway, when Mother was late picking me up from school to take me to Janie's party I was livid. I was pacing the school yard vowing to never again speak to her when the principal came to take me home."

Mike was looking at Samantha's hand as she had gripped the tuna sandwich so hard that it was oozing through her fingers. When she noticed where he was looking, she glanced down and saw the mutilated sandwich, then dropped it and used a napkin to clean her hand.

"Mother had been rushing so hard to get me to the party she'd run in front of a car. She was killed instantly."

"Sam—" Reaching out to her, Mike tried to touch her, but she pulled away.

"Mother had been rushing so fast that somewhere along the way she'd fallen against a radiator and burned her arms and legs. But a little thing like third-degree burns didn't make her stop to go to a doctor. Her only thought was to get her daughter to a party." Pausing, Samantha's mouth twisted bitterly. "A very important party."

"Was it a hit-and-run?" Mike asked quickly, not wanting her to dwell on her memories, but he needed to know what she was telling him.

"Heavens no." Looking across the picnic table at him, she tried to smile. "The man who hit her lived in Ohio, and he was very upset about the accident. He stayed in Louisville for two weeks after Mother . . . died and visited Dad and me, even showing me pictures of his own children."

"Samantha," Mike whispered, "I'm sorry."

"Yeah, thanks," she murmured. "It was a long time ago and I got over it. People can survive a great deal."

"Even husbands?" he asked, trying to make a joke.

She didn't smile. "One can survive husbands who betray them and mothers who die and fathers who die and grandmothers who desert them. One can even survive a father who has so little confidence in his daughter that he attaches strings to her inheritance. I find that one can survive almost anything." Getting up from the table, she started back into the house, but not before Mike caught her.

"Sam," he said, his hands on her shoulders as he turned her to face him. "If you ever want someone to talk to, I'm here."

She forced herself to smile at him. "There's really nothing to talk about. Nothing more than the ordinary person has to say, that is. I've had an extraordinary number of deaths in my life and one divorce and it'll take me a while to recover, but I will." She moved away from him. "Why don't I type more of your notes?"

Frowning, Mike watched her walk back to the library. No matter what he did, he couldn't seem to penetrate the shell that surrounded her, yet sometimes he glimpsed a Samantha that lay under the surface of the cool, calm, always-in-control person she presented to the world. When he had kissed her, he had seen a woman of passion. When she laughed, he saw a woman with a sense of humor. When she drank too much wine, he saw a woman who could tease and make bawdy jokes. But she never let her guard down for long. After each and every lapse, she drew herself back under control again. She was like a turtle that was being attacked and kept inside its shell, but now and then it stuck its vulnerable head out and looked around and soon retracted again.

Her father had said that when Samantha was a child she had been very different from the young lady she had grown into. Smiling, Dave had said that when she was a child, Sam had been a handful, that she had tangled herself into scrapes that had nearly driven her mother crazy. Samantha had been such a tree-climbing, sassy-mouthed, fearless little hellion—called Sam by one and all—that her mother said it took all her brains just trying to stay ahead of her rambunctious daughter.

Sometimes Mike caught glimpses of that little girl, but most of the time it was next to impossible. He wanted to do his best to get under her skin so he could see the imp her father had described. Smiling, Mike remembered the way Sam had tried to choke him when he refused to remember her lessons with the computer. He had no intention of learning to use a computer, because if he did, he'd have one less excuse to spend time with Samantha. Right now, his major goal in life was to get to know her, for being around her was like watching a rosebud unfold. Daily she seemed to change and blossom more. Now all he had to do was make sure that she didn't leave his house after their meeting with Barrett. That was two days away, and if she left him in a mere two days, he knew he'd never see her again. The thought of not seeing Sam again was not something he wanted to contemplate.

"Sam," he yelled as he followed her into the library. "Did you know that Maxie was a singer? She sang the blues."

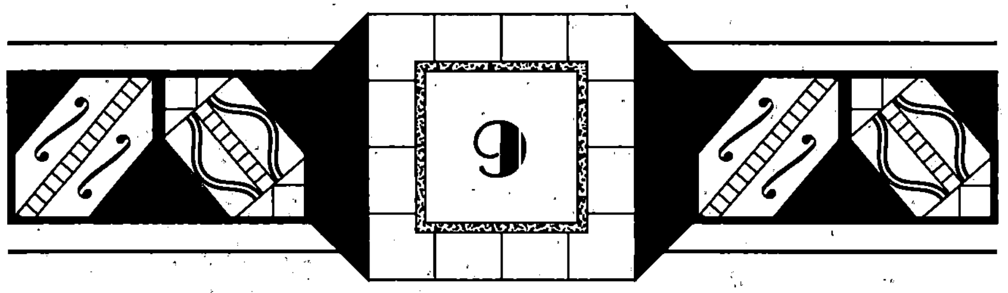

"I have a date tonight," Mike announced to Samantha. He was watching her with such intensity that she knew she was supposed to make some response, but she wasn't sure what.

"How nice. One of the young women I met with Daphne?"

"No, she's no one you know." His dark eyes never so much as blinked as he stared at her. "A chorus girl actually. A dancer. Legs, that sort of thing."

"I'm glad to hear that she has legs. Especially if she's a dancer."

From the look on Mike's face, she knew she had disappointed him. "What will you do while I'm gone? Sleep?"

"You may persist in your fantasy that I am on the verge of psychosis without your constant presence, but it doesn't happen to be true. I will probably wash my hair and watch TV. If that meets my guardian's approval," she said snidely. She was laughing at him because she realized that he wanted her to be jealous of his date. The truth was, Samantha was actually a teeny tiny bit curious about this leggy date of his. Not jealous, by any means, but curious. She knew he didn't like the women who'd arrived with Daphne, but what kind of woman *did* Mike like? Probably tall bimbos with big bosoms, she thought. Big bosoms, long legs, and no brains.

"Yeah fine," he half mumbled. "I don't think you should go out at night though."

"Of course not. And I won't allow any strangers in, no matter how much candy they offer me—unless of course it's a box of really good chocolate-covered caramels. I belong to the man who offers me caramels."

It was obvious from his expression that he didn't find her levity humorous—and he did want her to be jealous.

"Mike," she said, smiling, feeling a little flattered by his concern and his seeming to want her to be as possessive as he was. "Go on, go on your date. I'll be fine. Nothing will happen to me, and I won't do anything strange, so you don't have to worry about me. Go. Have a good time."

He hesitated, for he didn't trust her at all. If this appointment weren't so important, he wouldn't leave. "All right, I'm going, but lock the door behind me."

She shook her head at him, but when he was gone, she bolted the door, and when she turned back, the house seemed enormous and a little creepy with Mike gone. After drawing the curtains, she jumped when a siren screamed down Lexington Avenue. When the doorbell rang, she nearly came out of her skin, then laughed at herself. Waiting a moment for her heart to settle down before she went to the door, she opened the little panel and looked out.

A man was standing there, a tall, broad-shouldered, dark-haired, extremely handsome man. "Yes?" she said through the grill.

"Is Mike home?" he asked.

"Yes, but he's busy at the moment," she answered cautiously. If this man was a criminal, she could understand the high rate of crime in New York.

"Would you tell him that Raine wants to see him?" When Samantha made no response, he said, "Raine Montgomery. His cousin."

"Oh. Do you have any identification?" She watched him remove his wallet from inside his suit jacket and hold his driver's license up to the grill. Raine Montgomery. Thirty years old. Six foot one. Black hair, blue eyes. He looked authentic to her—authentically gorgeous. She unlocked the door.

"Actually, Mike isn't here," she said, opening the door. "He had a date and went out a few minutes ago."

The man smiled at her and she smiled back. He was very different from Mike, and all they seemed to share as cousins was dark hair. Mike was all fire and movement, whereas this man was quiet and mysterious.

"Actually, I came to meet you. That is, if you're Samantha."

"I am, but how . . .?"

He smiled again and she smiled broader in response. "Mike's mother called me from Colorado and asked me to have a look at you. Mike has mentioned you, and Aunt Pat wanted me to make sure you weren't a gold digger."

She found his honesty disarming. "Won't you come in?" she said, sweeping her arm toward the living room.

"I'd better not. It wouldn't be . . ."

"Proper?" she asked. Mike had said his Montgomery cousins had manners and here was proof. Here was a man in the twentieth century who was concerned about what was proper and what wasn't. Propriety was not something that seemed to concern Michael Taggert, for half of his day seemed to be spent lounging on Sam's bed—uninvited, unwanted.

"I think I'll return when Mike is here, but I shall call Aunt Pat this evening and tell her that she can rest her fears, that you are an imminently respectable and extremely pretty young woman."

Blushing under his praise, she followed him to the door. "I'm sure Mike will be sorry he missed you."

As he stepped onto the porch, the man laughed in a way that let her know he was fully aware of Mike's antagonism toward his cousin. He turned back to her. "You said Mike is on a date. I thought . . . I mean, I understood that you and he had moved in together."

Wanting to make herself clear from the start, she said, "I'm sure Mike gave his mother that impression, but actually I'm merely his tenant. I rent the top two floors."

At this information, Raine's eyes brightened. "In that case, would you like to go out with me tomorrow? Maybe in the afternoon? We could go to the park and eat ice cream and watch the kids play."

Samantha was sure she'd never heard such a romantic invitation in her life. So different from Mike's, let's-go-to-bed-and-screw-our-brains-out-honey type of invitation. "I would love to go out with you," she said sincerely.

Looking at her as though nothing in his life had ever pleased him as much as her acceptance, he smiled. "Tomorrow at two, then," he said and walked down the stairs to the sidewalk.

She was still standing in the doorway, watching him walk away when he turned back to her. "What color of balloons do you like best?" he asked.

"Pink," she answered, smiling.

Still smiling, he waved and kept walking down the block.

Going into the house, Samantha shut the door behind her. What a delightful man, she thought. What an utterly lovely, sweet man. Smiling, humming, she went upstairs to wash her hair.

"A Montgomery!" Mike shouted when Samantha mentioned her approaching date to him. "A goddamn nose-in-the-air Montgomery. You're going out with a mother—"

"Stop it," she yelled back. "I've told you a thousand times that what I do is none of your business. I am your tenant, nothing more than that. Your *tenant*! Your renter and that's *all*. You don't own me or have any right to tell me what to do."

"But a Montgomery! You can't—"

She turned on him. "As far as I can tell, Raine Montgomery is a very nice man. He—"

"You don't know anything about him," he snapped, as though he knew something dreadful about his cousin.

"I know that he has manners, which is more than I can say for you." She stopped shouting and drew a deep breath. "Can you honestly tell me anything bad about the man? Is he a criminal of any kind? Already married? Does he even have any bad habits?"

"He's perfect," Mike said with a curl of his upper lip. He was so angry he was shaking. Never before in his life had he felt so betrayed. In the last few days he'd put out five times the effort with Samantha that he'd ever expended on any other female, yet she'd given him less in return than any woman he'd ever met. The girl at the corner grocery was more obliging than Samantha was!

Seeing his anger, which had no justification whatever, she threw up her hands in frustration. "This is the strangest situation anyone has ever been in. Last night you went out on a date. Why is it all right for you and not for me?"

Leaning toward her, he put his nose close to hers. "Because my 'date' was eighty-six years old and in a nursing home. I'd been told that she once worked in the nightclub where Maxie sang. Maxie, remember her? *Your* grandmother. I was out on a Saturday night interviewing some old woman who couldn't remember who she was, much less what happened in 1928, while you were in *my* house flirting and heaven only knows what else with one of those goddamn Montgomerys."

She glared at him. "You're sick, you know that? You should see a doctor." Turning away from him, she started toward the stairs. "I have a feeling Raine is punctual. I will be down at exactly two."

In spite of her telling Mike that this was none of his business, his rage had upset her. Didn't it ever cross a man's mind to wonder if he had the right to be angry? Never in her adult life had she been angry that she hadn't asked herself if she *should* be angry. By any logic in the world Mike shouldn't be upset because she was going out with another man. She was an adult; she was unattached; there was nothing romantic between her and Mike. So *why* was he furious?

She gritted her teeth. Just once in her life she'd like to understand, really, truly understand, what went on inside a man's head.

Suddenly, she stopped ranting at Mike. How very odd, she thought, to be this angry at a man who meant so little to her. She hadn't been this angry after she'd found out what her husband had done, nor had she been this angry after she'd heard her father's will. She remembered wanting to throw something through a window when she'd heard the terms of her father's will, yet she'd been able to control herself.

But Mike could make her throw things. Michael Taggert made her want to tear telephone books in half with her bare hands.

Jerking the closet door open, she looked inside at the heavenly clothes hanging there and touched the sleeve of a soft, peach-colored jacket and remembered how nice Mike had been when they'd bought the clothes. He was half the most pleasant, easiest person she'd ever been around in her life and half the most infuriating, exasperating person she'd ever met. Sometimes she wanted to climb in his lap and tell him things she'd never told another person, and sometimes she wanted to hit him in the head with an axe—sharp side down.

All in all, she thought as she reached for a pair of linen trousers, it would be better for both of them if she left immediately after they saw Barrett. There had been too much turmoil in Samantha's life already for her to live in a house where she fought with her landlord.

10

Answering the doorbell to his cousin's ring, Mike stood for a moment with his hand on the doorknob, not allowing Raine to enter. "You touch her, Montgomery, and you'll never be able to breed any children."

Without a smile, Raine nodded, acknowledging what Mike meant: He had claim on Samantha.

Turning away, Mike left the room, for he didn't think he could stand to see Sam smiling at another man. But in spite of his noble intentions, he found himself standing at the front window the moment he heard the door close behind them, standing there watching the two of them walk toward Central Park. Physically, Mike thought, they were wrong for each other. Samantha's small curvy body didn't match his cousin's tall, thin, scrawny body.

Mike looked away from them in disgust, disgust at himself. Maybe Sam was right and he *was* crazy. Never before had he been eaten with jealousy as he was right now, and frankly, he didn't much like the feeling. Nor did he understand why he felt jealous, for Samantha had certainly never given him any encouragement to think that she belonged to him.

Her father had, he thought in his own defense. Her father had asked Mike to take care of his precious daughter after he was gone. The first month he had done a poor job of looking out for her, but since then he'd tried to make up for lost time.

Sighing, Mike thought of the lonely afternoon ahead of him. Who was going to be here to take delight in something as ordinary as ordering from a deli? Who was going to ask him questions and take an interest in his research? Who was going to smell the roses in the garden? Who was going to look him up and down whenever she thought he wasn't looking?

As Mike started to turn away from the window, he saw a man step from the shadow of a building across the street and start walking. In New York one saw people everywhere, but something about this man made Mike notice him. For one thing, he had been standing in that same place yesterday. Mike had noticed him because all men who worked out noticed other men whose triceps strained against the back of their shirt sleeves. This guy wasn't that big, he wasn't so big that his lats kept his arms from touching his ribs, but he did indeed know which end of a barbell to pick up.

Unlatching the window, Mike pushed it up and stuck his head out. After watching for a moment, he didn't know why, but he was ninety-nine percent sure that the man was following Sam and his cousin.

Mike didn't lose a moment, and was out the door in seconds, following the man across Park Avenue, Madison, then Fifth, and into the park. At the park, Mike was sure the man was following Samantha when he stepped behind the statue of General Sherman while Raine bought Sam an ice cream and a couple of balloons.

For a moment, Mike's attention strayed from the man, because Sam was looking up at his string bean of a cousin with a face drippy with sentimentality. From the look on her face a person would have thought that no one had ever given her anything as wonderful as that half-thawed ice cream and the cheap balloons. His stupid cousin was grinning back at her as though he'd presented her the head of a dragon.

"Give me a break," Mike said in disgust.

The next moment the two of them went strolling through

the park, not aware that anyone other than themselves existed, while Mike stayed back until he saw the man who was following them move. The man made no attempt at secrecy and at one point even walked ahead of them, sat on a bench, and watched them walk past.

As he stayed hidden, Mike didn't allow the man to see him, because if he'd been watching the house, he would recognize Mike.

For the next forty-five minutes, as Mike followed the man, he watched Samantha and his cousin. To give Raine credit, he never laid a hand on Samantha, but every time she so much as smiled at the bean pole, Mike wanted to smash him in the face. It was when the two of them stopped at the children's playground that Mike thought he was going to be sick. Deftly catching a swing with one hand, Raine helped Sam onto the seat as though she were an invalid, then gave her a little push, while Sam laughed in utter delight, as though he'd accomplished some great feat.

"I should have killed him the summer we were both twelve," Mike muttered.

Mike did have a moment of pleasure when Samantha stopped the swing and started to get out, because when Raine put out a hand to help Sam out of the swing, she moved away from his touch.

"It isn't just me," Mike said in satisfaction.

After the swings they walked along through the twisting paths and every time they disappeared from his sight, the hairs on the back of Mike's neck rose. It was when Raine stepped away from Sam to retrieve a baseball and throw it back to some kids that Mike realized the man who was following them was nowhere in sight. Mike's attention had been on whether or not his skinny cousin was touching Sam and had strayed from the real reason he was playing private eye.

For a moment, Mike looked about in panic, knowing that something was wrong. Where was the man? *Who* was the man?

Mike saw Samantha standing in the shade of some trees watching Raine with a syrupy expression on her face, and behind her, coming down the hill slowly so he wouldn't make a sound was the man.

Mike began to run. He ran across a blanket spread with food, causing the picnickers to yell at him; he leaped over a bench filled with people and they shrieked at him. When he hit the clump of trees he was still running, and when he hit the man with all his two hundred pounds of muscle, he flattened him. For several moments, hidden in the shadow of the trees, the two of them struggled, but it was no contest. Mike was much stronger than the man and soon had him pinned to the ground.

"Who are you?" Mike asked, holding the man down. "What do you want?"

The man had a look on his face that said he'd die before he said a word, and suddenly Mike knew the answers to his questions. "Barrett sent you, didn't he?"

There was the merest flicker in the man's eyes that let Mike know he was right.

"Why?" Mike asked, truly puzzled. "Does he want to know about his granddaughter?"

He never received an answer, because the man took advantage of Mike's puzzlement to pick up a rock and hit Mike on the head with it. The pain of the blow, as well as the unexpectedness of it, sent Mike reeling, and the man lost no time in disappearing. For a moment Mike sat on the ground, his hand to his head, his vision unclear.

"Michael Taggert! How could you do this? How could you spy on me?"

Looking up, he saw Samantha standing over him, hands on hips, and he thought her face was angry, but his vision was too blurry to be sure.

"This is really too much," she said as she went back down the hill.

As Mike blinked a few times, trying to clear his vision, a handkerchief appeared before his eyes. Taking it, he pressed it to his head in the general vicinity of the pain.

"Are you all right?"

He recognized the voice of his cousin and as Mike tried to stand, there was a strong arm placed under his to help him up.

"Mike?"

"I'm okay," he managed to say when he was standing and holding the handkerchief to his temple, feeling the warmth of the blood that was beginning to trickle down through his hair.

"You want to tell me what happened?"

"No," Mike said, not looking at his cousin. "Is Sam all right?"

Raine looked into the sunlit field where Samantha was

watching some children play. "She's fine. Is there a reason she might not be all right?"

"I don't know. I don't think anyone wants to harm her. There's no reason to hurt her." He looked at his cousin. "Watch out for her, will you?"

Raine nodded, then watched Mike walk away through the trees and saw him stagger once and catch himself on one of the many boulders in the park. After a moment, Raine went down the hill to Samantha and told her he had to make a telephone call. If he knew Mike, he'd not go to a doctor with his head wound, so Raine was going to call a doctor and request a house call.

11

It was an hour and a half later that Samantha walked into Mike's house and by then her temper was boiling. She'd had more than enough time to think about his following her, and she had strengthened her resolve to leave New York as soon as possible. Tomorrow afternoon she would go with him to see his old gangster, then early on Tuesday she'd catch a plane out of the city.

By the time she reached the town house, Raine close beside her, her only thought was to tell Mike what she thought of him. Standing at the door, she politely thanked Raine, even offered him her hand to shake. Instead of shaking it, he sweetly and expertly kissed the back of her hand. At another time Samantha would have been flattered by his attentions and his polite respect, but now her only thought was of getting to Mike and telling him what a lying, sneaking, rotten creep he was.

When Raine was gone, she unlocked the front door to the town house, her hands made into fists as she prepared herself for the coming argument. She had rehearsed how she was going to tell him that he was never to do anything like that again—not that she was going to give him the chance since she was leaving in under two days—but she wanted to let him know how childishly he had behaved.

The house was quiet, almost too quiet. If there was one thing Mike wasn't, it was quiet. She went into the garden, then into the library, where he was often sitting at his old-fashioned typewriter, then into the kitchen. Looking at the empty living room, she frowned, for it hadn't occurred to her that he wouldn't be in the house waiting for her.

It was when she was leaving the living room that she thought she heard a sound. Turning back, she walked fully into the room and saw Mike asleep on the couch.

"Michael Taggert," she began, "I want to talk to you about—" She broke off because she realized that he was asleep. But there was more to the way he was sprawled on the leather couch than mere sleep, for he was shirtless and shoeless, but he still wore his trousers, which were grass stained and dirty.

"Mike," she said, walking toward him, but he didn't move at the sound of her voice. She walked closer, and as she did, she stepped on his shirt lying on the floor. As she nearly always did, she picked it up—and saw the blood on it. Dark, dried spots of blood were on the collar and the right shoulder of his shirt.

After hanging the shirt on the back of a chair, she bent over him. "Mike," she whispered, and when he didn't stir, she touched his bare shoulder, but he still didn't move. On the table beside the couch was a brown bottle of prescription medicine, which she picked up, reading the name of a drug she knew to be a pain killer and a narcotic.

Putting her hand on his chin, she turned his head to face her and saw a large white bandage on the right side of his head. Stunned, surprised, even feeling a bit of fear, she sat down heavily on the floor beside him and sighed, "Oh, Mike, what in the world have you done?" She had a vision of his following her and in his blind obsession, falling against the boulders in the park.

He stirred in his sleep, his arm falling off the couch and landing against her. She started to place his arm on his chest, but there wasn't enough room on the couch for the width of Mike. Was there anything in the world more appealing than a strong man who was temporarily helpless? she wondered. While trying not to think of what she was doing, she touched his face, ran her fingertips over the rough whiskers just under his skin, and felt an almost uncontrollable urge to climb on the couch beside him to snuggle against him. He was in a drugged sleep so he'd never know what she'd done, she thought, and for a moment she'd have the wonderful feeling of touching another human being.

When he stirred again, he nearly fell off the couch, and Samanatha found herself with a great deal of Mike's weight leaning against her. If she moved, he'd fall to the floor, and if she didn't move, about two-thirds of her body was going to go to sleep in about twenty seconds.

"Mike," she said, then louder, "Mike!" She tried to push him off of her, but two hunderd pounds of sleeping male muscle was more than she could handle. "Mike!" she screamed, pushing as hard as she could.

Partially opening his eyes, he saw her and smiled. "Sammy," he said dreamily, putting his big hand into the curls of her hair. "You okay?" He didn't give her a chance to answer before he went back to sleep, still half on the couch, half off, still leaning on her.

"Michael Taggert!" she screamed. "Wake up!"

Reluctantly, he opened his eyes again and blinked at her.

"You're crushing me," she said.

With a sleepy smile, he pulled her up on the couch on top of him and, comfortable now, went back to sleep.

For a moment she lay where she was, full length on top of him, her cheek against his bare chest. How many years had it been since she'd been held by another human being? For a few months after she and her husband had been married, he'd made a pretense of loving her and wanting her, but the pretense had not lasted long. Within four months of their marriage they might as well have been roommates for all the physical contact between them.

Now, she might have been content to lie on top of Mike forever if his hand hadn't strayed from her back down to her buttocks. He obviously wasn't *that* thoroughly asleep.

Putting her sharp elbows into his ribs, she gouged as hard as she could.

Mike came awake with a grunt and a frown, but when he saw her on top of him, his face changed to delight. "Oh, Sammy, " he said, putting his hand on the back of her head to move her to kiss him.

Samantha moved her head to one side so his lips wouldn't touch hers as she pushed her elbows into his ribs again. When he yelped with pain, she scrambled off of him just as Mike made a lunge for her, missed, then fell to the floor with a thud that made the house shake.

He blinked up at her in drug-glazed bewilderment.

"Michael," she said softly, trying not to allow her voice to betray what she was feeling, that she wanted to stay with him, wanted to continue touching him. "I think you should go to bed. The couch is too small for you to sleep on."

Lying back on the carpet, he closed his eyes.

"Michael," she said again. "You have to get up." When he didn't move, she started to walk away, but he caught her ankle.

"Help me get up," he said, sounding weak and neglected.

She knew as well as she knew anything in life that he didn't need her assistance to get up, but at the same time she couldn't allow him to spend the night on the floor. Maybe he had been spying on her today, but maybe he had a reason to do so. Maybe he thought his cousin might harm her. As Mike had said a million times, he was supposed to take care of her, and perhaps in his mind, following her to the park *was* taking care of her.

Kneeling, she pulled his arm around her shoulders, then tried to help him stand up. It took quite some time to get him to his feet and even longer to get him all the way up the stairs and into his bedroom.

Once in the bedroom, she turned away as he unzipped his trousers and removed his socks then slipped under the covers. But there was a mirror, and she did just happen to see that he wore blue cotton underwear, the kind that were low cut on his hips. She also just happened to notice the way his thighs curved into his buttocks, the way there was no hair at the very tops of his legs.

When he closed his eyes as soon as his head touched the pillow, Samantha couldn't help herself as she tucked the cover about him.

"Don't go," he whispered as she started to leave the room.

"You need to sleep. Those pills are killers."

He smiled but didn't open his eyes. "Did you enjoy your date?" He sounded as though he were merely asking after her welfare and was interested in her afternoon, but he didn't fool her.

"We had a marvelous time. Raine is the most charming, the most handsome man I have ever met. I have agreed to bear his child."

Mike's eyes flew open, then after a momentary look of horror, he lay back on the pillow. "You are a cruel woman. Come over here and sit by me and tell me a story."

She knew she should stay away from him. After all, she was leaving in what was now a matter of hours and it was no good to get more attached to him than she already was. On the other hand, he had no doubt cracked his head open because of his misplaced sense of chivalry.

Primly, she sat on the edge of the bed, as far away from his warm, sleepy, nearly nude body as possible. "What story would you like to hear? About Peeping Tom?"

He didn't open his eyes. "Tell me one of your I-hate-men-and-I-especially-hate-marriage stories."

Blinking a few times, she laughed, but it didn't take her but a second to think of such a story. "I read a book that put forth the theory that the major cause of divorce in America is housework. The wives have to work at a job all day then come home and do all the housework too with no help from their husbands. After years of study, the author said she thought that modern women were marrying men, having two or three children, then getting a divorce. The husbands had served their purpose and were no longer needed, so the women got rid of them. Like the drones in the bee family, I guess."

"I hate to bring up matters that seem distasteful to you, but what about sex? Are the women willing to do without sex for the rest of their lives?"

"I didn't say the women were celibate, and besides, what does married sex mean anyway? He tosses your nightgown over your head and makes noise for four minutes."

At that Mike opened his eyes, looked at her, then began to laugh. He laughed so much and so hard that Samantha got off the bed, but he caught her hand and pulled her back to sit by him. She sat there, but stiffly.

"I am pleased that I amuse you so much." Her voice dripped sarcasm.

"You do," he said. "You amuse me a great deal, but I am also beginning to understand you."

She tried to snatch her hand away, but he held her fast. "You need to sleep and I need to pack."

"Pack for what?" he asked.

"For leaving this city. After we see Barrett tomorrow, I'm free, remember? You aren't going back on your word, are you? You *are* going to give me the money, aren't you?"

He opened his eyes fully. "Yes, I'm going to release the money if you visit Barrett with me. But, Sam, where are you going? Do you have anyone to look after you?"

She jerked her hand from his grasp. "I don't have any relatives, if that's what you mean. I'm afraid I wasn't blessed as you were with a relative on every street corner. I—"

"Cursed," he said. "Relatives are a curse. Always spying on you. Always—"

Suddenly, she came off the bed and glared down at him in anger. "You have no idea what you're talking about! You take everything for granted. You saunter into a store like Saks and expect your cousin to stop working and help you out. Your cousin Raine first came to your house to make sure I wasn't a gold digger out to rob you out of house and home. Your family *cares* about you, and I'd give anything in the world to have . . ." She stopped, realizing she was revealing too much about herself.

"To have what, Sam?" he asked softly.

"To have you stop calling me Sam," she spat at him, avoiding the issue. "Now go back to sleep. Tomorrow we visit your gangster." She turned to leave the room.

"What did you and my cousin talk about?"

You, she almost said, but caught herself. "Oh the usual, life and love and all the things that matter."

"What did he tell you about me?" Mike's voice was getting weak; he was falling asleep again.

"He said that all the Taggerts were rather poor, but that your family was excellent at breeding children and all of you could add and subtract very well."

Mike smiled sleepily, his eyes closed. "He was right about the kids part. I'll give you a free demonstration any time you want."

Trying not to smile, but failing, Samantha said, "Go to sleep," and left the room.

Samantha was dressed primly and properly in a beautifully cut Italian suit that she had no idea had cost Mike over four grand. Sitting in the back of the stretch limo, she kept pulling on the short skirt until Mike picked up her hand and kissed her fingertips while giving a look that asked her to please stop fidgeting. The man across from them glanced from one to the other but made no comment.

"The man is your grandfather," Mike said. "There's no reason to be nervous. And, besides, darling, I'll be there to take care of you."

Samantha shot him a look that said, "drop dead," and snatched her hand away. She wasn't nervous about meeting an old man who claimed to be related to her; her nervousness was caused by her asking herself what she was going to do after she left New York. This morning a groggy Mike had asked her if she was packed and if she'd made her plane reservations. It was her turn to lie and say that she had. Plane reservations to where? she wondered. There was nothing in Louisville for her; there was certainly nothing in Santa Fe. Maybe she'd go to San Francisco. Or maybe she'd travel for a while and see something of the world. After all, she was free to go and do whatever she wanted. But the idea of traveling alone didn't send any great charge of excitement vibrating through her.

Now she sat on the plush leather seat of the long limousine and wondered what she was going to do with her life. After this meeting, after Mike got what he wanted from her, there'd be no reason to stay in New York. No reason at all.

They rode through the country in the long, black car that Mike's old gangster had sent to pick them up. She and Mike had done little talking this morning, because Mike had walked into the kitchen with what Samantha could tell was a prepared story about the cut on his head. "If what you're about to tell me is a lie, I'd rather hear nothing," she'd said. She'd watched him struggle as he tried to form words, but at last he'd said nothing about his injury. Instead he had asked her if she knew how to make coffee. She said she didn't and had no intention of learning. She had been so furious with him that she'd spent the morning in the garden pulling weeds.

After a deli lunch that she'd refused to share with him, she'd dressed for the meeting with Barrett. At one-thirty there had been a call, and Mike came to tell her that the car would be on time.

"Why are you so angry with me?" he'd asked.

"You spied on me and you started to lie to me about what you'd done. I think that's reason enough for anger."

He hadn't been in the least contrite. Instead, he'd said smugly, "There are some things that you shouldn't know."

That had infuriated her more than what he'd done, and she was determined not to speak to him again, but then the long, black car stopped in front of the house. Mike had picked up her hand and started to slip a ring on it. Instinctively, Samantha drew back from him.

"If you're my fiancée, you need a ring. Will this do?"

In his hand was a gorgeous diamond ring that was about five carets of a pale yellow. She knew without being told that this was what was called a canary diamond. "Is that real?" she said under her breath.

"It belonged to my grandmother, and as far as I know, it's real."

She stared at it as he tried to slip it on her finger, but it stuck above her second knuckle. When the doorbell rang, she started to draw away from him, but to her consternation, Mike put her ring finger in his mouth and moved it around. Sam's eyes widened, for she'd never before experienced anything as utterly sensual as her finger inside this man's warm mouth. She watched Mike's lips, those lips that fascinated her, as he slowly pulled her damp finger out of his mouth then easily slipped the ring over her knuckle.

"That's better, isn't it?"

"Yes," she said, but her voice came out in a croak. Trying to get control of herself, she cleared her throat. "Ah . . . thanks."

"Anytime, Sam, my girl. Anytime, any place, any body part," he said as he slipped her arm in his and led her out to the waiting limo.

Now, as they finally reached Barrett's house, Samantha looked out the window in awe, for it wasn't a house but an estate, in the full meaning of the word. Huge gates that were flanked by high brick walls opened to a long drive that meandered through a tree-lined park. They seemed to drive for hours before they reached the house, which was as big as an institution.

Everywhere they looked there were muscular men jammed into too-tight suits with wires running from their ears down into the backs of their ill-fitting jackets. Two men with lean, hungry-looking dogs on leashes walked around the perimeter of the walls. As Samantha got out of the car, she thought that this must be how the president of the United States was protected, except that there looked to be more men here than she'd seen in photos of the president.

Standing for a moment looking about the place, Mike was trying his best to memorize every rock, every tree, and, more importantly, every face around him. He was the first and maybe only outsider to see this compound since Barrett had moved here many years ago, and he was going to have to describe it all in his book.

Mike dawdled as long as he could, even once bending to retie his shoelace. On the surface, everything about the place looked good, but on second glance, Mike saw evidence of neglect: gutters that hadn't been cleaned, a window pane that had been cracked and not replaced, flower gardens that needed weeding. Was it that Doc didn't care how the place looked? On the other hand, maintaining a place this size took a lot of money.

"Move it," the big man who had ridden with them—and not said a word during the entire trip—said as he gave Mike a shove. Mike had to force himself not to retaliate to the man's pushing as he followed Samantha into the house.

Inside, Samantha was looking about in astonishment. The rooms in the house were huge, made for a time of gracious living, and they were filled with antiques and paintings. Porcelains filled the niches in the walls.

While Samantha was feeling that she wished she had on a hostess gown and a few emeralds, Mike was looking at the place with the eye of one who has grown up in a house that made this one look like a pauper's den. For the most part, the antiques were fakes, as were the paintings and the porcelains. They weren't even very good copies, and there were a couple of places on the walls where the flocked wallpaper was lighter, as though a painting had been removed.

Also, there were no servants in sight, only the goons with the ear wires. Surreptitiously, Mike ran his hand over a table, feeling the dust on it as the guard motioned for them to follow him into another room.

The living room was big and light with windows looking onto the ocean, and at once Samantha went to them to look out, but Mike stayed where he was, looking about the room. There in a corner, sitting in a wheelchair, was the old man Mike had spent the last few years of his life reading and writing about. Mike liked to think he would have known him anywhere, although there had never been, to his knowledge, a photo made of the man, for Barrett had always had an aversion to photographs that verged on an obsession.

At first glance, Barrett looked like any very old man: shrunken, shriveled, dark brown skin—but his eyes gave him away. All the intelligence that had brought this man up from the slums of New York to controlling most of the crime in the city still showed in his eyes. The skin around those eyes might be old and wrinkled, but what was inside them was as young and alert as it ever had been.

Now those eyes were looking at Mike. He'd scanned Samantha and dismissed her, as though she were of no significance, but he was studying Mike, looking him up and down as though trying to judge his physical strength as well as trying to figure out what was in his mind. In spite of himself, Mike shivered. It was as though he'd just been subjected to some sort of otherworldly intelligence that could look inside a man and see what was in his soul.

"Won't you sit down?" the old man whispered. His voice was as frail as his body, and Mike had an idea that Barrett's physical disabilities infuriated him.

Samantha nearly jumped when she heard the man's voice as she had not known anyone else was in the room. Turning, she saw a small, thin old man sitting in a wheelchair. Immediately her heart went out to him, as she wondered if he was lonely here in this big house. Did he have friends and family? She smiled at him.

He gave her what looked like a smile, and she thought, Why, he's shy. Going forward, she offered him her hand and he took it. Holding her hand for a long while, he turned it over in his dry, leathery old palm and studied her young skin.

After a while he released her and motioned for her and Michael to sit down. Samantha did so, starting to take a chair, but Mike pulled her to the couch to sit near him. Giving Mike a bit of a frown that she didn't allow Mr. Barrett to see, she sat forward on the edge of the couch while Mike leaned back in silence.

"You have come to ask me about Maxie," Barrett said.

Samantha hadn't thought much about this meeting; she'd thought little past getting away from Mike and out of New York, but now she was interested. "My grandmother left my family the year after I was born, and I . . . We thought perhaps . . ." She looked down at her hands.

Pushing the controls of his electric wheelchair, Barrett moved closer to her and again took her hand. "And you want to ask if Maxie left your family to come to me."

"Actually . . ." Samantha began, then looked up at him. "Yes."

He smiled at her warmly. "I have not been so flattered in all my life," he said, squeezing her hand, then put his hand on her chin and moved her head so that the light played on her hair and cheeks.

At other times Samantha would have been annoyed at a stranger touching her, but now all she could think of was that this man might be her only remaining relative and that she had nowhere to go when she left Michael's house.

Barrett dropped his hand from her face. "You look like her. You look very much like her."

"I've been told so." Leaning toward him, she put her hand over his on the controls of the chair. "Do you know what happened to my grandmother?"

He shook his head no. "On the twelfth of May, 1928, she disappeared from my life and I never saw her again."

Letting out her pent-up breath, Samantha suddenly felt as though she'd lost something. In just a few minutes she had seemed to fill herself with hope. Never mind that she'd told Mike that she didn't care about a grandmother who'd committed adultery, she knew now that if an old woman who said she was Gertrude Elliot, also known as Maxie, had walked through the door, Samantha would have thrown her arms about the woman's neck.

"I didn't really believe . . ." she said, stammering over the words, then not knowing what else to say. She couldn't very well say, By the way, did you and my grandmother have a cuddle about that time and maybe, perhaps possibly, produce a kid that was my father?

"Come in here," Barrett said, leading the way in his wheelchair. "We'll have tea and I'll tell you what I know."

"Yes, please," Samantha said, quickly getting up and following him.

Mike, who she'd almost forgotten, slipped her arm in his. He was looking at her oddly, as though he were warning her about something, but she didn't have the time or inclination to try to figure out what was bothering him.

She followed the old man into a pretty yellow and white room that had a huge bay window looking out toward the sand and the ocean. Refusing to see the four men, two of them with dogs, walking up and down the area, she saw only the beauty.

The round table, with only two chairs at it, was set with a pretty teapot and two matching cups and saucers, and there was a large plate of little cakes that looked on the edge of being stale.

"Would you pour?" Barrett asked Samantha, pleasing her with his request. He refused to eat or drink, so she served only Michael and herself while Barrett sat quietly and watched her.

"With the right clothes and hair you could *be* Maxie," he whispered. "Even your movements are like hers. Tell me, dear, do you sing?"

"Some," she said modestly, for she had always liked to sing, but only for her family.

The three of them were quiet for a moment, Mike sitting on his chair looking like a preacher at a pornography convention. For some reason he seemed to be disapproving of everything she said and did. His absurd jealousy couldn't extend to this sweet old man, could it?

"Would you like for me to tell you about that night?" Barrett asked.

"Please do," Samantha said, sipping her tea and eating a small cake. "If you would like to tell us, that is. If you're not too tired." She ignored Mike's foot stepping on hers to tell her that this is what they came for. She was *not* going to tire a ninety-one-year-old man just so Michael Taggert could write some nasty book about him.

"It would give me great pleasure to tell you," he said, smiling at her. In the sunlight he looked older than he had in the living room, and Samantha had an urge to tuck him up on the couch so he could take a nap.

Barrett took a deep breath and began to talk.

"I guess it's an old-fashioned term and it seems out of place now, but I was a gangster. I sold whiskey and beer to people when the government had declared it illegal to sell liquor or even to drink it. Because of some bad things that happened, we sellers of alcohol got a very bad reputation." He paused to smile at Samantha again.

"I can't offer an apology for what I did. I was young and I didn't know any better. All I knew was that it was the Great Depression, and while other men were standing on bread lines, I was making fifty grand a year. And making money was important to a man when he was in love as I was."

Barrett paused a moment in memory. "Maxie was beautiful. Not loudly beautiful, but quiet and elegant, a real knockout." He smiled at Samantha fondly. "Like you," he said, making her blush.

"Anyway, Maxie and I had been a pair for months. I'd asked her to marry me hundreds of times, but she said she wouldn't marry me until I went legit. I wanted to, but I was making too much money and I couldn't see myself settling down somewhere selling insurance. But then came that Saturday night that changed so many lives. May the twelfth, 1928.

"When I look back on it, I wonder that I didn't have a premonition that night that something was going to happen, but I didn't. I was on top of the world. My right-hand man, Joe, a man who'd been my friend since we were kids together, had picked up the receipts that day and they were the best ever, so I bought Maxie a pair of earrings. Diamonds with pearls. Nothing big or flashy since Maxie didn't like showy jewelry, but these were real nice.

"I went to Jubilee's Place—that's where Maxie was singing—feeling on top of the world. Right away I went to Maxie and gave her the earrings. I thought she'd be happy, but she wasn't. She sat down on a chair and started to cry. I couldn't figure out what was wrong with her, and it took me a long time to get it out of her."

Barrett's voice lowered, as though what he was saying was very difficult. "She told me she was going to have our baby."

Drawing in her breath sharply, Samantha wanted to ask questions, but she didn't dare stop his story.

"Maxie was very upset about her pregnancy, but I was the happiest man in the world," Barrett said, continuing, "because I knew then that she'd have to agree to marry me. But I was wrong. Even when she was going to have a baby, she still said she wouldn't marry me unless I gave up the rackets."

Barrett gave what on a younger man would have been described as a grin. "I agreed that I would. I would have agreed to anything that night if it meant having the woman I loved marry me. But between you and me, I don't know if I would have stayed away from the rackets. Maybe in a year or so I would have gotten restless and gone back, but that night I meant it when I said I would get out.

"I wanted us to leave the club right then and go get married, but Maxie said she had to sing that night, that she couldn't let Jubilee down. I agreed only if she'd promise that it would be her last time to perform in public. In those days there was no talk of a woman wanting a career. All Maxie wanted was what I wanted: a home for the two of us and our children."

Barrett stopped and looked out the window. "She sang that night and I'd never heard her sing prettier. Like a bird.

"About ten o'clock, I guess, she took a break and I got up from my table to go backstage to see her. On the way I made a trip to the . . . you know, and when I was about to leave, just as my hand was on the door, I heard the first shots and the first screams. I knew right away what had happened. Back in those days I was small potatoes in the business. By that I mean I sold to only a few places, most of them up in Harlem. Most of the city was controlled by a man named Scalpini. I had already figured that Scalpini would have heard of our haul that day and I knew he'd be mad, but I thought he'd just send some of his guys over to try to work out a deal with me. But he didn't do that. He sent eight men to Jubilee's Place with typewriters—machine guns.

"I knew the men were after me, but all I cared about was getting to Maxie. I pushed open the door and already the club was full of screaming, hysterical, running people and blood—blood was everywhere. I had to push a woman's body aside to get the door open, then I had to walk over two people who were screaming on the floor. The bullets were flying everywhere and I took one in my shoulder then a second one in my side, but I kept going. I was afraid Maxie would leave her dressing room and come out or that maybe Scalpini's men would go after her because Maxie wasn't the kind of woman to think of herself first. She'd never run out the back door if she heard shots coming from the front.

"I almost made it to the back when something fell and hit me on the head. I think it was a chandelier. Whatever it was, it knocked me out cold. When I woke, it was hours later, and there was a man in a white coat bending over me. 'This one's alive,' he yelled and walked past me. I grabbed his ankle and tried to ask questions, but he shook me off. I think I passed out after that, because when I woke again, it was the next day and I was in a hospital, and my side and shoulder were bandaged. It was another day before I found out what happened. Scalpini had decided to get rid of me and all the men who worked for me, so he sent his men over to shoot all of us. It didn't matter to him that there were probably a hundred people in the nightclub that night and that most of them had nothing to do with me. Scalpini meant to kill us all and he very nearly did. I lost seven men that night."

He paused for a long while, and when Barrett spoke again,

there was a catch in his voice. "I lost Joe that night. Joe was my childhood friend, and he'd saved my life when we were kids. He was the only person I have ever before or since trusted. Joe was dead, took a bullet right through the forehead, so he must have died instantly. And there were twenty-five or so others either killed or injured that night. But worst of all, Maxie disappeared. No one knew what had happened to her. For a long time after that I searched for her, but I couldn't find any trace of her. She walked out, and I'm sure it was my fault. Maybe she knew I wouldn't be able to do anything that wasn't exciting, maybe she didn't want her child raised with a gangster for a father. I don't know. All I know is that I never saw or heard from her again."

He stopped talking for a moment, then took some long, slow breaths to calm himself. "I changed after that night. I'd lost the two most important people in my life—my best friend, my only friend, and the woman I loved. Samantha, can you understand how miserable I was after that night?"

"Yes," she whispered. "I understand what it feels like to lose everyone."

"It's better not to talk about the next few years of my life. I was not a pleasant person. I don't know what I would have become if this hadn't happened." He put his hands on the controls of the wheelchair. "I was in a car accident two years later, and my spinal cord was severed."

Comfortingly Samantha put her hand over his.

"I've done things in my life that I'm not proud of, but I think I would have been a different man if that night hadn't happened. I used to think about it a great deal, what would have happened if Maxie hadn't stayed to sing that night. If she'd left with me before Scalpini's men showed up, we probably would have been married before we heard the news of what had happened. If she'd left with me, Joe would have gone with us and he wouldn't have died either."

He looked off into the distance. "If Maxie hadn't wanted to stay and sing, everything would have been different." Reaching out, he touched Samantha's cheek. "Maybe if I'd married her and waked up to hear of the bloodbath at the club, maybe it would have scared me into going straight. Maybe . . ." His eyes grew misty. "Maybe now you would be my granddaughter, not just my biological granddaughter, but living here with me." He smiled. "Perhaps not here. Perhaps I'd be living in a house in suburbia somewhere, a retired insurance salesman." He touched her blonde hair. "Like Midas, I'd trade all my gold for the warmth of a child."

"I wonder what happened to her?" Samantha asked.

She and Mike were sitting in the backyard at the picnic table, eating from several white paper cartons of Chinese food that they'd had delievered.

"Happened to who?" Mike asked, although he knew very well who she was talking about.

"If my grandmother didn't leave my granddad Cal to go to Mr. Barrett, where did she go?"

"That's what your father wanted to know," Mike mumbled, looking down at his plate. Something was bothering him, and he wasn't exactly sure what it was. They had left Barrett's house immediately after the old man had finished his long, sad story. All the way into Manhattan Samantha had been very quiet, looking out the window with a slight smile on her face, as though something had pleased her very much. Now she wasn't eating but making little piles of her food on the paper plate.

"Do you think he lives alone in that huge house?"

"Probably. He seems to have killed most every person he's known over the years."

Samantha gave him a look of fury. "Why do you have to say so many bad things about him? I thought that writers were supposed to *like* the people they're writing about."

"Oh? How about the writers who do studies on serial killers? I don't like Barrett and I never will, but the man fascinates me. No one has ever tried to document what he's done in his life. No one actually knows what the man is capable of doing."

Samantha took a moment before she spoke. "He seemed like a nice man to me," she said softly.

Mike had to swallow before he could speak; he had to take a breath before he could say a word. "What is it about women and their love of a sob story? Some man you've never met hands you a tearjerker about true love lost and you fall for it. I especially loved the Midas part. I wonder if he rehearsed his little speech before he told it to you?"

Standing up, she glared down at him. "And I am sick of your jealousy! From the moment I first saw you, you have acted as though you own me. You have invaded my privacy; you have followed me and humiliated me and, in general, made my life miserable. And I don't even know you. You are nothing to me."

"I'm more to you than Barrett is," Mike said, standing up and leaning across the table toward her.

"No you're not," she said quietly. "He's my grandfather, my last living relative on earth."

Mike drew his breath in sharply. Now he knew what had been bothering him about the expression on her face when they had been riding back from Barrett's place. She had been smiling in contentment, smiling as though she'd found something that had been lost. "Sam," he said, putting his hand out to touch her.

But she drew away from him, not wanting to hear what he had to say. He could afford to be a know-it-all about her having found a living relative because he had what appeared to be thousands of relatives all over America. Someone like him couldn't possibly understand what it meant to be completely and absolutely alone in the world. He wouldn't understand the concept of Thanksgiving dinner with no one to invite or Christmas with no one to buy presents for. Someone who had so much family that he could afford to be cynical about them, could happily say mean things about them, couldn't understand. Maybe this man Barrett had done some awful things in his youth; maybe everything that Mike knew about him was true, but now he was an old, old man and he was alone—and Samantha was alone as well.

Turning away from this man who was a stranger to her, she started back into the house.

Stepping in front of her, Mike put his hands on her shoulders. "Sam, where are you going?"

"Upstairs. I do believe I am free enough to be allowed to do that, aren't I?"

Mike didn't release his hold on her. "I want to know what's in your head. I don't like the look in your eyes."

"I don't like the look in your eyes most of the time," she snapped. "Please let me go. I have to pack."

"I'm not going to release you until you tell me where you plan to go after you leave this house."

"As I've told you a thousand times, what I do in my life and what I have done are none of your business. I'll go where I want to go."

Mike bent to look into her eyes, but she turned her head away. "You're going to him, aren't you?"

"It's none of your—"

"Sam, you can't go to that man! He's a killer!"

She gave him a look of disgust. "He's ninety-one years old, and he's in a wheelchair. What possible reason would he have to harm me? I'm not rich, so it can't be that he wants my money. I somehow doubt that he wants sex from me. Maybe his whole story *is* a lie. Maybe he concocted the whole thing in an effort to get Maxie's granddaughter to live with him for his last few—very few—remaining years. If that's true, then what's wrong with it? He's a lonely old man and I'm . . ." She broke off, not wanting to say any more.

"Go ahead and say it. You're a lonely young woman." His voice softened, his hands dropping to her arms as he moved closer to her. "Tell me what you want, Samantha. Tell me what you want and I'll try to give it to you. Is it love you want? Then I'll—"

She jerked out of his grasp. "Don't you *dare* tell me you'll give me love. I've had all the love from greedy young men that I can take. What do I have to say to you, *do* to you to make you realize that I'm serious: I don't want to stay in this house with you. I don't want to go to bed with you; I don't want to have anything to do with you."

Mike stared at her for a moment, his expression changing from anger to bewilderment, then finally to resignation. "I can take a hint," he said with a little smile of mockery. "You are free to do what you want. In the morning I will go to the bank and get your money for you. Is a cashier's check all right with you?"

"Yes, fine," she said quickly, then turned away and started for the stairs toward her apartment. Stopping on the first tread, she looked back at him. "Mike, I do appreciate what you've tried to do for me. I sincerely believe that your heart has always been in the right place. It's just that you don't know me, not really. I think you have an image of me that I'm . . ." She took a breath. "That I'm one of your wounded birds. I'm not. I know what I want."

"Barrett," Mike said tersely. "You want that old man because he says he might be related to you. He's never—" He didn't say any more because Samantha ran up the stairs.

When she was upstairs, she closed the door behind her and turned the key in the lock. Not that locking the door would do any good, she thought with disgust, because he had his own key.

She dragged her big suitcase out of the closet, put it on the bed, and began to pack. With each of her new, heavenly garments she folded away, she felt sadness at leaving this apartment, at leaving this house that had become familiar to her. But she did her best to strengthen her resolve and kept packing.

When half of the suitcase was filled, she sat on the edge of the bed. Where *was* she going to go? It wasn't as though Mr. Barrett had asked her to come live with him, although she had seen that he very much needed a good housekeeper to take care of his neglected house. And it wasn't as though Michael Taggert wanted her for anything except sex. It always amazed her that men thought if they couldn't "conquer" a woman, then they had failed. Sometimes she thought that when a man was pestering her without ceasing, she ought to just lay down on the bed and give him what he wanted so he'd go away. Maybe that's what she should do with Mike. After he'd had what he wanted from her, he wouldn't care whether she stayed in his house, whether she went to live with a former gangster, or what she did.

Standing up, she continued packing. She didn't want to give

Mike what he wanted, didn't want to hear him say all the things that men say when they're trying to get under a woman's skirts: that he loved her and wanted to live with her for the rest of his life, that he was nothing without her, that she was everything to him. No, she didn't want that from Mike, because up until now, he'd been a friend to her. He'd been kind at times, if a bit autocratic. If she were honest with herself, she found his jealousy flattering. Mike had spent time with her. The day they had gone shopping had been one of the most joyous of her life. He had made her laugh, and at times he'd made her forget all the death that had followed her in her life.

She started to slip a pair of shoes into her bag, then stopped. All her life she would remember this time with Mike, remember the arguments they'd had, remember how he'd made her angry at every turn. She'd remember the way he looked after his shower, his hair wet, wearing only a pair of jeans, his feet and chest bare. She'd remember every touch, every look. She'd remember the way he smiled, just slightly out of one side of his mouth, as though his smile were tinted with sarcasm and disbelief that there was something to smile about.

She jammed the shoes into the case. Maybe she'd move to Seattle. Living around the rain forest might be nice. After the dryness of Santa Fe, her skin could stand living where it was foggy and cool.

She finished packing and set the suitcase on the floor. In the morning she would leave. What was she going to do? Have a taxi take her to the airport then go to an airline counter and say she'd like a ticket on the next available plane?

"Not exactly well thought out, are you, Sam?" she said aloud, then smiled at having called herself Sam. When she'd turned eleven and three-quarters, she had become aware of herself as a female and had declared to her family that she was no longer to be called a boy's name. From then on she was to be called Samantha. Her father and grandfather had readily complied, but her mother had infuriated her by laughing and continuing to call her Sam. After her mother died, no one had called her Sam—until she'd met Mike, that is.

Looking around the room, at her father's furniture, at her father's colors, for the first time she thought that maybe she'd like different curtains. Maybe rose-colored damask, she thought, and maybe she could put a matching spread on the bed.

She began unbuttoning her blouse, her nightgown over her arm, as she walked toward the bathroom to take a shower. In her next place of residence she could do whatever she wanted with the curtains and furniture.

There was no warning. One minute Samantha was asleep and the next there was a hand around her throat and she was fighting for her life. She clawed at the hand that was cutting off her breath, but even when she felt her nails tear his skin, he didn't move.

"Where is Half Hand's money?" the man whispered.

The moonlight coming through the window allowed her to see that he wore a stocking over his head.

"Where is Half Hand's money?" he repeated, but he didn't loosen the pressure on her throat to allow her to answer.

Samantha tried to kick him, but he was beside her in such a way that she couldn't reach his body. Besides, with no air getting to her lungs, she was losing strength. Michael, she thought, then used what little strength she had remaining to hit the wall with her heel. Once, she hit it. Twice. Three times. Then she began to fade out of reality as the pressure on her throat continued.

When the pressure was abruptly taken away from her throat, at first she still couldn't breathe. It was as though parts of her throat had been crushed beyond usefulness, and when she gasped, no air entered her lungs. Even when she sat up in the bed, her hand to her injured throat, she still couldn't breathe.

Turning quickly to the sound of a loud crash, she saw the shadow of Michael as he fought the man who had been trying to kill her. Mike was bigger than the man, stronger, and when Mike's fist plowed into the man's face, he hadn't a chance to survive the blow. As the man fell to the floor with a thud, Mike was beside her, his arms around her.

"Breathe, baby," he commanded her. "Goddamn you! Breathe!"

Hitting her on the back, he held her as Samantha gasped for air. Mike's strong hands clutched her shoulders, giving her a little shake as his eyes bored into hers. It was as though he were commanding her to do what she couldn't, yet she found herself wanting to breathe, if for no other reason than to do what he wanted. After what seemed to be hours, the air entered her lungs in a painful, jerking gasp.

Pulling her into his arms, her head on his bare shoulder, he stroked her back. He put one hand on her head, cradling it as she struggled with breath after breath, her chest heaving in little spasms.

Feeling Mike turn away when he heard a crash, she knew without looking that the intruder had regained consciousness and had leaped from the balcony.

"I hope he breaks his bloody neck," Mike whispered, but they both heard the man as he ran away across the garden below. No doubt he had leaped from one balcony to the next to reach the garden, then vaulted over the fence.

Still holding her, Mike reached for the bedside telephone and punched the buttons. "Blair," he said into the phone. "I need you. No. Strangulation. Get here quick." He put down the phone.

"Mike," Samantha tried to say, but he told her to be quiet and continued holding her.

He felt her shaking against him, felt the fear in her as she clung to him, clung like a frightened child to its father, as he soothed her, rubbing her back, stroking her hair. When she continued to shake, he slid down in the bed with her, then wrapped his arms about her body, pinning her arms against his chest. He moved a leg over her, as though to completely encase her in a cocoon of safety.

"I'm here, baby," he whispered, frowning into the darkness as she seemed to try to get closer to him.

A wounded bird, she'd said. She'd said that she wasn't one of his wounded birds, and he was sure she'd heard that particular bit of idiocy from Daphne. If Mike were into "wounded birds," he would have been madly in love with Daphne.

Samantha intrigued him; she'd intrigued him since before he'd met her.

After he found the newspaper clipping of Sam and Maxie in his uncle Mike's belongings and had searched out Dave Elliot, Mike had spent some time with Dave. Mike hadn't meant to stay in Louisville, but he and Dave had liked each other. Dave was lonely, what with his only child all the way out West and, as Dave said, happily married. Maybe Mike was a little lonely too since the death of Uncle Mike. Together, the two men had come up with the scheme to live together in New York in Mike's town house, where Dave could spend his retirement looking for his mother and helping Mike with the biography of Doc. Mike had liked the idea, liked having someone help him with the research.

Then, after Dave had commissioned Mike's sister to decorate the apartment just as Dave wanted, he had called Mike and said he wasn't going to be coming to New York after all. He wouldn't tell Mike what the problem was, but Mike knew something was wrong, so he got on the first plane to Louisville and appeared at Dave's door, suitcase in hand, and demanded to be told what was going on. Dave had blurted what he'd been told only a few days before: He was dying of cancer. Mike had wanted him to call his daughter and tell her, but Dave had said no, that Samantha had had enough death in her short life and she didn't need to see any more.

So Mike had moved in with Dave for a month. Dave had said he was fine, but Mike hadn't been able to leave him, for he couldn't bear to see the man alone when he knew he had so little time left.

For some odd reason, Dave had insisted that Mike stay in Samantha's room, not in the guest room. When Mike saw the room, he had laughed, for it was a child's room.

"Samantha and her mother picked out everything together," Dave said with a smile and a fond look about he room.

It was on the tip of Mike's tongue to point out that Samantha's mother had died when Sam was twelve, but he hadn't. He'd set his suitcase down on the rug that had little pink and white ballerinas dancing across it and looked at the bed: a white four-poster draped in gauzy pink cloth tied back with big pink bows. There was a little dressing table against one wall, draped in white-dotted swiss, the top of it covered with a child's dresser set. Looking about, Mike expected a ten-year-old girl to walk in the room at any moment.

Yet he knew Samantha had lived in this room until she'd left with her husband. Opening the closet door, he expected to find frilly little dresses, but instead there were adult clothes: boring, shapeless, obsessively neat clothes, but clothes sized for an adult.

Over the next few weeks, Mike's curiosity about this daughter who grew up in a child's room increased. Dave had pain pills that made him sleep a great deal, so Mike had time on his hands that he used to explore Samantha's room. At first he did so tentatively, knowing that what he was doing was none of his business, but as the days followed and he had little else to do, he grew less embarrassed at looking through drawers and cabinets.

Dave described his daughter as a feisty, opinionated, go-getter. If that was so, why had she spent all those years living in a child's room?

When Mike found a scrapbook kept by Samantha, he looked through it with interest. She'd cut out pictures of movie stars and rock singers; there were a couple of pressed flowers. It all seemed normal for a twelve-year-old—except that ten pages from the back of the book was a clipping from a newspaper: an obituary of her mother. After that there was nothing else in the book. Search as he might, he could find no scrapbooks that dated after her mother's death.

He found five diaries written by Samantha, all of them written in a child's round hand, all of them full of whispered secrets with other girls and who she loved at the moment and who her friends loved. She wrote of fights with her mother and how wonderful her father was.

Smiling, Mike remembered how, as a child, all his fights had been with his father. His mother was a saint, and he couldn't understand why his sisters sometimes got angry at her.

There were no diaries after 1975, after Allison Elliot died.

By the end of his month's stay, Mike was more puzzled than ever by what he'd found in the Elliot house. Sometimes it seemed as though Samantha and her father had stopped counting time on the day Allison had died. Dave talked about Samantha as a child, telling stories of her only during her first twelve years. He never mentioned what she had done during high school or when she'd lived at home and gone to the University of Louisville.

Mike had asked questions about Samantha, pointed questions, about her life after her mother's death, but he'd never been given any direct answers. Dave had been vague, often changing the subject.

It had been Mike who had insisted that Dave allow him to tell Samantha that he was dying. Mike said it wasn't fair to Sam not to know about her own father. At last Dave had agreed, but then, oddly enough, Dave had insisted that Mike not meet Samantha. He said Samantha could be told, but he didn't want Mike to do it, didn't want Mike calling her, and he wanted Mike out of the house when she arrived.

Mike couldn't help being hurt by this pronouncement. It was as though Dave thought Mike was an unsavory character, not good enough for his precious daughter. But Mike had done what Dave wanted and asked a neighbor to call Samantha, then Mike had boarded a plane and gone back to New York.

Two weeks later, Dave had called Mike and told him he was sending Samantha to him to take care of after he was gone. The way Dave sounded, he could have been talking about an orphaned child—or an express package.

Reluctantly, Mike had agreed to turn Dave's apartment over to Samantha, but truthfully, Mike had been dreading dealing with her. She must have a case of arrested development if her little-girl room was any indication of her personality.

But the woman he had met and the girl he'd been expecting were two different creatures. One moment she was hot and full of passion; she was the little girl in the diaries who wrote of arguments and escapades. The next moment she was terrified of her own shadow. And the next she was cold and hard, shutting the world out, not allowing anyone near her.

Yet, he thought, she wasn't cold and hard. She fought him; she pushed him away at every opportunity, but sometimes she looked at him with such need and longing in her eyes that he didn't know whether to reach for her or run away.

The day he'd bought her those clothes, she had looked at him with such gratitude that he'd almost been embarrassed. Most women would have been happy about the clothes, but Samantha had been more than happy. In fact, it wasn't the clothes that had delighted her, but . . . the attention? he wondered. It was almost as though she were grateful that someone had acknowledged that she was alive. He wasn't sure what had given her so much pleasure that day, but something had.

What happened to her after her mother died? he wondered. What had changed her from a normal, outgoing, gregarious child who had friends and went to parties to a young woman who could spend weeks sleeping?

Now, she was clinging to him in a way that he'd never seen

or felt in another person. Yes, she was frightened, and, yes, she had every reason to be, but there was something more to the way she clung to him. It was as though she needed him.

Maybe wanting to get away from his hometown was one of the reasons Mike had moved to New York, that and wanting to go to a place where he wasn't "one of the Taggerts" but a person in his own right. A place where he could be an individual, not part of the pack.

Smiling, Mike stroked her hair and kissed her forehead. When you grew up in a family as large as his, feeling that *you* were needed was not something you experienced very often. Early in life you found out that if you didn't do something, there were others to do it. If you didn't feed the horses, someone else would. If someone was upset there were at least a dozen people to offer comfort. As far as he could remember, no one had ever said, "Only Mike can do this job," or "I need Mike and no one else." Even in school girls had been as content to have one of his brothers as to have him. It didn't seem to make any difference to them.

But Samantha needed him, he thought, trying to pull her closer. She didn't need his money; she didn't need his body; she needed *him*.

He clutched her to him. Before he'd met her, when he thought of her living in his house, he'd thought of her as an obligation, a burden, actually, rather like a permanent blind date. Then, for a while, his only objective had been to get her into bed, and she'd rather forcefully told him she wasn't interested—forcefully, hell, he thought, she had been snide and nasty and downright insulting. He had lost interest in her for a while, letting her stay in her room and sleep. He'd allowed her to do whatever she wanted. Then Daphne had made him realize that Samantha wasn't just sleeping.

Mike put his hand over her ear. She was so small and so alone and maybe it was his vanity, but he felt as though he'd saved her life twice, once when he'd kept her from "sleeping forever" as Daphne called it and tonight when he'd had to break down a door to get to her. Tomorrow he'd have the windows measured for steel grills, grills to keep her safe.

"You're going to be safe, baby," he whispered. "I'll keep you safe." And I'll make you laugh, he thought. And I'll make you stop moving away from me when I reach out to touch you.

~

It was a while before Samantha could stop shaking, before she could breathe enough to think. Opening her eyes, she looked out the bedroom door. Down the hall, she could see the hole in the apartment door, the hole Mike had had to make to reach through the door to unlock it.

"How . . .?" she whispered, wincing at the pain in her throat. She was clinging to him, holding him as tightly as possible, as he was holding her. She didn't want to think about her fear, fear that was making her quiver.

"I heard you," Mike said. "I heard the thumps on the wall and I knew something was wrong. I thought maybe you'd fallen or hurt yourself. I didn't think—" He wasn't going to tell her what he'd felt when he'd seen the bastard trying to kill her. Now he marveled that he hadn't killed the man on sight, but his number one priority had been to get back to Sam, to make sure that she was all right, and he hadn't wanted to waste even a second pummeling the guy.

"Just be still," he said softly. "Blair will be here in a few minutes. I want her to look at you and make sure you're all right."

"A cousin?" Samantha managed to choke out, pulling her head back to smile up at him.

Mike didn't return her smile. Now that his immediate fear for her was under control, he could think. When he'd seen the man hanging over Sam, he hadn't given any thought as to why the man was there or why he was trying to kill her. Mike's only concern had been to save Sam, but now he wondered why the robber had been trying to kill her. Why couldn't he have taken what he wanted from her jewelry box or whatever without trying to commit murder?

"Sam?"

She moved her head against his chest. A few minutes ago she had been fighting for her life and now she'd never felt so safe.

"Did the man say anything to you? Did he call you by name or say anything to you?"

She shook her head no. Vaguely, she remembered the man saying something, but she didn't want to remember what it was. Right now she wanted to forget everything that had happened.

Her answer seemed to please him because she could feel

Mike relax against her when she told him no. When he put his hands on the side of her face and looked at her, she smiled at him and he smiled back.

"I wouldn't like for anything to happen to you, Sammy-girl," he said, kissing her on the forehead as he put her head back down on his chest.

A moment later the doorbell rang, and Mike gently laid her back against the pillows as he ran down the stairs. Soon a pretty young woman carrying a medical bag came into the room, then professionally, expertly, she examined Samantha's throat. As she did so, she talked to Mike who stood behind her, wearing only his very small cotton underwear, seemingly unconcerned at being nearly nude before two women.

"What happened?" Blair asked as she ran her fingers along the back of Samantha's neck.

"Some creep came in through the window," Mike answered. "Maybe Sam woke up and caught him rifling her jewelry box, I don't know."

Samantha shook her head. "I was . . . asleep," she said, frowning because it hurt to talk.

Mike didn't like to hear that, but maybe Samantha had moved or turned over, something to give the creep a reason to try to kill her. He didn't want to think that the man was a new serial killer. The Town House Murderer, maybe. Looking at the windows, he thought of what type of grills he'd order for them, but then he saw Sam's suitcase on the floor and knew that there was no reason for grills: She was going to leave in the morning.

Blair finished her examination. "I think you'll be fine. Just rest and don't talk. I'll give you a sedative so you can sleep tonight."

Nodding, Samantha took the pills the doctor gave her and drank from the cup that Mike held to her lips. Then her eyes widened as Mike scooped her up, blankets and all, and started down the hall with her.

"You spend tonight downstairs where I can watch over you," he said, and Samantha gave him no argument. She doubted that any sedative in the world would make her sleep comfortably tonight, knowing she'd lie awake imagining every shadow to be a man or men who wanted to kill her.

Downstairs, Mike put her in his bed, tucking her in as though she were a child, then went off with his pretty cousin and Samantha could hear them talking softly. Sam closed her eyes, feeling drowsy.

~

"How is she?" Mike asked his cousin.

"Fine," Blair answered. "She's strong and healthy, and there was no real damage done. She'll be fine in a day or two, a sore throat but nothing else." Snapping her medical bag closed, she looked up at him. "Mike, it's none of my business, but—"

"Are you going to start asking me what she is to me? That sort of thing? I can honestly say that I don't know."

"I had no intention of asking you anything about your personal life," she snapped, making Mike grin. "Doesn't it seem odd to you that Samantha isn't crying? If someone had tried to kill me, I'd be bawling buckets full. You don't think she's in shock, do you?"

Mike didn't know what to say, but now that he thought of it, maybe it was a little odd that she wasn't crying. His sisters seemed to cry over everything in the world. "I don't know. Maybe she cries in private."

"Maybe," Blair said. "But keep an eye on her. If she doesn't react to this tomorrow, call me. You may want to get her to see someone."

"A shrink?"

"Yes," Blair answered. Then, as Mike thanked her for coming over in the middle of the night, she said, "Let me look at your head. I'll take the stitches out next week." As she looked at his wound in the bright hall light, she said, "You seem to have had a great many accidents in the last few days. First someone creams you with a rock, and now someone tries to kill the young lady who lives in your house. You don't think the two are related, do you?"

"No, of course not," Mike said. But even Blair heard the false note in his voice.

"Mmmmm," she said as she kissed his cheek, then left the town house.

The frown left Mike's face when he went back to his bedroom and saw Sam curled in his bedclothes. Dreamily, she looked up at him, and he went to sit on the edge of the bed and picked up her hand. She was still wearing the engagement ring he had put on her finger.

"The man . . ."

"Ssssh, don't talk."

She smiled when Mike kissed the palm of her hand. "He said, 'Where is Half Hand's money?' "

It was a good thing her eyes were closed or she would have seen the terror on Mike's face; she would have seen the fear that came into his eyes.

"Good morning," Mike said brightly as he put the white wicker tray across Samantha's lap.

Sleepily, with the dull-brained feeling one has after taking sleeping pills the night before, she sat up in bed, wincing when she tried to swallow.

"I have vanilla yogurt, crushed strawberries, and fresh-squeezed orange juice. There are croissants too if your throat is up to it."

She frowned at him. He seemed awfully cheerful this morning after someone had tried to kill her last night.

She lifted a spoonful of yogurt to her lips and then frowned more at the pain in her throat when she tried to swallow, but Mike didn't seem to notice. He sat down on the edge of the bed—the way they often seemed to share meals—and ate a couple of strawberries.

"You know, Sam, I was thinking."

She opened her mouth to make a wisecrack, but it hurt too much to talk.

"I was thinking that you're right, that I've not taken into consideration what you want and what you've been through. Your father died recently, and a divorce must be an awful thing. On top of all that your father writes that will that makes you have to move to a city you hate and do something you don't want to do. It must have been terrible for you."

Samantha was watching him, and every cynical thought she'd ever had came into her mind. In her experience, when a man started projecting himself into a woman's feelings, he wanted something. She gave Mike an encouraging smile that she hoped looked full of self-pity.

"Yes, well, I was thinking that you need a vacation, a real vacation. Somewhere cool, away from the heat of New York. Somewhere by the ocean maybe. So, last night I talked to Raine—you remember him, don't you? My cousin you seemed so taken with? Anyway, Raine is going up to Warbrooke, that's a town in Maine. It's on the end of a peninsula and absolutely beautiful. Raine will be there with his whole family, and they have a guesthouse that's a wonderful place. You can rest and read and go out on boats and catch things out of the water and do whatever you want. You can spend the whole summer there if you want. I was so sure that you'd like this idea that Raine is coming by this afternoon to pick you up to drive you to Warbrooke. Doesn't this all sound great?"

While he was talking, Samantha was looking at him. His eyes were red-rimmed, as though he hadn't slept all night and, too, there was something in his eyes that she hadn't seen before. Why was he so intent on getting her out of the city? Why was he sending her away with a man who a few days ago he had been jealous of?

He was sending her to a tiny remote town on the edge of a peninsula, a place where his relatives could look out for her and could take over the care of her. She didn't for a minute believe that Mike was sending her away because he believed she needed a rest. A few days ago he seemed to think that what she needed was the opposite of rest.

Thinking about last night, she tried to remember everything she could about what had happened. Mike kept talking, telling her about a town he had previously described as nothing but a lot of water. Now he was telling her it was paradise, and that his Montgomery relatives were the kindest, sweetest people on earth. It was his repeated use of the phrase "they'll take *care* of you" that made her suspicious.

She reached across the tray to the bedside table to the note-pad and pencil there.

Who is Half Hand? she wrote.

Tearing off the note, she handed it to Mike. When she saw him turn white, she knew that in this question was the answer to a great deal.

"You have very nice handwriting, you know that? Nice round a's and o's. I tend to close mine."

Who is Half Hand? she wrote again and handed him the note.

Mike looked like a trapped man. He lay back on the bed, his eyes scrunched closed, as though in great agony. "Samantha," he said tiredly, and she was beginning to realize that he called her Samantha only when he was annoyed with her. "Samantha, this is not a parlor game. This is real and it's dangerous. I didn't have any idea that it was dangerous or I wouldn't have involved you, but now all I can do is get you out of here and into a safe place."

If you don't tell me who Half Hand is, I will call my grandfather and ask him, she wrote.

Mike's face lost its look of agony; now she saw real fear in his eyes. "You don't know what you're saying," he said softly in that tone a person uses when they're trying not to explode with rage. "You have to swear to me that you won't call that bastard."

Samantha frowned. *He is my grandfather!!!* she wrote.

Getting off the bed, Mike paced the room for a few minutes. "Sam, I made a mistake, a big one. I told you from the beginning that I thought your father's will was rotten and I should have done what I knew was right: I should have released your money without taking you to meet Barrett. But I was greedy; I wanted to meet him. No one's seen him in years and I—"

Breaking off, he wiped his hand over his eyes. "I don't know if Barrett is your grandfather or not, but I know what kind of man he is. I haven't told you much about him—I purposely didn't tell you because I was afraid you'd refuse to meet him if I told you the truth. And now I'm paying for it."

Removing the tray from across her lap, he sat back down on the bed, then took her hand in his. "You keep telling me that I lie to you. Maybe I have, but I thought I had a good reason."

He touched the bruises on her neck. "You could have been

killed last night, and it would have been my fault," he said softly. "I should have told you everything from the first and I should have given you your money immediately after your father died. I shouldn't even have allowed you to come to New York."

Putting her hand out, she took his, for he was genuinely upset about what had almost happened to her. When he looked at her, she smiled at him, but he didn't smile back.

"If I tell you what I know, will you leave the city? Will you go with my cousin and stay under his family's protection until I can solve this thing?"

How could she promise something like that? She didn't yet know what he was talking about. She thought a burglar had tried to kill her, but now she was beginning to understand that the man had wanted her specifically. Why? What did he think she knew that she should be killed for it?

Seeing her reluctance, Mike understood it. Maybe he didn't deserve her trust since he'd used her to get to see an old man. Mike swallowed. No book in the world was worth nearly causing the death of another human being.

"First I want to tell you about Barrett," he said softly. "I want to make you understand what kind of man he is. Sam, I don't want you to glorify this man. Just because he may or may not be your relative is no reason to endow him with godlike characteristics."

His lips tightened at the look on her face and at the way she scribbled furiously on the pad of paper.

He may have done some bad things in the past, but—she wrote.

He grabbed her hands before she could finish the sentence and held her wrists tightly for a second, but he released them, then calmed himself. "You've heard him called Doc, haven't you? Do you have any idea *why* he's called Doc? No, don't answer me. You'll probably say that he was given an honorary Ph.D. somewhere."

Pausing, Mike looked at her hard. "He's called Doc because it's a nickname for his real nickname. He's called the Surgeon."

She turned her head away from him, but Mike cupped her chin and turned her back to look at him.

"I don't care whether you want to hear or not, because I'm going to tell you anyway. When Barrett was nine years old, his prostitute mother abandoned him. I doubt if anyone ever knew who his father was. But whatever his mother was, Barrett seems to have been devoted to her, so maybe it unhinged him when she just walked out. For years the skinny little kid did what he could to survive. For the first year he nearly starved, but then he stole a cooking knife from a restaurant kitchen and learned to use it. There was a story that I couldn't verify that said he chopped off the fingers of another kid who tried to take food from the garbage can that Doc considered his."

"No," Samantha whispered, putting her hand to her throat in pain.

Mike continued. "When Barrett was fourteen, he was so malnourished he looked as though he were ten and he was sick of living hand to mouth every day. Scalpini was the crime boss of that day so Barrett decided to work for him. Barrett had a hell of a time getting through Scalpini's bodyguards, but he did one night just as Scalpini was sitting down to dinner at his favorite Italian restaurant. The bodyguards tried to kick Barrett out, but Scalpini said he wanted to hear what the kid had to say. Barrett said he wanted to work for Scalpini, that he would do *anything* for him, anything at all. All of them, including Scalpini, laughed at this kid who looked to be a child, but Scalpini, still laughing, said, 'Bring me Guzzo's heart, kid, and you got a job.' "

Again, Samantha looked away from him. She wasn't sure where he was going with his story, but she knew that she didn't want to hear it. Mike didn't say a word until she looked back at him.

"The next day, when Scalpini sat down to dinner, this scrawny, dirty kid tried to get through the bodyguards. Scalpini, probably liking the kid's perseverance and hero worship, waved him through. Barrett took a bloody ball of newspaper out of his jacket pocket and tossed it onto Scalpini's plate. Scalpini opened it and inside was a human heart."

Samantha didn't say a word for a while, just sat there looking at him, feeling the blood draining from her face. "How?" she whispered.

"Five days a week at four o'clock Guzzo visited his mistress for exactly one and a half hours. He liked to pretend he was making love to her for all of that time, but everyone knew the truth. He hardly ever touched the woman; his snores could be heard two blocks away. Barrett was so scrawny he slipped down the chimney into the bedroom, slit the man's throat while he slept, then cut out his heart. A few minutes later his mistress came into the room, saw her lover with a cut throat and a gaping, bloody hole in his chest, and started screaming. In the ensuing confusion, Barrett walked out the front door, stopping only long enough to wash some of the soot off his face and hands before he made his delivery to Scalpini. One of the bodyguards said the heart looked like it had been removed by a surgeon, and that's how Barrett got his nickname. Over the years the name's been dignified to Doc."

Mike stretched out on the bed, waiting, giving her time to digest what he'd just told her. "With what little I've been able to find out about Doc, I know that most of that story he told you yesterday was a lie. Or, maybe not a lie, just a stretching of the truth.

"First of all, Doc was trying to get your sympathy with all that about its being the Great Depression: 1928 was *before* the stock market crashed. Secondly, on that night when Scalpini shot up the speakeasy, it wasn't because Doc's receipts for that day had been especially good. It was because Doc had raided every safe, every till Scalpini had. The take was in the neighborhood of three million dollars."

When Mike turned to look at her, he saw that Samantha was listening, wide-eyed, to his story. "The man who picked up all the money from Scalpini was Doc's friend, the man Doc told you was the only man he had ever trusted: Joe, better known as Half Hand Joe."

Mike gave a little grin. "Want to know how Joe got *his* nickname?"

Samantha shook her head no, but that didn't stop Mike from telling her.

"Half Hand was older than Doc and as slow-witted as Doc was fast. No one knows whether Joe was born slow or came to be that way, because his father's hobby was hitting Joe on the head with whatever was handy. Joe met Doc when Joe was seventeen and Doc was ten, and Joe attached himself to Doc like a faithful old dog. When Doc started working for Scalpini, so did Joe. They went everywhere together, did everything together. When some rival hoods fired on Doc with machine guns, Joe pushed his little buddy aside. Joe took four bullets in the outside of his left hand and blew it away."

Mike held up his left hand to demonstrate, showing how

Half Hand was left with two fingers and a thumb. "He was called Half Hand after that night, and he was even more dedicated to Doc than ever. It's my guess that Half Hand realized that his future depended on Doc's safety, so he began sleeping outside Doc's door at night."

Mike took a breath. "Then came that night in 1928 and everything changed. Doc wanted to be the head of all the illegal businesses going on in New York, and in order to do that he had to get rid of Scalpini. Doc spent months planning the robbery and the killings it entailed. Everything went off on schedule except that Scalpini didn't wait to find out who had robbed him, he just took some of his boys and went to the speakeasy and opened fire. But they didn't get Doc. But they did kill Joe—Joe who was the only one who knew where the three million dollars was hidden."

Mike didn't speak for a moment, so Samantha wrote, *Why me?* and handed him the note.

Mike looked pained. "I don't know why I didn't think about others knowing the old story. In underworld circles the legend of Half Hand's money is like the Lost Dutchman Mine. There are a great many people who suspect that Maxie took it and that's why she disappeared that night. She wanted to get away from Doc and the gang; she saw an opportunity and she took it. Doc told you that Half Hand took a bullet in the head and died instantly. Some people said that Half Hand had been hit in the head so often by his father that a bullet couldn't pierce his skull. They say that he lived long enough to tell Maxie where the money was."

Turning, Mike looked at her. "What neither Doc nor Scalpini knew until years later was that the money they had, had been marked by the FBI. If it hadn't disappeared that night, whoever used it would have been holding evidence that could have convicted them. Whoever took it from Doc saved him from prison."

Was it found? Samantha wrote.

"Sort of," Mike said. "A hundred-dollar bill turned up in Paris in 1965."

Samantha had been listening to him intently, but the date jolted her. Her eyes widened.

"Right," Mike said. "That's the year after your grandmother Maxie left her husband and family. That was thirty seven years after the massacre, and no one was looking for the money. The old bill was spotted by a sharp-eyed clerk in the treasury office. After that one was found, they kept a look out for more bills, but no more showed up—not that anyone caught anyway. The clerk who spotted that one had just returned from a six-month leave of absence, so for all anyone knows the entire three million could have come through the treasury and not been seen."

There was too much information for Samantha to take in at one time.

Mike took the tray from her lap and started for the door. When he came back into the room, he said that he wanted her to sleep, that she needed rest after her ordeal and that her throat needed to heal. But as he started to tuck her in, he stopped. "When was the last time you cried?" he asked softly.

Samantha looked away from him, frowning.

Taking her chin in his hand, Mike turned her back to face him. "I'm not going to go away and I'm not going to allow you not to answer me." He handed her the pencil and notepad.

After a fierce glare of defiance, she wrote, *I was crying the day the principal came to tell me that my mother was dead.*

Samantha didn't leave New York that afternoon, but she had to promise Mike she'd obey him if he allowed her to stay with him for two more days—the amount of time Blair said it would take her throat to heal enough to speak. The truth was, she had a decision to make and she thought she could make it better if she stayed where she was than if she went to yet another unfamiliar place.

Mike wasn't easy to convince because he wanted her out of the city, wanted her in a safe place. He no longer wanted her to have anything to do with Doc or Maxie or any of what he was researching. Samantha wrote him a note asking him if he was going to continue writing his biography. When Mike said he was, Samantha did not point out that he wasn't any safer than she was, that someone might think he knew about Half Hand's money as well as she did. Nor did she mention that it was her grandmother involved, not his.

She simply didn't want to leave Mike's house, didn't want to get into a car with another man and drive to yet another place. She didn't want to leave Mike.

When she woke it was midafternoon and Mike brought her lunch on a tray. He looked tired and he hadn't shaved in two days. He wanted her to go back to sleep, but she pantomimed that she'd keep her lips zipped and throw away the key if he'd just let her sit on the couch and not have to stay in bed.

After reluctantly agreeing, he picked her up and carried her into the library and settled her on the couch as though she were helpless, a light blanket wrapped around her legs. When she was settled, he went back to his desk and started looking through his bundles of papers.

As Samantha watched him, she knew that she wanted to know more about the man who may or may not be her grandfather, so she wrote Mike that she'd like to type more of his notes. Refusing to allow her to sit at the desk at the computer and type, he asked her if there weren't small computers and she described a laptop. He asked her to write down what she needed so he could order it. Even though Samantha said a laptop computer would be too expensive and that she could sit at the desk, Mike refused to listen to her. At last she wrote down the name of a powerful little laptop, and on impulse, she wrote "King's Quest V and a mouse." Mike called a store and within two hours the equipment was delivered to the door.

After the equipment arrived, she got off the couch and installed the mouse and the graphics game on the color screen of the big computer while Mike was in the shower. When he entered the room, he was damp from his shower and wearing nothing but a pair of white tennis shorts. For a minute, Samantha thought her heart was going to stop at the sight of him, but Mike's eyes were on the computer screen and the opening graphics of the game. As though he were hypnotized, he walked toward the computer, touched the mouse on its pad, and when he saw the little man in the game move he was caught. Smiling at his beautiful, broad, bare back, Samantha saw that he couldn't figure out how to type notes, but within minutes, he had mastered the principles of a computer game.

That night, she found herself nodding off, and only when Mike started to pick her up did she wake. Out of instinct, she began to fight him, but he held her close. "It's me," he whispered. "Me, Mike, no one else."

It took her a moment to relax against him, sleepy, her throat still painful. But when he put her in his bed, she panicked, trying to get away from him.

Startled, Mike stepped back from her, his face full of anger. "I am *not* a rapist," he said through clenched teeth. "I'm not going to hurt you and I am not going to bed with any woman who doesn't want me in bed with her." Turning away, he went to the doorway, his hand on the light switch. "If you need me, I'll be next door in the guest bedroom." There was no warmth in his voice.

Samantha lay awake for a while in Mike's big bed, on pillows that he had slept on, and looked up at the ceiling. Inadequate, she thought. She had always been inadequate when it came to men.

When Sam woke in the morning, at first she didn't know where she was, but when she realized it was Mike's bedroom, a feeling of safety came over her. Someone, and she knew it was Mike, had placed clean clothes over a chair for her. Getting out of bed, she pulled on the jeans and T-shirt he'd left for her—there were no shoes, as though he thought she'd run away if given shoes—and went into the bathroom. This was Mike's bathroom, and the countertop had several bottles and jars on it, all neatly arranged, all clean. Picking up a bottle of aftershave, she smelled it, smiled, and put it down again, then found herself sliding back the glass door to the shower and looking inside to see his shampoo.

There was another door that opened into the bath, and when she opened it she saw another bedroom. The bed was rumpled, recently slept in. Obviously, Mike had spent the night in this room, the room closest to her.

After her inspection of the bathroom, she went back into the bedroom, and after telling herself she shouldn't, she opened his closet door. It was a large, walk-in closet and had been fitted with built-in cabinets to hold his clothes, which were all neatly arranged. He didn't have a lot of clothes, but what he had was all of the best quality. Touching the sleeve of a cream-colored jacket made of raw silk, she lifted the jacket from the rack, looking at the shoulders that were as broad as Mike's shoulders and the waist as narrow as his. There was no way on earth that he'd bought this jacket off a store rack; it had to have been made for him. Inside the jacket was the label of a store in London.

She put the jacket back, ran her hands across shirts and trousers, then touched perfectly polished shoes lined up on slanted shelves, each shoe with a cedar shoe tree inside it. Closing the closet door, she went back into the bedroom.

There was a big chest against one wall in the bedroom, and after a moment's hesitation, Samantha opened the drawers. Underwear, sweaters, a drawer full of workout clothes, socks. It was when she opened the bottom right-hand drawer that she saw a silver frame turned face down. She could no more have contained her curiosity than she could have willed herself to fly. Picking up the frame, she looked at the photograph of a very pretty young woman with lots of dark hair and an intelligent, almost aristocratic-looking face. "All my love, Vanessa" she'd written on the photo.

As Samantha put the photo back in the drawer the way she'd found it, she wondered why Mike had hidden the photo, why he hadn't wanted her to know that he had a steady girl who gave him all her love. Of course a man liked for a woman to think that she was the only one in his life, didn't he? She remembered last night and Mike telling her that he wasn't a rapist. He hadn't been making a pass at her, but Sam had thought he was.

After she finished dressing, she went into the kitchen where she found Mike sitting at the breakfast table. When she greeted him, he was distant to her, saying only that she should be in bed. She wanted to apologize to him for last night, for fighting him after he'd saved her life. She wanted to tell him that it wasn't him but her, that she was the one with the problems, but she couldn't bring herself to write what she felt. Quietly, she went back to bed and picked up a book, but didn't read it.

Later in the morning, Blair came and examined her throat and said she'd be all right by the next day, but if she could, she'd like for Samantha not to speak for another day. Blair went into the living room with Mike and minutes later Samantha got out of bed and followed them.

Blair was leaning over Mike and examining his head. Neither of them saw Samantha, so she slipped upstairs and put on some makeup. When she came down, Mike was in the garden, sitting at the picnic table, lunch food before him.

"You want something to eat?" he asked, but he didn't look at her.

Samantha opened her mouth to say something, then closed

it. How could she explain something that she herself didn't understand?

The sunlight glistened on his hair, and she could see the bare place where his scalp was white. When she stepped closer to him, reached out, and touched his hair, he didn't move. Encouraged, she stepped even closer and examined the wound. There were ten stitches holding the gash shut, and she knew without a doubt that his injury had something to do with why her throat was a mass of bruises.

On impulse, she kissed the sewn cut. Mike sat still, for once not grabbing her, not trying to wrestle her to the ground, not tearing at her clothes. His acquiescence encouraged her, and she smoothed his hair over the place, covering it completely.

Moving away from him, she went to take her seat on the opposite side of the table. He was looking at her oddly, as though trying to figure her out. She wanted to tell him to not try to figure her out, that she wasn't like other people, that she didn't fit into any mold.

Mike didn't say anything, just ate and kept his thoughts to himself.

At one o'clock the telephone rang and when Mike answered it, he broke into a smile. "That's great," he said, grinning. "Congratulations. Wait a minute and I'll ask Sam." Putting his hand over the phone, he turned to her. "Are you up for some company? A friend of mine just passed her bar exam and she's celebrating today. She and some others would like to come over."

Smiling, Samantha nodded yes, although she was leery of more of Mike's friends. So far she'd met strippers and rednecks. What kind of bar had this woman passed? Bar*tending*?

Not wanting anyone to see the bruises on her throat, Samantha put on a turtleneck knit shirt. An hour later, when she met Mike's friends, she was pleasantly surprised. There were four of them, one married couple, Jess and Anne, who had been married all of six weeks, and an engaged couple, Ben and Corey. It was Corey who had just passed her exam that allowed her to practice law. She said that she'd grown up in the same small town of Chandler, Colorado, that Mike had.

When the four ecstatic people, carrying bottles of champagne, entered the town house and saw Samantha on the couch, they immediately assumed that she and Mike were living together.

It was Mike who set them straight. "Samantha is my tenant," Mike said. "She has an apartment upstairs." He told them she'd fallen against the bannister and injured her throat so she couldn't speak. Sam fiddled with the turtleneck, afraid they would see the bruises that looked exactly like fingerprints.

When Mike said Samantha was no more than his tenant, his four friends looked from one to the other and wiggled their eyebrows. It wasn't the usual tenant-landlord relationship that had the tenant ensconced on the library couch wrapped in a quilt.

For Samantha it was good to have the presence of the other people, for their laughter broke the tension that had developed between her and Mike, and she got to see Mike as he was around other people.

Since she'd been twelve years old, Samantha had led an isolated life. Her mother had been the more social of her parents, the one who was always organizing barbecues, dinner parties, and church socials. After she died, Samantha had been left with her father, who rarely saw other people. Then there had been Samantha's marriage to a man who liked his socializing in private.

But Mike was a gregarious creature who was at ease in groups.

Jess liked computers, and when he saw the new equipment in Mike's library, he couldn't wait to turn it on. Mike gave Samantha all the credit for having chosen the equipment and for doing whatever had to be done to it to make it work.

Looking at the directory, Jess brought up the Sierra game and within minutes, the three men were moving the mouse about on the pad and arguing over bees and ants and robbers.

Lying on the couch behind them, Samantha watched Mike, thinking that it was odd that in such a short time all other men seemed to pale beside him. She watched him move, watched the way his muscles moved under his thin T-shirt, looked at the dark curls of his hair.

Suddenly, it hit her how close she had come to death. Remembering the man's hands on her throat, she could almost feel her life being squeezed from her. Yet, in the middle of that, she had known, *known*, that Mike would come to her if she could just make some sort of signal.

Now that she thought of it, she knew that hitting the wall

with her heel was a very weak signal to send to someone who was asleep. How had Mike heard her three puny knocks? How had he known they were cries for help and not just normal sounds? She could have turned over in her sleep and hit the wall.

Yet somehow, Mike had heard her and he'd come to her rescue. When she thought of the door to her apartment with the hole in it, she felt chills run up her spine. Mike had put his foot through the panel and had reached inside to the lock. He had come through a solid oak door with the force of a bulldozer. Or a superman, she thought.

Now, she looked at him, at his profile. Was he actually the most beautiful man on earth, or was that just the way *she* saw him?

Looking down from his face to his strong neck, to his bare arm, the tricep well defined, to his small waist, his stomach hard and flat, her eyes moved downward to his legs, hairy and brown beneath his shorts.

When she looked back up at his face, Mike had turned to her and was watching her. Samantha looked away from his eyes, not wanting him to know that she had been looking at him.

Moving away from his friends, Mike came to sit by her on the couch. Behind him the men were arguing over the game, and the women were outside looking at Mike's garden.

"Are you all right?" Mike asked, tucking the blanket around her, even though it was warm in the house.

She nodded, looking down at her hands.

Leaning toward her, Mike slipped her high collar down and put his hand on her throat, on the ring of yellow bruises there. As his fingers slipped around the back of her neck, his thumb rubbed over her lower lip.

Samantha's breath caught in her throat as she looked into his dark eyes. It was as though they were alone in the room, but at the same time she was well aware of the other people around them. When Mike moved closer to her, she didn't pull away, and when his lips were inches from hers, she still didn't pull away. His breath was warm on her lips, warm and sweet and fragrant.

When he touched his lips to hers, she closed her eyes, but when he moved away, she opened them. He was looking at her, looking at her in a way that she didn't understand.

"Sam," he whispered, then kissed her in earnest, kissed her

sweetly, not aggressively, but meltingly, as though he wanted to tell her something, as though he wanted to reassure her—as though he wanted to tell her that he cared for her.

She put her hand up to his neck. Ah, she thought, to touch Mike, to feel the warm skin that she looked at so often, to feel the curls of his hair about her fingers. She applied pressure to his neck with her fingertips and he moved his head, his kiss deepening.

Samantha lay back against the pillows, her fingers tightening on his neck, her mouth opening a bit as she felt the sweetness of Mike's tongue touch hers. He wasn't jumping on her, wasn't forcing her, wasn't overwhelming her.

It was he who pulled away. Her heart was pounding and her breathing was deep and fast.

"You like that better, sweetheart?" he whispered.

"I—" she started to say, but he put his lips to hers again and didn't allow her to speak.

Putting his hands on the side of her head, he ran his thumbs over her cheeks, then moved and touched her eyelids, her nose, her lips. After a moment, he pulled back and held up his hand. It was shaking. "You do something to me, Sammy-girl. I'm not sure what it is, but I've felt it since that first day."

It was the women coming in from outside that brought them back to the present. Straightening, Mike stood up from the couch, but the way he was looking at her with eyes so hot, eyes that asked so much of her, he may as well have still been kissing her.

"Have we interrupted something?" Anne asked. "Mike, you and your . . . tenant want us to leave?"

Mike grinned at her. "Actually, I'd rather you stayed. This house seems to get a little, ah, friendlier when there are people around."

Looking down at her hands, Samantha tried to keep anyone from seeing her blush. What Mike said was true: She felt safer when there were other people with them. When there was an audience, she was sure Mike wasn't going to do something that would take her where she didn't want to go.

At four everyone was starving, so Jess ordered food, enough for at least twenty people. When it was set up on the picnic table, Mike insisted on carrying Samantha outside.

"Shut up," he said when she started to protest. "You act like

I'm a sex deviant when we're alone, but you let me kiss you when the house is full of other people. If the presence of other people loosens you up, I will consider keeping the house packed. Now be still and let me enjoy myself."

She couldn't keep from smiling as she put her head into the curve of his shoulder.

Mike kissed her forehead. "Sam, you go to bed with me and I'll show you a real good time. I swear."

She laughed—but she wasn't tempted, not actually. She liked this much, much better than what people did in bed together. She liked the touching and the caressing, the kissing, liked the feel of Mike's breath on her lips, the sight of his muscles moving beneath his clothes. She liked sitting close to him, liked the way he leaned over her when he tucked the blanket around her. All in all, she liked the way a man treated a woman before he'd had what he wanted from her. After he got that, everything changed.

The five of them laughed and talked all through the meal. They talked of people Samantha didn't know, but they always made an effort to explain who the people were. Corey told stories about Mike as a child.

"Did you tell Sam what you did to your sister's friends' clothes?" she asked Mike, pointing a plastic fork at him.

With an embarrassed chuckle, Mike looked at his plate. "I somehow forgot to mention that."

"All those girls in those white clothes," Corey said, laughing.

At the mention of white clothes, Samantha became alert. She motioned Corey to tell the story, but Corey looked at Mike, at his pleading eyes, and said no, that it was Mike's story. Nothing anyone said could entice Mike to tell the story.

After dinner, they went into the living room where Mike put on Kiri Te Kanawa singing Puccini and talked. Samantha got Corey into a corner and wrote on her pad, *Tell me about Mike.*

"What do you want to know?"

Samantha put her hands palm up to signify that anything Corey told her would be all right.

"I don't know where to begin. He has eleven brothers and sisters, and—" She laughed when Samantha's mouth dropped open in shock. "There are a lot of Taggerts in Chandler."

Are they very poor? Samantha wrote.

Corey gave a snort of laughter, then began chuckling as she

put her hand on Samantha's arm. "You should ask him about that. Let's see, what else can I tell you? Mike's degree is in mathematics. He did all the course work for a Ph. D., but then got interested in his old gangster and never finished his dissertation." She looked at Sam. "His father would love for him to finish his degree. Maybe you could influence him."

Samantha shrugged to show that she had no influence over him. She and Mike were nothing to each other, just temporarily living together, and the fact that Mike spent a great deal of time trying to get her to go to bed with him meant nothing. As far as Samantha could tell, all men did that to all women. It meant nothing before the event and less than nothing afterward.

"Mike," Corey said as she picked up a calculator from a bookcase, "what's two hundred and thirty-seven times two thousand six hundred and eighty-one?"

Mike didn't look around, nor did he take so much as a second before he answered. "Six hundred thirty-five thousand, three hundred ninety-seven."

When Corey showed Samantha the calculator reading, she saw that Mike was correct. "The whole family is like that," Corey whispered. "In school we all thought they should have been in a circus." She pressed Samantha's arm. "Mike's a good guy, a really good guy."

Samantha looked across the room at him, and as she did so, Mike turned and winked at her. Sam smiled in return.

Why do you like white so much? Samantha wrote on her pad. She was once again in Mike's bed, and the house was empty and quiet, and she was very tired. In spite of the fact that she hadn't done much that day, it had been a tiring one. Now, she wanted to go to sleep and she didn't want to have to wrestle with Mike, didn't want him trying to continue what they had started on the couch in the library.

"You sure you want to know?"

She nodded as he tucked her in, then started to protest when he stretched out on the bed and put his head in her lap, but he acted as though he didn't hear her.

"When I was fifteen my sister, she was about nineteen, I guess, brought home four of her college friends to spend a week at our house. I thought those girls were the most beautiful creatures I'd ever seen. I followed them around everywhere and they teased me mercilessly.

"To this day I don't know what made me do it, but one day while they were out swimming, I gathered up all their clothes and took them downstairs, threw them in the washers, and added three cups of bleach to each load, then turned on the hot water.

"When the girls got back, they had nothing to wear except their swim suits and clothes that were white and tiny." He stared into space for a few moments. "They were beautiful. Tiny white shorts. Microscopic T-shirts. Skirts that only reached midthigh."

What did your parents do? Samantha wrote.

"It took them half a day to figure out who had done it—I do have brothers, you know—but when they found out, my mother said I should be blindfolded and stood up against an outside wall of the house and the girls should be given shotguns. But Dad said he'd take me outside and beat me. So we walked outside, he grinned at me, rubbed my head, and sent me off to spend the rest of the week with Uncle Mike, but he told me to limp whenever I saw my mother."

That's all that was done to you?!!!!! she wrote.

"Sure. Dad took the girls into Denver and bought them new clothes. After the girls left, my father gave me a small white shirt that had no buttons down the front. He said one of the girls had worn it to breakfast, and when she'd reached for something, all the buttons had popped off. He even saved a button for me."

Why didn't the girls borrow clothes from your sister or your mother and cover themselves?

Mike looked surprised, then smiled, then he laughed. "What a very, very good question. Maybe they liked my father and my brothers staring at them in open-mouthed admiration."

Still grinning, he rolled off of her and stood up. He stretched and yawned, with Samantha's eyes never leaving his body, especially when his shirt pulled up and exposed his bare stomach. Did he have any idea what he looked like when he did that? she wondered.

Abruptly, he stopped yawning and looked down at her, as though he knew very well that she was watching him. "That's your story for tonight. You wouldn't like to change your mind about . . . you know?" He nodded toward the empty side of the bed.

Sam shook her head no.

Then, as though it were the most natural thing in the world, he bent to kiss her lips. But Samantha turned her head away. When she looked back at him, he was bending over her, staring at her.

"Sometimes you remind me of those high school girls that you take out to drive-in movies. You go out one night and spend the whole night kissing and, after hours of work, finally getting your hand under her blouse. The next time you go out you think you're going to work on her skirt, but instead, she makes you start back at square one: She won't even let you kiss her."

In spite of herself, Samantha giggled. She could easily imagine Mike as a randy high school boy.

"Tell me, Sam, did the boys have to start over again with you with each date?"

When she didn't answer him, he handed her the pad and pencil. *I never had a date in high school,* she wrote.

Mike had to read her sentence three times before he looked up at her in disbelief, then taking the pencil from her he wrote, *Have you ever been to bed with any man other than the jerk you were married to?*

She didn't want to answer his question. *Why a jerk?* she wrote.

"He lost you, didn't he? Any man who'd do that has to be stupid."

Samantha laughed, then punched his shoulder. He was lying; he was flattering her, but still, having someone call her ex-husband a jerk pleased her.

"How about a goodnight kiss? Nothing more than that. I'll keep my hands on your shoulders. Trust me. I promise."

She wasn't strong enough to say no to kissing Michael, especially when he was looking at her like that. As he leaned on the bed, a hand on each side of her hips, she gave him a tentative nod, and he sat down on the bed again and put his hands on her upper arms. Slowly he brought his lips to hers.

With each kiss, she experienced wonder that something could be so lovely. As he'd done today, he didn't force her or try to leap on top of her. She began to sink into his kiss, began to trust him as she slumped back against the pillows, her eyes closed, her body relaxed.

"Good night," he said softly, and Samantha almost wished he wouldn't leave.

Getting off the bed, he turned off the light switch and went down the hall.

He asked her to trust him and she was beginning to, but, she thought as she snuggled down into the covers, would he trust her?

It had taken two days, but she had made her decision: She was going to look for her grandmother.

"I am going to look for my grandmother."

Samantha and Mike were in the bedroom of her apartment. She had slept downstairs in his bed, but early this morning, before she'd heard him stirring in the bedroom next door, she'd come upstairs to get dressed. When she'd come out of her bedroom, Mike had been standing in the living room, waiting for her. He thought she was getting ready to go with his cousin Raine to Maine, and it had taken all her courage to tell him that she wasn't going, she was staying here in New York with him.

Pretending he didn't hear her, Mike didn't even bother to answer. "Montgomery will be here any minute. All of them are punctual, so he won't be even a minute late. I bought you some chocolate chip muffins for the trip, because if I know the Montgomerys, they'll feed you something like broccoli and carrot soufflé. Maybe I ought to call Kaplan's Deli and get you a couple of pastrami sandwiches and a six-pack of beer. Beer's nice on a trip, and—"

"Mike," she said softly, "stop pretending you didn't hear me. I'm not leaving. I'm going to look for my grandmother."

"Like hell you are," he said, grabbing her tote bag in one hand and her elbow with the other.

"I am *not* leaving. And that's empty." She nodded toward the tote bag.

"No problem. When you get to Connecticut have Montgomery stop and buy you whatever you need. Better yet, wait until you get to Maine."

When Mike wouldn't release her arm, she did the only thing she could think of: She sat down on the floor. "I'm not leaving here and I'm not going to Maine. I am going to remain in New York to look for my grandmother."

Putting his strong hands on her upper arms, Mike lifted her. When Samantha remained rigid, he set her on the edge of the couch.

"Samantha," he began.

"It's no use trying to think of what to say to make me see your side of it. I have made up my mind."

Several emotions crossed Mike's face, then he sat down heavily beside her. "I'll close the house if I have to, then you won't have any place to stay."

"Fine. I'll rent another apartment."

Mike gave a grunt then a lopsided grin. "And who'll take care of you? The doorman? Sam, you're so terrified of New York you haven't even gone around the block by yourself. How do you expect to find your grandmother without me to help you? And I'm going to *refuse* to help you."

Turning her to face him, he took her hands in his. "Look, sweetheart, in any other instance, I'd love to have you with me, but this is dangerous."

She raised one eyebrow. "Men's work?"

He squeezed her hands. "Don't give me that women's lib crap! I'm not talking about who does the dishes, I'm talking about life and death."

"And what makes you think you'd make a better detective than me? You've been researching for two years, and I've found out more in a few weeks than you have."

Mike nearly choked on what he wanted to say. "Found out? You call the bruises on your neck 'finding out'?"

She tried to pull her hands away, but he held them tightly. "She is *my* grandmother, she was involved with a hideous man, and my father wanted me to look for her."

"Your father had no idea his mother was involved with gangsters—at least not *real* gangsters. Today gangsters sound kind of cute, and besides, your dad thought his mother ran away because of love."

"And why do *you* think she ran away?"

Mike put his nose nearly to hers. "Money. Murder. She knew something. It could be a million reasons—maybe *three* million reasons—but none of them are good, which is why *you* are going to Maine where it's safe."

She took a deep breath. There was no way in the world he was going to change her mind, but on the other hand, she wanted to stay in his house. It was comfortable here; the garden was pretty; it was a nice location. And, well, okay, she was rather familiar with Mike and if she did ever again need help—which of course she wasn't going to—he did have rather fast reactions.

"Mike," she asked, "why are you researching this man?" She narrowed her eyes at him. "The *truth*. I want the truth, not one of your lies, no matter how sweetly you tell it."

Releasing her hands, he stood up and walked to the window. "For my uncle Mike," he said, then turned back to her. "Remember when Doc said that Scalpini's men shot a lot of innocent people in the nightclub?"

She nodded.

"My uncle Mike worked there. He danced with the women whose husbands and boyfriends were too fat to dance, and he was on the dance floor when Scalpini's men arrived. He took thirty-two bullets below the waist."

"Thirty-two," she whispered. "And he lived?"

"Barely. It was touch and go for a long time, but he not only lived, he learned to walk on crutches. He and my grandfather were in the navy together and Mike saved Gramp's life, so when Mike needed help, Gramps gave it. He brought Uncle Mike to Chandler, hired the best medical people, and helped him get well. Uncle Mike lived in a little house behind ours."

"And he was your friend?"

"The *best* of friends. Sometimes a person can get lost in a family the size of mine, but Uncle Mike always had time for me.

He never lost patience with me, and he always took my side in any scrape—even when I was in the wrong."

"He sounds like a nice man."

"He was."

Looking up at him, she saw the sadness in his eyes and knew they shared something, this loss of people they loved. "And you want to bring justice to Doc because of what was done to your uncle Mike?"

"Something like that."

"Do you realize that if Scalpini hadn't shot Mike, you'd probably never have met him? In my case, my family was already formed, we were happy, but something that probably had to do with that night in 1928 broke my family apart. Don't I have a right to know what happened? To know what made my grandmother leave?"

He went to sit by her again. "Of course you do. I'll call you every day. I was going to anyway, but—"

"Were you?"

"Was I where?"

"No. Were you planning to call me every day?"

He gave her a look of disbelief. "You don't think I was going to send you into a town full of Montgomerys and not have daily contact with you, do you? Do you think I'm a *fool?*"

"And what would we talk about? Doc?"

Laughing, Mike reached out to touch her hair. "Sometimes, Sam-Sam, I think there are parts of your education missing. What do all boys and girls who have the hots for each other talk about for hours at a time?"

Turning red, Samantha looked down at her hands. It was the first thing he'd said that made her actually consider going to Maine. She recovered herself. "I am going to remain here and look for my grandmother," she said firmly. "And anything you—"

She quit talking because Mike had put his hand behind her head and drawn her mouth to his. He kissed her with such hunger that Samantha could feel herself beginning to tremble as she put her hands on his ribs, feeling the thick pad of muscle there.

"Don't you think I *want* you to stay here? Don't you think I love having you here with me? You're the only person besides your father who's shown any interest in my biography. My dad nags me about finishing my dissertation so I can get a doctorate. But for what? I don't want to teach and I don't want to work in an office somewhere. My brothers laugh at me and talk about my 'old gangsters.' Sam, maybe I don't want to do this biography just for Uncle Mike. Maybe I want to do it for myself because it's so difficult for me. In college, math was easy, too easy, but spending days alone in a library, up to my neck in falling-apart old books, then some girl in a short skirt walks by and she's got a rear end on her that . . ."

He grinned. "Anyway, writing has been a challenge, and I get distracted easily, but it hasn't been much fun until you came along. You sit with me and type my notes and we talk about things and I can bounce ideas off of you and—" Lifting first one hand then the other, he kissed her palms. "And sometimes you let me kiss you. It's been great, Sam, really great."

"And it will *continue* to be great," she said, squeezing his hands in hers. "Mike, we can work together on this. I *like* libraries; I *like*—"

"Yeah, and I like having you alive."

She pulled away from him. "You're going to lose this one. I am going to remain in New York and I'm going to search for my grandmother. As far as I can see, you have two choices: One, I stay here in this house with you and we look together, or two, I move to another apartment and I look by myself."

"This is too serious, Sam. This is too dangerous. *Why* are you doing this? We can drop this now and from the looks of him, Doc will be dead in a few years, then we can—"

"But that's just it, Mike," she said enthusiastically. "Don't you see? If Doc is still alive, then my grandmother might still be alive."

"That doesn't follow."

She looked at him hard. When she'd first met him, he'd been able to tell her lies and keep secrets from her without her detecting his deception, but now he couldn't. Right now there was an insincerity on his face, a tightness about his mouth that she was beginning to recognize. "You're holding something back," she whispered. "I can see it in your eyes."

Mike got off the couch, but Samantha put herself in front of him. "What do you know?"

"Nothing," he said angrily, turning away from her.

"Michael Taggert, if you don't tell me what you know I'll . . . I'll . . ."

"What?" he asked in disgust. "What else can you do to me? Put your life in jeopardy? Blackmail me? Run around in front of me in white shorts and T-shirt and yell rape when I touch you?"

"I'll kiss Raine Montgomery," she said. "I'll date him. I'll go out with him every night. I'll—"

Turning on his heel, Mike started to leave her apartment.

She caught his arm. "Mike, wait, please. Can't you understand? What if you found out that your uncle Mike wasn't dead, after all? Or that there was a chance that he may not be dead? Wouldn't you do everything you could to find him? To see him just one more time before he was gone? My grandmother is eighty-some years old, I don't have *time* to wait. Please tell me what you know. Please." Putting her hand up, she touched his cheek.

He caught her hand and kissed her palm. "Sam, you do something to me. You turn me into a kid again." He took a deep breath. "Your father told me that as of two years ago your grandmother was alive."

Samantha checked herself in the mirror in the foyer, making sure her clothes were straight and that her hair was arranged the way the hairdresser had taught her, then she put her purse on the narrow table and made sure that she had her new credit cards and cash. When she couldn't think of another thing to check or anything to do that would enable her to postpone what she planned to do, she put her hand on the doorknob, straightened her shoulders, and opened the door.

She was going to go out into New York all by herself. This time she was going farther than just around the block; this time she was going to spend the entire afternoon in the city by herself.

After locking the door behind her, she started down the stairs. This morning Mike had told her that her grandmother was alive as of two years ago. He'd explained that two years ago her father had received a postcard from his mother, and it was the card that had made David Elliot decide to try to find his mother. The postcard had been simple, saying only that she loved him, had always loved him, and that she hoped he'd forgive her. At the bottom, it had been sighed "Your mother."

At the time he'd received the card, Dave had had his accounting office to run and couldn't so much as take a vacation to New York, but immediately upon receipt of that card he'd started making preparations to take an early retirement so he could search for his mother.

Then, by a stroke of luck, fate, kismet, joss, or whatever one wanted to call it, six months after he'd received the card, Mike had appeared at his door and asked if Dave's mother had once had an affair with a gangster by the name of Doc.

That simple meeting had started a friendship that had eventually resulted in Dave turning the guardianship of his daughter over to Mike. "Ownership," Samantha had muttered when Mike had told her the story.

"Some ownership," Mike answered in mock weariness. "The deed's kept in a safe deposit box."

Mike had been very upset at Sam's telling him that she was planning to remain in New York, and she suspected that he had every intention of keeping her out of everything that he was planning to do. Knowing that he blamed himself for the murder attempt, she guessed that he planned to not allow her out of his sight, and his best way of controlling her was by keeping facts from her.

After their confrontation of this morning, she'd gone downstairs and seen Mike's gym bag by the front door, letting her know that he had obviously been planning to go to the gym after she left for Maine. When she asked him about the bag and his plans, he'd stubbornly said he was staying home with her. It had taken some fast talking on her part to persuade him to leave the house and go on his planned trip to the gym. She had to get him out of the house, because something he'd said was bothering her. Mike had said that she couldn't help him research because she was too afraid of New York to so much as leave the block.

What he had said was true, and Samantha knew she had to screw up her courage and get out into the city. After all, she couldn't spend her life hiding in Mike's town house, or for that matter, she couldn't spend her life hiding behind Mike. After—if—they found her grandmother, she would have to leave the city and Mike. How could she ever think of living alone if she was too frightened to leave the house?

Now, Mike was at the gym and Samantha was going out all alone into the maw of this notorious, noisy, dirty city full of strangers. No gladiator facing the lions had been more afraid than Sam was at this undertaking; no St. George facing the dragon had more misgivings than she did.

She walked down Sixty-fourth Street, breathing a sigh of relief when she crossed the street and no one had yet held a gun or knife to her throat. When she crossed the wide expanse of Park Avenue, which seemed to be mostly residential, she headed toward Madison, her head down, her courage screwed to the breaking point.

For the first two blocks she was so afraid that she didn't look at her surroundings, but by the time she neared Madison, she noticed uniformed doormen smiling and tipping their hats to her. Tentatively, she smiled back at them—at least they didn't look like muggers or drug dealers.

When she reached Madison, she took a right and headed north, walking three full blocks looking straight ahead, wondering how far she had to go before she had proved herself, proved that she could go out into this city without fear overcoming her. Her thoughts were occupied with imagining telling Mike defiantly that she had spent the whole afternoon alone on the streets of New York—and *she had survived*!

By the fourth block, she began to look at her surroundings, and since midtown Madison Avenue was all shops, this meant looking in the display windows at the merchandise. In Santa Fe most of the shops were full of goods for the tourists to take home: T-shirts with idiot sayings on them, mugs and badly made Indian dolls, coyotes on every conceivable surface. Everything was labeled handmade, as though people in other parts of the world had found robots to make cheap tourist goods. Besides the junk goods, there were also hundreds of galleries full of overpriced Indian art. The few "normal" stores geared toward the residents were filled with lowend merchandise: cheap rayon skirts, plastic picture frames, earrings that made your ears turn green.

What Samantha saw on Madison Avenue were shops full of beautiful goods: the best products the world had to offer. She saw stores that contained clothes so expensive that guards stood at the door, selectively admitting customers who passed their scrutiny. When a handsome young man in a beautiful suit smiled and held a shop door open for Samantha, she felt as though she'd passed membership into a world of the rich and powerful. Entering the store, she saw lush gray carpet, mirrored walls, and merchandise that cost the yearly income of some people—mostly women who were overworked and underpaid, she thought with a grimace.

She went into a shop full of exquisite sleepwear, Montenapoleone, and, on impulse, spent much too much on a white nightgown made of cotton so fine that it was transparent. Little pink threads were tied into bows about the neckline.

She passed Giorgio Armani, Gianni Versace, Yves Saint Laurent. It was in Valentino's that she realized how much money Mike had spent on the clothes she had bought at Saks, for she saw a suit just like one she had and the price was thirty-four hundred dollars.

"Are you all right?" the pretty young clerk asked in concern.

"Yes," Sam managed to say as she sat down and took the cup of cool, bottled water that was offered to her. There was part of her that felt she should be angry at Mike for deceiving her and part of her that glowed with pleasure, for what woman didn't like to receive presents? She couldn't help wondering when he'd worked out the details with his cousin Vicky to dupe Samantha into thinking that the clothes were something she could afford and that she was going to be able to pay for them herself.

Leaving the store, she wasn't sure what she should do. Go to Michael and confront him with his knowledge of what she'd found out? Then again, it didn't seem very nice to yell at him for doing something so sweet as buying her thousands of dollars worth of lovely clothes. So maybe later she'd figure out a way to say thank you.

With her head up (it didn't hurt her pride or self-esteem to now be aware of the fact that she was wearing about five grand in clothes), she continued on her excursion into the wild, untamed streets of New York. As she looked in a shop window of antique jewelry, she thought, The *real* danger in this city is the merchandise.

At Seventy-second street, Sam went into the wonder of a store that Ralph Lauren had created and wandered all the floors looking at the furnishings as much as at the goods. She used the very pretty lavatory in the basement, then went back upstairs and bought a marcasite pin that looked Edwardian.

After leaving his store, she looked west toward Fifth Avenue where she saw the green of Central Park. Turning toward the park, she thought she might wander through it, but if New York beat Santa Fe in merchandise, nowhere on earth could beat Santa Fe for scenery.

Instead of going into the park, she took a left and went down Fifth Avenue, looking up at the windows of the buildings facing the park and wondering what famous people lived in the buildings. Just at the end of the park, she stopped into F.A.O. Schwarz and bought a stuffed monkey, thinking the funny little creature might relieve the seriousness of her apartment.

Across the street from the toy store she saw the Plaza Hotel and there she encountered Bergdorf Goodman's—lovely, beautiful Bergdorf's, which she instinctively knew deserved a day all its own, so she limited herself to the first floor, where she thought she couldn't get into too much trouble. She underestimated Bergdorf's, for she left the store with a shopping bag full of socks and hose and a leather belt with a silver buckle. Past Bergdorf's she saw Fendi's and the barred, fortress-looking jewelry store of Harry Winston, which made her think of the Duchess of Windsor. Moving south, she saw Charles Jourdan, Bendel's, and Elizabeth Arden's red door.

Smiling in fond memory as she looked across the street at Saks, thinking of the lovely day she'd spent there with Mike and what he had done for her that day, she turned into Rockefeller Center and saw the gold statue of the flying man that she'd seen a thousand times on TV. Leaning back against the rail that overlooked the area that in the winter was the skating rink, she set down her heavy shopping bags by her feet and rubbed her hands. She had been walking for hours and she should have been tired, but instead, she felt wonderful: She had faced the enemy and found the enemy to be a delightful, entertaining new friend. As she looked at the people around her, at the windows of the Metropolitan Gift Shop, she couldn't help but smile. What a lovely place, she thought.

After buying a hot dog from a street vendor, she left Rockefeller Center and walked further south, where she looked in the window of a shop and saw a four-inch-tall bronze statue of a Japanese samurai. The little warrior was strong and armor-clad, but he had a particularly engaging smile that reminded her of Michael. Thinking of all Mike had done for her, she very much wanted to buy a gift for him, and this statue would be perfect. She went into the store and asked to see the statue.

It was in this store that Samantha learned what every true New Yorker knows: that everything in New York is for sale and what the price tag says has nothing to do with what an item actually costs.

Contrary to the world's opinion, there is no human being on earth nicer than a New York merchant when he's showing his wares to a richly dressed customer. The man looked at Sam's expensive designer suit, her Mark Cross purse, her Bally shoes, and the big diamond flashing on her finger and smiled sweetly as he handed the little statue to her. It wasn't a false smile, for no one has ever loved anything or anyone as much as a true New Yorker loves buying and selling.

"How much is it?" she asked.

"Seven fifty," the man said.

Sam's face fell. She wanted the statue, but that was far, far too much to pay.

The merchant, who had a good eye for tourists—who were so naive they could be talked into anything at any price, in fact, tourists often bought things they didn't want just to get the merchant to stop badgering them—thought Samantha was a New Yorker. She dressed like a New York woman, even had the nails of a New York woman. (In the rest of America, manicures were something only the richest, idlest, most vain women had, but in New York, thanks to the Koreans, manicure parlors were five to a block and eight dollars a session.) He thought Sam was acting when she said the price was too high; he thought she was playing the game.

"It will be a hardship to me, but I can let you have it for five fifty."

Samantha looked startled. She'd not expected him to lower his price. "I'm sorry, that's still too much."

Born in the city, the merchant thought. "Is there anything else in the store you like?"

Thinking that was a very odd question, Samantha didn't try to understand it but pointed to some garnet earrings that she liked and the merchant took them out of the window so she could look at them.

She thought the earrings were lovely, but she refused to allow herself to covet them. It was better that she bought something for Mike to say thank you for all he'd done for her. "They're nice but I'd rather have the statue, but it costs too much," she said honestly.

"How about five fifty for both of them?"

Again Samantha looked startled, but she was beginning to understand. On impulse, she said, "Three fifty."

"Four twenty-five," he said, taking the earrings off the counter.

"Three seventy-five for both of them. Cash." She held her breath, for that was every penny she had on her. She couldn't go up even a nickel.

"Four hundred and that's all I can do."

Sam's face fell again, and she looked as sad as she felt. "I'm sorry but three seventy-five is all that I can spend." Slowly she turned toward the door.

"Okay," the man said in disgust. "They're yours. Three seventy-five. Cash."

When Samantha left the store, she was feeling a little stunned, as though she'd just done the strangest thing of her life, and she walked for half a block before she realized that it was beginning to rain. Looking at her watch, she saw that it was nearly six o'clock. She knew without a doubt that Mike would be home waiting for her and he'd be furious.

Having learned about bargaining, Samantha now learned about taxis: At the first drop of rain, all New York cab drivers headed for shelter. At least that was the theory proposed to explain why there were never any vacant cabs on the street when it rained, or maybe the rain might wash the cars, then they'd no longer deserve the name of New York cab. Standing at the curb side, she held her hand up, but no cab stopped for her. Well, she thought, perhaps New York isn't perfect after all. Readjusting her grip on her shopping bags, she put her head down against the rain and started the long walk back to Mike's town house.

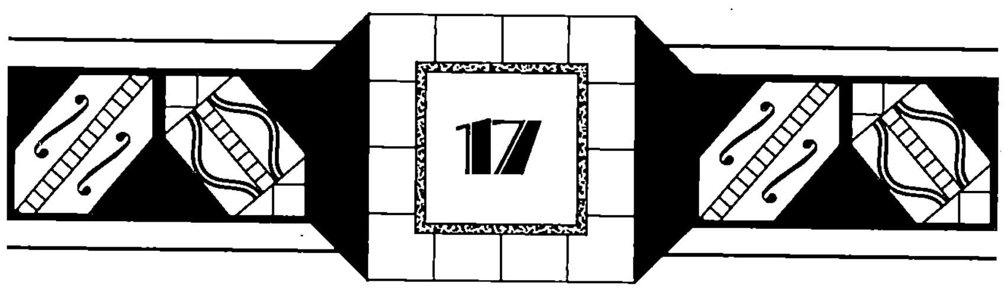

As soon as she turned the corner onto Sixty-fourth Street she began to run. The rain was coming down hard now and she was getting wet, but that had nothing to do with her hurry—she was hurrying toward Michael. He might be angry that she'd left without telling him where she was going and he'd rant and rave a bit, but she knew that he'd be waiting and he'd be glad to see *her*. He'd be glad that she was safe and he'd want to hear about what she had been doing, what she had seen, what she'd bought. He'd want to know everything. She didn't know how she was sure of this, but she was.

He opened the door before she was on the top step. Obviously he had been watching for her. In spite of his immediate blustering, she was grinning at him.

"Where the hell have you been?" he said, sounding angry, but she could hear the underlying relief in his voice. She also detected something else: curiosity. "If you'd been gone another minute, I'd have called the cops. Don't you realize that this city is dangerous?"

"Oh, Mike," she said, laughing and running her hand through her wet hair. "There are thousands—millions—of women out there without a big, strong man to protect them."

She could see that he was partially mollified by her calling him a "big, strong man."

"Yes, well, *they* know what they're doing, but you—"

He stopped because she sneezed and the next minute he took her by the arm and led her to the bathroom they shared. "Out of those wet clothes. Now."

"Mike, my dry clothes are upstairs. I need—"

"After today I'm afraid to let you out of my sight, even to go upstairs. I'll get you something to put on." He shut the bathroom door.

For a moment Samantha stood looking in the mirror. Even to her, she looked flushed and happy, which is how she felt. Quickly she began to undress, hesitating over whether or not to remove her underwear, then, on impulse, she took it off too and rubbed herself with a towel. There was a knock on the door, and Mike opened it enough to hand her a bathrobe. Taking the robe, she saw right away that it had never been worn. The robe was too new, and it wasn't something that Mike would wear. It was navy blue silk charmeuse with burgundy piping, the kind of robe a woman would buy a man, then become frustrated when he wouldn't wear it. Only David Niven could wear something like this robe and feel comfortable in it.

Slipping her arms in it, she hugged the silk to her. It was Mike's and it felt good.

When she left the bathroom, she was toweling her hair dry. Mike met her in the kitchen, a drink in his hand.

"No," she began, but he pushed the drink toward her and she took it.

"Now," he said sternly, "I want to know where you have been. What caused you to run off like that and scare me half to death and—?"

She took a deep swallow of her gin and tonic. "If you don't stop complaining, I won't show you what I bought you."

That statement made his eyes widen.

She smiled. "Come on," she said and led the way into the breakfast area, where they could sit and watch the rain through the glass doors. She left him there while she went back to the foyer to get her bags, and when she returned he was sitting at the table.

"Close your eyes and hold out your hands," she said.

After a moment's hesitation, Mike did what she asked as she unwrapped the little samurai and put it in his hands. When he opened his eyes, she watched his face to see if he was pleased.

Mike didn't say anything for a moment as he held the little statue. He liked the sculpture, liked it very much. In fact, it was something he might have bought for himself, but more important than his liking the statue was the fact that she'd given it to him. Never before had an unrelated female given him a gift when it wasn't his birthday or Christmas. All of the other presents he'd received from females had been impersonal, a sweater or a tie or a wallet. And the gifts were usually followed by the female saying, "Let's go out to dinner and show it off," which meant that he'd spend more than the present had cost.

"Do you like it? I thought he looked rather like you. You know, kind of fierce, but rather sweet, too . . . smiling."

He was looking at her as though seeing her for the first time. From what he saw on her face, he might as well have been seeing her for the first time, for she looked different: She looked happy. "Yes, I like it," he said softly, puzzled by the pleasure his words seemed to give her. Could giving a gift to another person please someone that much?

Leaving his chair, he walked to the glass doors and examined the man in the light, looking at his facial features, studying the intricate carving of his clothes. When he looked up, Sam was standing beside him.

"He's the nicest present I've ever received in my life," Mike said truthfully. Normally, when he received a gift from a woman, he kissed her, then, after an expensive dinner, took her to bed, but now he just smiled at Sam as his hand curled about the little statue—and that smile, at that moment, seemed more intimate than what he'd shared with other women in bed.

They went back to the table and when she began to talk, he watched her as much as he listened to her. She was telling him of the great and wondrous experience she'd had when she'd bargained for the purchase of the man. To hear her tell it, she had fought her way through enemy territory to explore new frontiers.

"What else did you buy?" he asked, looking at her shopping bags.

As she began to pull out other purchases to show him, Mike knew without being told that this showing of what she'd bought was a new experience for her. How odd, he thought, because his sisters and his mother, and sometimes it seemed that every female in the neighborhood, used to gather in their dining room to look at each other's purchases.

Extravagantly admiring everything she showed him, he made comments about all of it. He listened with interest and pleasure as she told him about Madison Avenue and Fifth Avenue and what the other women had been wearing and what she had seen and how she'd eaten a hot dog from a street vendor—all of it so ordinary, but seen through Sam's delighted eyes, all of it so wondrous.

When she'd shown everything except the white nightgown, she seemed to run out of words and she sat down, all her purchases on the table about her and sipped her drink. Smiling, she looked out at the rain.

"Oh Mike," she said, "I haven't been this . . ." She seemed to search for the words. "This happy, in years."

"The shopping made you happy?"

She laughed. "Yes and no. The selfishness of this city, of having my hair done and my nails polished, of living here in this house and not having to cook and having you look at me as though—" She broke off, then after a quick glance at him, said no more.

After a while, he spoke. "What did you do in Santa Fe?" he asked, genuinely curious, for as far as he could tell, nothing she'd done since coming to New York was unusual. His sisters, his mother, and all the females he'd ever known seemed to spend their lives fooling with their hair and nails.

"I worked," Samantha said, knowing she should keep her mouth shut, but the drink was making her relax. "I worked at ComputerLand five days a week, and two evenings and Sunday evenings I taught an aerobics class at a local spa. The time I wasn't at work I did housework and bill paying and groceries, that sort of thing."

"And what did your husband do?" He hadn't meant it to, but the word *husband* came out with a sneer.

A humorless little laugh escaped Samantha as she held her

drink aloft in a mock toast. "He was writing the Great American Novel."

Her words gave Mike some insight as to why she'd once made a snide remark about writers. "And what did you do when you lived with your father before you got married?"

Downing the last of her drink, she looked back at the rain, and when she spoke, he could barely hear her. "I saw a TV show once where someone asked a man why he remained married to his terror of a wife. He was such a *nice* man, you see. The man said that sometimes he thought he was like a clock and that his wife kept him wound up and that he was afraid if he didn't have her, he'd sit down somewhere and never get up again, that he'd be like a clock that no one remembered to wind. I think my father and I were like that man. My mother was an outgoing, social person and I think she wound my father and me up. After she died, we . . . we sort of unwound."

Mike wasn't sure he understood what she was saying. All of his life he'd had to fight for privacy and time alone so he really couldn't imagine just two people living in one house. When he was a kid and one of the younger kids had invaded his room and messed with his stuff, he'd thought that being an only child must be divine.

Now, looking at her, snuggled in the chair, overwhelmed by the size of his robe—he'd always hated the thing, but right now it was his second favorite possession—he didn't think being an only child was so good.

He smiled at her. "Tell me more about today. Tell me about Santa Fe."

She laughed at that. "You wouldn't believe me if I told you. Santa Fe is the strangest place on earth. Shall I tell you about the Soul Quest seminars or our brand-new escalator?"

"All of it," he said.

As she began talking, Mike listened and laughed as the rain coming down outside isolated them. It was an ordinary evening, just two people sitting at a table, sipping drinks, and talking, but to Mike it was one of the most pleasant evenings of his life. For once he was with a female, and there was no pressure on him to entertain her or make her think he was great. There was no need to try to impress her. Holding up the little samurai, he looked at it, then closed his fingers tightly around it.

"What?" he asked. Samantha was looking at him expectantly.

"I want to know about Colorado and your eleven brothers and sisters, if you don't mind telling, that is." She spoke shyly, as though she were asking something she shouldn't.

"Where should I begin? Think of always being in a crowd. Think of noise and confusion and no privacy. Actually, think of living in a circus, complete with clowns and monkeys."

Sam leaned forward on her elbows, her face eager. "Did you have arguments? Did you have lots of friends? Did you have pets? Did you go to movies? Did your sisters have slumber parties?"

He grinned. "Want to hear about the time my brother Kane and I hid under my sister's bed waiting for her slumber party to begin?"

"Yes," she answered eagerly.

It was late when, after seeing Samantha yawn, Mike suggested that they go to bed. She headed for the stairs, but he told her no, that he wanted her to sleep downstairs near him, at least until Monday when the grills were to be installed on the windows.

After escorting her up the stairs to her apartment, he stood in her living room waiting while she got some of her night things to move downstairs into his bedroom. His, he thought with a smile. This morning when he'd tried to shave he'd had to move a bottle of perfume, two pots of pink stuff, one of purple, and at least six little brushes. Her stockings were draped over the shower rod, and there was a bra hanging off his bathroom doorknob.

After he'd moved out of his father's house, away from his many siblings, Mike had never wanted another person to live with him. Even in college he'd refused to have a roommate, and he'd never wanted any of his girlfriends to live with him. It wasn't until the last two years that he'd begun to feel as though he missed the company of other people. After he'd met Dave, it had seemed natural to invite him to live in his house; they'd be together, but they'd have their own apartments, so it seemed to be the ideal situation.

After Dave had called and asked Mike to take care of his

daughter for a year, Mike had dreaded having a female in the house, because he knew that a female would need lots of looking after and cause him lots of problems. "You never guessed half of it, Taggert," he said aloud to himself.

"Did you say something?" Samantha asked, coming out of the bedroom and holding yet more bottles to be put in his bathroom. What did women *do* with all that stuff? he wondered.

"No, I was just looking. It's dark in here, isn't it?"

Samantha looked about the room, at the dark greens, the hunting prints, and the plaid on the furniture. When she'd first entered this room she had loved it, but now she thought she might buy a slipcover for the largest chair. "I saw some lovely rose damask in a shop on Madison," she said. "Maybe . . ." She stopped, for what she was thinking seemed to be disrespectful to her father. After all, he had chosen everything in this room, and, too, it didn't make sense to spend money on the apartment when she was going to be leaving in such a short time.

She looked at Mike, then had to look away. It was better not to think of leaving and going somewhere where she knew no one.

"Rose damask, huh?" he asked, taking her arm in his, offering to take the bottles from her, but Sam said no, then asked him to get a beat-up old hatbox from inside the closet. He didn't even want to know what was in it, probably some more female-only products, he thought.

Downstairs, as he helped her put her things on the bathroom counter, which was already packed, she looked at the counter in dismay. "You'll have your space back when they put the grills on."

A minute before, Mike had been thinking with regret of his lost space, but now he didn't want to think of her moving back upstairs.

"And, Mike," she said softly, "about the ring." Holding out her left hand, she looked at the big diamond sparkling, thinking that it was so beautiful that she didn't want to part with it. Reluctantly, she began tugging at it. "I meant to give it back, but—"

He put his hand over hers. "Keep it. As long as you want to wear it, it's yours."

"I couldn't do that. I mean . . ."

"I'll just have to take it back to the bank and put it in the safe, and it'll just rot there. Mother says that jewels react better to being used than to sitting in a safe deposit box. Besides, it looks better on your skin than in the ugly gray box."

"Mike . . ." she began. "No one has ever—I mean . . ."

Leaning forward, he kissed her softly and gently. "If you again tell me thanks, I'll get angry."

When she looked up at him, there was gratitude in her eyes—and he didn't like it. He'd never done anything but shown her simple human kindness, kindness that she should have expected. "You want to spend the night in bed with me?" he asked.

For a moment Samantha looked startled, feeling betrayed that he'd expect her to thank him in that way, but then she realized he was teasing. She laughed and the moment of tension was broken. "I'm not *that* grateful."

"The gratitude comes *after* you spend a night with me," he answered, grinning at her.

"Get out of here," she said, laughing, then quickly he stole another kiss and left the bathroom.

Mike went into his bedroom and began to undress, smiling all the while. Damn it, but he was glad she hadn't left, glad she hadn't gone with his skinny cousin to Maine. Sometimes it was difficult to remember that there was danger if she stayed here, and sometimes all he could remember was Sam with his friends, all of his friends. He had been surprised but pleased when she hadn't snubbed Daphne, and Sam had liked Corey and the others. He knew she would like his family in Colorado and that they'd like her. He could imagine her and Jeanne talking about rose damask together.

At the thought of his family, Mike frowned, remembering her story of tonight. What had she meant with her little story about clocks winding down? He had an idea that if he asked Sam for further explanation, she'd tell him another story and another and another, and he just might never find out the truth. She called *him* a liar, but she could give lessons.

Picking up the telephone extension, he called information in Louisville, Kentucky, giving the operator the name of Dave's attorney to get his home number. Mike knew it was late in Louisville, but he didn't know anyone else who might be able to answer his question of what had happened to Sam after her mother's death.

When the attorney answered, Mike quickly apologized for its being so late, then asked his question. The attorney jolted him by saying that Allison's death had sent Dave into a clinical depression that had lasted for years.

"He was so bad that a couple of us wanted to commit him," the attorney said, "but we couldn't bring ourselves to do it. Dave stayed in the house in the dark—he couldn't bear any light in the house—ate only enough to keep alive and saw only Samantha. She was his little substitute wife, doing all the cooking and cleaning. The poor kid gave up everything that a kid does. Dave had some savings so he didn't have to go to work, and he couldn't stand for Samantha to be out of his sight except to go to school. Poor, poor kid. If she'd grown up in a mausoleum she would have had more fun that she had in that house with Dave."

"When did it stop?" Mike asked.

"Dave never did get back to what he was before Allison died, but his savings ran out and he had to go back to work. By then Samantha was a teenager, and Dave was so dependent on her that she continued taking care of him and the house until she got married. All of us were glad to see her get married, see that she would at last have some life of her own." He hesitated. "But her marriage didn't work out, did it?"

"No, her marriage didn't work out," Mike said softly, then thanked the attorney and put down the telephone, feeling that he understood a great deal more now than he had. He now understood Sam's fascination with his family. He understood her pleasure at the smallest bit of attention; he understood why she sometimes seemed as though she were seeing the world for the first time.

As he thought of Sam, he remembered seeing her in Dave's apartment, remembered the look she had given that plaid chair. In the next moment he picked up the phone and called his sister in Colorado. Jeanne lost no time in getting to the point: Samantha. Eyes rolling skyward, Mike had no doubt that Samantha was a major topic of conversation with his family.

"What's this Samantha look like?" Jeanne asked, not trying to hide her curiosity.

Mike didn't hesitate. "A modified Bardot; skin like cream; eyes the color of Kit's '57 Chevy; hair the color of that palomino you had when you were fourteen; a body that belongs on the cover of *Sports Illustrated*." He stopped because Jeanne was laughing, but he grinned into the telephone.

"Mike," Jeanne said, still laughing, "does she have a brain?"

"Yeah and a real smart mouth."

"I think I like her already. Tell me what you need."

"You still have the floor plan for the top two floors of my house? The apartment you did for Dave Elliot?"

"Yes. Mike, I was sorry about his death. I know you liked him a lot."

"Thanks. I want you to redecorate the apartment and I want it done fast—real fast."

"Two weeks?"

"Overnight. I take Sam out for a day, say next Monday, and come back to a new apartment."

Jeanne didn't say anything for a moment as she thought of her sources in New York. She could buy most of the furniture off the showroom floor, a lot of it at Tepper Galleries, put it in storage, then move in a day. "I can't get curtains made or paintings done, and you'll have to pay retail for some things."

"All right," Mike said without hesitation.

Jeanne gave a low whistle. "You *must* be in love." When Mike was silent, she asked, "What style is she?"

"She lives with me, but she's only let me kiss her a few times, no hands."

"Ahhh. Old fashioned. English chintz. Rose silk cushions. Aubusson rug. A four-poster bed draped in slate blue damask. Tassels. Eighteenth-century antiques."

He interrupted her. "Sounds good to me. Hey, Jeanne," he said as he was about to hang up, "make the bed *big*."

Laughing, she hung up.

Samantha awoke in the morning and, half asleep, staggered into the bathroom, only to be brought up short by the sight of Mike standing before the mirror wearing only a towel about his waist and shaving lather on his face.

"Sorry," she murmured and started back into the bedroom.

"It's okay," he said. "I'm decent. What do you want to do today?"

Turning back toward the bathroom, she blinked to clear her sleepy vision. He was certainly something wonderful to see so early in the morning, with his broad back and that tiny towel barely hanging onto his hips. One tiny tug and . . .

"You're going to get into trouble if you keep looking at me like that," he said, watching her in the mirror.

Samantha smiled at him, but instead of going back into the bedroom, she went to stand by him to watch him shave. Both her father and her husband had used electric razors, so it was new to her to see a man shave with lather and a blade.

"You don't like electric razors?" she asked, picking up a

bottle of his aftershave, English Leather, opening it, and smelling it.

"I inherited my father's thick beard, an electric won't touch it."

Standing there, leaning against the wall that ran beside the mirror, playing with the bottle, she watched him stroke the razor over his face, then rinse the blade in the sink. Once, he looked at her in the mirror and winked.

Smiling at him, she thought, What a lovely moment. Sometimes she felt more married to Mike than she ever had to her husband. Her husband had had ironclad rules, and one of his rules was that a man and woman were never to be in the bathroom together.

"Have you decided?"

"Mmmmm?" she asked dreamily, watching him.

He finished shaving, then held a washcloth under the hot water and wrapped his face in the cloth for a minute before wiping away the last of the lather. Turning to her, he bent so his face was close to hers. "What do you think?" He turned his face first one way, then the other.

Smiling, Samantha put her hands on his cheeks, feeling the freshly shaved skin, and was tempted to run her thumbs over his lips, maybe even to kiss him. "Baby soft."

"Are you sure?" Bending closer, he rubbed his cheek against hers, first one side then the other.

Putting her hands on his shoulders, she felt his warm skin and closed her eyes for a moment.

"No stray whiskers to hurt a lady's skin?"

"No, none," she said softly, leaning her head back against the wall. "Perfectly smooth."

Abruptly, he moved away from her, and in spite of herself, Samantha frowned. Usually he tried to kiss her, but he didn't kiss her this morning. She had no way of knowing that her early-morning nearness was more than Mike could bear. If he wasn't to touch her, he had to step away. But Samantha didn't understand Mike's abrupt movement, so on impulse, she looked in the mirror—then squealed. Her mascara was under her eyes, and her hair, damp when she went to bed last night, was standing on end. Grabbing one of Mike's combs, she ran it under water then tried to make her hair lay down. Behind her, he laughed, then kissed her neck.

"You look beautiful," he said honestly.

"As beautiful as Vanessa?" she asked, then put her hand over her mouth in disbelief. She had *not* meant to say that.

Mike raised one eyebrow. "Been snooping? Going through people's drawers? Looking at people's private possessions?"

"Most certainly not. I . . . I wanted a pair of socks, that's all. I didn't want to disturb you, so I thought I'd look in the cabinet. I had no idea you would object to lending me a pair of socks." She stopped because he was smirking at her. With her nose in the air to let him know what she thought of him, she pushed past him to leave the bathroom. "I couldn't care less who Vanessa is. I'm sure you have a thousand girlfriends. What do they matter to me?"

When he was silent, she turned around to see him standing in the bathroom doorway, leaning against the jamb, smiling at her in a know-it-all way. "Would you leave? I need to get dressed."

"So do I and my clothes are in here, but I have an idea you know that."

"I know nothing of the sort." She started toward the door that led into the hallway, but he caught her arm.

"Where are you going?"

"To my own apartment, not that it's any of your business."

Catching her in his arms, he held her loosely while she struggled against him. "Now look what you've done," he said.

Samantha was *not* going to look, because she knew very well that his towel had fallen to the floor. Resolutely, she kept her eyes on his. "I would like for you to release me," she said stiffly, holding herself rigid.

"Not until you answer me." He bent forward as though to kiss her neck, but Samantha turned her head away.

"I *have* answered you: I care nothing about Vanessa."

Laughing, Mike pulled her a little closer to his big, warm, naked body. "I didn't ask anything about 'Nessa, you did. I asked you what you wanted to do today."

He was holding her loosely, but when she moved, she was almost close enough that her breasts were touching his chest. Because he was now completely and absolutely naked, Samantha kept her eyes fixed on a place to the right of his head. She wasn't going to start wrestling with him, but she did think of telling him that he shouldn't have spent time in the sun to get the golden color to his skin, then she wondered if perhaps that was his natural color of skin and he was golden all over. "I have a very interesting book I plan to read," she said, her lips pursed together.

Mike was looking down at her body that was about a quarter of an inch away from being pressed against his, at the very thin fabric that separated them. "You know, I may change my mind about blue nightgowns. I like that one. Is it silk?"

"Cotton," she said stiffly. "Old-fashioned, boring, or, as you say, Rebecca of Sunnybrook Farm cotton."

"Oh? Vanessa wears—" He didn't finish his sentence because Samantha hit him in the ribs with both her fists.

Wincing, he gave a grunt of pain, then laughed, but he didn't release her from the circle of his arms. "Sammy, baby, you're the only woman in my life. Vanessa was a long time ago."

"It doesn't matter to me at all. Would you stop playing Tarzan and release me? I'd like to go upstairs and get dressed."

Moving just a bit forward, he put his face close to her neck so she could feel his warm breath on her skin. "Tarzan? How about if we stay in today and play Indian brave and uptight missionary's daughter? All your family could be killed by Indians, then I'd save you, but you'd hate me at first until I made you cry out in ecstasy, then we—"

Try as she would, she couldn't keep from laughing. "Oh, Mike, you're crazy. And what in the world have you been reading?"

"Crazy with wanting you," he said, nuzzling her neck, but he still kept a breath of space between them, as though he *had* to keep distance between them. "If you don't like Indians, I could show you a few tricks with red silk scarves. Or I could be a pirate and . . ." He stopped talking because his mouth was on her neck.

When he began to relax, Samantha ducked under his arm and moved away from him, hiding a smile at the groan of misery he emitted when she left the circle of his arms. Keeping her back to him so she wouldn't see him in his present bare state, she left the bedroom and went upstairs to get dressed, smiling all the way.

She had no more than pulled on a pair of jeans than Mike knocked on the outside door of her apartment. His knocking was certainly only a formality as the door had a foot-size hole in it. Even at that formality, he didn't bother to give her time to open the door before he entered and made himself at home in the living room. When Samantha entered the room, still buttoning her blouse, Mike was sprawled in a chair, his feet on the ottoman.

"You make up your mind yet?"

"You mean about which book I'm going to read? There's what looks to be an excellent biography here on Captain Sir Frank Baker, the Victorian explorer. I thought I'd start that."

Mike's frustration showed on his face. "What does a guy have to do to get a date with you? My bony cousin—"

"Raine asked me," she said pointedly. "He asked me politely and gave me twenty-four hours' notice. Women appreciate that sort of thing. *Asking* a woman on a date shows a little more finesse than saying, 'Uh-oh, my towel has fallen off,' or 'Let's play doctor.' "

Slowly, Mike got out of the chair and stood before her. Taking her hand in his, he kissed the back of it with exaggerated politeness and courtesy. "Miss Elliot, may I have the honor of a day spent in your company?"

"With or without red scarves?" she asked with narrowed eyes.

"It is milady's choice," he said, again kissing her hand, but this time he touched her skin with the tip of his tongue.

Smiling in spite of herself, Samantha looked down at his tumble of black curls. "What will we be doing on this date?"

Mike looked up at her in disgust. "*Not* swings and ice cream." After kissing her hand a third time, he smiled up at her mischievously. "We could always visit Vanessa."

"Only if I can bring Raine," she shot back at him with an equally impish grin.

Mike laughed and straightened. "How'd you like to see more of New York? Chinatown, Little Italy, the Village, that sort of thing. Believe it or not, there's more to this city than Fifth and Madison avenues—both of which, I might say, you have adjusted to with amazing adaptability."

"Let me change clothes and—"

"No, jeans are perfect for where we're going." He slipped his arm in hers and in another minute led her out the front door.

Samantha had her first experience of New York on the weekend. It seemed that on the weekend, midtown Manhattan emptied of all the beautifully dressed and groomed people and was refilled with what were unmistakably tourists. There were women wearing baggy dresses or shapeless trousers with elastic waistbands hanging onto big-bellied men with four cameras strapped over their polyester shirts.

"Where have they gone?" Sam asked.

"Country houses and neighborhoods around the city," Mike answered, leading her north. First he took her to a street fair on Sixty-seventh near First Avenue, and Samantha saw table after table full of costume jewelry from the thirties and forties. She fell in love with a silver basket filled with flowers created out of colored stones. "It's Trifari," the woman said as though that meant something. Samantha wanted the pin, but she'd already spent too much the day before, so reluctantly she put the little basket down.

Mike didn't hesitate as he bought it for her, but when he handed it to her, Samantha protested that he shouldn't have, that he'd already done too much for her. When he urged it on her, she refused to take it. "You've done so much for me, I can't take any more."

Mike shrugged. "Okay, maybe Vanessa would like to have it."

With a glare at him, Samantha snatched the pin out of his hand, closing her palm around it so tightly the pin bit into her flesh. Smiling, Mike lifted her hand, pulled her fingers from around the pretty pin, then fastened it onto the collar of her shirt. The sparkling pin wasn't right for her casual attire, but she couldn't have cared less as she happily took the arm Mike offered and walked beside him.

They walked down First Avenue together to Sutton Place. Mike led her into a pretty little park that had a few women with baby carriages; the women were obviously nannies and the town houses around them were obviously for the very rich.

As Samantha stood at the wrought iron fence and looked up at the bridge over the East River, watching the barges along the river, Mike came up behind her and slipped his arms about her waist. As she always did when his touches became too intimate, she started to move away, but he said, "Don't, please," in a rough voice that she couldn't deny. She stayed where she was, allowing him to hold her, the back of her body pressed down the length of the front of him, and for a moment she allowed herself to enjoy his nearness.

As he pointed out things to her across the river, they stood locked together, his arms around her, her hands on his bare forearms. Leaning her head back against his shoulder, she could feel the warmth of him, the solid sturdiness of him, knowing how safe she felt when he was near, as though nothing or no one could ever hurt her again. "Mike, thank you for the pin."

"Anytime," he said, his voice soft and low, as though he were feeling some of what she was.

Samantha started to say more, but a child, a toddler about two years old, came hurtling toward the fence, running on unsteady legs and not looking where he was going. His nanny yelled, but the child didn't stop running. As easily as though he'd done it a million times, Mike's hand scooped down and caught the child's head, keeping him from hitting the fence.

Safe but startled, the child looked up at Mike, then his eyes widened and welled with tears, while Mike knelt in front of the child. "You were running pretty fast there, Tex," he said. "Might have made a hole in that fence. We couldn't let that happen, could we?"

Nodding, the child sniffed and smiled at Mike just as his nanny, at least seventy pounds overweight, came trudging up to her charge.

"Thank you so very much," she said, then took the child's hand and led him away. The little boy looked back over his shoulder and waved at Mike, who waved back.

When Mike turned to Sam and held out his hand for her, she didn't hesitate in entwining her fingers with his. They started walking south, leaving Sutton Place behind.

"Do you know that I've never so much as changed a baby's diaper?" she said, thinking of how familiarly Mike had dealt with the little boy.

"It's not exactly a highly skilled task," Mike said, then looked at her. "I'll tell you what, we'll go to Colorado and visit my family, and you can change all the nappies you want. I'd place money on it that my whole family will let you learn on their kids. Inside a week you'll be an expert."

"I'd like that," she said seriously. "I'd like that very much."

Squeezing her hand, he led her to the curb, caught a cab, and gave directions to the driver to take them to Chinatown.

By four o'clock Samantha was tired, but very happy, for she had spent yet another heavenly day with Mike. They had walked until her legs hurt and seen and done more than Samantha could remember. Mike had fed her until she was ready to pop. He had made her laugh, made her see things she never would have seen without him. He took her to tiny, out-of-the-way stores, such as the Last Wound Up, which had nothing but wind-up toys. He showed her statues and parks and street fairs; they listened to street musicians and saw performers who were very, very good. She tried on hats at a stall and talked Mike into buying a shirt made of Balinese cotton. And as they walked and saw things, they talked.

The talking was what had pleased Samantha most. For the first time since she'd met him, Mike didn't try to be Sherlock Holmes and get every little piece of information out of her that he could. He didn't ask her a single question about her father or her husband or about what her years in high school had been like. The absence of questions made Sam relax, and as she relaxed, she asked him questions about his life and childhood. Mike didn't seem to have a secret in the world—with the exception of other women, that is. If she'd not been able to look at him, not seen the way other women in the street looked at him, she would have thought he'd never so much as had a date before, for all the mention he made of the women in his life.

He told her about his brothers, all eight of them, and his three sisters; he told of his parents and his many cousins. He told about what he'd studied in college and his many years of graduate school. He told her anything and answered everything she asked, but he didn't mention women.

At four o'clock they sat down at an outside table in a little restaurant, and when a very good-looking, well-built young man walked by, Samantha glanced up at him, only to turn back to see Mike scowling at her. "Think he's a bodybuilder?" she asked with exaggerated innocence.

Glancing over his shoulder at the man as he took a drink from a glass of beer, Michael Taggert, who, if allowed, would eat nothing but beef and beer, muttered, "Looks more like a bellybuilder to me."

Laughing, Samantha gave her order to the waitress.

Over Cokes and muffins, Samantha fiddled with her straw and said idly, as though it meant nothing to her, "You haven't been married?"

He didn't answer, so she looked at him. He was staring at her intently, with no humor in his eyes.

"Sam," he said softly, "I'm thirty years old, and I'm heart-whole. I've had affairs with women—Vanessa and I were together for two years—but I've never been in love. In my family we take marriage seriously; we actually believe in those vows a man and woman exchange. I've never asked a woman to marry me; I've never met one I wanted to spend my life with. I've never met a woman who I thought was good enough to be the mother of my kids." Reaching out, he took her hand in his. "Until you."

Her breath held for a moment, she pulled her hand back. "Mike, I don't—"

"If you're again going to give me that crap about not wanting to commit, save it. I don't want to hear it." He looked down at his plate. "Sam," he said softly, "I want to ask you a question and I want you to answer me honestly."

She braced herself. "All right."

"Did your father ever . . . touch you? Sexually, I mean."

For a moment, she felt anger race through her, but then she calmed herself. In a time when every magazine brought a new confession of some woman who had been a victim of incest, it wasn't a bad question. "No," she said, smiling at him, "my father never crawled into bed with me, never touched me in any way except with affection and love. He was a very good father, Mike."

"Then why . . .?" he began, but closed his mouth. He had started to ask her why she was so turned off by him, but he didn't want to hear her answer. Maybe it was just him. Maybe she didn't like *him* and that was the reason she continually pushed him away. "Is it me?" he said in spite of himself. "Do you like a different type of guy?" He looked up at her. "Raine maybe?"

"Mike, you're the most beautiful man I've ever seen in my life. Why would any woman like Raine better than you?"

He didn't smile. In fact, her answer seemed to make him more confused. Although he'd found out a great deal about her, there were still missing pieces of the puzzle that was Miss

Samantha Elliot. But the more time he spent with her, the more he was sure she was worth the effort.

Standing, he put money on the table. "You ready to go? I have to get back and get cleaned up. I have a date tonight."

Slowly, she stood. He talked to her about marriage vows and children in one breath, then told her he had a date in the next.

In the silence in the taxi on the way back to the town house, Samantha had time to think, but at first all she could do was feel, and what she felt was old-fashioned, gut-wrenching jealousy. This was a new emotion for Sam, and it didn't take much analyzing to know that she didn't much like the sensation. Of course, to be jealous, she told herself, you had to feel as though you owned another person, that you had a right to that person's time and attention . . . and love. But she certainly didn't own Mike and he didn't own her. Wasn't this lack of ownership, this freedom from possession, what she had worked so hard to achieve? Hadn't she fought him at every turn just so she *wouldn't* be tempted to have any feelings for him?

Samantha was well aware that right now she was as vulnerable as a person could get. After all, she'd recently lost the last person on earth who had any connection with her; her husband, her relatives, all of them were gone. Being alone in the world and grieving could make a person do odd things, such as *think* you were in love with a person when actually you were merely very grateful. That's what she was to Mike: grateful. She'd told him that when he'd kept her from sleeping for whole days at a time, she was merely tired, not depressed, but even then, even when she'd said it, she'd known she was lying. She had been so depressed that she hadn't wanted to continue living; although she had never actually comtemplated suicide, she had wanted to sleep without waking up.

Mike had taken her out of herself and forced her to wake up by using a combination of enraging her and just plain, ordinary paying attention to her. He had also given her hope, which was something that had been missing from her life after her father died. Mike had given her hope that she would be able to find her grandmother, that she could find the last person on earth who had a link to her.

Of course, to Mike's way of looking at it, everything he had done, all the kindnesses, all the attention, had backfired because he'd involved Samantha in something that had turned out to be dangerous. But Sam didn't regret any of it. If her life was going to be threatened, she'd rather have it threatened by an outside force than by her own hopelessness.

Now, looking at Mike in the taxi, she did her best to squelch her feelings of jealousy. He had said that he was heart-whole, that he wasn't in love with another woman, but then you didn't have to be in love to go out on a date, did you? Of course it was none of her business whether he dated or not since she was just his tenant, but it seemed odd that he seemed to enjoy her company but now wanted to spend time with someone else.

"Have you had this date a long time?" she asked, trying to sound as though she were just making conversation. Maybe his mother had arranged a date with a friend's daughter.

"Three weeks," he said tersely.

"Ah. Then you *must* go?" Is it an obligation? is what she really wanted to ask.

"Yes." He turned to her. "Jealous?"

She saw that he was trying to be lighthearted, to be his usual teasing self, but Samantha sensed tension under his words. He's hiding something from me, she thought, trying not to frown. There's something he doesn't want me to know. Immediately, her first thought was, he's going out with Vanessa and he doesn't want me to know about it. How silly that he should try to hide it, she told herself. What he does with his time is absolutely and utterly none of my business. He could date actresses, models, whomever, and it would mean nothing to her.

As she thought about Vanessa or any other woman who might be in Mike's life, she realized that every muscle in her body was rigid. This is absurd, she told herself, utterly ridiculous. Mike and I are . . . friends, that's all. We've been forced to spend a great deal of time together and we've made the best of it, and that's all there is between us. Of course he was probably lonely living in that big house by himself and he was grateful to have some company, which is why we've spent so much time together going places, doing things, laughing together, touching each other, kissing—

She broke off as she looked at his profile. Mike would never in his life be lonely. He was too likeable, too gregarious, too caring, too—

"Don't look at me like that," he whispered, not even turning to look at her.

Self-consciously, Samantha turned away to look out the window of the cab. Something was bothering him, but she didn't know what it was. In that moment she knew what was wrong. He's lying, she thought. He doesn't have a date. But *why* is he lying?

She knew the answer the moment she thought about it. He's lying to protect me. Warmth spread through her. Not just warmth, but joy, pure undiluted joy ran through every vein in her body. Just as she'd known that if she could signal Mike when the man was choking her he would come for her, she knew that now Mike was trying to keep her safe. What was it Mike had said to her? "Your father gave me the care of you and I mean to be worthy of his trust." She knew he felt that the attempted murder was his fault because he'd not considered the old gangster legend about the missing money. Since the attempt on her life, Mike had done everything he could to get her to safety. He'd so much wanted to protect her that he'd been willing to send her away with his cousin Raine, who he disliked—at least Mike disliked Raine when it came to Samantha, she thought.

Leaning her head back, trying not to smile, she remembered the last time Mike had gone out on a date. That night he'd wanted her to be jealous and had been disappointed when she hadn't been. Later he'd told her that his "date" was an eighty-six-year-old woman who he thought had worked in the nightclub where Maxie had worked.

"I'm going with you," she said just as they reached the town house.

"Like hell you are," Mike answered, and the way he said it made Sam sure she was right: Wherever he was going tonight had something to do with Maxie. She would have been hard-pressed to be able to think of a time in her life when the knowledge that she was right made her so thoroughly happy. She could have danced a jig in the street and run along the top of the fence railing crooning, "Singin' in the Rain."

But she behaved herself. As Mike paid the fare, she sedately walked up the stairs and got out her door key, but Mike elbowed her aside and used his own key. Smiling, she watched him, guessing that his old-fashioned ethics extended to door locks. She could see that he was angry, and the more angry he was, the happier she became. If he were going out on a "real" date, he wouldn't be angry, he'd be laughing at her.

"What do you think I should wear?" she asked brightly. "A suit or a nice pair of trousers?"

"A nightgown and a bathrobe," he said through clenched teeth as he closed the door behind them. "That's all you need for staying in tonight and watching TV."

"There is absolutely nothing on on Saturday night, so I guess I'll just have to go with you."

"Samantha," he said, giving her a threatening look. "You are *not* going with me."

"Vanessa might be annoyed?"

For a split second, a look of puzzlement crossed his face, then he grinned, but Samantha knew him well enough by now to know how false that grin was. No Vanessa. Hallelujah. "For your information, I'm meeting Abby for dinner."

"Where?"

"You wouldn't know the place. Upper West Side. Very posh. I probably won't be home until late, or maybe I'll spend the night."

"The nursing home will allow you to do that?"

The quick, horrified look on his face made Sam know that she'd guessed right. He managed to get his face under control quickly, but not before Samantha was looking at him smugly. While he was saying things like, "Abby doesn't live in a nursing home" and "She's one hot lady," Sam just stood there and smiled at him. No Vanessa. No actress. No model. No anybody else at all. Just Mike trying to find her grandmother.

"Damn you, Samantha," Mike said, sounding as though he were on the verge of tears. "Damn you to hell and back. You can*not* go with me. This woman may have known your grandmother. Doc's men might be watching her. She might—"

"She might *be* my grandmother for all you know."

When he turned away from her, she knew that he was trying to think of arguments to persuade her that she should not, could not, go with him, and she knew that whatever he said was going to have no effect on her decision. "I don't know why you're looking so pleased with yourself," he said when he turned back.

Stepping closer, she smiled up at him. "I don't know why I ever thought you were an accomplished liar. You're not at all good at lying."

Mike's face and body expressed his rage: His eyes flashed, his nostrils flared, his hands were fists at his side. "Maybe not, but I'm damned good at tying up little girls who are too stupid to know what's good for them." He took a step toward her.

Samantha swallowed, for he did indeed look as though he meant to do her bodily harm. "You couldn't hurt anyone if you tried," she said with as much bravado as she could muster. She held her ground when he was standing so close he was touching her, looming over her.

Mike's anger dissolved in a rush, and he pulled her into his arms, holding her so tight she almost couldn't breathe. For once, Samantha made no effort to get away from him, but instead, held onto him, snuggling her cheek against the hollow in his chest. They fit together so well, she thought. Her ex-husband had been tall and thin. They had looked odd together; they hadn't fit at all. But Mike was perfect.

"Look, baby," he began, "I don't want you involved more than you already are. I don't even like leaving you here in the house alone tonight. In fact, I was going to suggest that you spend the evening with Blair or Vicky or—"

"Raine?" she asked, her eyes closed, smiling as she thought of the thousand times she'd wanted to snuggle with Mike. He felt better than she'd imagined.

"No, the idea of your spending the evening with that stick

never crossed my mind." Still holding her, he bent his head back to look at her. "You don't *really* like that guy, do you?"

"No," she answered honestly for the second time that day, but who was counting? Smiling, he put his head back on the top of hers.

"Okay, here's what I'll do. I'll go see this old woman by myself since this is probably a wild goose chase anyway." He shook his head in disbelief. "This woman will be the seventh old lady I've been to see. With each one somebody had sworn to me that she'd been at the club the night Scalpini's men shot the place up, and each time either the woman was daffy or she was too young or she'd never heard of Jubilee. It's all been a waste of time, and I'm sure this one is too. I'll take you to Blair's—she lives on the West Side—then, after I see this old lady, I'll come back and pick the two of you up and take you out to dinner. I'll take you anywhere in the city you want to go. We could go to the Quilted Giraffe or the Rainbow Room or—"

"No," she said. "I'm going with you."

"Sammy, sweetheart, please listen to me." He was stroking her hair and her back as his big body was leaning over hers so she was nearly encased in him. She hoped he would spend the next three hours trying to persuade her not to go with him.

"Mmmmm, I'm listening. Maybe we could go out to dinner after we meet her. I'd like to go to the Sign of the Dove."

Mike released her; he was really angry now. "You're not going with me."

"All right, then I won't go with you. If you don't want us to search for my grandmother *together* then I'll have to go by myself. How many nursing homes on the Upper West Side can there be? And, by the way, west side of what?"

Standing there, Mike stared at her for a moment, his face running the gamut of emotions, knowing that she would do what she said. He'd never in his life seen anyone as stubborn as she. "Wear a suit," he said tightly as he turned away from her.

"So we can go out to dinner afterward?" she asked, but he didn't answer.

Samantha didn't like the nursing home. For one thing, it was ugly, sterile ugly. Everything in it had been chosen for use with no consideration for beauty. The floors were those hideous gray plastic tiles that some creature from hell had invented, and the walls were painted in a white that was so glaring it could have been lit with neon. All the lighting was overhead and fluorescent, and every tube in the building hummed with that sound that was guaranteed to drive a sane person crazy within three days.

Besides the look of the place, there was the smell: disinfectant and medicine. Samantha sometimes wondered how people managed to make a place smell of medicine. Did they empty pills out of those little brown bottles on the floor then crush them?

Holding her hand, Mike looked down at her and saw the disgust on her face. "This is one of the better homes," he said. "Some of them smell like urine."

Shaking her head in disbelief, Samantha looked at the ceiling. The "designer"—desecrator, actually—of the nursing home had managed to completely disguise the fact that the "home" was in a beautiful old building. High above their heads were lovely moldings, and the walls were that heavy, thick plaster that helped to make old buildings quiet. But the walls were covered with horrid photocopies of rules and schedules: no lights after nine in the evening; no loud music, in fact, no rock and roll at all; no dancing in the dining room; no running; no chewing gum. While Mike was at the desk asking about the woman he was to see, Samantha read the notices and wondered what had happened to cause notices to be put up outlawing gum and dancing and rock and roll.

"Oh, Abby," the nurse was saying with a little smile. It was the smile you used when speaking of a wayward pet that often got into trouble but you were fond of the mischievous little darling anyway. The nurse was standing behind a desk covered in plastic laminate that was chipped, scarred, and tattooed with marks from a thousand ball-point pens.

"Abby's doing all right now. For a while we thought we were going to lose her, but she pulled through. Come along, I'll take you to her, but don't be surprised if she's a bit contrary. She's a feisty one."

Samantha walked with Mike, following the nurse down the hall, and wondered whether Abby was retarded or senile.

The nurse opened a boring gray door, and they stepped into

a room that was as ugly as what Samantha had already seen. The room was so clean that Sam thought a little dust would be a nice decorative touch. Overhead, florescent tubes whined, and their light showed every barren inch, from the gray tiles to the bare white, white, white walls to the stainless-steel furniture.

"There we are," the nurse said in a hearty-hearty voice. "I hope we're feeling good tonight, for we have visitors."

"Drop dead," said the woman in the bed, her voice strong.

"Now, now, Abby, you mustn't say those things in front of your company. They've come a long way to see you."

"East Side, huh?" The woman's voice was heavy with sarcasm.

As the nurse chuckled, Samantha looked around her to get a look at the woman on the white-painted metal bed, lying on the white sheets. The only "color" in the room was the gray tiles.

She was a small thin woman, and there was a tube running out of her arm and wire hung from under the sheet, leading into a dial-laden machine that perfectly matched the rest of the decor. The woman was old, her cheeks were sunken, and her skin was wrinkled, and she had an unhealthy greenish-gray cast to her skin. In spite of the unhealthy look of her, Samantha could see that she'd once been pretty. Even though her body now seemed to be giving out, there was intelligence in her eyes.

The woman was looking up at the nurse, but when the nurse moved to one side, she saw Mike, looked him up and down, dismissed him, then looked at Samantha. For a moment she stared at Sam, almost as though she were surprised by her, then abruptly she looked away and back at the nurse. "Get out of here," she said. "I want to talk to my guests alone."

Turning away, the nurse winked in conspiracy at Mike, as though to say, Isn't she cute? then left the room.

"Hello, I'm Michael Taggert. I contacted you some time ago, but they said you were recovering from surgery and couldn't see me."

"Probably told you I was going to die, didn't they?"

Mike smiled at her, but Abby didn't take her eyes from Samantha. "And who is this lovely young lady?"

Samantha said the first thing that came to her mind. "I don't like this place and I don't like that woman."

Her eyes sparkling, Abby chuckled. "I can see that you and I agree on many things. Why don't you come over here and sit by me? No, not in the chair, on the bed beside me so I can see you. My old eyes, you know."

Samantha didn't hesitate. Some people are afraid of older people—maybe they remind them of what they will someday become—but Samantha wasn't. She'd spent a lot of her life with her grandfather Cal and with her father when the cancer was making him age daily. Now, she didn't think twice as she climbed on the bed beside the woman and wasn't surprised when the woman took her hand and held it—held it rather tightly.

Abby looked at Mike. "I take it you were the one who wrote me about Maxie."

"Yes," Mike said softly, standing at the foot of the bed, looking from one woman to the other, watching their movements. "I want to know what you know of her."

"Why?" Abby shot out, and Samantha saw the needle on the machine flicker.

For some odd reason, Mike just stood there watching the two women and didn't answer Abby's question.

"He's writing a biography of Doc," Samantha answered for him. "And he wants to know about Maxie. And I want to find her too because Maxie is probably my grandmother." Her voice lowered. "It was my father's dying wish that I look for his mother."

Abby didn't say anything, but the needle on her machine went all the way to the right and stayed there for a second or two.

"Maxie's dead," Abby said after a moment. "She died about eighteen months ago."

Samantha let out her pent-up breath. "You're sure?"

"Absoultely. We were friends since the twenties. Well, not really close friends since then, but back then we used to be close and we kept in touch over the years. She died out in New Jersey somewhere and the home where she stayed sent me notice of her death." She looked up at Samantha. "Why in the world would a pretty young thing like you want to know about an old woman like her? You ought to marry your young man here and have babies and forget about the past."

Sam didn't look at Mike. "He's not my young man."

"Oh?" Abby said. "Then what's this?" Lifting Samantha's left hand to the light, the big diamond sparkled.

"Oh. That. I . . . Well, we . . ."

"My uncle Mike wanted me to look for Maxie," Mike said, breaking his long silence.

"And who would your uncle Mike be?" Abby asked without much interest in her voice.

"Michael Ransome," Mike said softly.

Slowly, Abby turned to look at him, her eyes hard, glittering like dark coals. Her body might be ill, but her spirit and her mind were obviously very healthy. "Michael Ransome died that night. Died on the twelfth of May, 1928."

"No, he didn't," Mike said. "Scalpini's men nearly shot his legs off, but he lived. The day after the massacre, he called my grandfather in Colorado, and Gramps sent a plane for him, then saw to it that the world thought Michael Ransome was dead."

After a long, thoughtful moment in which Abby seemed to be digesting what Mike had said, she narrowed her eyes at him. "If your grandfather could do that, he must have some money—and power."

"Yes, ma'am, he does."

"And what about you? Can you support this lovely child?"

"Yes, ma'am, I can. Would you please tell me about my uncle Mike?"

Abby, still holding Samantha's hand, leaned back against the clean, crisp, sterile pillows. "He was a handsome man. Handsome Ransome all the girls called him."

"As handsome as Mike?" Samantha asked, then lowered her eyes, embarrassed at blurting out her first thought. "I mean . . ."

Abby smiled. "No, dear, not quite as handsome as your young man, but Michael Ransome was wonderful in his own way."

"Where did he come from?" Mike asked, utterly serious. "Uncle Mike would never tell anyone about his past."

"He was an orphan. No family. All he had were his looks and the ability to dance as though he were floating on air." She paused, then almost whispered. "And he had the ability to make women love him."

"Did *you* love him?" Samantha asked.

"Of course. We all did." It didn't take anyone with ESP to know that Abby was being evasive, as though she didn't want to tell anything about herself.

"Did Maxie love him?" Mike asked.

Abby fixed him with a sharp, piercing look, as though she were trying to read his mind. "Yes," she said after a moment. "Maxie loved him very much."

Taking her purse from the chair beside the bed, Samantha withdrew a photo from inside, a photo that was yellow with age and had one corner burned away. She handed the photo to Abby. "Is this Michael Ransome?"

When he saw the photo, Mike nearly jumped out of his skin in surprise as he snatched it from Sam's hands before Abby could get a good look at it. The photo was one of those studio portraits of a handsome man, a very suave-looking man wearing a tuxedo, a cigarette in his hand. Mike had only known his uncle when he was older, but he knew that the man in the picture was the man he'd loved so much. "Where did you get this?" he demanded of Samantha.

She didn't like his tone that said she should have shown him the photo before presenting it to someone else. "For your information, my father left me a box full of my grandmother's things and this was in it. Dad stuck a note on it saying that when he was a little boy his mother had burned a bunch of things and he'd managed to save this from the pile."

"Why didn't you show it to me before?"

"For the same reason that you keep secrets from me," she snapped, glaring at him. "Every day you reveal something else that you've kept from me so why shouldn't I keep a few things from you?"

"Because—" Mike stopped, his face turning red with embarrassment when he heard Abby begin to laugh.

"He's not your young man?" Abby asked, teasing, as she looked from one to the other.

Samantha wasn't embarrassed in the least. "He *thinks* I'm four years old and that he's my guardian and my protector. He throws fits if I so much as go out shopping by myself."

Before Abby could say a word, Mike said softly, "One of Doc's men tried to kill her."

That statement, that one statement that told so much, wiped the smile from Abby's face. For a moment she lay back on the pillow and did nothing but concentrate on trying to breathe. The needle on the machine fluctuated wildly, moving from one side of the dial to the other then back again. After a while, a time during which Samantha stroked her hand and held onto her firmly, Abby lifted her head again. "Yes, that's Michael Ransome," she said softly, her voice weak. She took a few breaths and tried to sound cheerful. "And now I'm glad I've been able to solve the mystery for you. Maxie died over a year ago. I have your mailing address, young man, and I'll send you the letter I received from the nursing home saying Maxie died." Her tone was a dismissal, but neither Sam nor Mike acted as though they understood.

"What was her real name?" Samantha asked.

"Maxine Bennett," Abby shot out, frowning.

"I wish I could have met her," Samantha said, stroking Abby's hand, her eyes with a faraway look in them. "I heard so much from Granddad Cal about her and from my father."

"Cal," Abby said softly, her frown disappearing and a slight relaxed, peaceful smile taking its place. "Maxie spoke of him. Was he all right after Maxie left or did he die in a place like this?"

"No," Samantha said brightly, happily. "He stayed with us, with Dad and me, the last two years of his life. I was going to school so we had to hire a nurse/housekeeper for him."

"Was his nurse nice?"

"No, she was dreadful and Granddad Cal made her life miserable."

Abby smiled but didn't say anything, so Samantha continued.

"She was a horrible, bossy woman and she treated Granddad Cal as though he were a stupid child. He would have fired her, but he said that getting her back gave him a reason to live. He used to do awful things to her, such as putting salt in her shampoo so it'd sting her eyes. One day while she was outside mowing the lawn he made a big pitcher of iced tea for her, only it wasn't iced tea. It was Long Island tea, you know, that stuff that's all liquor. She drank three big glasses of it then passed out on the kitchen floor. While she was passed out, Granddad Cal shaved her mustache."

Both Abby and Mike laughed.

It was at that moment that the nurse reentered the room. First she scolded Samantha for sitting on the bed and not on the chair, then she scolded Abby for making her machine fluctuate.

"They *love* patients who are in comas," Abby said. "They're the only ones who obey all the rules."

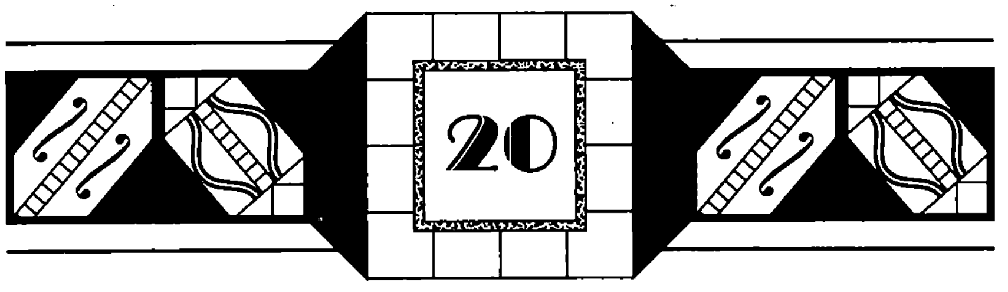

"Where are you taking me for dinner?" Samantha asked happily as they left the nursing home. "I saw an Italian restaurant, Paper Moon, on Fifty-eighth, and it looked very pretty."

Grabbing her elbow, he said, "We're going home for dinner," then narrowed his eyes at her. "We're going home and you're going to show me the box of things your father left you."

"But, Mike, I'm hungry."

"You can order in, like you always do. Call up Paper Moon and order, whatever you want to do, but tonight, you're showing me that box."

As Mike hailed a cab, Samantha couldn't resist a little smugness. "It doesn't feel very good to have people keep secrets from you, does it?"

His hand on her arm, he squeezed hard. "Do you realize that the secret to why whoever tried to kill you may be in that box?"

"No . . ." she said slowly.

As he opened the taxi door, he asked, "What *is* in the box?"

When she was silent, Mike gritted his teeth. "You haven't looked inside it, have you?"

"Going through a dead person's effects is not my idea of a good time. Maybe you're ghoulish that way, but I'm not. I opened the box—it's the old hatbox you carried downstairs for me—saw the photo on top, took it out, and that's all. The box looked to be full of old clothes, clothes that belonged to someone who might have run away with a gangster."

"A box full of things that may tell us a lot. It might tell us something that could keep someone from again attempting to kill you."

In spite of herself, Samantha put her hand to her throat. "You don't think I'm still in danger, do you?"

"Yes," he said softly. "I think that with every person we talk to, you're more in danger than you were before." His voice lowered. "I think it's possible that you're in so deep now that even if you went to Maine you'd still be in danger."

Samantha turned away, looked out the window, and took a deep breath.

Thirty minutes later they were in Mike's house, and he had the hatbox on the breakfast table. Sam had insisted upon ordering dinner before they opened the box, and Mike had reluctantly agreed. Had she tried, Samantha wouldn't have been able to explain her reluctance to open the box. She knew it was full of her grandmother's possessions, and in other circumstances, she would have been curious to see what was in it, but she wasn't at all sure that she wanted to see the contents of this box. Pandora's box full of the world's evils. Somehow, she was sure if they opened this box, they would start something that would have to be played through to the end.

When Mike reached out to pull the lid off the box, Samantha put her hand on the top.

Watching her, Mike waited while she took a few deep, calming, breaths. After a while, she nodded and stepped back, holding her breath while Mike lifted the lid.

Standing over it, he peered down into it, a frown on his face, until Samantha, curious, stepped forward. "What is it?" she whispered.

"I don't believe it," he said, his voice sounding apprehensive.

"What?" Stepping close to him, she looked down into the box. When Mike grabbed her arms and said, "Gotcha!" she jumped two feet. Her hand to her heart, her face red, she hit him on the shoulder. "You!"

Laughing, Mike reached into the box. "I don't know what you're afraid of, it's just an old dress." He pulled out a red silk dress and handed it to her.

At first Samantha didn't want to touch the dress, but when Mike moved his hand, she saw something sparkle. Taking the dress from him, she slowly let it unfold, holding it up by the shoulders to look at it. "Lanvin," she whispered in awe, reading the label at the back of the neck, speaking in reverence of the Paris couturier's name.

It was a beautiful dress, red moiré with a fitted bodice, narrow shoulder straps, and a heavenly draped bias-cut skirt that was hemmed to midcalf in front with a bit of a train in back. On the right side of the waist was a sunburst design done in diamanté.

"Looks like you got over your fear," Mike said sarcastically, but she ignored him as she looked at the dress, admired the way it flowed when she moved it.

Mike took a pair of shoes from the box. They had been made to match the dress: red moiré T-straps with diamanté running down the vertical strap and Louis heels. Samantha knew the moment she saw them that they were exactly her size.

"Look at this." Mike handed her a small box covered in blue velvet. Resting on the velvet inside were a pair of earrings, but not just any earrings: These were long and pear shaped, diamonds from the earlobe to the base, with three large pearls hanging off the bottom edge.

Mike gave a low whistle.

"Doc's earrings," Samantha whispered. "The ones he said he gave Maxie the night she disappeared."

Mike pulled underwear from the box: a peach silk crepe de Chine bra trimmed with delicate ecru lace and matching panties. A tiny sexy garter belt and flesh-colored silk hose were folded together.

In the very bottom of the hatbox were tossed a long string of pearls and two diamond bracelets. Holding the bracelets to the light, Mike examined them. "I'm not a jeweler, but it's my guess that those are real," he said as he handed them to Sam, then ran the pearls across the back of his fingernail. Rough enough to use for emery boards, a roughness found only in genuine pearls.

"Real?"

"Absolutely," he said, adding the pearls to the pile on the table.

Samantha put the bracelets down, and the two of them looked at the articles on the table: the red evening gown, the matching shoes, the fabulous earrings, the bracelets, the necklace, and the underwear. It was obviously everything a woman had been wearing from the skin out on a night in 1928.

"If these things were in your father's possession," Mike said, "it removes any doubt that your grandmother was Maxie."

"Yes," was all Samantha could answer, but she didn't have to make another comment because the doorbell rang and the food arrived. They sat at one end of the table eating, not saying much as they looked at the pile of clothes and jewels draped across the other end of the table.

Both their minds were on that night in 1928 when, for whatever reason, a young woman, clad in silk and diamonds, had walked out of a bloodbath and not been seen again. Pregnant, she'd traveled to Louisville, Kentucky, and three days later had married a man who could not have children. She stayed with her husband, bore a child, had seemed to be happy, then in 1964 she had once again disappeared.

"Mike," Sam said, "wouldn't you like to know what happened that night? Wouldn't you really, truly like to know?"

"Yeah," he said. "I really would."

"Doc said Maxie's baby was his, but Abby says Maxie loved Michael Ransome."

"I'd put money on Uncle Mike. I can't see Doc sharing even sperm with someone."

"Mike!" she said, not liking his crudity. "Maybe he did love her. She could have been Doc's mistress but in love with Michael Ransome too. Maybe she loved both of them."

Mike didn't answer as he was looking at the dress, at the way it was reflecting the light. "Did you see the stain on the dress?"

"Yes," Samantha said quietly, looking down at her plate of food. She'd seen the stain and instinctively knew what the discoloration was.

Leaving the table, Mike picked the dress up and held it to

the light. "It's blood, isn't it? It looks like someone tried to wash it out, but you can't remove blood."

"No, at least not that much blood."

"Wonder whose it is?"

"From your accounts of the massacre, it could belong to any of several people."

Mike kept looking at the gown under the floor lamp. "Doc said Maxie was in the back of the club when Scalpini's men opened fire and she didn't come out again. If that's true, it couldn't be Uncle Mike's blood; he never left the dance floor. He was shot there and stayed there until the medics took him away. And, according to Doc, he was in the john most of the time." Mike looked up at Samantha. "I'm going to send this to Blair and have her have it analyzed. If we get a type on this blood, maybe we can match it with hospital records of the people who were shot that night."

Samantha got up and took the dress from him. "Will they cut the dress up?" she asked sadly.

Mike wanted to point out that she'd had the box for months and not opened it, had even seen the dress and not cared enough to take it out and look at it. Now she looked like a child whose teddy bear was being donated to charity, but he didn't point that out to her.

"Naw, they won't hurt it, but I don't think we should let it out of our sight until we've made a record of it."

"Record? Oh, you mean photograph it. I guess I can hold it up for you, or we could tape it to the wall."

"That won't work," he said, frowning, as though trying to figure out a solution. "I know. Why don't you put it on? Would you mind? The whole outfit looks as though it might fit you."

A couple of hours ago the idea of looking inside an old box had repulsed Samantha. She wouldn't have been able to think of anything she'd like to do less than rummage through old clothes. Except maybe put on a blood-stained dress.

Then again, thinking of musty old clothes stained with blood was one thing and being presented with Paris couture and diamonds and pearls was something else again. She touched the lace on the peach-colored underwear. "Do you think it would help you with your biography if I put the clothes on?"

Mike had to put his hand over his mouth to hide his smile. "It would be a personal favor to me if you'd wear them. Just for a few minutes. Why don't you go put them on while I get the camera? I'll have to set it up on a tripod so take your time."

He hadn't finished speaking before Sam gathered the clothes in her arms, put everything back into the box, and headed for the bedroom.

Once in the bedroom she hurriedly stripped off her own clothes and put on Maxie's bra and panties. The silk against her skin seemed to change her. Standing up a little straighter, she pulled her stomach in a little tighter and tilted her chin up, then moved just a bit to feel the silk slither against her skin. When she'd first come to New York, during the time she stayed alone in her room, she had listened to her father's music, the old blues singers. Now, standing in Maxie's underwear, she began to hum an old Bessie Smith song.

The garter belt came next; propping her foot on a chair, she rolled the silk hose ever so slowly up her legs. When one leg was silk clad, she stretched it out, adjusting the seam down the back. After opening the door to Mike's closet, she moved the chair before the full-length mirror and watched herself slide the second stocking up her leg. Peach silk bra, loose-legged panties, silk hose, bare thigh between silk and silk.

What was it about a garter belt and hose that was so incredibly sexy? she wondered, straightening, turning this way and that to look at herself and liking what she saw. Panty hose that encased a woman in nylon from waist to toes didn't feel sexy; they made a woman feel as though she were a sausage encased in a wrapping. But with several inches of bare thigh above the silk, she felt seductive, alluring, as though she were a vampy singer in a Harlem nightclub and handsome young men were coming to hear her sing.

In the bathroom she looked at herself in the mirror, seeing that her face was too clean, too much the young-lady-I-met-in-church, and her hair was too modern, too fluffy with hair spray.

Turning on the tap, she wet a comb and ran it through her hair, and once she began, she couldn't stop. Parting her hair on the left side, she wet it thoroughly and plastered it to her head, forming stylized curls in front of her ears, then, to make sure her hair stayed in place, she coated it with spray. She used her darkest eye pencil to heavily outline her eyes, then drew a sharp line through her brows, strongly emphasizing them. With a lip pencil she managed to make her lips sharply pointed on top, as she'd seen in pictures of Clara Bow.

Stepping back from the mirror, she studied herself and nodded. She could almost imagine herself as Maxie, getting ready to go on stage—and her lover and the man who bought her diamonds were both waiting for her.

When she slipped the dress over her head, the silk slid over her skin, and she wriggled to make it fall into place. For a moment she stared at herself in the mirror. "Maxie," she whispered, seeing not herself, but another woman, a woman who was sure that she was of interest to men. When she buckled on the shoes, she tossed her foot onto the countertop then ran her hand up her leg.

"Sam!" Mike yelled. "Aren't you ready yet?"

"Keep your shirt on, buster, this baby's worth the wait," she yelled through the door. She fastened Doc's earrings on her ears, slipped the diamonds on her wrists, then wrapped the pearls twice about her neck.

As she was about to leave the bedroom, she glanced at a couple of Balinese puppets Mike had on the top of the dresser, noticing the foot-long carved stick attached to the hand of one puppet. Carefully, she unscrewed the stick, then used the little brush in a bottle of Mike's white typewriter correction fluid that he'd carelessly left in the bedroom to paint four inches of the end of the stick. When she was finished, she had what was a good facsimile of a cigarette holder complete with fake cigarette. Putting it to her carmined, bee-stung lips, she opened the door enough to tell Mike to turn out all the lights except for the single floor lamp and had to ignore his country-boy cry of "Alll riiiight."

When she left the bedroom she was no longer the innocent, respectable Samantha, but Maxie, a singer who had men fighting each other to have her.

When Mike saw her slinking down the stairs, he gave a low whistle—and completely forgot about taking a photograph. The Samantha he knew, *his* Samantha, didn't walk the way this woman was walking with her hips pushed forward and her body undulating in seductive movements as she made her way toward him, the diamonds in her ears and on her wrists sparkling. This woman was as different from the woman he knew as Daphne was from an Indiana housewife. Mike found himself backing away from her, for this woman was a bit intimidating; she made him feel as though he should be wearing a tux and offering her gifts that came in long black velvet boxes. When Samantha put the fake cigarette holder to her newly shaped lips, Mike sat down on one of the chairs by the breakfast table and watched this woman who he felt that he'd never seen before.

When Sam was a few feet in front of Mike, she began to sing an old blues song she'd heard Bessie Smith sing.

Bad luck has come to stay
Trouble never ends
My man has gone away
With a girl I thought was my friend

Many people seem to think that an ability to sing the blues comes from skin color, but it comes from having experienced misery in life—and Samantha had had more than enough heartache and sadness in her short life to be able to sing the blues as well as any other person on earth. Her voice, albeit untrained, was strong from inherited talent, and it was filled with emotion.

Lordy can't you hear my prayers
Lady Luck, Lady Luck, won't you please smile down on me
There's a time, friend of mine
I need your silver feet

Mike watched her and she made him *feel* the words she was singing, made him feel the sorrow of a woman whose man had been stolen by another woman. She was saying the words as only someone who had experienced the emotion could sing them; she sang them the way they were meant to be sung, the way they had been written. It wasn't as though she were a modern folk singer enraptured with the cute songs the blacks used to sing and trying to imitate them for an audience of WASPs. Samantha was the type of woman for whom the song had been written and she sang it with her heart as much as with her voice.

I've got his picture turned upside down
I've sprinkled slough-foot dust all around

Since my man is gone I'm all confused
I've got those Lady Luck Blues

The mournful song was short. When Samantha finished, all Mike could do was stare at her, blinking in confusion, feeling that he was looking at a stranger in a slinky red dress that slithered over her curves.

To his consternation, Samantha walked toward him in a way he'd never seen any woman walk and put the tip of her high-heeled foot on the chair edge between his legs, leaned toward him, and inhaled on her cigarette holder. He was sure he actually saw the smoke she blew out the side of her mouth.

"Well, honey?" she said, and it was *not* Samantha's voice. This woman's voice was lower, raspy almost, and it was very, very provocative—bewitching, the voice of a siren who was quite capable of luring men to their deaths.

"Samantha?" he whispered, and to his embarrassment, his voice broke like a teenager's.

With a sultry laugh that would have done justice to Kathleen Turner at her throatiest, she moved her foot and turned away from him. As she walked away, he couldn't take his eyes from the undulating back side of her, the skin of her back glowing and perfect in the soft light of the single lamp.

"Sam," he said, calling out to her when she started back toward the bedroom, but she didn't turn. "Maxie," he whispered and drew in his breath when she smiled at him over her shoulder, and it was a smile of a seductress, a woman who knew what effect she had on men.

When Samantha disappeared up the stairs into the bedroom, Mike let out his breath, then rubbed his arms. He'd been holding his breath and his muscles were tense. Trying to ease the tension in his body, he walked to the glass patio doors and looked out at the night. The woman who had just appeared in this room was one he hadn't known, a woman who had many secrets, a woman who was capable of all manner of things—and Mike wasn't sure she was a woman he especially liked. Maybe she was a woman he'd like to take to bed, since every pore of her body oozed sexuality. Then again, maybe he'd rather not go to bed with her, for the woman who'd just sung for him probably knew more about sex than he did. She was the kind of woman who would fake an orgasm, would fake love for a man. She was the exact polar opposite of Samantha with her openness, her sweetness, her ability to give.

"Well?" Samantha said from behind him.

When he turned, she was Samantha again, face washed shiny clean, hair a tangled mess, her nifty little body concealed under his bathrobe. On impulse, he went to her, surrounded her in his arms, and kissed her soundly, not a kiss of sex or passion, but a kiss of relief, a kiss of welcome home.

"Mike?" she asked. "Are you all right?"

He was holding her so tightly she could scarcely breathe, and it was a while before he could recover himself enough to speak. With a chuckle that even to him sounded forced, he said, "You make me believe in split personalities." Holding her away from him so he could see her face, he searched it. "Are *you* all right? You were so . . . so different. You were . . ."

"Maxie," she said. "I put the dress on and I seemed to become her. Did I do a good job?"

He pulled her head back down to his shoulder. "Too good. Much, much, much too good."

"Mike! Is something wrong? All I did was sing a song and, well, maybe vamp it up a bit."

He wouldn't release his tight hold on her. "It was more than that. You changed. Really changed."

"A little change never hurt—"

Kissing her again, he silenced her. "Sammy, I don't want you to change. I like you just the way you are."

As she snuggled against him, Samantha was not at all sure what had upset him so much, but she rather liked his concern. And she liked his compliment. "Mike," she said softly, "I like you too." It wasn't until later that she realized the extent to which he was upset because, for the first time, when they went to bed, he didn't try to get her to spend the night in bed with him. Something about his reluctance made her smile as she glanced at herself in the mirror over the dresser. Maybe she should be Maxie more often, she thought. Maybe she should not be so predictable, so very boring, a woman without surprises. Stroking Maxie's dress that was draped over a chair, she smiled, then, on impulse, she took her new pretty sheer white nightgown from where she had hidden it in the bottom of one of Mike's drawers and put it on. Maxie would have worn a white nightgown if she'd wanted to. White or black, lace or satin, big and transparent, or tiny and skin-exposing, Maxie would have worn any nightgown in the world—if she'd wanted to.

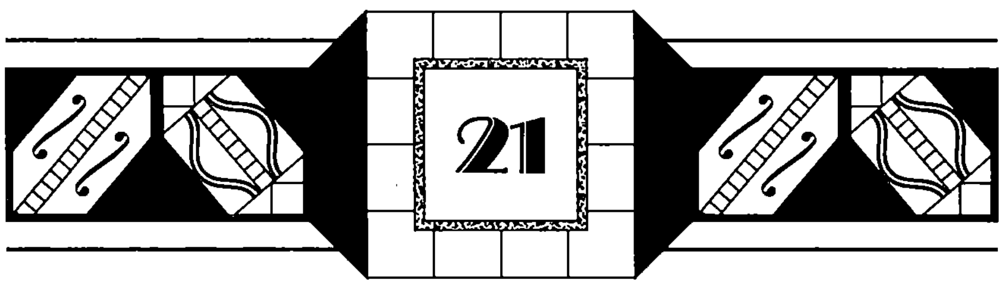

21

At five minutes to nine on Sunday morning, Samantha was sitting in the center of Mike's bed, knees to her chest, wearing her new white nightgown and trying to give herself a pedicure. The fact that the implements she was using had been in her possession since she was ten years old—they were fitted into a pink plastic case printed with tiny white poodles with blue ribbons on their tails—didn't help the process. So far she hadn't heard a sound from Mike's room, so she assumed he was still sleeping.

At nine, she picked up the remote control off the bedside table and flicked on the TV to watch Charles Kuralt's "Sunday Morning." She'd been watching the show since they had taken Mr. Kuralt off the road and nailed him to a chair in New York. It interested Samantha to see if he was ever going to get that melancholy look off his face, the look that said, I'd rather be on the road.

In the first few minutes of the show Charles went over the stories that they were going to do that morning, giving each one his special tone of, Can you believe this? Samantha didn't pay much attention to what he was saying until she heard the word *Jubilee,* then her head came up sharply, and her eyes widened as she hung on every word Charles Kuralt was saying.

> The Jubilee Massacre isn't as well known as the St. Valentine's Day Massacre, but then nothing that happened in New York during Prohibition is as well known as what happened in Chicago. Maybe it's the cynicism of New Yorkers, but what happened that hot Saturday night on May the twelfth, 1928, wasn't even called a massacre by New Yorkers. Some wit—dare we say half-wit—dubbed it the Changing of the Guard as one gangster mob boss killed the gangsters of a man who would be boss. The shoot-out backfired and the sympathy of the people—crooked cops and such—went with the man who had been shot at. Doc Barrett, then a twenty-eight-year-old hoodlum, took over control of illegal liquor sales after that night, after that dreadful shootout in which seventeen people were killed and more than a dozen wounded. Doc gained but he also lost, for his childhood friend, the man he said was the only man he would ever be able to trust, a man with the colorful name of Half Hand Joe—we are told he lost half his left hand saving Doc from a bullet when they were kids—was killed that night.
>
> It all happened in a glamorous speakeasy in Harlem known simply as Jubilee's Place. Doc may have gained that night, but Jubilee lost everything he had. His club was destroyed by over three thousand bullets—and by a few thousand souvenir seekers over the next few days.

While the newsman was talking, the camera showed pictures of the exterior and interior of a falling-down old building in a horrible area of Harlem. Rats scurried across the floor as the camera zeroed in on bullet holes in the walls.

"Jubilee still owns his club," Charles Kuralt continued, "but what with property values as they are today, he hasn't been able to sell it or rent it, so today it sits empty."

Charles put down his paper and gave his Mona Lisa smile to the camera.

> And some people say haunted. But we're not here today to talk about a massacre, even a massacre as violent as that one sixty-three years ago. We're here today to talk about Jubilee Johnson and his music, for not even a massacre that took everything he owned could keep a man like Jubilee down. Today he's a hundred and one years old and still playing, still singing, . . . and still jubilant.

Leaping out of the bed, Samantha tore through the bathroom and into Mike's bedroom where he was on his stomach, buried under the covers and about six fat down-filled pillows. "Mike! Wake up. You have to come see what's on TV." He didn't stir so she knelt on the edge of the bed and touched all of him that she could see, which consisted of about a quarter inch of bare shoulder and a curl of black hair.

"Michael! Wake up! You're going to miss it." He didn't so much as move a muscle; if he hadn't been so warm, she would have thought he was dead. Climbing into the bed with him, she grabbed his shoulders and began to shake him. "Jubilee's on television. Maxie's Jubilee is on Charles Kuralt! Get up!"

One minute he seemed to be sound asleep and the next minute he had grabbed her, pulling her into the bed beside him and began rubbing his sharp-whiskered face into her neck, making her squeal in laughter while he held her down.

"What are you doing waking me up?" he growled in mock fierceness. "It's Sunday and a man should be allowed to sleep."

Laughing, Samantha was trying to get away from him as his whiskers scraped her skin. "Mike, Jubilee's on television."

It was then that Mike's face changed and he pulled away from her, moving from hugging her and holding her close to not touching her at all.

"What's wrong?"

"Get out of here." There was no more play in his voice; he was in dead earnest now.

She could tell that he was very angry, but she didn't know why. Was he angry because she'd waked him up? Some people took sleep seriously, but she hadn't realized that Mike was one of those people. Backing off the bed, she began to apologize. "I'm sorry. I guess I shouldn't have awakened you, but I wanted you to see the show, but maybe I'll go upstairs and set the recorder and you can see it later."

He turned his head away from her. "Take off that gown."

It took Samantha a moment to understand what he was saying, for at first she thought he was demanding that she strip, but then she realized that she had on her brand-new, very pretty, very thin, very, *very* white nightgown. Even as the feeling of pleasure began to flow through her, she felt rotten about not remembering his "problem" with white, well, maybe not *too* rotten, but a little bit bad. Had the sight of her in this plain cotton gown affected him *that* much, to make him turn pale, to make him unable to continue looking at her?

"I . . . I wasn't thinking, Mike," she said slowly, but even to her own ears the apology sounded insincere. Any man who looked as Mike did, who was as sexy as Mike, who was as sweet and kind and as much fun as Mike was, who was as smart as Mike was, who was as all round wonderful as Mike was, could have his choice of any female on earth. Yet, she thought, he was turned on by *her*—so much so that he couldn't even look at her while she was wearing white.

"I came in here to tell you about the TV show and I forgot what I had on. I didn't mean—" She stopped because he had turned to look at her—and what she saw in his eyes made her take a step backward, for his eyes were filled with something she wasn't sure she understood. There was need and desire and longing in his eyes, but also desperation, as though he were in need of something she had and he'd die without getting it.

Putting her hand to her throat, Samantha took a step backward. It had been a long while since she'd been afraid of Mike, but she was now. As he moved across the bed toward her, she took another step backward. "Mike," she began, but he didn't speak, just looked at her with those eyes and kept coming toward her with the stealth of a wolf.

Samantha, in a cowardly move, gave a little squeal of fright and ran from the room, shutting the bathroom door behind her, then the bedroom door. She leaned against it, her breast heaving. Maybe Maxie could handle young, handsome men stalking her, but Samantha wasn't quite ready.

It took her a moment to calm her breathing, then she tore her new nightgown off and put on her jeans and a long-sleeved, high-necked shirt that covered most of her skin and went to the library to watch the TV in that room.

It was nearly twenty minutes before Mike appeared in the

library and when she looked up at him, she started, for his skin and lips looked nearly blue.

"Are you all right?" she asked, going to him to feel his forehead. His skin was as cold as a salamander's. "Mike!"

Pushing her hand away, he sat on the couch. "Cold shower," he murmured, obviously embarrassed by everything that had happened that morning. "Has the segment come on yet?"

"No," she said, trying not to smile, but his reactions to her made her feel good. Of course, she thought, this was how all men felt *before* they went to bed with a woman—especially before they went to bed with her. It was much better to allow Mike to fantasize about her than to do what he seemed to think he wanted her to do and go to bed with him, because if she did, he'd probably ask her to leave his house forever. Or maybe he'd just fall asleep during the process of bedding her.

"No," she said, "you haven't missed it. I think it's on next." She handed him half a toasted bagel slathered with cream cheese, which she'd had delivered.

Sitting beside her on the couch, he ignored the bagel and, instead, took her chin in his hand and lifted her mouth to his. He kissed her for a long time, sweetly, not aggressively, no thrusting tongues, no tearing at her clothes, no hands on her body except those warm fingers on her chin, and that long, long kiss of yearning was almost her undoing. Turning to him, she put her hand on his shoulder and opened her mouth under his. Her body seemed to liquefy, to turn into something warm and soft and yielding as her neck bent back into what should have been an impossible position, but she wanted to blend into him, to lose herself in him.

When he pulled his lips away from hers, she was too weak to sit up and would have fallen back against the couch if Mike's hand hadn't caught her.

"Why, Sam?" he whispered. "Why do you tell me no? How much longer am I supposed to wait? You want a marriage proposal first? Because if you do, then will—?"

She put one finger over his lips, not wanting to hear the rest of that sentence. She didn't want to talk about her reasons behind what she did, didn't want him to know the truth about her, at least not yet, not when what they had was still so fragile. Maybe someday, maybe later, she could tell him the truth about herself.

Uttering a curse word, Mike grabbed the bagel that was still in her hand, except that now the bagel was a bit crushed from where Samantha had clutched it during Mike's kiss, and there was as much cream cheese on her fingers as on the bread. She had the disconcerting experience of Mike picking up her hand and slowly, languorously, sensuously, licking every morsel of cheese off her fingers.

"Your show's coming on," he said, her little finger in his mouth.

"Huh?"

"Your show. Jubilee, remember?"

"Huh?" He was licking her palm.

"Maxie. Jubilee. Death. Destruction. Massacre. Remember?"

"Huh?"

Putting her now-clean hand on her lap, Mike turned her to face the TV, but it was some minutes before she could focus clearly enough to see the program about the life and career of the ancient musician. The camera showed Jubilee, who, for all his hundred and one years, looked energetic and spry, and his mind was obviously as good as it ever had been.

Mike pulled her back against him as they watched, as they saw the trashed-out building that had once been an elegant nightclub done in blue and silver in the Art Deco style. Jubilee talked some about the club, about the entertainers, about how the ladies had worn their furs and the men had brought their mistresses, but it had ended after the massacre, and he'd never had the money to rebuild the place.

At the end of the segment, Samantha put the mute on the TV and turned to Mike. "Is Harlem very far away?"

"In philosophy or miles?"

She grimaced. "Miles."

"New York's an island, remember? Nothing's very far from anything else."

"So if I told a cab driver that I wanted to go to Harlem, he'd know where to take me?"

Mike didn't say anything for a moment, just looked at her. "Tell me you're not thinking what I hope you aren't."

She got off the couch. "I'm going to visit Jubilee, if that's what you mean. And I'm going to do it now, before anybody else realizes that the man is still alive."

Standing in front of her, Mike put his hands on her shoulders. "You mean the man who tried to kill you, don't you?"

She pulled away from him, not wanting to think about that time. "Maybe Mr. Johnson knows something about that night, about why my grandmother had to leave her family, about what justified her causing so much unhappiness in our family. Maybe—"

"Is there anything in this world I can say to persuade you not to go?"

She shook her head. "No, Mike, there's not. I would like it if you went with me, but if you don't want to, I'll go by myself."

"To Harlem? Tiny blonde you to that area of the city by yourself?"

"Is it as bad as on TV?"

"Yes."

She swallowed then took a deep breath. "Yes, I'll go by myself if I have to." Even as she said it, inside, she was begging Mike to go with her. There was a limit to a person's bravery.

"Okay, get dressed. Wear something plain, not something with a label."

Nodding, she turned away and went upstairs to change.

There was already a crowd outside Jubilee's brownstone when she and Mike arrived, not in a taxi but in a car that Mike had hired that was to wait for them. The driver of the car was a very large man with skin the color of coal and a long pink scar that started on the back of his neck and disappeared into his shirt, and he seemed to be a friend of Mike's. Nervously, Samantha just smiled at him a lot, which seemed to amuse him a great deal.

On the trip north to Harlem, Samantha did not look out the window, for it was much too frightening. Poverty on such a scale, poverty so close to such immense wealth as there was in midtown Manhattan, was not something that she could really understand.

When they at last arrived at Jubilee's house, the only nice-looking house on the block, Samantha gave a sigh of frustration, for it looked as though a riot were about to begin. It seemed that most of New York watched Charles Kuralt's television show, and they'd come to see Jubilee—or come to borrow money from him or sell him something or get him to look at the songs they'd written.

In the doorway stood a big, tall woman with iron gray hair and a look of fury on a face that had once been handsome. Holding aloft a broom as though it were a weapon, she was trying to discourage the watchers from climbing the front steps. Samantha saw two men get smacked in the face with the broom.

Mike put his hand on her elbow. "I don't think now is the time," he said as he began ushering her back toward the car.

Samantha twisted out of his grip. "No! I'm going to talk to him now. I don't think I'll have enough courage to come back here again."

"That's the best piece of news I've heard yet."

"Mike, can you get me through that crowd? If I can get near enough to that woman, I want to tell her that I want to ask Jubilee about Maxie."

Mike thought about wasting time arguing with her, but the futility of the exercise didn't appeal to him. Besides, the truth was, he wanted to meet Jubilee too and wanted to know if the old man knew anything of importance about Maxie and why she had left her family. Looking over her head, Mike nodded in question to the big black man standing by the car, and the man gave an answering nod.

Within minutes, Samantha had her hand firmly clasped around the back of Mike's belt as he plowed his way through the people, the enormous black man behind them. When Samantha got to the bottom of the stoop, the woman with the broom made for the three of them. But the black man caught the broom handle before it touched them, thus giving Mike and Samantha time to call out that they wanted to ask Jubilee about Maxie.

From the look on the woman's face, she had heard the name before. With a grimace, she nodded to a child standing behind her, and the boy scurried into the house. Moments later he returned and waved his arm for them to enter. Mike with Samantha close behind him entered the house while their driver returned to the car.

The inside of the house had the used, worn look of houses that had been bought many years ago, decorated then, and not touched since. The baseboard and the ceiling moldings had been painted probably thirty or forty times over the years and were never washed in between, so the paint, over dirt, was peeling and flaking. The thickness of the paint hid most of the detail of the wood.

They followed the child up steep, narrow stairs to the top of the house, where it was hot and sunny and looked as though it hadn't changed since Jubilee was born. It was on the second landing that a man stepped out of the shadows and nearly frightened Samantha to death. He was a tall black man, extremely good-looking, and he had the angriest eyes Samantha had ever seen on a human being. He wasn't just angry at the moment but angry for a lifetime, angry forever, angry at everyone and everything.

After an arrogant, flared-nostril look at Samantha, he disappeared down a hallway. Swallowing, and after a reassuring glance back at Mike, Samantha continued to follow the child up the stairs.

The child opened a door at the top of the house, allowing Samantha and Mike to enter, then left them alone in the room. The instant she saw the room Samantha loved it. Two walls were covered, floor to ceiling, with shelves containing hundreds of piles of what she knew to be sheet music. From the looks of the torn, yellowed covers, the music probably comprised the years from now back to the Flintstones. Dominating the room was an enormous grand piano, one of those black, glossy pianos that men wearing tailed tuxedos played. It was obviously an instrument that was loved, for it was polished and without so much as a scratch on it. A couple of old upholstered chairs with the stuffing protruding comfortably from the arms sat across from the piano.

Both Samantha and Mike were so intent on looking about the room that they almost missed the tiny man sitting on the piano bench, his head barely visible above the music stand. The TV camera had managed to hide a few of Jubilee's wrinkles and the lighting had softened the fact that there was no meat on his body, just dark, leathery skin over bones. He looked more like a mummy than a human, and his sparkling eyes were incongruous in his ancient body, as though some showman had found a way to make *his* mummy exhibit look more realistic.

Samantha grinned at him and he grinned back, showing a rather fabulous pair of false teeth.

"My name is Samantha Elliot and I'm Maxie's granddaughter," she said, extending her hand to him.

"I would have known you anywhere. Look just like her." His voice was good, and Samantha had an idea that he'd never stopped using it, but his hand felt as much like skin as a good-quality piece of leather did. As he spoke, his fingers played softly with the piano keys in an absentminded way, as though he weren't conscious of what he was doing; playing the piano was like breathing to him.

Mike stepped forward and began to tell Jubilee why they were there, about Doc and Maxie, about Samantha's father, about the biography he was writing.

As Jubilee listened, he continued to tinkle with the piano keys, a faraway look in his eyes. When Mike stopped speaking, he looked at Samantha. "Maxie used to sing the blues. Sang them as well as any woman alive."

Smiling, Samantha sang the words to the song Jubilee had been playing, "Gulf Coast Blues," ending with the words,

You gotta mouth full of gimme,
a hand full of much obliged

The first look of disbelief on Jubilee's face was replaced by joy, but a special joy, for here was an old man seeing something that he thought had gone from the earth. For just a moment there looked to be tears in his old eys. "You sound like her, girl!" he said and turned to the piano fully, both of his old monkey hands going to the keys. "Know this one?"

"Weepin' Willow Blues," she said softly as the man began to pound out the notes. There couldn't be much strength in that frail body, but what there was, was in his hands.

Samantha opened her mouth to sing, but closed it when, through the window, sounding like a ghost, came the mournful wail of a trumpet with a mute on it. For a moment she looked at Mike to reassure herself that she was still in the nineties, for a muted trumpet was not a modern sound.

"Don't pay him no mind," Jubilee said impatiently. "That's just Ornette. You know this or not?"

Samantha knew without asking that the horn player was the ferocious-looking young man she'd seen on the stairs, and she also knew that she was being tested. If that young man could play something as old and obscure as "Weepin' Willow Blues," then he had to have learned it out of love, not to make money on it. She also knew without being told that he didn't believe a little blonde woman could sing the blues.

Opening her mouth, Samantha began to wail the old song about a woman who'd lost her man. At the end came the staccato verse:

Folks I love my man
I kiss him mornin' noon and night
I wash his clothes and keep him clean and try to treat him right
Now he's gone and left me after all I tried to do
The way he treats me, girls, he'll do the same thing to you
And that's the reason I got those weepin' willow blues

When she finished, Jubilee didn't say a word, but Samantha could tell from his face that she had indeed sung the song correctly. There was that look that needed no words to explain it: You sound just like her, hung in the air.

On impulse, while both Jubilee and Mike were staring at her in wonder, she went to the window and yelled angrily in challenge in the direction of the horn player, "Did I pass, Ornette?"

At that, both Mike and Jubilee burst into laughter, Jubilee sounding like an old accordion that had a few holes in it.

"Sassy like her too," Jubilee said, nearly choking. "Maxie was never afraid of anybody."

"She was afraid of something," Mike said soberly, "and we'd like to find out what it was."

Jubilee would tell them nothing about Maxie. He kept playing the piano, asking Samantha if she knew this song and that and repeating that he hadn't seen Maxie since the night she disappeared. When Samantha asked him if he had any idea *why* Maxie had disappeared that night, he mumbled that no, he didn't.

A hundred and one years old, Samantha thought, and he *still* couldn't lie convincingly. She tried to calculate how many times she was going to have to visit him, how many Bessie Smith songs she was going to have to sing, before he told her what he knew about Maxie.

When she and Mike told him good-bye, Samantha kissed the old, leathery cheek and said she thought she'd probably see him again.

On the landing, waiting to lead them downstairs again, was

the little boy, but he did what Sam thought was a rather odd thing: He slipped his hand into Mike's. She'd already seen that Mike had a natural rapport with children, but still, there was something unusual about this. It wasn't until they were outside and she saw Mike slide the hand the child had been holding into his pocket that Samantha realized that the child had given Mike a note. From Ornette, she thought, and she knew without a doubt that Mike was going to keep whatever was on that note a secret from her.

In the backseat of the car, all the way back downtown, she acted as though she knew nothing about the note. "Ornette," she said lightly. "I think I've heard that name before."

"Ornette Coleman. Alto sax," Mike said, looking out the window.

When they were back at the house, Mike instantly disappeared into the bedroom and Samantha was sure he was looking at his secret note. When he came out, he was dressed in shorts and a T-shirt and had the Sunday *New York Times* under his arm. They ate lunch (deli delivered) outside in the garden, both of them looking at the paper. Later, they sat in wooden deck chairs, Mike still with the paper, seeming to spend hours on the financial section, while Samantha put the laptop computer on her knees and tried to write down all the facts she knew so far about Maxie.

There wasn't much. Maxie maybe had been and maybe hadn't been in love with two men, or three if you counted Cal. However many there had been, in the end, she had left them all. Where had she gone and why?

Every few minutes she would get up from her chair, mumbling something cryptic, such as, "I need another floppy," then disappear into the house, where she took as long as she dared to search for the note the child had given Mike. She searched the clothes he had worn that morning, looked in every box in the guest bedroom he was using (and felt a little pang of guilt that she had run him out of his bedroom), and even looked in the toes of his shoes.

It was on her sixth foray into the house that she dared to look in his wallet. Somehow that seemed to be the ultimate invasion of privacy, and she hesitated before picking it up off the dresser. But once she looked inside it, she made a thorough search. He had three credit cards, all gold, and twelve hundred dollars in cash, the amount making her draw in her breath a bit. There was nothing else in the wallet, no list of phone numbers or account numbers, nothing, but then she thought that maybe a man who could multiply as Mike could might be able to memorize the numbers he needed to know.

Just as she was about to put the wallet down, she remembered that when she was a child her father'd had a wallet with a "secret" compartment, and he used to allow her to find treats in it. Digging around in Mike's wallet, she found a hidden compartment and pulled out the piece of paper she found inside.

She nearly had to sit down when she saw that the hidden document was a photo of herself—a picture of Samantha when she was in the fifth grade, and she knew that Mike had to have taken the photo from her house in Louisville. Was it a gift from her father or did he take it from her room where she knew he had stayed? Why was he carrying it in his wallet?

Guiltily, she put the photo back into its hiding place, but when it wouldn't slide back in smoothly, she knew without a doubt that she'd found the note.

Nelson—Paddy's Bar in the
Village—Monday—Eight

With the speed of lightning, she put everything back the way she'd found it and went back into the garden to sit with Mike. Her curiosity got the better of her, and after sitting quietly for a few moments, she asked him what his father's office telephone number was. Without looking up from his paper, Mike answered.

"Your oldest brother's telephone number."

"Home or mobile unit or the office in Colorado or the office in New York or the house in the mountains?"

"All of them."

Mike put down his paper and looked at her. "Is this a test?"

"What's my Social Security number?"

With a crooked grin, he told her.

"Do you know my bank account number as well?"

He put his paper back in front of his face as he told her, then he told her her secret password for using her cash card at the bank machine, but he would *not* tell her how he had come to know that number.

"Vanessa's number," she snapped out.

"Stumped me on that one. In fact, I'm not sure I ever knew it."

He was lying, of course, but when she looked back at her computer screen, she was smiling.

At three o'clock, Samantha left her chair and went to the kitchen where she began rummaging in the cabinets trying to find what she needed.

When Mike heard Sam in the kitchen, he wondered what she was doing so he got up to see. He found her sitting on the floor, surrounded by half a dozen pans and looking puzzled. "Trying to figure out what to do with them?" he asked with a male smirk.

"I am trying to figure out how to make a sidecar."

"Hire a welder."

"Very funny," she answered, rising, starting to put the pans away. "I was hoping you had one of those drink-making books."

"Ahhh, *that* kind of sidecar. Are you planning to get drunk?" he asked, hope in his voice.

"No, I'm going to make a pitcher of sidecars and take it with me when I visit my grandmother this evening."

That announcement stopped Mike from speaking as he stared at her in astonishment. "W . . . what do you mean?"

She stopped moving to look at him. "For some reason, Mike, you seem to think that I'm not altogether very smart and that you can keep things from me, but I knew that Abby was my grandmother the moment I saw her. She looks like my father, moves like him. She even quirks her mouth exactly like my father did." She leaned toward him. "And *you* knew who she was too. It was written all over your face. You were so taken aback you could hardly speak."

Catching her hand in his, Mike held her fingers tightly. "I didn't say anything, not because I don't think you're smart but because . . ."

"I know," she said, smiling at him, squeezing his hand in return. "You don't want anything to happen to me and you think it's dangerous for me to visit her."

"Exactly."

She took a deep breath. "Mike, you are so lucky. You have so many people who belong to you, but my people are all gone. Only Maxie and I are still alive, and she's there in that horrible place alone day after day and I'm here and . . . and she won't be there much longer."

When she began to tremble, he pulled her into his arms. "Hush, sweetheart. It's okay. We'll go see her if you want."

"You don't have to go with me." As they always did, Mike's arms made her feel safe.

"Sure," he said, stroking her hair. "I'm going to let you go by yourself. You'll probably get stuck in a revolving door."

Smiling, she looked up at him. "I was hoping you'd go." She pushed away from him. "Now," she said, businesslike, "how do I make a sidecar?"

"Samantha, you can't take her booze. I don't want to have to point out the obvious, but she's a very sick lady. I don't think her doctor will allow—"

She put her fingers over his lips. "My granddad Cal said, 'When you know you're dying, what can hurt you?' He hadn't smoked since the fifties, but on the day the doctor told him he was dying, he bought a big box of very expensive cigars and smoked one a day until he died. My father put the ones he didn't smoke under the lining of his casket."

Mike could only stare at her; she had experienced things that he couldn't imagine. She had grown up surrounded by dying people, and her father, when he wasn't dying, had demanded that no sunlight be allowed into the house.

Without a word, Mike reached into a cabinet above her head and took down a yellow book that turned out to be a collection of drink recipes. "Let's see. A sidecar: Cointreau, lemon juice, and Cognac. I think we can manage that."

"Oh, Mike, I do love you," she said, laughing, then was embarrassed at what she'd said.

He didn't look up from the book. "I should hope so," he said, sounding as though what she'd said meant nothing to him, but the color of his neck was a little darker than normal, almost as though he were flushed.

Busying herself with getting the lemons from the refrigerator, Samantha began talking quickly to cover her embarrassment. "I do hope the nursing home doesn't give us any trouble and will allow us to spend some time with her. You know what I want to do, Mike? I want to take photos to her. Upstairs I have a big box full of albums and loose photos of my father and mother and Granddad Cal and me, most of them taken after

Maxie left. My goodness, but I can't keep calling my own grandmother by her name. What do you think I should call her?"

"Abby," Mike said seriously. "Until she wants you to know that she's your grandmother, I think you shouldn't let her know that you know." He grimaced. "The poor woman probably thinks that keeping her identity from you will help keep you safe."

With a startled look at her, he stopped talking. "Sam, from the first your goal—or rather your father's goal—has been to find out what happened to your grandmother. You've found out: She ended up in a nursing home plugged into machines. If you know that, then why did we go to Jubilee's this morning? Why did you ask him questions about Maxie if you already knew the answers?"

"I know where she is but not *why* she's there," she said softly.

Mike groaned. "Samantha . . ."

She knew that he didn't want her to do any more searching, but the more she found out about Doc and Maxie and Michael Ransome and Jubilee and everyone else, the more she wanted to find out what happened that night in 1928. At one point she'd thought of her grandmother with what was close to hatred for leaving her family, for leaving without so much as a backward glance. But she'd met her grandmother now, and she had seen the tears in Maxie's eyes when Cal was mentioned, making Sam sure that Maxie had loved him very, very much. What's more, Maxie loved her granddaughter. That was evidenced by the way she'd reacted when Mike had told her that someone had tried to kill Sam.

"I wish I knew what my grandmother liked to eat," she said. "I wish I could take her . . . chocolate cake or something like that, whatever she really likes, something that's bad for her, something that I was sure that insufferable place wouldn't give her to eat."

Putting his hands on her shoulders, Mike looked into her eyes. "Can I say anything to make you stay away? What if I told you that whoever tried to kill you might still be watching you and you might lead them to Maxie? I don't think that woman's body is strong enough to withstand an attack such as you had."

Samantha had thought of that and had weighed the possibilities. "How long do you think she has?"

Mike wasn't going to lie to her. "When I first contacted her, the doctor told me she had three months left, tops."

Samantha took a deep breath. "If you were she and you had had no one for many years, and now you had a chance to spend a few weeks with someone you love, would you risk it?"

He wanted to point out that just because Maxie had left her family in Louisville twenty-seven years before didn't mean that she had necessarily been alone since then, but he didn't say that. In fact, remembering Maxie in that loathsome place, he wondered if maybe Sam wasn't right and Maxie *had* been alone all those years. She may have run away because she was afraid of being discovered, so it wouldn't have made sense for her to leave one place and become a social whirl and therefore highly visible elsewhere.

"Any pictures of you naked mixed in with those photos?"

Laughing, she moved away from him. "On a fuzzy rug when I was eight months old," she said.

"How about eighteen years old? Young, nubile—"

"What does that mean? That I'm not young now?"

Mike shrugged. "Young body, old mind. Hey! you think Maxie would like caviar? We could stop at the Russian Tea Room and get blinis."

Samantha was still thinking about his "young body, old mind" comment. "I would imagine she would love caviar, at least it sounds good anyway. I just hope the home doesn't give us too hard a time."

When what he hoped was an inspired idea occured to Mike, his face lit up. "You leave the home to me. I'll see that they let her eat whatever she wants and that she's treated very well from now on."

It was almost six o'clock when they arrived at the nursing home. Samantha was wearing her red Valentino suit and Manolo Blahnik high heels and carrying a red Chanel bag. Now that she knew how much her clothing cost, she was almost afraid to wear it and she dreaded getting into one of those filthy New York cabs. So she asked Mike if he was maybe, hopefully, going to hire a private car again, but he told her that no, he wasn't.

Because of his answer, she was not prepared for the long black limousine that pulled up in front of the town house. Her mouth was still hanging open in astonishment when the uniformed chauffeur got out and she saw that he was Mike's cousin, Raine.

"Good evening, Miss Elliot," Raine said politely, tipping his cap to her.

"Get the blinis?" Mike asked, his arm around Samantha's waist so tight you would have thought Raine was a pirate trying to kidnap her.

"Yes, sir!" Raine said smartly, clicking his heels together, then preceded them down the stairs and opened the back door for them.

"You're sure you know how to drive this thing?" Mike asked his cousin, obviously doubting his ability to do so. "Frank will kill both of us if you so much as scratch it."

"Who's Frank?" Samantha asked as they got inside.

"My oldest brother."

Once inside the car, Samantha tried her best to sit very still and behave herself, for she was sure that women who wore designer clothes were used to stretch limos and didn't crawl all over them exploring, but Mike laughed at her. "Go on. Frank won't mind."

She opened little doors, looked in cabinets, and turned the TV on and off, then Mike sent a fax to Colorado and received one from his grandfather that said, "Michael, my boy, when are we going to meet your Samantha?"

Wide-eyed, Sam looked at Mike for an explanation as to what his family knew about her, but Mike just shrugged in reply.

After a while she settled back in the seat and thoughtfully looked at Raine so skillfully driving the car. She felt that she was beginning to know Mike and to understand a little about the way his family functioned. "If he's doing this for you, what are you going to do for him?"

"Looking over his portfolio."

"His investment portfolio? Why would he want *you* to do that for him?" She wanted to know more about Mike, for she was finding out that he was good at giving away very little about himself.

"Because none of the Montgomerys knows anything about math." Begrudgingly, he said, "They're okay with words but not with numbers."

"You still haven't answered my question: Why does he want *you* to look at his portfolio?"

"Because I'm good at it, that's why," he answered, and Sam knew that that wasn't really an answer at all.

When they arrived at the nursing home, Mike wouldn't allow her to get out, but made her sit in the car for ten minutes. "I want every one of them to see us," he said, looking out the dark tinted windows through which no one could see at the faces that were peering out at them from the windows of the home.

After a long while, Raine opened the door for them and

Samantha, moving as regally as she felt alighting from such a car, walked ahead of the two men. Mike was wearing his beautiful Italian suit, and Raine, in his chauffeur's uniform, his arms laden, looked like a bored rich girl's dream-come-true. By the time they reached the desk, every mobile person in the nursing home had crowded into the hall to see them. Four women and two men were attached to stands with bottles hanging from them, and one woman was in a wheeled bed pushed by two other women.

With Samantha's arm tucked firmly in his, Mike stopped in front of the plastic-laminated counter and looked at the shapeless nurse behind it. She was obviously the person in charge; she looked so "in charge" that the words may as well have been written across her forehead.

"We're here to see Her Royal—" Mike began, then when he saw Samantha's shocked face, he patted her arm. "I'm sorry, my dear, I know I keep forgetting that she doesn't want anyone to know the truth. What name is she using now?"

Samantha blinked at him.

"Abby?" Mike asked. "Is that the name Her Royal— Oops! I was about to do it again. The princess will *never* forgive me if I reveal her secret." Leaning across the counter, he gave the ugly nurse a look of such lasciviousness that Samantha wanted to hit him. "But I'm sure that you already know all about . . . ah, Abby, don't you?"

The woman blushed like a girl, but it lost something in effect since all the blood rushing to her face made the hairs on her chin stand upright. "O' course. We know about the . . . the princess."

"And you're taking good care of her, aren't you? Not that you need to curtsey, she *hates* all that fuss. When one has a childhood of nurses and nannies curtseying to one, it makes one come to hate such formalities. You understand, don't you? But—"

"Whatever happened to the sapphire bracelet she gave her last nurse?" Samantha asked. Two could play this game. "Remember that nurse who was so nice to her?" Leaning over the counter, she smiled at the nurse in conspiracy, as though what she was saying was just between the two of them, but when Sam spoke she was loud enough to be heard to the far end of the corridor. "Her generosity is going to be the death of this family.

If she tries to give any of her jewelry to the staff, would you please report it to us?"

"W . . . why, yes, of course I will," the nurse answered.

"Now, may we see her?" Mike asked. "Undisturbed?"

"Yes, certainly. Right away. Move it!" she snapped at a man in a wheelchair.

With all the expertise of an experienced doorman, the nurse opened the door to Maxie/Abby's room and closed it behind them.

Abby, half asleep in her bed, looked up and had a moment's trouble focusing. "I . . . I didn't expect to see you two again."

Samantha had the box of pictures in her arms—in fact, she had transferred them into the hatbox that had contained Maxie's dress—and walked briskly forwad. "I've come to ask a favor of you. You're the only person in the world who I can find who knew my grandmother, and I wondered if you would mind going through some old photos with me."

"Photos?"

"Of my family. I know it's a terrible imposition, but I thought you might be able to tell me something, I'm not sure what, but maybe my grandmother might have told you something about herself."

"Why do you want to know about her?"

"Because I love her," Samantha said simply. "And I think she would have loved me if she'd met me. Jubilee said we're very much alike."

"Met him, have you?" Abby was starting to come fully awake.

Stepping forward, Mike put the big picnic basket down on the edge of the bed. "She gets her nose into everything. This morning she was yelling out the window at Ornette, Jubilee's grandson, and—"

"Ornette is Jubilee's great-grandson," Abby said, then made a little face that said she wished she'd kept her mouth shut. To cover herself, she said, "What do you have in there, young man?"

"Sidecars," he said, removing a tall stainless-steel flask from the basket. "And caviar blinis."

For a moment Abby looked as though she were going to cry with a combination of happiness and regret—for she well knew that Samantha should not be there. "You two are fools, you know that?" she said softly, her remark addressed to Michael.

"Yes, ma'am, I know that very well, but Samantha is, as far as anyone can tell, just like her grandmother. Sassy is what Jubilee calls her, and she wanted to show you her photographs, so we're here. She had an idea that if her grandmother were still alive Maxie might like to see what she'd missed, might like to see her son and her daughter-in-law, see her grandchild growing up, and she might like to see her husband as he grew older. Think Maxie would have liked to have seen that?"

"Yes," Abby said softly. "She would have."

"Oh heavens!" Samantha said. "You'd think this was a funeral. We're having a *party!* Michael, pour the drinks and roll those pancakes. And . . ." She hesitated. "I don't know what to call you. If Maxie were alive, what do you think she'd like me to call her?"

"Nana," Abby said instantly. "I think she said that was what she wanted her granddaughter to call her."

"Would you mind very much if I called *you* Nana?"

"I wouldn't mind at all. Now, where is my drink? I haven't had a sidecar in years."

Samantha climbed on the bed beside Abby, pulled the box of photos across her knees, and opened it, while Mike rather awkwardly rolled thin pancakes around red caviar and sour cream, then served them to the two women with crystal glasses of the cognac mixture.

Within thirty minutes all awkwardness between the three of them was gone. After the first drink, Abby got very sloppy at saying that Maxie would like so and so. Instead, she was saying things like, "I remember that. We kept the lawn mower in that old shed. Did Cal ever tear that thing down?"

Mike teased Samantha mercilessly about pictures of her when she was a child, laughing at one where she was obviously furious and hadn't wanted her picture taken. Abby defended Samantha, saying she had been the sweetest baby alive.

Refilling Abby's glass, Mike said in the most mournful tones imaginable that, for all he knew, Samantha was *still* the sweetest baby alive.

"Michael!" Sam snapped.

But Abby took Samantha's side. "You mean, a big, strapping hunk like you hasn't persuaded this dear little thing to go to bed with you yet?"

The words, as well as the sentiment, were so very funny coming out of the mouth of an eighty-four-year-old woman that Sam and Mike laughed uproariously.

"Why does every generation think it's invented sex?" Abby asked in mock exasperation.

"Why don't you tell us about sex in *your* generation?" Mike said encouragingly. "At least, that way, I'd be able to experience *somebody's* fantasies."

"You'll get no lessons from me, Michael Taggert. You'll have to find out on your own."

The evening got more funny when Samantha showed pictures of herself, as promised, nude on a rug. Both Abby and Sam giggled at Mike's heartfelt groans at Sam's "pinup" pictures.

When Raine entered the room, Samantha knew that the party was over and so did Abby. For a long moment, they clung to each other, Samantha's strong, healthy young body holding the frail, weakening body of her grandmother.

"Don't come back," Abby whispered. "I'm not sure it's safe."

Pulling away from her, Samantha acted as though she hadn't heard her. "I'd love to return. Thank you so much for the invitation. Are you ready, Michael?" She left the room without looking back, not seeing Mike kiss Abby's cheek, then slip a piece of paper with his phone number and the private numbers of some of his family members on it into Abby's hand before leaving the room.

On the drive back to the East Side and Mike's town house, Samantha was quiet.

"Enjoy yourself?" Mike asked.

"Mmmmm," was all she answered.

"Are you okay?"

"Certainly. I couldn't be better. It was great spending the evening with my grandmother. I'm just a little tired, that's all. I think I'll go to bed early tonight."

Mike didn't say any more on the ride home and at the house, she went inside while he stayed outside talking to Raine. When he entered the house, Samantha was nowhere to be seen so he assumed she'd gone to bed. For himself, he was a little too wound up to go to sleep, so he fixed himself a sandwich and a beer, took it into the library, and turned on the TV.

Samantha walked in so quietly that he didn't know she was near him until he looked up and saw her standing there, wrapped in his bathrobe, her face shiny clean, looking about twelve years old. He could see that she had something she wanted to say to him. Instantly he turned off the television and looked up at her.

Tentatively, Samantha sat on the edge of the couch a few feet from him.

"Mike," she said hesitantly, looking down at her hands in her lap. "I want to ask you something."

"Sure."

Holding tightly onto her hands to still them, she said, "I look at this house and everything in it and I know it was expensive and I know that you paid for my new clothes and you told my grandmother that your grandfather was a man of some wealth and that you could support a person." After that pauseless sentence, she took a breath, trying to stop her heart from racing, for she was filled with embarrassment at asking for something else from a man who had already given her more than . . . more than was necessary.

She looked up at him. "Mike, do you have any money? I mean, enough that you could spare some?" Her eyes were pleading and apologetic at the same time.

"Yes," Mike said after a moment, but not wanting to elaborate on the answer. He liked thinking that she knew nothing about his finances, because women had dated him for his money. A couple of them had gone so far as to say that they loved him when they meant they loved his money.

"I want to ask a personal favor of you. Will you lend me some money? A few thousand? Ten at most, I think. I'll pay you back whenever I can."

He tried to keep from frowning. "Whatever I have is yours. May I ask what you want the money for?"

"I want to buy some furniture."

"For your apartment?" The words came out sharper than he'd meant them to as he thought of having asked Jeanne to redecorate Sam's apartment.

"No, of course not!" Samantha snapped, annoyed that he thought she was such a frivolous, ungrateful person as to ask him, who had given her so much, for something she didn't need. "It's not for me, it's for my grandmother. I want to make that dreadful room of hers beautiful. I want to buy some pictures for the walls—nice pictures—a chair and a few accesories, but I want them to be of good quality, very good quality. My grandmother used to wear Lanvin and real diamonds and real pearls." Samantha paused for a moment then said very softly, "Maybe we could rent the furniture. She won't need it for very long."

Putting his hands on her shoulders, Mike kissed her hard, a kiss that told her he was proud of her. "We'll buy whatever you want. Tomorrow we'll go shopping at a few antiques stores where they know my sister."

"Michael," she whispered, not meeting his eyes. "I'm so afraid. I don't want to see another person I love die."

Putting his fingers under her chin, he tipped her face up and looked at her in silent question, as though asking her what she needed. Then, as though he knew the answer, he opened his arms to her, not in desire but in warmth and comfort—and perhaps in love.

Without a thought, she moved onto his lap, her body as close to his as possible as she drew her knees into her chest, his big arms wrapping about her, making her feel safe, letting her feel the very aliveness of him. She could feel his heart beating under her cheek, and when she pressed even closer to him, she thought she could feel the blood coursing through his veins.

"Hold me, Michael," she whispered. "Hold me tightly. Let me feel your strength, your . . . health." Her voice was ragged with emotion.

He held her as tightly as he could without breaking her bones, spreading his hands to cover her head and as much of her back as possible. In his mind's eye, he saw what she must have seen: Her grandfather slowly wasting away, gradually moving toward death, then her father eaten by the same illness, dying in her arms exactly as her grandfather had. Now she'd found her last blood link on earth, and Mike well remembered the dry, nearly lifeless skin of the woman, the grayish pallor of her. Death was hovering over Maxie, already pulling at her, trying to take her from earth—and from Samantha.

In spite of how tightly Michael was holding her, Samantha began to tremble.

"Sam!" he said sharply in alarm, but his tone had no effect on her as her trembling increased, so he pulled his hand away from her head and held it in front of her face. "Look at my hand! Do you hear me? *Look* at it!"

Slowly, she lifted her head. She was trembling so violently now that her teeth were almost chattering. She had no idea what Mike was doing as she obediently looked at his hand.

"Strong. Healthy," he said, holding his hand inches from her face. "Alive and well. See it?"

His hand *was* strong, glowing with the health of youth and exercise and just plain love of living. To Mike's utter consternation, she pulled his hand to her face, held his palm to her lips, and breathed deeply, as though reassuring herself that he was indeed alive and was going to stay that way. Moving her head slightly, she put his warm, calloused palm to her cheek, closed her eyes, and rested her head against his chest, listening to the beat of his heart while Mike held her as tightly as he dared.

Holding her as he stroked her back, he wished he could help her, wished that he could take some of her pain away, wished he could stop what they both knew was going to happen. But he could do nothing. No amount of money, no amount of love can stop a person from dying.

Even after Samantha fell asleep in his arms, Mike continued holding her, allowing her to relax against him, wanting to feel her warm little body next to his.

Sometimes, when he thought about how much he loved her, it was almost a physical ache inside him. He was to the point where he could hardly stand to be away from her, as though he were afraid he'd miss one of her smiles or even one of her frowns. It would have been impossible to describe the pleasure he received from watching her blossom, seeing her change from the little rabbit he'd first met to the woman who could yell out the window at someone like Ornette. He liked to see the joy she gave to other people, such as when she kissed Jubilee or when she befriended Daphne or when she climbed onto the bed with Maxie and hugged her.

Yet she terrified him with this continued pursuit of the people who had been involved with Maxie and with her need to know what happened so long ago. Right now Mike wished he'd never heard of Doc, had never heard of Dave Elliot. But if he hadn't, he reminded himself, he wouldn't have met Sam.

In her sleep she relaxed against him, her trust of him complete and absolute. It was this trust that was beginning to drive him insane. For the life of him, Mike couldn't figure out why she wouldn't go to bed with him. He'd asked every question he could think of, investigating her past under a microscope, doing what he could to find answers, to make her talk to him. From the way she reacted when he touched her, he'd have thought she was raped when she was a child or some other traumatic thing had happened to her so that now she couldn't bear a man to touch her.

But Samantha allowed Mike to touch her. Brother! did she allow him to touch her! Hand holding, snuggling, kissing, cuddling together on the couch, she seemed to want to touch him every minute of every day. He was sure that if it were up to her she could perfectly well sleep in the same bed with him every night and not even be tempted to go any further than sleeping in each other's arms.

He had fantasies—awake or asleep he had fantasies about making love to her—but his major fantasy was about persuading her that sex wasn't so bad. He thought about kissing her until she was limp, then gradually going further, but Sam always seemed to read his mind; when sex was his intent, she pushed him away.

Now he was finding that his patience was nearly at an end, for he was beginning to feel that his love for her wasn't going to be returned. From talking to her father and from what Samantha had told him Mike knew that her ex-husband was very different from him, and maybe that's what she needed: a different kind of man. Maybe she could only respond to men like her ex and not men like Mike. Maybe she needed some CPA-type guy: structured, formal, tidy . . . boring.

Maybe, he thought, and his gut twisted at the idea, maybe she thought of him as a "friend." Sometimes women had stupid notions that a sexually healthy man and woman could be platonic friends without the "complications" of sex. Maybe that's what Sam thought about him, thought that they could remain living together in this house as roommates.

Both of these theories had many holes in them, such as why she was so damned jealous of any other woman he so much as glanced at and why she looked at him as though he were a combination of Apollo, Conan the Barbarian, and Merlin. It was an easy guess that a tenant didn't usually look at her landlord with eyes that made him seem as though he could do anything, accomplish anything, become anything.

So why the hell wouldn't she go to bed with him?

At midnight, he picked her up and took her into the bedroom, carrying her as she clung to him as though she were a nine-year-old and he her father. When he put her on the bed, she smiled at him in her sleep. Now what was he supposed to do? Put her jammies on her?

"Samantha," he said, "I'd like to be one of those altruistic, storybook heroes who can undress the heroine without jumping on her bones, but I can't. You'll have to undress yourself and put on your own nightgown. I want to make love to you too much to be able to even look at your bare body and still be able to control myself. I just might turn into that rapist you've always thought I was."

By the end of this speech, her eyes were wide open as she looked up at him standing over her. "Mike, thank—"

But he'd shut the door sharply before she could say the words he'd come to hate..

In the morning, Samantha sensed that Mike was different the moment she walked into the breakfast room where he was seated and looking at the newspaper. He didn't put down his paper and smile at her as he usually did, didn't wink at her as he often did. Instead, he kept the paper in front of him, reaching out for his coffee cup without looking up. When she said good morning, he still didn't look at her.

For a moment she thought he might be angry at her because she'd once again imposed on him, but he'd been so very nice to her last night. Of course Mike was always nice, always kind . . . always the most wonderful human being on the face of the earth, she thought.

Moving to stand behind him, she put her hand on his shoulder. "Mike, about last night—" she began, then to her astonishment, he moved away from her touch. He did not want her to touch him!

Samantha was so stunned by his movement that she had to leave the room. When she returned later, dressed for the day, she hoped she had her facial expression under control. With all the years she'd spent living with her ex-husband, acting, pretending every moment, shouldn't she be good at acting by now?

He was still sitting at the table, still hidden behind the newspaper. "Mike, about last night," she said, this time without touching him. "I didn't mean to impose on you. I didn't mean to ask more of you than you've already given, and, about the money for the furniture, you don't have to lend it to me and—"

"Samantha," he said firmly, "I don't want to hear it. Money is the least of my problems and as soon as I get dressed, we'll go buy Maxie some furniture. We need to get out of the house anyway because my sister is going to be here today and I don't want to be in her way."

With that he left the room, without so much as turning to look at her.

It was a strained day. Usually they talked so much that they tended to talk over the top of each other, but today, there seemed to be nothing to say. Mike did just as he'd promised and took her to Newell's where she saw floor after floor of heavenly antiques, and he took her to the Antiques Mart where they went to shop after shop, but she wasn't having very much fun. Doing her best to think of Maxie and not herself, she bought a couple of pretty bed jackets, a bottle of perfume, and even some earrings, but she could think of little else except that Mike was angry with her.

The worst part of the day was when Mike jumped away from her if she got too close to him, as though he couldn't stand for her to touch him. By the afternoon, Samantha was weary with it all, weary with what was happening now, weary with her memory of the past, for her ex-husband had done the same thing to her. In the beginning of their marriage they had held hands and kissed and had enjoyed touching, but after the first few months he couldn't seem to bear her touching him. Now it was turning out to be the same with Mike. But it was a great deal more understandable with Richard, because she'd been to bed with him. Go to bed with Samantha Elliot, she thought, and be turned off sex with her forever.

By late afternoon she was so nervous that when she accidently touched Mike's hand, she jumped. "I'm sorry," she said. "I didn't mean to touch you. I know you don't want me to touch you. I didn't mean—"

Turning toward her, Mike said, "Oh, Sam, you don't understand at all, do you?" Pulling her into an empty corridor of the Antiques Mart, he drew her into his arms and kissed her sweetly, longingly, her body pinned between the wall and his big, warm torso.

When he drew his lips away from hers, she put her head on his shoulder, her heart beating wildly. "I thought you hated me. I thought—"

He didn't want to hear what she thought, nor did he want to talk about what was bothering him, he didn't want to have to put it into words. "I'm taking you to Blair's and leaving you there because I have to go out tonight and you can't return to the house."

All she could do was nod, so glad that he was again looking at her.

In the taxi he was silent and she wished he'd tell her what was bothering him, but no matter what questions she asked, she couldn't get him to talk. At Blair's apartment building, he practically dropped her at the curb, waiting only to see that she got inside under the care of the doorman.

"You look as though you could use a drink," Blair said as soon as Samantha was inside her apartment, which was small and neat and furnished with comfortable, modern furniture. "You and Mike have a fight?"

"I . . . I think so," she began as she took a seat on Blair's couch. "But, actually, no, we didn't." Looking at Blair, her face showed her distress. "I don't know what's wrong, but Mike's angry at me and I don't know why."

"Sex," Blair said quickly. "With men at this early stage of courtship it's always sex. They think of nothing else."

Taking the gin and tonic Blair held out to her, Samantha grimaced. "It couldn't be sex because there isn't any."

For a moment Blair didn't understand what Samantha was saying, then she laughed. "Poor Mike. I'll bet this is a surprise to him. Since he was a teenager I doubt if any female he's wanted has taken longer than twenty-four hours to fall into bed with him—and that includes high school."

"If he fell into bed with me, he'd never want to see me again," Samantha said heavily.

Blair had been trained as a physician, but right now her experience as a woman was of more use to her, and she could see that something was wrong with Samantha. Viewed from a distance, it was odd that Samantha and Mike weren't spending every minute of every day in bed together, since she'd never seen two people more enraptured with each other. Seeing the two of them together was enough to nauseate a healthy individual. They laughed uproariously at each other's slightest witticisms, got nervous when one left the other alone in a room, making weak excuses to follow. They looked at each other with eyes so big and drippy they'd make a cocker spaniel's eyes seem cruel.

As far as Blair could tell, since Samantha had moved into Mike's house, the two of them hadn't been more than a few feet apart from each other, except for the day Samantha had gone out with Raine and Mike had followed them and been hit over the head with a rock by a passing stranger—a story which Blair didn't believe for a second.

Last night Raine had come by her apartment and told her about driving Mike and Samantha to see Sam's grandmother. Raine had had a good laugh about how besotted his cousin was and said he looked as though he'd walk across fire if Samantha wanted him to—or if he thought it would impress her. "I hope to hell *I* never fall as hard as Mike's fallen," Raine had said. "I think Mike would have gone after me with a shotgun if I'd so much as touched the hem of her skirt, which I wouldn't mind doing given the legs under that skirt. I do rather envy him his nights."

Now Blair was hearing that Sam and Mike had never gone to bed together. It was rather like finding out that Romeo and Juliet had been faking their love for each other.

"Where did Mike go tonight?" Blair asked.

"To find out more about my grandmother," Samantha answered and explained a bit about the note. "He doesn't want me to go with him because I'm not suitable for a bar. You know what he said about me? He said that I have an old mind in a young body. He thinks I'm . . . that I'm the motherly sort, the little church girl. I'll bet Vanessa went to bars with him."

"What do you know about Vanessa?"

"What do *you* know about Vanessa?"

Blair laughed. "Did you know that Vanessa slept with other men while she was going out with Mike and that Mike knew about it and didn't care?"

A bit stunned by that news, Samantha blinked a couple of

times. "Since Mike is the most jealous man in the world, that's a little difficult to believe. He's jealous of Raine and this city and everything that I like that isn't him. Sometimes I think he's even jealous of computers."

"Well, he wasn't jealous with Vanessa. She was a showpiece and she was there when Mike wanted her and left him alone when he didn't want to be bothered. But then, it's my opinion that Vanessa would have done anything Mike wanted, because she liked his money more than she liked him."

"Is Mike wealthy?"

"Yes." Blair was pretending that her attention was on her drink, but actually, she was watching Samantha intently.

"But Raine said all the Taggerts were poor."

"Compared to the Montgomerys, they are. Mike inherited around ten million on his twenty-first birthday, and by now, with his skills at investing, I wouldn't be surprised if he'd tripled the amount."

With a big sigh, Samantha finished her drink. "I was beginning to think that was the case."

Blair laughed at her tone because she sounded as though she'd been told Mike had some great, unchangeable flaw. "Mike's money isn't a tragedy, you know. It gives him a lot of freedom."

"Freedom to have any woman in the world," she said heavily. Blair nearly laughed again. Mike wasn't the only victim of the green-eyed monster. "I think Mike is . . . is . . ."

"You don't have to tell anybody what you think of Mike; it's in your eyes for everyone to see."

"I wish it were on my body," she muttered, then looked up at Blair sharply. "You know what I'd like to do?"

"What?"

"Look like a slut."

"What!?" Blair nearly choked on her drink.

"I think maybe I have some talent as an actress. I put on a dress my grandmother had worn in the twenties and I sort of, well, turned into her. Actually, I was an altogether different person. I sang an old blues song for Mike and I think he was a little shocked, and, truthfully, maybe I was too. Anyway, I wish I could put on a minuscule outfit and high heels and go to this bar and pick up Mike. I couldn't do that as myself, but maybe if I were another person, dressed as another person, I would have some courage. I'm not sure what I'd do with him once I'd picked him up, but—"

"I have every confidence that my oversexed cousin will help you figure out something to do with him. You know, I might have a few pieces of clothing that could be just what you're looking for. How does red lycra sound?"

"Like a leotard."

"This is much smaller than a leotard. In fact, I've seen finger bandages larger than the skirt I have in mind."

"It sounds perfect. Could I see it?"

"Sure. I'll get a magnifying glass and we'll start searching in my closet."

Laughing together, the women headed for Blair's bedroom.

"Would you look at that?" Nelson said, cigarette smoke curling about his head.

Mike didn't turn to look at what had to be the fiftieth girl this creep had declared to be the most sensational creature on earth. Taking a drink of his third beer, Mike leaned toward the skinny little man. "You planning to tell me what you know in this century or not?"

He was sounding belligerent now because he was feeling belligerent. For two hours he'd been here in this sleazy bar trying to buy, sweet talk, bully, whatever he could think to do, information from this old alky. So far, he'd had no luck, and he was beginning to think that the anonymous note-writer at Jubilee's had been lying when he'd hinted that Nelson knew anything.

"She's buying a pack of cigarettes now," Nelson said, his eyes to the right.

Pulling another fifty from his pocket, Mike slipped it across the table. "That's the last of it. You don't tell me anything after this, I'm leaving."

"Keep your shirt on, muscle-boy. Can't you spend a little time with a guy who's down on his luck?"

Nelson was one of those people who had been born down on his luck. No doubt he'd found something wrong in his childhood, his mother spoke too sharply to him or some such, and now he used it as an excuse to wallow in grief and spend his life in bars cadging drinks. He was little, thin, dirty, and weasly looking, and he felt the world owed him a life.

"I guess you got better things to do than sit here with the likes of me." His voice was a self-pitying whine. "Maybe you got somebody at home waiting for you." The implication was that Nelson didn't have anyone and that's why he was so unhappy and had to drink and make those marks shooting whatever it was into the inside of his arm.

"Yeah, I got somebody," Mike said, and thought of Samantha, of the pure cleanliness of her, and right now he very much wanted to be at home with her. Jeanne should be finished with her apartment by now, and Mike wanted to show it to Sam, to see her face when she saw it. Maybe, when she saw the rooms, she'd be so happy that she'd turn to him, throw her arms around him, he'd kiss her, then—

Nelson was snapping his fingers in front of Mike's face. "You leavin' me, boy? My God, but I think she's comin' this way. You gotta see her. Real Classy. And a body like I've never seen before."

At one time Mike might have been interested in seeing this woman, at least in looking, if in nothing else, but he wasn't interested in anything that patronized this dive.

"One of you boys have a light?" came a deep, sultry voice from Mike's left. With a grimace, he picked up a book of matches from the ashtray, struck one, and turned to light the woman's cigarette.

What he saw made him freeze. Samantha, sweet, perfect, innocent little Samantha, was dressed in a red-sequined tank top that was cut so low in the front that he could see nearly all of her breasts, and she wore a tight red skirt that, as far as he could tell, covered nothing whatsoever. All eight or so feet of her legs were showing beneath the "skirt."

When she bent forward, he could see the deep, exquisite cleavage made by her large, round, beautiful breasts—the same cleavage that all the bums in this place could see. Samantha put her hand over Mike's to hold the tip of the cigarette to the match flame. Lighting it, she stood, her hips thrust out, and looked down at him, fluttering her lashes a bit. "Mind if I sit down?"

Too intent on gawking at her to pay attention to the flame, Mike dropped the match when it burned down to his fingertips.

"Sit by me, baby," Nelson said eagerly. "You're new in here, aren't you? Who you work for?"

Holding the cigarette between her two fingers, her elbow resting on her hip, Samantha looked down at Mike. "You going to invite me to sit down or not?"

"I'm going to kill you," he said under his breath, but he moved over on the seat so she could sit by him.

When she was seated she tried to take a draw on the cigarette, but since she'd never smoked in her life, she gave a couple of very unseductresslike coughs.

Angrily, Mike took the cigarette from her. "Just what do you think you're playing at?" He started to stub the cigarette out in the ashtray, but on second thought, he put it to his lips and took a very deep draw, a draw that burned the cigarette half way down to his lips.

"Mike, I didn't know you smoked."

"I don't," he said tightly, letting out the smoke slowly. "I quit two years ago, but then there's a lot you don't know about me. A few more weeks around you and I may take up drinking."

"Ditto," she said, looking him in the eyes.

"Mike," Nelson said, "looks like you two know each other. You wanta introduce me or you gonna keep her all night? You can't keep her *all* night, can you?"

"You hear that, Samantha? Nelson thinks you're a prostitute."

Leaning toward Mike, she let her lips come near his. "And what do *you* think I am?" she practically purred.

"All show," he said, drinking the last of his beer. "Let's get out of here."

Samantha was not going to leave yet. If she went home with him now, nothing would have changed. For whatever reason he was angry at her, he was still angry. Signaling the waitress to come to the table, she ordered a double shot of tequila gold. "And a quartered lime and a Dos Equis if you have it, and do you have some salsa and chips?"

Before Mike could say another word, a man came to the table and asked Samantha to dance with him. "I'd love to," she said, starting to get up, but Mike put his hand on her shoulder, holding her on the seat. "I guess not," Samantha said to the man apologetically.

When her drinks came, she turned to Nelson. "So what do you know about my grandmother? I assume you are Nelson, aren't you?" Well aware of Mike's eyes on her, Samantha knew that he realized she had to have looked inside his wallet to have seen the note.

"Not as much as I'd like to know about you, baby," Nelson answered in what was meant to be a provocative manner.

Mike was still looking at Samantha, waiting for her to turn to him, but she didn't. Instead, with all the ostentation, all the sexiness she could manage, she made a fist of her left hand, slowly licked the web of it, poured salt on the wet place, sensually licked the salt away, then lustily tossed back the tequila in one shot, after which she juicily bit into a lime wedge.

"Lord help us," Nelson whispered, but Mike didn't say a word, just kept looking at her profile.

Picking up a chip, she reached out to the bowl of salsa.

"Careful of that!" Nelson warned. "Paddy's stuff is lava."

Samantha scooped a lot of the salsa on the chip and ate it while Nelson watched in awe. "In Santa Fe we'd feed this to the babies," she drawled as she drank some of the dark brown Mexican beer. "Let me give you some advice, Nelson. If someone in Santa Fe warns you that something is hot, be careful, but if a New Yorker says it's hot, laugh."

"That's enough," Mike said, grabbing her upper arm and pulling her out of the bench. Leading her onto the dance floor, he surrounded her in his arms and began a slow dance. "What are you trying to do? Out-macho the guys? If that's your goal, you've done it."

Rubbing her hips against his, a very serious look on her rather heavily made up face, Samantha said, "Do you think Nelson is the type of person who really *cares* about the South American rain forests?"

"What's wrong with you? And who gave you that getup you have on?"

"Don't you like it?"

"Not on you."

"Want to take it off?"

Holding her at arm's length, he looked into her eyes. "How much have you had to drink?"

"Not much." She put her head back down on his shoulder. "Mike, why have you been angry at me today?"

Her words made him soften, or maybe it was the feel of her in his arms, with her hips moving with his, her breasts rubbing against his chest, or maybe it was the sight of her in this outfit that wouldn't have adequately covered a three-year-old, but he couldn't remember why he'd been angry at her. "Ahhh, sweetheart."

She seemed to melt into him further. "You haven't called me anything but Samantha all day. No Sam-Sam or anything else."

"You're killing me, you know that? You're driving me insane. I think we ought to talk about where we stand with each other."

"Isn't that what the female is supposed to say? Then you're supposed to say that you don't want to commit, then I say—"

"Why don't you shut up?" He was becoming involved in the slow undulations of the dance now, his hands moving up and down her back, fingers edging down over her buttocks. For all that either of them were aware of the other people in the bar, they may as well have been alone.

"Do you have any idea how much I want you?"

"I feel some of it right now."

"Don't laugh at me, Samantha."

"Oh, Mike, I'm sorry, it's just that . . ."

"What?" he said rather sharply. "What is it? Tell me!"

Pulling away from him, she went back to the table, downed the last of her beer, and turned to leave. It had been a mistake dressing up like a tart and trying to entice Mike, because under the sexy clothes, she was still plain ol' Samantha Elliot, not a femme fatale. She may have been able to turn herself into a chanteuse while wearing Maxie's clothes, but even Blair's micromini couldn't make her unafraid of sex, unafraid of ruining everything she had with Mike.

As she turned away from the table, Nelson shoved a piece of paper at her that contained a name and a telephone number. "Call Walden," he said. "He can tell you lots about Maxie."

Taking the paper, shoving it into her bra—where it itched—she nodded and turned away.

Mike caught her elbow. "You're not going without me." He didn't say another word as he pulled her outside.

But Mike had other ways of communicating besides words. One minute they were standing on the curb waiting for a taxi and the next Mike had pulled her into the alley beside the bar, his arms going about her as he hungrily began kissing her neck. After the first moment of his passion, Samantha tried to move away from him. When Mike didn't seem to understand that she didn't want him to touch her, she had to use force to push away.

Mike, utterly and absolutely frustrated, as well as confused, leaned back against the brick of the building wall, his hands raised above his head, palms out, as though he were nailed to the wall. "Why?" he asked. "Why, Sam? What is it that you have against me? Was that husband of yours so great in bed that you want to enshrine him? You can't think of another man besides him?"

At that Samantha laughed, and Mike, his face full of anger at thinking she was laughing at him, started to move away from the wall, but Samantha leaned toward him. She'd had too much to drink, first at Blair's apartment and now here, and her slightly inebriated state made her dare to do things that she would not do otherwise.

Almost as though to tease her, his shirt was open halfway to his waist, and now she put her hands inside it, touching his skin. Mike was angry, seriously angry, she knew that, and he didn't respond to her touch, but kept his hands against the wall as he watched her.

"You don't understand, Mike," she said softly.

"Then why don't you explain it to me." There was no softness in his voice.

Since she'd first met him, Samantha'd had a nearly uncontrollable desire to touch him. Now, sliding her hands inside his shirt, she felt the sculptured muscle across his chest. Some women looked at the bodybuilders on TV or on a beach and thought they were too muscular, but not Samantha. When she was in Santa Fe and leading her aerobics classes, there were times when the men in the free-weight side of the room so distracted her that she missed her rhythm. One evening a man named Tim, who had performed in bodybuilding competitions, was squatting five hundred pounds. With two men at either end of the bar, which bowed under the weight of the plates, Tim did a deep knee bend with the full five hundred pounds. After he'd completed his squat, the women in Samantha's class had burst into laughter, because Samantha had been so engrossed in Tim that she'd forgotten to lead the exercises. Embarrassed, Samantha had given her attention back to the women.

Now, she was touching one of those muscled men, one of those godlike creatures who looked as though he could lift buildings with his hands.

"How much do you squat, Mike?" she whispered.

"Six fifty," he answered, having no idea why she should ask something like that now. His friends, the ones who'd been to college, pretended that Mike's power lifting didn't exist. Their attitude was, Mike's got a brain in spite of the fact that he's got some muscle.

"Bench press?" She was running her hands over his chest, around toward his back, feeling his lats, the muscles that made his back so very wide, made it curve.

Mike didn't move from the wall, nor did he make any motion to touch her, for he didn't want to scare her away. If his acquiescence was what she needed to get her to touch him, then he would remain in one position if it killed him. "Four fifty," he answered.

His shirt was old and soft and the buttonholes were loose, and when she touched the buttons, they slipped out of the holes, opening the shirt to his waist. Samantha's hands slipped lower, down to his stomach, his hard, rippled stomach.

"Dead lift?" she whispered, meaning the lift where he picked up a weight from the floor to his waist.

"Seven hundred. Strength has to do with bone density and the bones of the people in my family are a bit more dense than the average Joe's. Look, Sam, if you want stats—"

She kept rubbing her hands over his skin. How long had it been since she had really touched a man? For that matter, had she ever really touched one? She had certainly never wanted to touch one as much as she had wanted to touch Mike since the first day she'd looked into his dark eyes, since she'd first felt his lips next to her own. "I want to explain to you."

"Yeah, well, I'm listening." His voice was ragged, as though he were under great strain, but he still had his hands up, away from her. Had anyone seen them, they would have seen what looked to be a man being held at gunpoint by a woman.

"It's me, not you. Don't you understand that? At first I was afraid of you." Her hands were at his waist, moving toward his back, moving over all that muscle that had not an ounce of fat over it. "Well, maybe not afraid, but I didn't want anything to do with another man."

"You've made that abundantly clear. Sam, you want to say what you have to say? I don't know how much more of this I can stand."

"I don't want to ruin what we have between us." Sliding her

hands up his chest to his shoulders, she moved down over the tops of his arms. In another minute she would have the shirt completely off him. His skin felt so very good, so warm, so smooth, so strong, skin that was tightly draped over yards of heavy muscle. She would have liked to put her lips to his skin, to taste it. Was it salty from the sweat of dancing?

"What *do* we have between us?" His voice was harsh, strained, and he closed his eyes for a moment. All his life girls had been easy for him, but the girl he'd most wanted, Sam, seemed to be impossible. She made him think appalling thoughts of taking her out on a lonely road and forcing her, but he knew he'd never be able to live with himself afterward—but, more importantly, neither would she.

"All the sweetness," she said. "We have kindness and talk and friendship. We laugh together. Do things together. We—"

Abruptly, Mike moved his hands down from the wall and put them on her shoulders as he looked into her eyes, searching them. "You think all that will end if we go to bed together?"

She liked him when he stood still and allowed her to touch him, but she wasn't drunk enough to not know the truth. "Mike, if you went to bed with *me,* it would end," she said in disgust. "I'm rotten at sex."

For a moment Mike stood still, not at first understanding what she'd just said, then the first bud of enlightenment came to him. "Yeah, I bet you are," he said softly, then slipped her arm through his. "Too bad they don't have a piece of software to teach sex, then you could learn all the right moves and positions." For the first time in a week he felt good because he understood now, knew what her problem was—but, best of all, he knew how to fix the problem. Never in his life, through many years of mathematics, had he looked forward to a solution more than he did now.

Leading her toward the street, he put up his hand for a cab.

Samantha giggled. "That's a great idea, Mike. Who can we get to write the software program?"

When a taxi stopped, Mike opened the door for her. "I might have some ideas of what could be put in your software."

"Do you, Mike? What research books did you read?"

"I made up my own positions," he said companionably. "My own positions, my own motions, even my own feelings. I've never read one book on sex."

As Samantha got into the cab, she moved to the far side of the seat. "I have. I've read many, many books on the subject."

"Oh? And who asked you to read these books?"

"Richard. He said they might help me." Turning, she looked at him in the dim light from the streets, but his face was turned away. He was staring straight ahead, as though he didn't want to look at her. "Do you understand now?"

"Yes," he said softly. "I now understand everything."

He didn't say another word to her on the ride back uptown to his town house, and with every click of the cab meter, Samantha grew more depressed. She shouldn't have told him. What was that saying? Better to allow people to think you're a fool than to open your mouth and remove all doubt. Well, she'd opened her mouth and told Mike about her sex life. He'd said she was all show and she *was*. She could dress the part of a woman of the night, but she didn't know how to act the part.

By the time they reached the house, she was planning what she'd say to Mike, that she'd move out in the morning—that is, if he didn't want her to leave tonight—and she was sorry she'd cost him so much in time and money and inconvenience.

Very calmly Mike paid the driver, unlocked the front door, allowed her to go inside, then locked the door behind them.

"Mike," she began, ready to recite the little speech she'd prepared, but Mike didn't give her a chance, for he began to stalk her—stalking being the only way to describe the stealthy, predatory way he moved toward her. "Mike? Are you all right?"

"All this time I thought it was men you didn't like. There were times when I thought the problem was me, that I turned you off, but you never turned away from me when I touched you—unless I seemed to want more."

"Of course not." Backing up, she moved toward the living room. "Mike, you frighten me when you look at me like that."

"Like hell I do. I'm not sure *anything* frightens you. You aren't afraid of me, not in the normal sense, anyway." He narrowed his eyes at her. "You're afraid men won't like you."

Samantha could feel herself turning red from the tip of her toes to her hairline. Maybe in the red dress he wouldn't notice the color of her skin. "You are the most stupid man," she said, trying to sound nonchalant, trying to make it sound as though she were in control. "Just because I turn down your advances you start to play psychologist and decide that I think men don't like me. Ha!"

"You don't just turn me down, you turn down *all* men."

"I'd rather be safe than—" She stopped talking because she was now up against the east wall of the living room.

Standing very close in front of her and not allowing her to get around him, Mike leaned closer. "Why did you divorce your husband?"

"I hardly think that's any of your business." When she tried to move away from him, he put one hand on the wall on each side of her head.

"Why, Sam?"

"It's not—"

"Maybe it's not any of my business, but you're going to tell me anyway."

"Incompatibility," she said quickly, but was not able to meet his eyes.

"You're a bad liar."

"Unlike you. You can lie—"

"Why, Sam?"

"He . . ."

"He what?"

"He had another woman!" she flared at him.

"Then he was a fool," Mike said softly. "Why would he want another woman when he could have you?"

She looked away from him, but there was gratitude for his words in her eyes. "I've told you, so please move your hands."

"Yes, I'll move my hands," he answered as he grabbed her into his arms and began kissing her. Using all her strength, she tried to get away from him, but he held her to him. "What happened to you, Sam?"

"Leave me alone, please," she whispered, not looking at him.

"Did you turn to him in the night, but he wanted nothing to do with you?" As he spoke, she still struggled against him. "The bastard. He was all worn out from someone else, wasn't he?"

Ceasing her struggles, she glared up at him. "Yes. Yes, yes, yes. Is that what you wanted to hear? He slept with her twice a day, but he never touched me. Me, the sexless one. I'm the cook, the cleaner, the little money-maker, but I'm not—" When she couldn't continue, Mike kissed her. "No, please let me go."

"Why should I let you go?"

"Because I don't want—"

"Don't want to make love with me? Like hell you don't. You've wanted me from the first day we met, but you've acted as though you hated me. I didn't—"

His words were silenced as his hands roamed over her body, over her breasts, down her thighs, her throat, her arms, between her legs. But Samantha stood still, rigid, unmoving, willing herself not to respond to him.

"How long can you hold out against me, Sam? If I do this?" Bending his head, he kissed the top of her breasts, and it was no difficult matter to pull the stretchy fabric down over one breast as he gently took the peak in his mouth. "Or this?" Moving his mouth downward, he caressed her breast with his thumb.

"Please . . ." she whispered, eyes closed, head back against the wall.

"Please what? Tell me what you want. I'll do anything you want, anything."

"Then let me go."

"Anything but that." His lips moved down her body, down to her waist, then back up to her face while his hand moved under her top, his long fingers on the skin of her stomach. "Please, Sam. Don't hold back."

"I can't."

Kissing her ear, one hand on her breast, the other inching up her thigh, his hand slowly moved up under her skirt. "What do you want? Tell me. Gentle? Sweet?"

Suddenly, he pulled away from her and looked at her face, at her closed eyes, at the expression of control she was wearing, as though she was determined to contain herself.

"No," he said. "You want what I want: Sam, I need you."

At that he grabbed the front of her panty hose and pulled at the same time that he somehow managed to unfasten his trousers and drop them to the floor.

It was at the feel of Mike's hands on her bare flesh that made Sam's years of pent-up desire come to the surface. One moment she was standing still, unresponsive, self-contained, and the next her hands and mouth seemed to be everywhere on him, tasting his skin, licking, sucking, clawing.

For just a moment, he was startled by her, startled by her sheer hunger, then his mouth was on hers, his hands grabbing at her, responding to her with the same need that she was exhibiting.

Abruptly, Samantha stopped moving as a sense of déjà vu overtook her. Looking up at Mike, she half expected him to be Richard and to be wearing that bored look, that half-asleep look, that Richard had always worn when they were in bed together. But he wasn't her ex-husband, this man was Michael, and the expression on his face was of desire and longing and need and . . . caring, caring that she receive as well as give. He looked like she felt.

Understanding her thoughts, Mike said, "It's me, Michael Taggert," as he grabbed a handful of her hair and pulled her head back to apply his teeth and lips to her throat. "And I'm a different man."

When he picked her up to set her down on his manhood, Samantha nearly cried out, but she wrapped her legs about his waist, locked her ankles, and hung on as he pounded into her, her back against the wall. Stroke after deep, deep stroke, she held on, her nails biting into the skin of his back, her mouth sucking on whatever part of him she could reach.

When he finished and gave her one last thrust before limply collapsing against her, his head on her shoulder, she almost screamed in frustration, but she kept her noises to herself and hugged him to her.

Pulling away from her, Mike looked into her face as though searching for an answer. "Sorry, baby, I wanted you too much. The next one is yours."

Although she had absolutely no idea what he meant, she liked it when he kicked his trousers off and carried her up to the bedroom to stand her by the side of the bed. She liked it when he undressed her and kissed her breasts. When he removed his shirt and held her, skin to skin, he kept looking at her, as though he expected something from her.

At last, frustrated because she had no idea what he wanted, she said, "Michael, I don't know what to do. I don't know how."

"Baby, there *is* no how. There's no right or wrong, except maybe making your partner feel bad."

"I don't want to displease you. I want—"

Very gently, he kissed her breast. "You like that?"

"Yes. Yes, very much."

"Tell me if I do something you don't like."

Kissing her all the while, he ran his hands over her thighs, but he still seemed to want answers that she didn't have. "But *I* like *all* of it," she said at last.

Halting, hands on her hips, Mike looked at her in disbelief. "You're afraid you'll do something to me that *I* won't like?" His incredulousness sounded in his voice."Okay, try me. Start touching, start kissing. Whatever you want to do to me, you may. I'm yours."

Anyone else might have laughed at his words, but not Sam. Years of Richard saying, "Not *there*. Men don't like to be touched *there*." Or, "That's not the way to touch a man, don't you know *anything?* Most women your age know this stuff. Why don't you?" had made her wary. Her ex-husband had made her shy and uncertain from years of trying to remember his rules.

"I . . . I guess I would like to touch you." When Mike just stood there staring at her, she said, "Is that all right?"

Mike kissed her softly. "And people doubt if there's a heaven. There is and it's here in this room. I'm yours, baby."

Holding her hand while she remained standing, he stretched out on the bed, but Samantha couldn't look at him. The front of him was too . . . too intimate, too private, and his eyes kept watching her. Seeming to read her mind, he turned over, face down, so she could look at him in comfort.

Tentatively reaching out, she ran her hand over his shoulder. There was one dim lamp on in the room, and it made Mike's honey-colored skin glow. With his face turned away from her she could look at him to her heart's content, look at and touch the full, long, nude, muscular length of him.

He was the most perfectly formed man she'd ever imagined. He was movie stars, men in underwear commercials, guys at the gym, the construction worker in the red T-shirt who'd whistled at her but she'd pretended she hadn't heard; he was the men in three-piece suits whose brains were as sexy as their bodies; he was lazy, insolent seventeen-year-old boys whose muscles bulged out of their clothes, rodeo stars, and those smooth-cheeked, eyeglassed men who held their children tenderly. He was all of them.

Running her hands over his body while he lay still, so still he might have been asleep, she began to kiss the back of him. When her lips had kissed him from the nape of his neck to the soles of his feet, she straddled his legs and began rubbing her hair over his skin. Stretching out on top of him so she could feel her breasts on his skin, she fit her torso into the hills and valleys of his body.

Somewhere along the way she stopped thinking about him as a person, even about whether she pleased him or not, and began to think only of herself. Remembering seeing that soft bit of skin where his legs joined his buttocks, that hairless, enticing little patch that she'd once seen in the mirror when he'd walked away from her, she hadn't realized then that she'd wanted to kiss that bit of skin. So now she did kiss it: kissed it, sucked on it, ran her tongue over it while Michael lay absolutely still.

It was some time later when Samantha lay beside him, her body vibrating, her breath short and shallow. She wanted him, wanted him inside her, but she was afraid to tell him so. Once, after she and her ex-husband were first married, she'd asked, "Could we do that again?" Instantly he had become furious, telling her that she was saying he was a bad lover. "Don't you know anything? Men *can't* right away. It's physically impossible."

Now, she was timid with Michael, not wanting to insult him or make him angry. "Michael," she said softly, but it was difficult to control her voice. "I was wondering if maybe, we could, well, possibly, do that again—if you can, that is."

With the fury of a storm at sea, Mike roused from his seeming acquiescence to jump on her, his hands on her hips, fingers digging into muscle and skin, as he slammed into her so hard she was sure he'd loosened a couple of back teeth. Samantha saw stars.

Mike halted instantly, hovering over her, looking as though he was afraid he'd killed her. "Sam, baby, are you okay? Did I hurt you?"

Samantha blinked up at him in surprise. "Golly, Michael, I think you *can.*"

"Imp," he said as he stretched out on his back and pulled her on top of him.

In the manuals she'd been given, Samantha had read about different positions, but missionary was the sum total of her experience. Sitting on Mike, she looked down at him with an expression of, Now what do I do?

Lacing his fingers, Mike put his hands behind his head and gave her a look of, You figure it out.

Samantha did.

~

Lying still beside Mike, her skin sweaty, every muscle in her body limp, Samantha smiled dreamily. "What was that?"

There was a little smugness in Mike's voice when he spoke. "Sam, my dear, you have just experienced what is commonly known as an orgasm. Like it?"

She chuckled. "Michael, had I known you were capable of producing such an effect, on the first day I met you I would have grabbed you by the neck, pulled you into the house, and had my way with you on the foyer floor."

"Then we would have been in perfect accord, because that's just what I had in mind for you."

"Ahhh, but would you have respected me in the morning?"

"Speaking of respect, we have two alternatives now: One, we can snuggle together and go to sleep or, two, we can fill the tub with hot water, put in some of your smelly stuff, wash every nook and cranny of each other's bodies, get out, dry each other off, come back in here and I can give you what I think will probably be your very first lesson in oral sex."

Opening her eyes just a bit, Samantha gave a jaw-cracking yawn and said, "I'm awfully tired, Mike. Maybe we should sleep." His face fell, making him look like a boy who'd just been told that he wouldn't get to go to the circus after all. Yawning again, she scratched her ribs. "On the other hand, I could use a bath."

He had her in the bathroom before she could say another word.

It was in the bathtub that Mike asked her why she'd waited so long before going to bed with him. He tried to make his question sound as though the answer didn't matter to him, but she wasn't fooled by his tone.

"Richard told me I wasn't any good at sex and that's why he had to go to another woman."

"And you believed him?" Mike sounded as though he thought she were the dumbest person in the world.

"How the hell was I to know that he wasn't telling me the truth?" she fairly shouted at him. "He'd been to bed with lots of women; I'd been to bed with him and only him. What was I supposed to do, get a second opinion? Was I supposed to go to a bar or somewhere, pick up a man, go to bed with him, and find out whether I was actually bad in bed or not? Let me tell you something, Mr. Confidence, when you believe you're not desirable to men, you bloody well *aren't* desirable."

It was later, after the extraordinary success of Mike's very special lesson, that he asked her more questions about her ex-husband. Now, rather like boxers resting between rounds, Samantha snuggled her cheek on Mike's bare chest.

"You want to tell me about your ex-husband?" he asked.

"No."

"Um-hmm."

"What does that mean?"

"It means that I've never yet met a woman who could resist telling anyone who'd listen what a jerk her ex-boyfriend or ex-husband was."

Lifting her head, Sam glared at him, but he pushed her head back down. For a moment her pride and her wish to talk warred with one another. She didn't want to tell him about her marriage or her divorce because they both made her feel like a failure, but at the same time she'd like to tell someone the truth—not the sugar-coated version she'd told her father, but the *truth*. Spilling her guts won out over pride.

"The first two years my marriage was all right, I guess. We never had any great passionate affair, but we learned to adjust to each other. Richard had a partnership with two other men in a CPA firm, and I worked at ComputerLand.

"Everything was fine, I thought, but one day he came home and told me he was profoundly unhappy. Profoundly. Not very unhappy or extraordinarily unhappy but *profoundly* unhappy. He went on to say that the reason he was unhappy was because he had always wanted to write the Great American Novel, and he knew he wasn't going to get to because he had to spend all his time earning a living."

She shook her head. "I was shocked. It was the first time I'd heard of this great ambition of his, and I felt guilty because I'd lived with the man for two whole years and had no idea he wanted to do anything except calculate people's taxes. We sat up all that night and talked."

Pausing, she thought about that night. "I think that night was the closest we ever were before or at any time afterward. We made a bargain that night that for one year I was to support the two of us while he devoted his time to writing. Part of the bargain was that he was to take care of the house since I'd be holding down two jobs."

She couldn't seem to keep her anger from rising. "I don't know what happened. It started out all right, but then I'd come home from work and the kitchen would still be a mess from breakfast, so I'd clean it up before going to my evening job at the spa, then the laundry would pile up so I'd wash it on Sunday. By the end of a year I was doing everything—housework, earning the living, everything. But I didn't mind because every Sunday afternoon Richard would read me descriptive passages from the marvelous book he was constantly working on. He'd never tell me the plot, he'd just read me those elegant, isolated paragraphs."

She had to take a breath before going on. "We used to talk about what we were going to buy and where we were going to go when he received his multmillion dollar advance for the book. Planning our future helped make me feel less tired so that I didn't mind doing housework and earning the living."

As Mike stroked her hair, she realized that the time with Richard was beginning to fade in her mind. "But the agreed-upon year turned into eighteen months, then into two years, and by the end of two years I was so tired I'm not sure I was even alive."

Mike felt her body tense as she continued speaking. "But then one day I was at the store and received a call from my father's neighbor."

Mike didn't say anything, but he had been with Dave then. He was the one who had persuaded Dave to allow the neighbor to call Sam.

"The neighbor told me my father was dying, and when I heard, I just wanted to go home to Richard and have him hold me." She gave a little snort of derision. "When I heard the news of my father's impending death, I thought I'd reached my breaking point.

"Anyway, when I got home Richard wasn't there. I must have been a little frantic because I began searching through his desk looking for something that might tell me where he'd gone. When that turned up nothing, I went to his bookshelves. Looking back on it, I think Richard must have thought I wouldn't dare look at *his* books because he hadn't gone to a lot of trouble to hide his conspiracy. The books had markers in them and passages highlighted. One by one I read all the passages he'd read to me during the Sunday afternoons. Not one of them had been written by him, all of them were by other writers."

She took a breath. "By the time I figured out that he hadn't been writing, I wanted to know what he had been doing for those two years, so I looked at his computer. One of the first things he'd asked me to do when I'd set it up for him was to show him how to encode his files so a person had to know a password to read them. It took me only seven words to find his password—the name of a dog he'd had when he was a boy—and I looked to see what he'd been writing."

She took a while before going on, and Mike didn't say a word, just waited patiently for her to continue. "On the screen was a detailed diary of his sexual liaisons with the woman who used to be his secretary. To this day, Mike, I don't understand why he chose her over me. I don't want to sound vain, but I'm better looking than she is and a great deal more intelligent, and I have a sense of humor whereas she has none. I still don't understand it. I tried very, very hard to please Richard. I tried to give him whatever he wanted. Where did I fail?"

"When did he give you the sex manuals to read?"

"Oh, that. I put my foot in my mouth. After we'd been married a few months, we went to see a movie—I don't remember what it was—but afterward I thoughtlessly said that I didn't understand what all the fuss was about, as sex was so boring. Richard said that maybe our sex lives wouldn't *be* so boring if I just knew a little about sex."

"And how did you do at your jobs? Successful?"

She smiled. "Yes. I was always being promoted at ComputerLand, and at the spa they had me teach the instructors."

"And how was Richard's CPA business?"

"I see what you're getting at. He did all right for a while, but then he lost some clients and I think his partners were planning to get rid of him."

"Sounds to me like you terrified him."

She sighed. "You know, that did occur to me a few times. I learned to tell him only of my setbacks and my frustrations. He'd listen to my account of something that had gone wrong, then lecture me about how I *should* have done so and so, and afterward he'd be nice to me for days. I kept promotions to myself, but he saw them reflected in my paychecks."

"Maybe this other woman looked up to him, thought he was her big, strong hero."

"Jackrabbits would seem brainy to that woman. I used to spend Friday afternoons trying to help Richard by teaching her how to run the office, how to answer the phone by saying something other than, 'Yeah, what'd'ya want?' She was stupid, plain, thick-waisted, thick-ankled, and never washed her hair. She was rude and tasteless and couldn't comprehend a joke—and she took *my* husband away from me. When we were getting the divorce, Richard said she was a great deal better in bed than I was. He said that plastic dolls were better in bed than I was."

"And he knew that from experience?"

Samantha giggled. "Maybe a doll would give him someone pretty to look at now and then. Oh, Mike, I don't understand it. Why would someone want to hear of the failures but not the successes of someone they loved? I knew Richard was frustrated in his job. That's why I agreed to support us and give him a chance at big-time success, but he never even *tried* writing. I don't think he so much as wrote a single chapter. He used the two years to ski and play tennis and . . . and . . ."

"Bang his secretary."

"Yes! If he disliked me, why didn't he just ask me for a divorce, *then* have an affair? Why did he have to make me so miserable?"

"Maybe he thought it was fair to make you unhappy since you were making him wretched."

"Me? But I did *everything* for him. I supported him, cooked for him, cleaned for him, ironed his shirts, hand-washed his sweaters—"

"You did all that and *still* managed to be a success at *two* jobs? It's a wonder he didn't kill you."

"You're taking his side!" she half shouted as she started to move away from him.

But he pulled her back to him. "Your ex-husband was a stupid, frightened coward, and his lifelong punishment is that he lost you."

She hugged him, kissed his shoulder. "Oh Mike. I tried so hard to be what he wanted me to be."

When Mike spoke, there was a definite whine in his voice. "You don't try very hard with me. You haven't hand-washed anything for me, and I didn't even know you *could* iron."

She didn't laugh in return but was utterly serious. "As far as I can tell, all you want from me is laughter and sex."

"Found out at last. Meet Michael Taggert, the personification of shallowness."

Looking up at him, her eyes were filled with what she felt for him. "No, Michael, you're not shallow. Richard was shallow. Shallow and superficial and petty. You . . . you know how to love."

As he kissed the top of her head, he put his hand on her bare breast. "Especially right now. Wanta play 'sit on the tent pole'?"

"Not *again?*" she said, giggling. "I don't know if I'm ready again so soon."

"Want me to talk you into it?"

"Yes, please," she said politely, sounding as though she were asking for a second watercress sandwich. "If you wouldn't mind, that is."

But Michael had his mouth full and couldn't speak.

Samantha woke after only about an hour's sleep, but she'd never felt better in her life. She had to pry her body from under Mike's, lifting his sleep-heavy arms and legs from over her body before slipping out of the bed. Taking the robe she'd appropriated from the back of the bathroom door, she slipped it on and started to leave the room. But she turned back to stand beside the bed, looking down at him as he slept, limbs sprawled across the sheets, relaxed.

Her life was changed now, she thought. Changed forever. Irrevocably changed.

Last night with Mike had changed her, had made her feel freer inside than she had ever felt. Smiling down at him, she realized that she had been changing from the first moment she'd met Mike. The prim, frightened little mouse who'd ridden in her first cab was not the same woman who had done the incredible things she'd done with Mike last night.

It was odd that she was one way with her ex-husband and another with Mike. Richard had not approved of Samantha when she'd laughed too loud or been exuberant about anything, whether she was happy about a promotion or a book she was reading or anything at all. Maybe Mike was right and her being anything but sedate frightened Richard.

For a moment Samantha leaned over the bed and touched Mike's hair. She didn't frighten Mike because he was sure of himself, sure of who he was and what he was, and Samantha's vitality pleased him rather than scared him.

A curl of his hair twined about her fingers. If angels were real, she thought, they'd have hair just like Michael's.

Smiling at her own sentimentality, she left the room to go upstairs to her apartment to get some clothes.

The first thing she noticed about her apartment was that the door Mike had put his foot through had been replaced, but she'd known he was going to have it done so it didn't surprise her. After opening the door, she halted, thinking she was in the wrong room and turned away, but then she turned back. Of course this was her apartment, she told herself, but it was now very different.

The walls of the living room were still dark green but now the curtains were of cream-colored chintz printed with big dark pink roses gathered on a ribbon of green the exact shade of the walls. A fat club chair, upholstered in the same chintz, was next to a large couch covered in a rose pink the same shade as the roses in the chintz. An Aubusson rug picked up the pink and green of the furniture. Behind the couch was a long, narrow table of light-colored wood, marquetry baskets on the leaves and the top. Two black paper-mâché sewing tables, their surfaces wrinkled with age, were at either ends of the couch.

Walking slowly, as though if she moved too fast, the dream might evaporate, she went toward the bedroom, and upon entering, she drew in her breath.

The bedroom was done in shades of blue, what looked to be hundreds of shades of blue, ranging from very dark to so light as to be hardly discernible as blue. The walls were papered in a stripe of two shades of ice blue and the windows were curtained with a dark blue silk that was almost purple. In the middle of the room was a huge four-poster draped in an airy cotton of the palest blue imaginable. When she walked near the bed and looked up, she saw that the underside of the canopy was done in what she knew was called a sunburst design, with the fabric radiating from a central medallion in tiny gathers out to the edge of the frame. The spread of the bed was a fine, soft blue cotton trapunto-stitched in a design of flowering tendrils.

"Do you like it?" Mike asked from behind her.

She turned to him, so overcome with emotion that she was unable to speak. That he'd done this for her, done this beautiful thing, was beyond her understanding. As she looked at him she remembered the night she'd spent in his arms and she knew that now she was free to touch him, touch him any time she wanted.

Her arms slid around his neck, hugging him to her. "Thank you," she whispered. "Thank you very much."

"Want to try out the bed?" he asked, kissing her neck.

She laughed. "I wouldn't want to mess it up."

"We'll be careful," he said enticingly as he took her hand and started leading her toward the bed.

It was as she was climbing onto the bed that she looked at the pretty blue clock on the bedside table. "Mike! It's nine-fifteen. The furniture is to be delivered to the nursing home at ten o'clock."

"They'll figure out where to put what," he said, drawing her onto the bed.

But Samantha pulled back. "We have to be there."

With a groan, Mike lay back against the pillows, each of them edged with Battenburg lace. "I'll go only if you promise to spend the afternoon in bed with me."

"If I must," she said with a big, weary sigh.

When Mike made a lunge for her, she squealed and ran for the bathroom, where she pulled up short. The bathroom still had dark green fixtures and the countertop was still covered in dark green marble, but now all the accessories, even the light fixtures, were in the palest pink. Pink glass jars ranged along the back of the countertop and along the wall of the tub; beautiful pink towels monogrammed with SE hung from the racks; and the walls above the green tile were papered with a design of pink roses.

She turned to Mike standing behind her. "Who did this?"

"Jeanne."

"Your sister?"

When he nodded, Samantha started asking questions about how she'd been able to do it all in so short a time, when had

Mike arranged it, and how had he known this was exactly what she liked? On and on the questions went as she ran from one room to the other looking at everything, Mike behind her, basking in her obvious pleasure.

During the night she had told him that Blair had told her about his money, and he had been very glad to see that it hadn't seemed to affect her. Now, he thought that he was freed from keeping secrets from her. He no longer had to be careful not to mention the family jet; now he could share with her the good news when a stock split and earned him a quarter of a million dollars; now he could buy her that little gold watch she'd nearly swooned over in Tiffany's windows.

"If you don't get dressed," he said, "you're going to miss the delivery of the furniture."

After one more very grateful kiss to Mike, a kiss that almost made them even later, Samantha ran to get dressed. It was while she was in Mike's bathroom, where her makeup was, that she said to him, "You know what really bothers me about that nursing home?"

Reaching around her, trying to get to his shaving lather, he said, "Besides the smell of the place, besides the personnel, besides the ugliness?"

"Yes, besides all of that. There is nothing to *do* in that place. I don't remember seeing so much as a magazine anywhere. If Jubilee had been put in a place like that and his piano was taken away from him, I doubt if he would have lived past eighty."

Mike looked at the three square inches of mirror that Samantha had left him and said, "If you hurry and get dressed we'll have time to stop on Fifth Avenue and pick up some books to take to your grandmother."

Samantha laughed. "Michael Taggert, is that a bribe to get me out of your bathroom?"

"Will it work if it is?"

"Yes," she said, and after planting a kiss on his shoulder, she scurried into the bedroom.

Minutes later they entered the revolving door of a big Fifth Avenue bookstore. Mike was surprised to see that Sam was not only no longer afraid of revolving doors, but seemed to have mastered them.

When they were inside, Samantha turned to Mike, feeling a little shy. He'd said she could buy magazines, but how many?

What with her several shopping excursions, she envisioned her credit card being run through the little machine and the machine, like a cartoon character, clutching its belly and laughing. "Uh, Mike," she began, "what kind of budget do I have?"

"Money or time?" he asked impatiently.

"Both."

Looking at his watch, he said, "You may buy everything that you can get to the cash register within twelve point six minutes."

"Point six?"

"It's now point four."

Samantha had once read that where women made their big mistake in marriage was the morning after the wedding. In an effort to please their husbands, they often made them breakfast and served it to them in bed, thinking that *this* morning was special and that they would only do this on "special" mornings. But the man took the breakfast in bed as an indication of what to expect for the rest of their married lives and was therefore disappointed over the coming years whenever he had to eat breakfast at a table.

It wasn't as though they'd been married yesterday, but they'd, well, experienced some togetherness. Now Mike wasn't looking at her with lust, but looking at her as though he were her . . . well, her husband. He was being patronizing and she didn't like it. No doubt he thought she'd pick up a couple of books and a few magazines, then he'd smile in a fatherly way and say something like, "Are you happy now?"

Samantha smiled at him. She was going to show him that she wasn't going to be like the bride who brought her husband breakfast in bed, and she was going to teach him a lesson in the process. He was rich enough to afford what she was going to do to him in the next twelve minutes.

"Okay, Mr. Got-Rocks, you're on," she said with one eyebrow raised in challenge as she turned to the clerk behind the register. "I need two shopping bags, FAST!" The bored young woman handed them to her.

Samantha first made her way to the mystery section, since she knew something about those books. Grabbing all of the Nancy Pickard, Dorothy Cannell, Anne Perry, and Elizabeth Peters books off the shelves, she dumped them into the open bags at her feet.

Standing near her in the science fiction section was a tall, well-dressed man who was pretending that he wasn't watching what she was doing. Samantha had noticed in the time she'd lived there that New Yorkers liked to pretend that they were sophisticated, that they'd seen everything there was to be seen, but the truth of the matter was that they were insatiably curious—in fact, nosy. They were always aware of what the person next to them was doing, always trying to see something they hadn't seen before, for New Yorkers seemed to Samantha to love anything out of the ordinary. It's just that it takes a lot to do something a New Yorker considers extraordinary.

When this man saw Samantha frantically dumping books into the bags, he asked, "Are you entering a contest?" Curiosity always overrides manners in a New Yorker.

"Yes," Samantha said. "I'm with a nursing home and I get to keep all the books I can buy within twelve minutes."

At that the man's face lit up. "May others help you?"

"Of course," Samantha said. Mike had said nothing about others helping or not.

"I might be able to choose science fiction for you and my wife could help with the bestsellers list."

Within four minutes flat, everyone in the store knew about the lady in the contest and everyone wanted to help. Two tall black boys with razored haircuts (one of them with a Z on his temple) asked if she wanted some magazines.

When Samantha said, "One of each," the boys looked as though they'd won the jackpot. With a jump, they slapped hands, then took off for the big magazine stand.

A man with two children volunteered to select games, and a woman said she'd buy audiotapes. A very nerdy-looking young man said he could pick out videos for her.

When the twelve minutes were up, Samantha skidded to a halt before the register with her arms full of Silhouette romances and the stacks and stacks—and stacks—of books, tapes, magazines, and videos in front of the check-out counter startled her. But she wasn't going to back down.

"Is this all yours?" the clerk gasped, her eyes wide. When Samantha—not looking at Mike who had been watching her in disbelief—nodded, the girl said she had to get the manager.

By the time the manager got to the register, everyone in the store, most of whom had participated in the buying, were standing to one side and watching solemnly.

"I hope you can pay for all of this," the manager said sternly.

Samantha nodded as the clerk picked up the first book and held the electronic eye over the code bar, but then Samantha yelled, "Wait!" and everyone drew in his collective breath. Was Samantha going to chicken out?

"What kind of discount are you going to give me?" she asked the manager.

At that the New Yorkers burst into approving applause, for they recognized one of their own. It was a bit later, after quite a bit of discussion that involved several people, that a discount of twelve and a half percent was agreed upon.

After all the purchases were rung up and Mike had paid with his credit card, the people helped carry the many bags into the street to get a taxi. They had the misfortune/luck to get one of the rare taxis with a native New York driver who told them they could not put all that stuff in his vehicle. There is nothing a New Yorker likes more than controversy so there erupted a bit of a "discussion." Tourists began taking pictures of the real, live, honest-to-God New Yorkers having an argument in the middle of the sidewalk. They'd heard about such things happening but hadn't really believed it was done; *their* mothers had taught them to argue only in private.

"I did it," Samantha said when she and Mike were alone in the taxi. But then maybe alone wasn't the right word, for covered wagons hadn't been packed as solidly as this car was. She had two bags in her lap, four under her legs and two behind her back. A Judith McNaught audiotape was protruding from her purse (she thought she might listen to it before passing it on) and gouging her right kidney rather painfully. "Twelve minutes flat. Right on time."

Mike was looking over the very long register tapes. "Twelve minutes to drag half the store to the counter, eleven minutes to haggle over the price with all the gusto of an Egyptian camel merchant; seventeen minutes to tie up three registers and use four rolls of paper, and thirteen minutes to pack the taxi while half of New York gave me directions on how to do it. Yes, Sam, we're right on time."

Leaning across two shopping bags, she smiled at him. "Do you mind?"

"No," he said honestly, reaching out to caress her cheek. The patronizing look was gone and in its place was again that look of desire.

Still smiling, Samantha leaned back against the bags. It didn't look as though Mike was going to expect her to be a docile little thing who served him breakfast in bed.

Since the movers didn't bother to arrive on time, Sam and Mike arrived only twenty minutes after they did to find Maxie sitting up in bed and giving orders to the three robust young men who were sweating as they hauled the furniture into the room. A doctor had a stethoscope to her heart.

"Lady, we already told you that we just move things, we don't hang pictures," one of the men was saying.

"Well, Nana," Samantha said upon entering the room, "it looks as though you have everything under control." She kissed Maxie's cheek as the doctor straightend up, then after he'd left the room, Samantha started telling her all about what Mike had done to her apartment, then how Mike had bought so many books and magazines and how Mike said this and did that and—

Mike left the room with the doctor. "How is she?"

"Failing," the doctor said, then grinned. "But she's happy while she's here. I wish all my patients had a couple of fairy godmothers like the two of you. But go easy on the booze, all right?"

"She brought chocolates today."

"Fine," the doctor said, then grew serious. "I hope your wife is prepared for Abby's death."

"Yeah, Sam's prepared for death," Mike said, no longer smiling. "She's had lots of rehearsal time. Lots."

It was three hours later when the telephone beside Samantha's newly decorated bed began ringing and Michael realized that it was his own line and pushed the appropriate button. After removing Samantha's ankle from his ear and replacing it with the telephone receiver, Mike said, "Hello?"

"Michael? Is that you?"

"Mom! Good to hear your voice. You sound so close."

Samantha untangled herself from Mike with the speed of a preacher's daughter caught naked at a revival meeting and sat up primly, the covers clutched to her neck.

"Oh, God, no," Mike was saying, his voice filled with trepidation, then looking up at Samantha, he saw that she'd gone white—as though she thought he'd just heard of someone's death. Mike put his hand over the receiver. "My family has come to New York to meet you."

After the long moment it took for the meaning of those words to sink into Samantha's brains, she collapsed back against the bed. She almost, *almost* wished it had been a death.

"How many of you are there?" Mike asked then paused. "Oh? That many, huh?" Pause. "Dad come too?" Pause. "Great, it'll be good to see everyone and I'm sure the kids will have a good time." Mike's face changed from mere dread to horror. "Mom, Frank didn't come, did he? Tell me Frank didn't come too." Pause. "Well yes, of course I'll be glad to see him, and no, Raine and I didn't stratch his precious car." Pause. "Sam? Oh, she's here with me."

Samantha watched Mike's face turn red.

"Mother! I'm shocked by you. Okay, okay, we'll be there just as soon as we get dr . . . er, ah, as soon as we can. See you in a few minutes." As he hung up the telephone, Samantha could hear Mike's mother laughing.

For a moment they lay on the bed, not touching, both looking up at the underside of the canopy.

"Why?" Samantha whispered.

Mike rolled on his side and ran his finger down her bare stomach. "I told you: They want to meet you."

"*Why* do they want to meet me? What have you told them about . . . us? Did you tell them that we . . . that we . . .?"

Mike grinned at her. "One of the major reasons I left Colorado was because of things like that call. But it didn't do any good to come to New York, they still know everything about me. But to answer your question, no, I didn't tell them about us, but I'm sure Raine did and Blair did and Jeanne and Vicky did. I don't know why I left Colorado, since it's a regular convention of Taggerts and Montgomerys right here in New York."

She rolled toward him. "Oh, Mike, I'm scared. What if they don't like me?"

"How could they not? I like you."

"But you've wanted to go to bed with me."

"What does that mean? That I'm indiscriminate? That if she's pretty and sexy and I want to go to bed with her, then I'll *like* her?"

"How in the world can you separate pretty and sexy and wanting to go to bed with someone from liking them?"

Mike gave a shrug that was the male equivalent of, I don't know and don't plan to analyze it.

Samantha got off the bed. "What am I going to wear? The pink Chanel or the red Valentino or the gray Dior?"

"Jeans. They're in Central Park having a picnic, and there's over a hundred of them."

Samantha sat down heavily. It would have been nice if there had been a chair placed where she sat, but there wasn't.

Moving to the edge of the bed to hang over the side and look down at her sitting on the floor, stark naked, legs crossed, Mike smiled. "You want to try the guest bedroom before we leave?"

Samantha groaned.

"Come on, Sammy-girl, how bad can it be? A hundred people inspecting you, asking you personal questions, my mother wanting to know if you're a fit person to live with her precious son, the other wives looking you over, my father—"

She hit him in the face with a pillow.

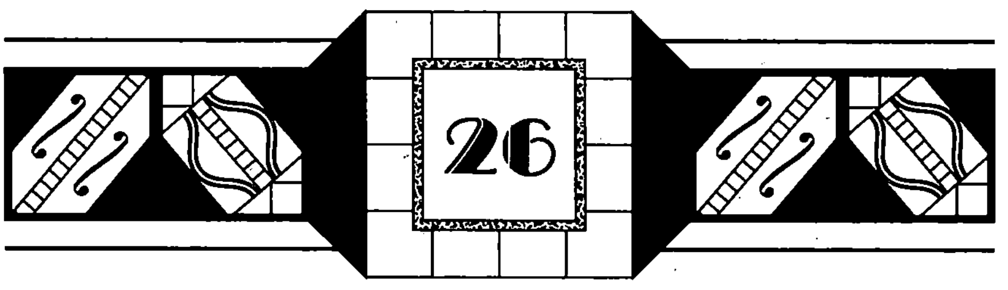

It was over an hour before they made it to Central Park because Samantha and Mike nearly had a fight when Mike wanted her to wear skintight jeans and a red T-shirt with no bra. Perhaps the argument had gone farther than it need have because she'd as soon have a fight as go to the park and be put under the scrutiny of a hundred of Mike's relatives.

When they finally did reach the park, Mike pointed. "There they are."

It took Samantha a moment to realize that the group of people she'd assumed was the entire population of one of those oddly named European countries was Mike's relatives. There weren't a hundred of them, there were at least four hundred, maybe five, she thought. Without a conscious thought, Samantha turned on her heel and started back toward the safety of Fifth Avenue, but Mike caught her arm. Smiling and teasing her all the way from the town house to the park, he seemed to be enjoying himself immensely, so it took a moment for him to see that she wasn't kidding, that she was indeed petrified with fear.

Turning to look at his family, at the zillions of kids running around, at the chumminess of them all, he thought that maybe Sam was right to be a little nervous.

"Stay here and I'll get something to calm you down," he said as he started toward his family.

"Michael!" Samantha hissed at him. "I do *not* want something to drink!" But Mike didn't hear her or else he ignored her, as he was already at the first table that was set up under the trees. Half behind a bush, half exposed so she could watch, Samantha saw Mike walk to a woman sitting on a chair under a tree, holding what appeared to be a nursing infant. Mike spoke to the woman for a few minutes, she nodded, then pulled the child from her breast and handed the baby to Mike.

As though the sight of Mike taking a child from its mother's breast weren't enough, the fact that no one at the gathering said anything to him was, in Samantha's eyes, quite odd. She knew he hadn't seen any of them in at least two months and they had come all the way from Colorado and some from Maine to see him, so why did they say nothing when he walked into the midst of them?

A moment later he was in front of her and was offering her the drowsy baby as though he were a bouquet of flowers.

Samantha took a step backward. "Mike, I don't know anything about babies."

"You didn't know anything about sex either but you learned," he said, smiling lecherously. "Take him."

Looking at the baby he held, she thought she'd never seen anything so beautiful as this pink and white creature. There was milk on the baby's chin, and she used the blanket edge to wipe it away.

"He needs to be burped." Watching with great interest, she saw Mike expertly unwind the blanket from the baby, exposing fat arms and legs, a plastic-coated diaper, and a little shirt. Draping the blanket over Samantha's shoulder, he then pressed the child to her until she was forced to take it into her arms.

Instinct and desire went together to make Samantha gather the child to her.

"A perfect fit," Mike said, leaning forward to kiss her mouth softly. "Now jostle him around a bit, thump him on the back, and get a belch out of him."

"Like this?"

"Perfect."

When the baby gave an enormous burp, she looked at Mike with eyes that said she'd accomplished the most wondrous feat in the world, making him laugh, but she could tell that he was proud of her.

"You're Uncle Mike," said a voice some distance below them. They looked down to see a very pretty little girl, about eight years old, golden brown hair perfectly curled and arranged, wearing a divine little white dress with hand-embroidered rosebuds across the front and white shoes and stockings.

"Well, Miss Lisa," Mike said, "aren't you the fashion plate for a picnic? Where'd you get that dress?"

"Bergdorf's, of course," she said smugly. "It's the only place to shop in New York."

"Aren't you a little snob?"

Unperturbed, the child looked up at her uncle with flirty eyes and stuck out her foot. "But I got the shoes at Lamston's," she said, speaking of a popular dime store in New York.

Laughing, Mike scooped her off the ground, buried his face in her neck, and began to make disgusting noises. The noises seemed to be a silent call for children, for they seemed to emerge from every part of the park, from behind trees and rocks, running across fields—and they all attacked Mike. One sturdy little boy attached himself to Mike's leg, sitting on his foot, while two identical twin girls took the other leg. Mike held Lisa with one arm while she fought the children who tried to climb up Mike, yelling, "I found him first!" Within minutes Mike looked like a Zuni storyteller doll with children hanging off the front of him, arms around his neck, legs hanging down his back, and two boys swinging from the arm that wasn't holding Lisa.

Laughing, Samantha watched him walk toward the picnic tables, dragging screaming, laughing children with him.

When four children ran up to him and were disappointed that they couldn't find a square inch of Mike that wasn't already taken, Mike said, "Bring Sam."

With trepidation on her face, Samantha backed away from the approaching children who collectively outweighed her, as they, with impish grins, started for her. Holding the baby to her protectively, she looked as though she were facing a pack of wolves.

One minute she was on the ground and the next she and the

baby were swept into a pair of strong arms. After an initial gasp of shock, she looked up into her rescuer's eyes: eyes that were like Mike's except older.

"Ian Taggert," he said, as though they were being presented to each other in a ballroom instead of her now being carried by him. "Mike's dad," he said unnecessarily. "And who do you have there?"

"I don't know," she answered, looking down at the baby.

"Plan to give him back?"

Samantha turned red as she realized that she was still holding the baby as though someone meant to harm him and she was going to protect him with her life. She didn't know it, but that gesture won her a place forever in Mike's father's heart. Ian had never liked any of Mike's other girlfriends; they always worried about their clothes getting dirty, but he liked this one.

"Get your own girl," Mike said and took Samantha from his father's arms.

"Michael Taggert, put me down!" she said under her breath as he carried her to the table and everyone, all eight hundred of them, gathered around to look at her.

After the first twenty names, Samantha didn't try to remember who they were, and she was grateful when she saw a few familiar faces: Raine, Blair, and Vicky—who managed to look elegant even in a pair of jeans. Sam noted Mike's very pretty mother, his sister Jeanne who had decorated her rooms, and she noticed Mike's oldest brother, Frank. Frank looked like the rest of the men in his family, but he was an example of how expression could change a person's features. The honest, open eyes, so like Mike's, were narrowed, as though he were scrutinizing everything and everyone, and the beautiful, soft Taggert mouth was drawn into a firm line.

As Frank shook her hand, he didn't flirt with her as Mike's other brothers had, instead, he looked at her speculatively and said, "You will, of course, be willing to sign a prenuptial agreement?"

Putting his arm around Samantha's shoulders, Mike told Frank to stuff it as he led her toward the trees. "You've met the worst of the family, now meet the best." As they walked she asked him questions about his family and was told that Frank planned to be a billionaire by the time he was forty and it looked as though he was going to make it. Samantha laughed at the way Mike spoke of millions and billions the way the rest of the world spoke of tens and twenties.

Sitting under a tree, a little apart from the noise of the rest of the family, was a very pretty young woman, about twenty, who looked as though she'd stepped out of the pages of a children's storybook. She was the beautiful princess the knights risked their lives to save, the princess who knew that a pea had been put under her mattresses. She wore a long draped skirt of layers of chiffon, a gauzy blouse, and a big picture hat like the one Scarlet wore to the barbecue. Beside her was a straw bag full of romantic novels and on her lap was an exquisitely dressed, picture-perfect baby, who Samantha found out later belonged to one of Mike's cousins.

"Jilly, honey," Mike said softly, "I want you to meet Samantha."

Jilly looked at Samantha; Samantha looked at Jilly. Mike, with a smile, excused himself, for he knew that Sam had found a friend in his overwhelming family. Samantha sat under the tree with Jilly talking about books they had read. Within minutes there were four children sitting near them, just sitting and listening as Jilly and Samantha talked.

One by one the women of Mike's family came to sit with them, so Samantha got to exchange a few words with each of them. She was pleased to tell Jeanne how much she liked the apartment, how the colors were perfect, how everything was perfect. She again thanked Vicky for helping her that day in Saks and apologized for her naïveté about the cost of the clothes.

She was a little nervous about talking to Mike's mother, and Pat made it worse when she said, "What do you think of my Michael?"

Samantha didn't hesitate. "Except that he lies constantly, never picks up his clothes, pretends to be dumb when he wants to get out of doing something, and has the ability to be utterly oblivious to the fact that I am doing nearly *all* the housework in *his* house, I think my Michael is perfect." There was an emphasis on the word *my*.

Laughing, Pat squeezed Sam's hand affectionately and said, "Welcome to the family," then went off to play with her grandchildren.

In between visits with the others, Samantha and Jilly talked, or rather Samantha talked, telling Jilly all about Mike and Maxie and about all that had happened since she'd come to New York.

It was late afternoon when Samantha felt secure enough to leave the haven of Jilly and move to the picnic tables. It was while she was talking to a young woman named Dougless, who was a Montgomery and married to a very nice man named Reed and looked to be in her fortieth month of pregnancy, that she had an experience that she never again wanted to have happen to her.

As Samantha straightened from reaching for an olive on a platter, Mike put his arms about her shoulders and kissed her on the neck. "Thanks a lot for coming today, Sam-Sam," he said.

It was a perfectly ordinary encounter, perfectly acceptable—except that the man who was touching her wasn't Mike. He was wearing clothes just like Mike's and he was approximately the same size as Mike, but he didn't feel like Mike, didn't smell like Mike, didn't kiss like Mike.

"Release me," she said, standing stiffly in his arms.

"Nobody minds." He continued nuzzling her neck.

Samantha had done her best to be polite, but she did not want this stranger touching her. As she opened her mouth to say something stern to him, she felt his hand slip down her back to just above her buttocks—and the hand was moving lower. She panicked. "Stop it!" she yelled, beginning to fight him. "Stop it this instant. Let me go!"

Even knowing that Mike's family was staring at her in open-mouth astonishment, she didn't care. Let them think of her what they would.

"Get away from me. Don't touch me!"

Releasing her, the man stepped back, looking at her in astonishment. *Everyone* was looking at her as though she'd lost her mind.

Just when Samantha was wishing the ground would open up and swallow her, Mike, walking with a couple of his cousins, a football in his hands, stepped into view, and she ran to him.

Putting his arm about her protectively, he held her, but from the way he was laughing, she had no doubt that he'd known all along that another man planned to touch her. "Sam, honey, meet my twin brother, Kane."

Mike was grinning at her, as was Kane, and they seemed to expect her to smile at the two of them and forgive them their little deception. She had no doubt that this game of pretending with each other's girlfriends had been played many times before.

But Samantha didn't feel very forgiving. When she turned to Mike, her eyes were blazing in anger. "Do me a favor and drop yourself off the nearest cliff."

As she turned on her heel and walked away from him, away from the entire group, Mike's family burst into laughter.

Samantha was nearly out of sight before Mike caught up with her.

"Sam, honey—" he began.

"Don't speak to me." When he reached out for her, she said, "And don't you even think of touching me." She started walking again, Mike beside her.

"What are you so angry about?"

"I've been trying to make a good impression on your family and you . . . you make a fool of me by putting your brother up to pawing me in front of them. It was humiliating. Didn't you think about how I'd feel?"

"No," he said, smiling. "People can't tell us apart. I thought you'd think Kane was me."

Pausing, she stared at him; sometime between yesterday and today his brain had fallen out of his head.

"Sam, Kane and I are identical twins. We're exactly alike, even down to moles and birthmarks."

Samantha gave him a look that said, Tell me another one. "Mike, tell me," she said with great patience, "was the person who delivered you and your brother one of your relatives?"

"As a matter of fact she was, but what's that got to do with anything?"

Giving him a look of great patience, she explained. "Because, just like you, she's a liar. She lied to you and your whole family. Your brother doesn't look like you at all. If you're twins, you're fraternal twins, or maybe one of you is a nine-month baby and the other is an eight-month one. If that's the case, then you're just brothers, nothing else."

Mike gasped at her in disbelief. "Sam, Kane and I have won contests for being the most identical twins."

"Then the losers must have been different colors. Now would you mind—"

She didn't say anymore because Mike grabbed her in his

arms and began to kiss her, and when she tried to push him away, he wouldn't let her. "Sammy, sweetheart, I really didn't mean to humiliate you, honest. Kane and I have been playing jokes on people since we were kids. It's a kind of initiation into the family."

"And I failed," she said gloomily.

He laughed. "Failed? You passed with glowing colors. Come on, let's go back to my family. You'll see how well you've passed."

She allowed him to keep his arm around her shoulders, allowed him to lead her back to the others, but as they reached the picnic tables, she saw Kane talking to his mother. "Your brother touches me again and he'll be sorry."

Mike kissed her cheek. "No, I won't let him touch you." There was pride in his voice, such pride that Samantha refrained from asking him why he had never bothered to tell her that he had a twin brother.

One thing Mike hadn't lied about was that his family would be pleased with her for knowing which brother was Mike. The fact that, as far as she could tell, none of *them* could tell Mike and Kane apart made her understand why his family had not greeted Mike when he'd first arrived—they'd thought he was Kane. It occurred to her to tell them all that they needed a good eye doctor if they thought Mike looked like his brother, because Kane didn't look anything like Mike. In fact, Kane was rather ordinary looking. He was handsome, yes, but he didn't have the beautiful mouth that Mike did, his hair wasn't as curly, he didn't move as Mike did, and Kane was just a wee bit fat, not muscular like Mike was.

For the rest of the day, until sundown, Samantha had to put up with one little test after another, with every family member except Mike's parents and Jilly referring to Mike and his brother by each other's names. Twice Kane put his hand on Samantha's shoulder, once when she had her back to him. Heavens, but the man didn't even *feel* like Mike.

It was in the early evening, when the children were getting sleepy and the men had gathered away from the women to talk, that Samantha had a chance to sit quietly on a chair and look at the group. There were more people here named Taggert than Montgomery, but there were enough of each, and she'd spent enough time around both families that she was beginning to be able to tell them apart.

The Montgomery men and the Taggert men were very different from each other, both physically and in their personalities. The Montgomerys were taller, but the Taggerts were prettier. The Taggert men, ranging in height from five eight to just six feet, were all big men, big and thick and heavily muscled. The men together looked like a convention of weight lifters or a crew of construction workers. What made them different, what set them apart from other brawny men, was the prettiness, in a way, of their faces: big eyes, full lips, the sweetest smiles imaginable. For all their size and muscle, not one of them looked as though he could hurt a fly.

The Taggerts were men that a woman could curl up with, men a woman could go to for help, men a woman could trust to protect her, to pull her from a burning building without giving a thought for his own life. They were sexy men. Samantha had no questions as to why each woman who married into the family seemed willing to bear a countless number of children. She had no doubt that every Taggert father was close to his children from birth to first love to grandchildren. These weren't men who went off with the boys on Sunday afternoons. In fact, looking at them, Samantha wondered if any Taggert man who had children ever went anywhere without one of them. These were men who knew how to give and receive love, not just tell a woman he loved her, but really, truly love her through sickness, through the good times and the bad, through turmoil and peace, through sadness and happiness. The Taggerts were men a woman could depend on to always be there, men a woman could trust.

The Montgomery men were different from their cousins, for the Montgomerys were as elegant as the Taggerts were down-to-earth. Samantha thought that a Montgomery man would know if one made a mistake and said an opera aria was by Puccini when it was actually by Verdi. They'd know when a person goofed and used the butter knife on the fish. They'd recognize a Chanel copy from a Chanel. They were, without exception, quiet, reserved men, all of them tall, all of them handsome in a sharp sort of way, with unreadable eyes, sculptured cheekbones, and jaws that were almost belligerent. The only softness in their faces was their mouths. Samantha couldn't help wondering if, when they fell in love, their whole faces softened. All in all, they were rather fierce-looking men, men who could lead in wars, men who would die protecting the men under them—or their wives and children, she couldn't help thinking.

She wondered what the private lives of the Montgomerys were like, did they love with all the fierceness she saw in their eyes? She had no doubt that when they did fall in love the recipient was selected very carefully. Did the Montgomery men laugh? Did they cry? Did they play ball with their sons and talk to their daughters about their Barbie dolls? She wondered if she'd ever know the answers to her questions, for she knew without being told that a Montgomery would allow a person to know only what he wanted a person to know about him.

"And what have you decided?" Pat Taggert asked, taking a chair next to her, making Samantha aware that she had been watched and that Pat knew what she was thinking. Maybe when Pat had been contemplating marrying Mike's father, she too had compared the two families.

"That I wouldn't mind having an affair with a Montgomery but I'd rather marry a Taggert," she answered, then realized that what she'd said shouldn't have been said.

Pat smiled, seeming to like the honesty of her answer. "Exactly the same conclusion I reached some time ago."

Samantha looked down at hands. "You didn't . . . I mean . . ."

"I didn't, but I do like to mention Raine's oldest brother to Ian now and then." The women laughed together.

Later, as it began to grow dark, people started taking their leave of each other, and Samantha realized that she felt at home with these people. As she helped clear the tables, all the leftover food to be taken to a homeless shelter, she chatted companionably with them.

Coming up behind her, Mike slipped his arms about her waist. "Okay, everybody, Sam says she's never changed a diaper so who's going to lend us a kid overnight?"

"Me," said a Montgomery cousin.

"I will."

"Mike, you can have both of my boys for as long as you want."

"How about my twins? She ought to learn on twins."

"I use cloth diapers, Mike. And safety pins with little ducks on them. Sam should learn on cloth diapers."

As Samantha stood blinking at the deluge of offers, Mike said, "Take your pick."

"How many children may I take?" she asked.

That response brought a hush to the Taggerts, for if there was one thing they were serious about, it was children. There were no wives in the Taggert family who didn't have children, in fact, it was a joke of strutting pride that Taggert men could impregnate any woman in the world, no matter what doctors had told her. They had impregnated women who were on the Pill and women who'd had IUDs inserted. One Taggert, after six children, had had a vasectomy. When his wife became pregnant two years later, he'd had some doubts about her fidelity. After the child was born she'd insisted on having a DNA test to prove the child was his. He had apologized with a new house and a three-week trip to Paris where she'd bought a trunk full of new clothes. (Since then, some of the other Taggert wives had been suggesting that their husbands get vasectomies.)

"You can take one or two or all of them," Mike said in response to her question.

Samantha looked at the nearly silent group of people, at all of the children, ranging in age from a tiny creature that looked to be only minutes old to big, hulking teenagers who looked as though they were dying to get away from their relatives. She was seriously tempted by a fat, smiling baby about eight months old, but at last she pointed. "Those two."

Her choice was a couple of little boys about four years old who were far and away the dirtiest children at the picnic, their faces sticky, their hands and clothes looking as though they'd rolled in mud. But under the dirt were cherub faces with black curly hair and big, innocent eyes and mouths of sweetness.

When Samantha chose the two boys, Mike let out a groan that made the whole family burst into laughter. She looked at Mike in question.

"Do you have to have those two?"

"Mike!"

"Those brats are Kane's boys, and they're bad even for Taggerts. How about Jeanne's little girl? She's adorable."

Samantha glanced at Jeanne's little girl, at the pretty child's clean dress, her angelic smile, then back at the twins who were at that moment trying to kill each other. "I want the boys."

As Mike groaned again, Kane put his arm around his brother. "Ah sleep," Kane said. "Sweet sleep. That's what I'm going to get tonight and you're not."

Mike turned to Sam. "Samantha . . ." he began, but she stopped him.

"They remind me of you, and when they're cleaned up, I imagine they'll look just like you."

This brought more laughter from the family. Pat smiled fondly at her two grown sons. "There *is* some justice in the world after all if it means you boys are going to have children as bad as you were. Yes, Samantha, dear, Kane's boys are *just* like he and Mike were as children, and may heaven help you if you want to learn about children on those two."

After a noisy leave-taking, with lots of kissing and hugging and hundreds of invitations to come to Colorado and to Maine, Samantha and Mike set off toward Mike's house, each holding the hand of a dirty twin boy.

Later, at the house, Samantha sent the boys into the garden to play while she prepared a late snack for them—and Samantha got her first experience of what had made Mike groan when she said she wanted to take the twins.

It wasn't that they were bad children. They didn't play pranks on their elders or see what they could get away with. Truthfully they seemed to be happy with just each other and didn't seem aware that Samantha and Mike were there. What caused the problem was that they were so very, very active and the fact that there were so very many of them.

Samantha glanced out at the flood lit garden and saw one child climbing the fence, ready to fall to his death, while another child ran up the fire escape as fast as his stubby legs could carry him, while a third child was climbing up the side of the house, beside the fire escape, and was now at the top of the first story, also on the precipice of death. A fourth child was eating the roses, thorns and all, while number five was climbing onto a lawn chair that was balanced on one leg on the edge of the brick walkway.

"Mike!" Samantha yelped in desperation as she stood at the glass doors and looked out in helplessness. "They're going to be killed—all eight of them. Or is it twelve?"

Mike didn't look up from his newspaper. "Those two are in a class all their own."

"I think you should—" she began, her voice filled with fear since one child was now moving up the wall of the town house toward the second floor.

"You wanted them, now you have them."

Turning to Mike in disbelief, she saw that his face was hidden by the newspaper. Obviously he wasn't going to help her. She went outside into the garden to see what she could do to prevent the children from killing themselves.

Contrary to what it seemed, Mike was very aware of what was going on and very interested in what Samantha was planning. Standing to one side of the glass doors, he unabashedly spied on her, watching as she at first tried talking to the boys as though they were adults, reasoning with them that they were on the very precipice of death and should control their baser urges. She suggested paper and colored pens and lemonade. When that had no effect, she gently tried to take a child down from the wall. Gentleness had no effect on the sturdy four-year-old who was now out of Samantha's reach.

Watching, Mike saw that, for a moment, Samantha seemed to have no idea what to do, but then his nephew gave it all away by laughing, letting Samantha know that he saw her dilemma and was enjoying being the cause of it.

"You little scamp," she said, narrowing her eyes at him as the boy kept working his way up the rose trellis on the wall. In the next minute, Samantha was after him, and the child, still laughing while his brother shrieked encouragement from the ground, led Samantha on a chase across the side of the wall, like two crabs moving on a perpendicular surface.

Stepping into the yard, Mike was ready to catch one or the other of them should they start to fall, but Samantha caught the child by the seat of his pants and the imp turned to look at her as if to say, Now what are you going to do? Mike could see that Sam had no idea how to get the big kid down, but she was trying not to let the boy see that. He saw, and he delighted in her consternation.

"Are you going to let a four-year-old defeat you?" Mike asked from the ground.

Without looking down at Mike, Samantha gave the child an I'm-bigger-than-you-and-I'm-going-to-win grin and the next minute she had him in her arms—all of what had to be a hundred pounds of him. Somehow, she got him to the ground. Of course Mike was there for those last few feet, catching them both in his strong arms when a rose branch broke and setting them upright on the lawn.

The minute the child's feet touched earth, he scampered off with his brother while Samantha rubbed her arms. They were aching from the exertion and from hundreds of rose thorn scratches. "Now I understand why you lift weights. It's to prepare you for dealing with children. Do you think I should give them a bath?"

Smiling, Mike gave her a soft kiss and pulled her into his arms. "Mike, where are the boys?"

"Mmmm," he said, caressing her back. "You said the bad word."

" 'Boys?' How is that a bad word?"

"No, you said, *bath*. They've disappeared, and you'll have to find them if you mean to clean those two up. Half the time Kane admits defeat and throws them into a horse trough. His theory is that they'll take a bath when they discover girls, so why bother until then?"

She pushed away from him and when she looked at him, her mouth was set. "My grandmother dealt with gangsters, so I think I am capable of dealing with two little boys. What we need here is a cunning mind and the strength of Hercules. Stand over there," she ordered and when he was at one side of the garden, she said, "My goodness, it's Donatello and Michelangelo and Raphael and Leonardo right here in our garden!" When two dirty little boys appeared from nowhere, Samantha grabbed one about the waist then the other. Bowing under the weight like an Olympic bar across a squatter's shoulders, she held on through ferocious wiggles.

"You fibbed!" one child yelled, startling Samantha for she didn't know the boys could talk.

"Yes I did," she answered calmly. "I learned how from your uncle Mike. He's the best fibber in the world."

For a moment both boys stopped struggling to look at their uncle Mike with new respect, but he looked just the same, just like their dad, so he wasn't of much interest. They resumed their attempts to get away from Samantha. She wasn't very big, but she seemed extraordinarily strong.

"You two are going to have a bath, then I'm going to read you a story and you're going to bed." When the boys kept struggling, nearly tearing Samantha's arms out of their sockets, she said, "It's the goriest story you've ever heard. Lots of blood and people being chopped in half and—"

The boys stopped wiggling as they listened to Sam tell them about what she was going to tell them all the way up the stairs.

It was as she was bathing the twins, trying to get what looked like years of dirt off of them while they bashed each other with soap and washclothes and drenched Samantha, that Mike stood in the doorway and watched her. The boys were so much alike, as Mike said, down to moles and birthmarks.

"How are Kane and I different?"

"Michael Taggert, if you're fishing for compliments—" She broke off as she dodged a bar of soap flying through the air.

"Maybe I am, but wouldn't you be curious if all your life people had told you that you were identical to another person, then someone told you that you weren't even similar? How are we different?"

"He's smaller than you for one thing. And the expression in his eyes is different. You're . . . you're a nicer person than he is. Softer."

"Maybe when I look at you my eyes are different."

"Maybe." She turned toward him. "But your eyelashes are definitely longer. And curlier."

At that Mike laughed. "Curlier?"

Embarrassed, she turned away. "I knew I shouldn't have said anything. You are not like your brother. Not like him at all." Mike seemed to be satisfied with that as he left the bathroom, which was rapidly resembling a place that should apply for national relief.

After the boys were bathed and at long last in bed, she and Mike went to bed—together, in his bed. Samantha was very tired and would have thought she could expend no more energy during the day, but she walked out of the bathroom wearing her white nightgown and took one look at Mike's eyes, and they were on each other ravenously, tearing at clothes and skin, mouths and hands everywhere.

It was an hour later that they lay side by side, sated, Sam's head on Mike's shoulder, his arms around her.

"This is all so new to me," Samantha said. "I mean, I've done this . . . Sort of." She laughed. "Mike, the difference between sex with you and sex with my ex-husband is, as Mark Twain says, the difference between lightning and a lightning bug. I had no idea sex could be enjoyable, fun, and so very . . . fulfilling."

Mike said nothing.

Idly, she ran her fingers over the hair on his chest. "I guess you've done this a thousand times with a thousand different women. I guess this is nothing . . . unusual for you."

"Sam, when I was fourteen my father gave me the first of many talks about using protection during sex. He talked to me about sexually transmitted diseases and unwanted pregnancies. Since then, every time I've gone to bed with a woman I've used protection, a thin little membrane that separated me from her. I've used it even if she *said* she was on the Pill or whatever. I'd rather be safe than sorry. Until last night I'd never been, I guess you could say, skin to skin with a woman before. Maybe you could even go so far as to say that I was a virgin until last night."

She was hesitant. "Was it better? Without, I mean?"

"*Much* better. Much, much, much better. Never experienced anything like it. Had no idea sex could be so good."

Holding up his hand, she looked at it, comparing it in size to her own, caressing his fingertips with hers. "So now I guess, well, later, with other women you won't use any protection. You'll always want to be . . . skin to skin."

"That's true."

Her fingers laced with his and tightened. She could not let herself think of life without Mike, of Mike being with another woman.

"But then, Sam," he said very softly, "I think the buck stops here."

She was afraid to ask what he meant, but his words made her heart beat faster. Then, abruptly, she turned toward him. "Michael! If you're not using any birth control, I could get pregnant!"

"Really?" He sounded as though he were unconcerned about the possibility of pregnancy, then just slightly, his hand tightened on hers. "Would you mind?"

She ignored his second question. "I think this is extremely irresponsible of you. You should have used something."

"Me? Why not you?"

"I would have, but that first time you didn't exactly give me time to think, and besides, I was a little too tipsy to think clearly."

He grinned down at her. "Know what the mating call of the southern belle is? Ooooh, I'm soooo drunk."

"I'll get you for that," she said as she jumped on him, trying to tickle him, her nightgown wrapping around both of them.

But they were interrupted by two very clean little boys standing by the bed and staring at them. There was no need for the children to say anything because what they were feeling was in their eyes: They were away from home and their dad and they wanted reassurance. Neither Sam or Mike hesitated as they pulled the boys into bed with them. The children snuggled together like the two halves of an egg that they were between Mike and Sam and went to sleep instantly.

Samantha had an idea that sleeping with children cuddled close was nothing new to Mike, but it was to her, and the feeling called to something deep within her.

"Mike," she whispered, "do you make twins?" She tried to make the question sound light, but she couldn't. She wanted Mike, and she wanted the children he could possibly give her.

Mike knew what she was asking: She wanted to know if the two of them could have kids together, and Mike knew that an affirmative answer from him was a lifetime commitment. But then he'd made a commitment the first night they'd made love and he'd used no birth control, which had been a very conscious decision on his part. "Probably," he said at last. "Want a couple?"

"I rather would, yes," she answered as though it were not the most important answer she'd ever given in her life.

Above the heads of the sleeping children, their fingers entwined, holding to each other tightly.

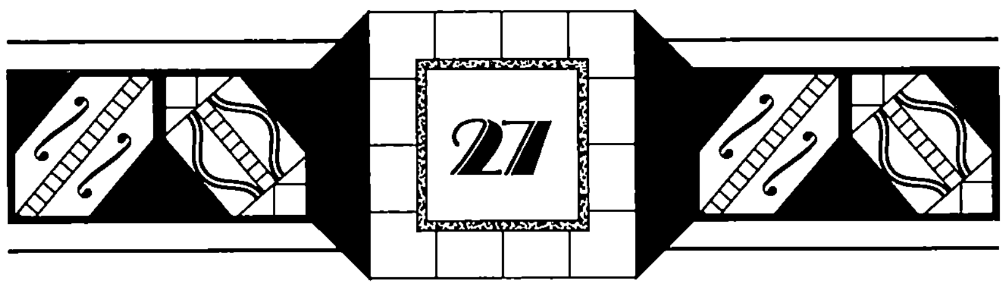

Mike woke when he heard the soft sound of a key turning in the front door lock. Since the attempt on Sam's life, he never seemed to sleep soundly; he always had one ear alert and listening. Now he knew that the person coming in the front door had to be his brother Kane because, for all his brother's act of nonchalance, the truth was, Kane was mad about his two boys and could hardly bear them to be out of his sight.

Easing out of bed and tiptoeing from the room, Mike was still pulling on his trousers when Kane entered the town house. "I see the place is still intact," he said. "Did my brats give your lady nightmares or did she do the sensible thing and leave you?"

Without a word, Mike put his finger to his lips and motioned for his brother to follow him. Silently, he opened the door to the bedroom he shared with Sam and allowed him to look inside. Samantha was on her back, and in the crook of each arm was one of Kane's sons, one on his stomach, his face pressed into Sam's arm, while the other boy was on his side, half on her, half off.

"It's been so long since I've seen them clean I'm not sure I would have recognized them." As Mike started to close the door, Kane looked at his brother and what he felt was in his eyes. "God, how I envy you!"

Mike smiled but with a touch of sadness at the memory of the death of his brother's wife. His sadness was soon erased by the cry of "Daddy!" and the hurtling through the air of one small body then another. Catching one then the other of the heavy, sleep-warmed children, Kane started for the living room.

"Sammy!" one of the boys yelled, putting out his arms for Sam to come with them, but Mike put his hand over the door as a barrier.

"Oh, no, monster, you've had her long enough. She's mine now." At that he shut the door, locked it, turned to Samantha, who was just waking up, and stroked a pretend mustache. "And now, my beauty . . ."

"Mike," Samantha said, sitting up in the bed. "You can't . . . I mean, there are people out there."

"A common occurrence in my family," he said as he made a leap onto the bed and grabbed her about the waist, pulling her to him.

"Mike, really, you can't. Your brother—"

"He knows all about the birds and the bees." He was fumbling for the edge of her nightgown, but fumbling in an expert way as she made halfhearted attempts to push his hand away. Halfhearted because what if she *won*?

When Samantha finally left the bedroom, she found Kane in the breakfast room buried behind *The Wall Street Journal* and the twins sitting on the floor eating.

"What are they eating?" she asked, although she could very well see what they had been given to eat; but she wanted Kane to admit it. She was having a difficult time liking this man.

When Kane spoke, he didn't seem very concerned, for he didn't even look around his paper. "Cookies. Diet cola."

Without asking their father's permission, Samantha took the paper towels laden with cookies from in front of the children along with their cans of cola.

Kane looked around his paper at her. It wasn't that what she was doing was so unusual, heaven knew that every female in his family had tried to get his sons to eat properly, all without success. What surprised him was that Samantha had taken away the boys' food and they weren't screaming in protest.

Kane watched as she put pillows on chairs at the table—his boys did *not* eat at tables—towels over the pillows to protect them, then lifted the boys to seat them on the pillows.

Giving up any pretense at pretending to read the paper, Kane saw his rambunctious boys sit quietly while Samantha scrambled two eggs, toasted whole wheat bread, and poured two glasses of milk. Kane was now fascinated because to his knowledge, his sons had not eaten anything except grasshopper legs and rose thorns and sugar for years. Twice he managed to catch the eye of one of his boys, raising an eyebrow in question, but his son merely gave him an angelic smile, as though their eating eggs and toast and sitting at a table without spilling anything was what they did every day.

After the meal Kane watched Samantha wash their hands and faces—another first—then kneel and hold up two cookies.

"What do I get for these?" Samantha asked.

"Kisses," the boys chorused, sounding like something out of a 1950s model-child training film.

Smiling, the boys each kissed one of Samantha's lovely cheeks, then held theirs up to be kissed by her. When the boys went scampering into the garden, Samantha called after them that if they got dirty she'd have to bathe them again and rewash everything.

"Genitalia, too?" one of the boys asked.

Samantha turned to Kane, her eyes wide in shock.

"He means toes," Kane said, shrugging. "He heard the word on 'The Simpsons' and I told him it meant toes."

"Yes, you darling child," Samantha said. "I'll wash your toes too and further, if you get dirty, I'll trade all your Teenage Mutant Ninja Turtle bandages for boring grown-up ones. How's that for punishment?"

Giggling, the boys ran into the garden.

Kane's mouth was hanging open as he looked at Samantha as she cleaned up the breakfast dishes.

Turning to him, her face stern and judgmental, she said, "You really shouldn't let them eat cookies for breakfast, and diet cola is all chemicals. And their hygiene leaves a great deal to be desired."

Picking up his paper, Kane put it back in front of his face. "You can't have them, Sam. They're mine. Get Mike to make you some of your own."

Samantha didn't answer him. When she went to the kitchen, she was blushing, for the thought that Kane, who she knew was a widower, might possibly leave the boys with her until he found a mother for them had indeed been uppermost in her mind.

"You want to tell me about you and Nelson?"

"Nelson?" Samantha asked vaguely, for her mind was on the twins, the dear boys Kane had taken away immediately after breakfast. It was almost as though he were afraid that if he left the boys with her any longer, she might succeed in taking them away from him.

"The guy in the bar. You remember him? You met him when you paraded yourself before half of New York while wearing practically nothing."

Samantha laughed. "Ah, yes *that* Nelson. Mike, do you think I have the qualifications to be one of those five-hundred-dollar-a-night call girls?"

Mike grunted in answer. "Are you planning to tell me what Nelson wrote on that piece of paper he gave you or not? Of course, I could be like you and snoop through all your possessions to find it, but I have more ethics than that."

As she picked up his dirty lunch plate, she kissed the tip of his nose. "Couldn't find it, could you?"

For a moment, Mike looked away, not meeting her eyes, then he left the table to follow her into the kitchen. "Samantha," he said, "what are you up to?"

"The paper had a name on it, Walden, and a telephone number."

As he watched her load dishes into the washer, he realized that she was avoiding his eyes. Putting his hands on her shoulders, he turned her to face him. "And what have you done about this name and number?"

"I called the number and it seems that Mr. Walden is an attorney and I have an appointment to see him today at three."

"Were you planning to go alone? Maybe you were planning to tell me that you wanted to do a little shopping, then sneak away to the appointment?"

"Mike, it's not as though I was planning to secretly meet somebody like Doc by myself. This man is an attorney, and he's young, at least he's younger than most of the people who know anything about Maxie are, so he couldn't have been *too* involved with what happened in 1928. Mr. Walden is only fifty-five."

"And how do you know that?"

"I, well, asked his secretary. I told her I thought he was a man I'd met at a singles' bar and described him as about twenty-six, blond, and tall. She informed me that Mr. Walden was fifty-five years old, married with four grown children, and five feet six and had gray hair and a potbelly. If he's that young, what can he know about my grandmother? Do you think he handled some legal work for her or do you think he does actually know something?"

"I guess there's only one way to find out, isn't there? Get dressed and we'll go see him."

"Mike, you don't have to go. I can meet him, then come back here and tell you what he had to say."

It half enraged Mike and half pleased him that she was trying to protect him, for he knew that's exactly what she was trying to do. He'd made it clear that he wanted her to stop sticking her nose into the mystery of what happened to cause Maxie to leave her family. Now she was continuing to search but was trying to keep her searching from him.

He kissed her softly. "Do you realize that it's after two o'clock now? If you plan to get into one of those suits of yours and spray your hair with that epoxy stuff and paint your face and—" Samantha was already running toward the bathroom.

At three-fifteen, Samantha and Mike were ushered into Mr. Walden's office by his thin, pinched-looked secretary. Through a process that Samantha found infuriating (Mike had sent Samantha off to the restroom while he sat on the desk of a very pretty receptionist, looked at her through lowered lashes, and asked her questions about Mr. Walden) they had found out that Walden was a criminal defense attorney; he took on the cases of the most reprehensible men and kept them out of jail. The receptionist had shuddered prettily as she described some of the underworld characters who sometimes came into the office. She said that Mr. Walden didn't seem to mind the fact that his brilliant defenses kept the most awful people on the street.

"Underworld connections," Mike said. "No wonder Nelson knows him. What's wrong with you?"

Samantha was walking beside him so stiffly that her legs hardly bent. "Absolutely nothing is wrong with me. Why should anything be wrong with me? Just because you were looking down that woman's blouse is no reason for anything to be wrong with me."

Smiling, Mike took her arm and wouldn't let her move away. "She had a nice pair of—"

"If you like cows!" Samantha said through clenched teeth, jerking her arm away and walking ahead of him.

When they were ushered into Walden's office, Samantha was angry and Mike was chuckling. Mr. Walden, who was exactly as he'd been described, took one look at the two of them as they sat down and said, "I don't handle divorce cases."

With a laugh, Mike reached for Sam's hand resting on the arm of the chair in front of Mr. Walden's desk, but she snatched it away. "Actually, we've come here on another matter. Your name was given to us indirectly through Jubilee Johnson."

For just a second the expression of joviality on Walden's face changed. It was odd to think of this man as a defender of criminals, because put a white wig and beard on him and a red suit and he'd be every child's picture of Santa Claus. "Ah, yes, Jubilee. I hope he's well and his family is doing all right."

It was at that moment that Samantha saw Walden's left hand.

When she'd entered the room, she'd been so upset with Mike that she hadn't really looked at Mr. Walden or noticed much of anything about him except that he was such a pleasant-looking man that she immediately thought that he could know nothing about Maxie.

Now she was staring at his left hand. His hand had been tattoed a solid black from his wrist upward, covering his smallest finger and the one next to it, and those two fingernails were polished with black enamel.

"Half Hand," she whispered, because at first glance his hand looked as though half of it were missing. "Half Hand," she said louder, interrupting whatever Mike and the man were saying.

Stepping around the desk, Walden smiled at her, then held out his hand, palm down, and she took it in her own, looking at it. Releasing his hand, she looked up at him. "Who are you and what do you know about Maxie?"

Mr. Walden chuckled, sounding like the man he resembled. "I was born with the name of Joseph Elmer Gruenwald 3d. Since my father was called Joe, I was called Elmer. Ugly name. It's difficult to get ahead in this world with a name like that because you spend a lot of your life hearing jokes about Elmer Fudd. To counteract the name I think I spent a lot of time thinking about my gangster grandfather."

It was Mike's turn to speak. "Half Hand."

"Yes," Mr. Walden said. "Half Hand Joe was my grandfather. My father was nine when Half Hand was killed and I think he glorified him. Rather than facing the facts that his father was nothing more than a hired killer, my father tried to make him into a hero, so I grew up hearing about how great Half Hand was." He hesitated. "When Half Hand died, my father was given some money, but my grandmother went through it within six months."

Holding his left hand up, Walden studied it. "When I was sixteen, I got drunk for the first time in my life, and when I woke up I found that I had gone to a tattoo parlor and had this done to my hand in memory of my grandfather. When I was sober I wanted to have it removed, but my father said it was an omen."

When both Samantha and Mike looked puzzled at that, Mr. Walden chuckled. "My dad had a rich fantasy life. He got married when he was little more than a kid and I was soon on the way, so he never had a chance to go to school. After he saw my hand, he said I was destined to become an attorney and save men like my grandfather. I don't know how a sixteen-year-old with a hellacious hangover and a tattooed hand equaled attorney to my father, but the whole scheme sounded good to me. I went to law school thinking that I was going to be spending my life saving misunderstood men and women, but I find that I defend the dregs of humanity."

His words and his expression were at odds with each other, for he looked well pleased with himself.

"Why?" Samantha asked.

"Money, my dear. The scum-of-the-earth wouldn't do scummy deeds if it didn't make them a lot of money, and defending them has made me a rich man. My parents lived in a two-room apartment with five kids. I have a penthouse on Fifth Avenue and an estate in Westchester. I've sent my four daughters to Ivy League schools, and my wife has her clothes made for her in Paris."

He smiled at the innocence of the two handsome young people before him, for their faces were readable, telling him that they would never sell their souls for money. But, then, from the looks of the way they were dressed and from the way they carried themselves, neither of them knew what it meant to be hungry or cold or have the landlord evict them in the middle of the night for nonpayment of rent. His daughters were like this pretty little Samantha, well groomed, well fed, not haunted by memories of poverty. Inadvertently, the garbage he defended had done this good deed and helped put something clean and good on earth.

"When I was twenty-one, I changed my name to H. H. Walden, a nice WASP name that I used all through law school. It helped me with the blond tennis players, and later, I could tell the bums I defended that the H. H. stood for Half Hand, so it helped me there too."

"Because they had heard of Half Hand's lost three million," Mike said, making Walden smile.

"You've done some searching, haven't you?"

Mike told him about the biography he was writing and about Maxie being Sam's grandmother. "What can you tell us about her?" he asked.

"Nothing," Mr. Walden said, his eyes locked with Mike's and never flinching.

A practiced liar, Mike thought. "Not even the name of the nursing home she's in?" Mike asked. "Do you have any idea who's paying her bills?"

At that Walden put his head back and laughed uproariously. "Caught me, did you? Yes, I know where Maxie is, but I'm not paying her bills. If you want to know that, you should ask her where the money comes from."

"She pretends she's someone named Abby and won't even admit she's Maxie."

"Ah, well, that's understandable. She's probably afraid for the young lady here, afraid Doc will do something to her, or if not Doc, then someone else. The legend of Half Hand's money is still alive in some circles. Of course, you do know that her name really is Abby, don't you? No? It's Mary Abigail Dexter. When she signed on with Jubilee to sing in his club, she initialed the contract, but instead of using her initials of M.A.D., she wrote M.A.X. Jubilee's bookkeeper, who needed glasses, thought her name was Maxie and the name stuck."

Mike gave Walden a hard look, for he had a feeling the man was withholding information, information that he had no intention of telling them. "Someone broke into an upper floor of my house and tried to kill Samantha."

Walden didn't so much as blink, but then he lived with death and murder and mayhem on a daily basis. "Did they now? You catch him?"

"No," Mike said tightly. "You have any idea who it could have been? Someone you know?"

Walden smiled. "It could have any one of thousands of people I know. There isn't a person I've defended who isn't capable of climbing into a window and trying to kill a pretty girl. You just have to tell me a time and a place, and I can match a murder with it."

Samantha opened her mouth to speak, but Mike beat her to it.

"February 1975, Louisville, Kentucky," Mike shot out, but he didn't turn to look at Samantha who was glaring at him. That was the time and place when her mother had died.

"I'd like to go now, Mike," she said softly, but Mike kept looking at Walden and didn't move from his chair.

After looking from one to the other of them, Walden punched a button on his phone and told his secretary that he wanted anything she had for the date and place Mike had given him. "She has everything on computer so it should take only a minute," he said into the silence that had developed after Mike asked his question.

For five long minutes he sat back in his chair and looked at the two of them, trying to figure out what was going on besides the writing of a biography. He wondered if they knew the full extent of what a nasty creature Doc was, or if they thought he was a sweet old man merely because he had defied the devil long enough to reach the age of ninety-something.

When his secretary placed a single fat file folder on his desk, Walden leaned forward.

"Ah, I remember this creep well. He went to the gas chamber about ten years ago and never was there a more deserving occupant. I defended him, but I was glad to know that there was no way I could win the case. On the night before he was executed, he asked me to come to his cell so he could tell me all about his life. I'd like to tell you that he was remorseful, but he said he wanted me to write everything down so he could be put on TV or in the movies like Al Capone was."

Walden flipped through the pages of notes. "I wasn't going to tell him that I'd die before I made him into a folk hero, but I recorded everything he said in case I later had someone accused of something he'd done."

Running his finger down the pages he said, "1975. Ah, here it is. My, my, but he was busy that year. Four, no five killed by him, all of them gang members. No, wait, here's one."

Glancing up at Mike, he said, "Louisville, Kentucky. February." He looked back down at the pages. "Nasty, nasty, this one. Good lord! I had forgotten about this. He was looking for Half Hand's money. I think someone hired him but he wouldn't say if he was hired or on his own. I think he wanted me to think he was smart enough to kill people without someone else telling him who, what, and where."

"What did he do?" Mike asked quietly.

"He killed a woman. He said he had a tip that someone in her family knew about Half Hand's money, so he went to Louisville, kidnapped the woman, and tortured her a while to get her to talk. Let's see . . . He held her against a hot radiator, but when he realized that she didn't know anything, he took her out and ran her over with his car. He bragged about how the woman begged him not to hurt her little girl, so after he killed her he stayed in town a few weeks and talked to the kid and asked lots of questions to see if she or her father knew anything. He decided they didn't, so he left town."

H. H. looked up at the two of them. A moment before they had been healthy-looking and pink fleshed, but now they appeared pale and sickly. The man reached out and took the woman's hand where it was gripping the chair arm, and it was then that H.H. realized that the tortured woman was probably this young woman's mother.

"I . . . I . . ." he began, and H. H. Walden, the man who was never at a loss for words, could think of nothing to say.

Mike stood up. "Mr. Walden, thank you so much for your help. I think we'll leave now."

"Look, I'm sorry I told you that story. I didn't mean . . ." There was nothing else he could say as he watched the two of them leave his office.

"Are you all right?" Mike asked when they were on the street.

Samantha nodded. "Fine. Really, Mike, I'm fine, but I think I'd like to take a little walk now. By myself. So I'll see you later."

"Are you sure?"

"Absolutely." When he continued looking at her anxiously, she gave him a reassuring little smile and put her hand on his arm. "Mike, it happened a long, long time ago. I've had many years to get over my mother's death, and it really doesn't matter how she died. Dead is dead, whether it was an accident or murder. I'd just like to be alone now. Maybe I'll go to a church for a while." With a little squeeze on his arm and another little smile, she turned away.

Mike caught her arm and spun her around. She was a good actress, he had to admit that, and if he hadn't known what she'd just found out, he'd never have known she was suffering. But he was beginning to know Samantha, know her well. Most of her life had been spent keeping grief and despair to herself, sharing it with no one. "You're going with me."

"No, I . . ." She tried to get away from him, but he caught her arm and held her to him.

Curling his bottom lip around his teeth, he gave a piercing whistle that made a cab come screeching to a halt. Mike opened the car door and pushed Sam inside. When she tried to speak to him, he told her to be quiet. As they neared the house, he took her chin his hand and turned her face to the light to look at her. Her skin was pale and clammy to the touch; her breath was uneven.

When the cab stopped, Mike paid and got out, pulling Sam behind him as he ran up the stairs, taking them two at a time, half carrying her when she couldn't keep up with him. Shoving the key into the lock, he flung the front door open and once inside, he ran with her toward the bathroom.

He barely made it before Sam began vomiting into the toilet. With one big hand on her forehead, the other arm wrapped around her ribcage, he held her while she heaved and heaved and heaved, her stomach convulsing, jerking in its attempt to bring up more. When there was no more, when she was hanging over the bowl with her stomach moving in spasms, he went to the sink and soaked a washcloth in cold water, then pressed it to her forehead as he flushed the toilet and put the lid down.

He had to help her off the floor to sit down. "I'm fine," she whispered. "Really, I am."

"Like hell you are." Leaving her alone for a moment, he got her some orange juice, then had to make her drink it. "And this." He held out a mint and when she shook her head no, he squeezed her chin and popped it into her mouth.

Taking the washcloth from her, he rinsed it, wrung it out, and wiped her hot face. What did one do in situations like this? he wondered. How did one deal with such devastating news as Samantha had just received? He tried to imagine how he'd feel if he'd just been told that his mother had been tortured and killed at the whim of some criminal who thought she might know where some money was.

"When you were a child," Mike asked, tenderly stroking her hot face with the cool cloth, "and you were sick, who took care of you?"

"My mother," she whispered.

"And after you were twelve?" Pausing in wiping her face, he waited for her answer, but she gave none.

Sam turned her face away. "I think I'd like to lie down now," she said as she started to rise.

"Go to bed? By yourself?"

"Mike, please. I really don't want to—"

He would not allow himself to be angry because she seemed to think that he'd demand sex from her at a time like this. Remembering that she'd said that when she found out her father was dying all she wanted to do was go home to her husband and have him hold her, he caressed her cheek. But her husband hadn't been there when she'd needed him, and after her mother had died and she'd needed her father, he'd failed her too. Mike thought that it was time that a man *didn't* fail her. "Sam-Sam, I'm not going to leave you alone. Your father may have left you alone to be an adult, but I'm not going to." Picking her up in his arms, cradling her like a child, he started out of the bathroom.

"Put me down," she said, struggling against him.

Stopping in the hallway, he looked down at her. "I'm not going to allow you to be alone. Call me autocratic, call me a male chauvinist pig. Call me whatever you want, but tonight you aren't going to be alone. This time you aren't going to have to deal with death by yourself." When she pushed against him, he pulled her closer. "You aren't big enough to fight me."

He started walking, not toward his bedroom as she'd thought he meant to, but toward the back garden, and as he walked, he pulled an afghan from the back of a chair. When he was in the garden, he sat with her on a chaise, holding her on his lap as though she were a child, and put his hand on the side of her head as he pulled her head down to his shoulder.

"Tell me about your mother," he said.

Burying her face in the muscle of his shoulder, Sam shook her head. Right now the last thing in the world she wanted to think about was her mother, about her mother being held to a hot radiator, her mother begging for the safety of her child.

"What was her favorite color?"

He waited, but when Sam didn't speak, he said, "My mother's favorite color is blue. She says it's the color of peace, and with all of us kids peace is what she most wants in life."

Sam was silent as he tucked the afghan over the two of them. It was a balmy, warm day, but Sam's shock had made her body cold to the touch, as though all her warming blood had retreated to somewhere deep within her. Stroking her damp hair back from her temple, Mike pulled her closer, trying his best to cover all of her with his own body. He didn't know why he was so adamant about it, but he felt it was imperative that he get her to talk.

"Did your mother sing to you?" he asked. Sam didn't answer. "Did I ever tell you that my great-great-grandmother was a famous opera singer? She was called LaReina. Ever hear of her?"

Sam shook her head no.

"My father has some records she made. Pretty good voice if I do say so myself. It amazes me, though, that no one in my family can sing a note. Not fair, is it?"

She was silent as he rubbed her back and held her so very tightly, so very securely to his big body. Samantha remembered what she had worked so hard not to remember: No one had held her after her mother died. After her mother's death, her father had spent three years sitting in a darkened room. Most days he didn't bother to shave or change out of his bathrobe, and he ate only enough to keep himself alive. Sam had done her best to cheer him up, but whatever she did, she never allowed him to see her own loneliness. She had never let him see her own sadness, never let him know how much she needed him, and how much she missed her mother.

"Yellow," Sam whispered. "My mother liked yellow."

Mike held Samantha for hours as she talked to him and told him about her mother and about how much her mother had meant to her. Remembering the story she'd told him about her father and her being like clocks that ran down after Allison Elliot died, Mike began to hear something else in Samantha's words: She blamed herself for her mother's death. She'd said that to him once, that she had killed her mother with her demands to go to a children's party, but she'd covered herself by saying that she knew that wasn't true. He now realized that had been an intellectual response. On a gut level, Samantha really and truly thought her mother's death was her fault. What's more, she thought that her father also believed she was responsible. Why else had Dave shut her off, not looking at his only child, not talking to her, not comforting her? The selfish bastard! Mike thought. He'd thought only of his own grief and not his daughter's.

After Kane's wife had died, Kane's grief had debilitated him, but he'd done his best to be there for his boys who'd waked in the night crying for their mommie.

But Samantha hadn't cried and she wasn't crying now. She was pale and cold and so weak she could hardly move her hands, but she was dry eyed. Denying herself the release of tears was the way she had punished herself for causing her mother's death and her father's grief.

"As a child I was a terror," Sam was saying. "I was selfish and demanding and always had to have my own way. Once my mother bought me a beautiful pair of blue velvet shoes, and I was so rotten, I wouldn't even try them on. I'd wanted red patent leather shoes."

"What did your mother do?"

"She told me that she was not going to drive all the way back downtown to purchase different shoes for me. She said she was not raising a prima donna and that I was to take what I could get."

"Did you get your red shoes?" he asked softly, already hating this story. It was the third one she'd told in which her normal, childish selfishness was blown up into making Samantha sound like a child demon.

"Oh yes. The next day, I told my mother how pretty her hair was and how blue her eyes were. I told her I was pleased she didn't look old like my friends' mothers who were without exception fat and ugly. I told her she should dress like the beauty she was. She smiled at me and asked what I had in mind, so I told her I remembered seeing a dress on a mannequin in the window of Stewart's Department Store that would look fabulous on her."

"And she took you back downtown?"

"She said that such sincere flattery and such cleverness in trying to get what I wanted deserved to be rewarded, but she warned me that there had better actually be a dress in Stewart's window or I'd catch it."

"I guess there was."

"I sweat all the way downtown. I was afraid Stewart's would have a display of men's clothes only, but they didn't let me down.

I got my red shoes and Mom got a new dress." Samantha was silent for a moment. "It was the dress she was buried in."

Mike continued holding her, continued stroking her hair, continued listening to one story after another, but with each story his resolve hardened. Blair had suggested that Samantha go to therapy. For what? So some guy could tell her over and over that it wasn't her fault that her mother died? Tell her that her father's depression wasn't her fault? It was going to take more than words to make Sam actually *believe* that what had happened wasn't her fault.

Somewhere in one of her stories she mentioned how her father had brought Richard Sims home for her to meet. It took Mike a few questions to realize that she'd married him mainly because her father seemed to have wanted her to. And why not? She'd dedicated her life from the age of twelve to twenty-three to her father in an attempt to make it up to him for what she thought she'd done to him, so why not marry to try to please him?

Her father's attorney had said that Sam gave up all her outside life to spend time with her father and help him with his depression. Sam had been so isolated during that time that the attorney thought maybe Samantha had been the victim of incest, but he hadn't wanted to get involved so he didn't really know for sure.

Alone from the time she was twelve, without her mother who had been, as far as Mike could tell, her best friend, Sam had had no one to turn to, but she'd tried to be the best little girl in the world in an attempt to make her father love her again. It was understandable that she'd marry whomever he wanted her to marry. Maybe marrying a man chosen by her father would make him love her again.

When Samantha's marriage had turned sour, she'd had no one to turn to. She couldn't very well call her father and tell him that the man he'd chosen for her—and Mike found out that it was Dave Elliot who had funded Richard's share in the CPA office in Santa Fe—was using her like a pack mule. Since Sam had spent her childhood isolated and burdened with secrets, she'd not learned how to make friends, friends she could tell her problems to.

Thinking back to the first month she'd been in his house, he now understood her depression, understood why she'd wanted to retreat into a room and never come out again. Retreat into her father's room, he thought. Her father had deserted her when he was alive, but maybe she'd hoped to find him after he was dead.

Over and over again the question of what could he do went through his mind. What could he do to make Sam realize that her mother's death wasn't her fault? That Dave's depression wasn't her fault? Mike had heard that depression was anger turned inward. What could he do to make her turn that anger outward? He wanted to see her smash things, wanted to hear her curse her father for deserting her, wanted to hear her scream about what her ex-husband had done to her. He wanted to see her cry.

Getting up from the chaise, he carried her into the house. Samantha thought he was going to take her to bed, and she hoped he was because she was very, very tired. Instead, he started for the front door.

"Where are we going?" she asked tiredly.

"I'm taking you to your grandmother. I think it's time for the charade to stop; I think it's time for some questions to be answered."

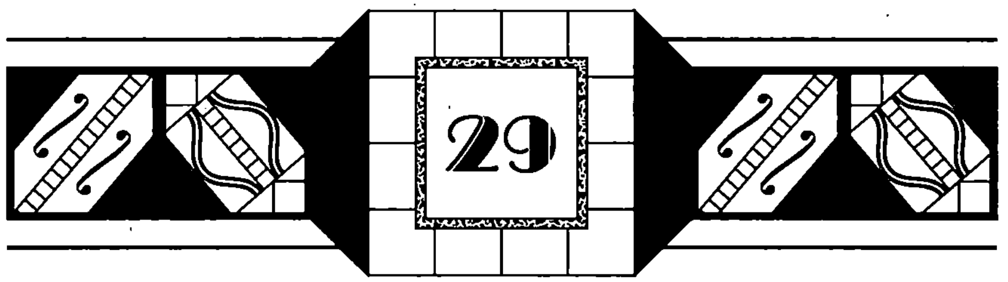

29

It was morning when Mike returned to Maxie's room at the nursing home. Not that he'd left the place last night. After he'd taken Sam to her grandmother last evening, he'd told Maxie that she was to tell Sam the truth. Mike had said that life was too short, too much an unknown, for the two of them to continue pretending not to know who the other was. He'd been angry and he may have said some things he shouldn't have, but Sam needed her grandmother for as long as she had her—and Maxie needed Sam.

He'd left them alone after that, and they had spent most of the night talking while Mike had spent the night, sleeping very little, on a hard cot in what was euphemistically called the "guest lounge." Mike didn't know what they had talked about for so many hours, but every time he had checked on them throughout the long night they were still at it.

"How is she?" Mike asked when he entered, looking at Sam curled into Maxie's arms. He hadn't shaved and he was still wearing the clothes, now rumpled, dirty, and wrinkled, that he'd worn when they saw Walden yesterday. Smiling, he looked at Samantha, sleeping the way one slept after great emotional trauma: with her mouth slightly open, her breath hiccuping now and then, her limbs as flaccid as an infant's.

Moving forward, Mike said, "Here, let me take her. She's heavy and your arm must be dead by now."

For a split second, Maxie gave him a look of such ferocity that he took a step backward. When he recovered himself, he grinned at her. "I guess she's not too heavy after all."

Embarrassed, Maxie chuckled. "No, she's not too heavy. I wish I could have held her when she was a child. I wish I'd been there after—"

"After her mother died?"

Maxie looked away, for she knew that Allison's death had been her fault, for if she hadn't married Cal, the Elliot family would have had no connection with Doc and Half Hand.

"The doctor gave Samantha a shot to make her sleep," Maxie said. "He didn't want to, but the other residents bullied him into it." Smiling, she looked at Mike with love and gratitude. "Since you bought the books and games and all the other things for this place, not to mention what you did for my room, I think these people would do anything for you. To them, you're a combination saint and superman."

"Don't let Sammy snow you. None of this has been my idea. Until I met her I led the quintessential life of a bachelor. I spent my days figuring out how to add more money to the already horrendous amount I have and my nights cavorting with one beauty after another—none of whom I gave a damn about."

Stroking Samantha's arm, Maxie put her hand to Sam's cheek. Maxie looked older today than she had when they'd first met her, for what Samantha had told her yesterday about Allison's murder had taken its toll on her. "And now your life is different?"

Mike moved to stand by the bed so he could smooth the hair back from Sam's forehead. "Now my life is very different. Now I feel as though it has . . . This is corny."

Maxie's eyes were bright, intense. "I like corny, especially when it comes to my granddaughter."

"Now I feel as though my life has a purpose. Does it make sense to say that I think I've been waiting for Sam? And do you know something? I think her father knew that I was waiting."

"David," Maxie said softly. "My beautiful son." For a moment she looked away, her eyes misty as she thought of all she'd missed: her granddaughter's life, her son's death. And if she'd been there in 1975, it might have been her who was killed and not the mother of a young girl.

Picking up Maxie's hand from where it rested on Sam's shoulder, Mike held it. "Dave wouldn't let me meet his daughter. At the time I thought it was odd that he wanted me out of his house before she arrived, especially since he'd had me stay in her little-girl's room instead of the guest bedroom." Mike paused for a moment because he understood that room now, understood that, for Dave, time had stopped on that cold February morning when his wife had been so brutally murdered—and as a consequence, time had been made to stop for his feisty little daughter.

"Dave chose Samantha's first husband for her," Mike said, looking Maxie in the eye.

It took a moment for her to understand what he was trying to tell her. "And you think he chose you for Sam, too." It was a statement, not a question.

"Yes, I do. Dave kept saying that he wanted to make up to her for what he'd done. I am ashamed to say that for a while I thought he'd molested her. Now I think he meant that he'd chosen the wrong man for her the first time. Looking back on it, I think Sam knew when she first met me that I was another arrangement made by her father, and I think that's part of the reason for her initial hostility toward me. Her father'd done a very bad job of choosing for her the first time."

Teasingly, Maxie smiled at him. "But he didn't do such a bad job the second time?"

Mike didn't return her smile. "He almost made a very bad mistake. For the first month Samantha lived with me, I let her stay alone in her room. I don't know what would have happened if my friend Daphne hadn't pointed out that Sam was . . . was . . ." He took a breath. "I think she may have been on the verge of suicide."

Reassuringly, Maxie squeezed his strong, young fingers. "You've made up for lost time." Her voice brightened. "So now that you're the rescuing hero, how do you feel? Like you've done a great, selfless deed?"

At that Mike laughed so loud Samantha stirred in her sleep.

"I did at first. At first I felt like a martyr. There I was helping her, saving her from herself, and the ungrateful brat wouldn't even go to bed with me to say thanks."

Maxie laughed. "You solved that one, didn't you?"

"She solved it. She solved everything. She's made me see how lonely I've been over the last years and how bored I'd become with everything. Sam looks at life as though all of it is new and wondrous. You should see her when she goes shopping. It's the same ol' stuff but to Sam it's as though she's exploring a new planet. I guess nobody who has lived through what she has takes the good parts of life for granted."

He caressed Samantha's cheek. "You should have seen her at the picnic with my family. She fit in with them as though she'd been born with them, and all the kids loved her. Kids don't like bad adults, they can sense them, but she and my baby sister had children all over them."

Stepping away from the bed, Mike examined a Victorian oil painting of an impossibly idyllic landscape, but Maxie could tell that he wasn't really looking at it. "Did she tell you about the picnic?" he asked.

"Some. She seemed to have had a wonderful time." Even if Samantha had given Maxie a minute-by-minute account of the day, Maxie wouldn't have said so, because it was obvious that Mike wanted to tell her something and she wanted to hear what he had to say.

"I was furious with my mother for planning the thing because I knew, but Sam didn't, that Sam was being tested. Did she tell you that I have an identical twin brother?"

"No."

Looking back at Maxie, Mike grinned. "She didn't tell you because it's not important to her." For a moment he paused. "All the things that have been important to other people about me—maybe you could say the things that define who I am—seem to mean nothing to Sam. She doesn't care about my money or that I'm one of a pair. Being a twin is great most of the time, but sometimes it feels as though you're not a unique person, that, unlike everyone else in the world, you're only half of a whole. One of the reasons I came to New York was because I was sick of living in my small town where even my own relatives constantly asked me which one I was."

Pausing for a moment, he ran his hand over the polished

top of a cherry table. "There's a saying in my family. It's a stupid, ridiculous saying and I don't know how it got started, but it goes, You marry the one who can tell the twins apart."

When Mike didn't continue, Maxie looked at him, trying to figure out what he was saying. "Your family came here to see if Samantha could tell you from your brother? That was the test?"

"In a word, yes. About five years ago, my twin brother, Kane, called my mother from Paris and said he'd fallen madly in love with a beautiful young French woman and was going to marry her. My mother congratulated him, then got off the phone and told me to get on the Concorde and go to Paris to meet her. She never said the words, but then she didn't have to, because we both knew why I was being sent to France."

"You were to see if your new sister-in-law could tell you from your brother."

"Yes."

"And could she?" Maxie asked.

"No. Kane didn't know I was coming, so I went to the address where he was staying and it turned out to be her parents' house. I knocked, but no one answered so I walked to the back garden, and there she was, as beautiful as Kane had described her. But the moment she saw me she leaped out of her chair, ran to me, threw her arms around me, and gave me an incredible kiss. By the time Kane got there, she had my shirt half off."

"Was your brother angry to find you like that with his fiancée?"

"No, we're not like that. He knew what had happened, but he would hardly look at me, because he also knew that she had not been able to tell us apart—and she never could. Every time I was near her, she'd ask me if I was Kane or Michael."

"What happened to her? You speak of her as though she were in the past."

"She died in an accident, and Kane was devastated. He was crazy about her, but—"

"But what?" Maxie asked.

"My family never met her, but I think there was the feeling that she'd died because she wasn't the right one for Kane, his . . . his soul mate, so to speak."

"What happened at the picnic here?"

Mike grinned at her. "Sam knew my brother wasn't me. She knew it immediately, but I don't think Kane could really believe it. All day long he kept testing her. He'd walk up behind her and put his hand on her shoulder, but Sam wouldn't so much as look at his hand—she seemed to *sense* who he was, and she'd say something like, 'What do you want, *Kane?*' She'd say it in a rather nasty tone."

If possible, Mike grinned wider. "I don't think she likes my brother very much."

"What does he think of her?"

Mike thought a moment and remembered seeing his brother watching Sam with his kids, remembered seeing him looking at her at the picnic. "If I dropped dead tomorrow, I think my brother would ask her to marry him. No, I think he'd beg her to marry him."

Mike stuck his hands in his pockets. "Kane has made me realize how lucky I am and how much I owe Sam. If she hadn't come into my life, I probably would have married someone like my last girlfriend, then drifted through life, not happy, not unhappy, but feeling vaguely unsettled."

Reaching out, Maxie took his hand in hers. "You have answered a prayer for me. If I could have one wish, it would be to leave this world knowing that my granddaughter had someone to take care of her, someone to love her."

"You don't have to worry about that. I love her more than I can understand. I can't remember what my life was like before I met her. I've thought about it and I can't seem to clearly remember what I used to do with my time." He smiled. "Maybe, as I said, I was just waiting for her to come to me, waiting for fate—and David Elliot—to hand her to me."

Looking about the room, now filled with antiques, paintings on the walls, rugs on the floor, he gestured. "All of this is her doing. You know what she does? About every ten minutes she tells me, 'Thank you,' and every time she says it, I feel guilty. All I've done is hand over some money, which I can well afford, but she gives of herself. She gives to me, to you, to my lonely brother and his barbarian children. Even when she thought she hated me, she worried about me when my head was split open."

"So what do you plan to do with her now?"

"First on the list is to impregnate her."

Maxie laughed so hard her machine needle started bouncing back and forth, as though it too were laughing. "You are a wicked young man."

"Anything like Sam's grandfather?" His voice lowered. "Anything like Michael Ransome?"

"How long have you known?"

"Since I got her clothes off of her, which, I might add, wasn't very long ago. She has the same birthmark on her shoulder that Uncle Mike had." He gave Maxie a hard look. "Have you told her yet?"

"Yes, I told her. I told her everything she needs to know. I wish you'd take her away. Take her to that town in Colorado of yours and keep her safe."

"We're in too deep now. Too many people think that we're hot on the trail of Half Hand's money—or whatever it is that people want from her. Sam's mother wasn't safe in Kentucky and Sam won't be safe in Colorado."

"What are you going to do?" There was fear in Maxie's voice.

"I'm going to solve the mystery. I'm going to find out what happened that night. I'm going to find out the truth—all of it."

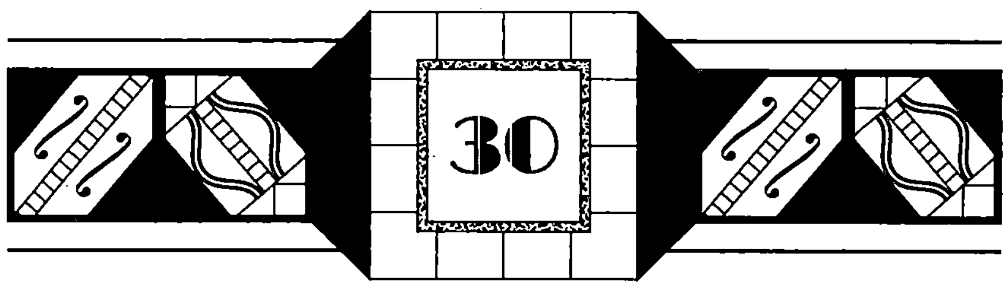

For three days Mike treated Samantha as though she were made of glass. She spoke only in answer to his questions, ate practically nothing, and had no interest in anything, not books, not computers, and, to Mike's dismay, not sex.

On the fourth day he couldn't stand it anymore and called in the heavy artillery: Kane's sons. At six in the morning the door to the bedroom opened and both Sam and Mike were awakened by two flying bodies screaming, "Sammy! Sammy!"

Kane stood in the doorway watching them, Sam hugging the boys, who were filthy, and receiving wet kisses, while Mike was trying to keep booted feet out of his face.

"When do rehearsals start?" Kane asked.

At that question, Mike darted out of bed and quickly ushered his brother from the room. It was after Samantha had bathed the twins, fed them, and sent them into the back garden to play that she looked at Mike and said, "What rehearsals?"

It was the first time she'd shown interest in anything in days. Mike wanted to tell her, but at the same time he was afraid to tell her what he had in mind. He very well knew that he'd already burned his bridges behind him; he couldn't go back now.

"I've tried to think of what could be done to find out what happened that night in 1928," Mike said. "I think people—myself included—want to protect you, so they do their best to keep their knowledge to themselves. But I've realized that you can't be protected until it's ended and it can't be ended until everything that happened that night is out in the open."

Samantha sat down at the table across from Mike and his brother and looked from one dark pair of eyes to the other. Speaking of hiding things, speaking of lying, she knew that that's exactly what they were doing. "I want to hear all of it, every word, with nothing kept back."

Mike and Kane began to talk over the top of each other. "Frank's bought Jubilee's nightclub and Jeanne's already buying the stuff to redecorate it and Dad's going to lead the gangsters and Vicky's taking her vacation time to outfit everyone and Mom's working on the food and you're going to sing with Ornette and H.H.'s going to play his grandfather and—"

It was at the mention of her singing with Ornette that she stopped them and made them explain. Interestingly enough, it was Kane who did the explaining. She could see in Mike's eyes that he was concerned about her reaction to his idea.

Kane, who, as far as she could tell, had been told everything there was to tell about what had happened with Doc and Maxie, told her that all the principles were lying. "Jubilee won't tell what he knows; H.H. won't tell what he knows; Maxie is too afraid for you to tell; Doc tells but no one can believe him."

What Mike had come up with was a way to solve the riddle: He and his family and Sam were going to recreate the night of May the twelfth, 1928. They were going to rebuild and redecorate Jubilee's Place as it had been on the night of the massacre, then reenact the entire evening, machine guns and all.

After his initial explanation, Kane sat back and listened to his brother further rationalize his idea to Samantha. The brothers had talked well into last night, with Mike explaining about Samantha's life, how Samantha had been such a good little girl since her mother died, a dear child who never caused anyone any bother, never asked anyone for help, and, as a consequence, had never been helped. She had done everything she could to gratify her father, even marrying a man she now knew she had never really liked, and she'd gone on to try to satisfy her husband—and become angry at herself, not him—when she couldn't please him.

Now Mike was telling Samantha that he wanted to recreate what happened on that night so long ago so he could complete his book, but the truth was, Mike was hoping to shock Samantha into facing what had been done to her. He wanted to shock her into expressing her sorrow, her grief, and, most of all, her rage.

After Kane was told what had happened to Samantha's mother, Mike said that after each of these horrifying revelations, Samantha would retreat into herself for a while, then after a few days, she'd act as though nothing had changed. For years the events of Samantha's life had been an endless list of disasters—a list that was now so long that most people could not have survived it. Yet Samantha not only survived, she went about her daily life as though nothing had happened to her. Mike had said he felt sure that if his only goal was to find out what transpired that night, Maxie could tell them everything, but Mike had a vision of Sam sitting primly in one of the little suits she was so proud of and silently listening to yet another story of unspeakable tragedy, then getting up and saying, "Where shall we go for dinner tonight?" No matter what Maxie told Sam, no matter the depth of the evil described, Mike was sure Sam would internalize the information, suppress what she felt about it, and continue with her life, apparently unaffected.

Mike's fear was that someday, maybe twenty years from now, she was going to be like those women in the papers who at fifty, after a seemingly normal life, suddenly became suicidal. If they endured, they had to at last confront abominations that had been inflicted upon them during their childhoods, incidents they had forbidden themselves to see when they were happening.

Mike was afraid for Samantha, afraid of what would happen to her if she didn't release the rage that had to be seething within her. Mike feared that, like a volcano, if Sam didn't explode now, she would later. The only fact for certain was that eventually Samantha had to release what she had repressed for so many years.

So Mike had planned this reenactment, telling Samantha that the reason for it was that he wanted to know what had transpired that night, but Kane well knew that if it were up to Mike, he'd walk away from all of this, content to never again hear the name of Doc or even of Maxie. Long ago Mike had lost the desire to know what had occurred so many years ago; now his only concern was Samantha and her future well-being. Mike's feeling was that if there were any way in the world to help Samantha and to give her what she needed, then he was going to do it, no matter what the expense, the time involved, or the people he had to recruit to help him.

It wasn't easy for Mike to put her through this theatrical production. He suspected that, at best, it was going to be an ordeal for her, but he also knew by something he called gut instinct, but Kane very well knew was nothing more than deep, unselfish love, that this was the only way that Samantha could ever possibly attain the peace she so desperately needed.

Because Mike saw it as the only way—abhorrent to him as it might be—he was going to say whatever he had to, to get Samantha to participate. He couldn't very well tell her that he thought the sight of blood and having to hear all the gory truth of what some gangster had done to decimate her family would be good for her, so in essence, Mike was telling her that the night was to be an amusing little diversion that would give his relatives something to do and would entertain everyone.

Mike was lying, as Kane knew that Sam often accused him of, but Mike knew that Samantha would never take part in this drama if she thought it was just for her. She would do it for Mike, but she'd never do this for herself.

Silently, Kane listened as his brother threw out a long line of bull about Jubilee having secrets and H.H. knowing more than what he was telling, and how, if Mike could find out answers to his questions, he would fulfill a lifelong goal of writing this book. But Kane knew exactly what his brother was doing, and he'd never been so proud of him in his life as he was at this moment. With identical eyes that reflected the pride and love he felt, he looked at Mike; Mike saw and, as always, he understood exactly what his twin was thinking. Turning a bit red, Mike looked away, but he smiled, pleased with his brother's unspoken praise.

After Samantha heard what Mike had to say, she knew that if she hadn't already been sitting she would have had to. "Who are we going to use for an audience?" she asked, eyes wide in astonishment. "How can we get enough actors to participate? And even if we found them it would take months to rehearse them." The unspoken words that Maxie doesn't have months filled the room.

"We'll use relatives," Mike and Kane said in unison—something that she was beginning to learn that they often did—and they said the words as one would say, We'll use mannequins.

"Mike," Samantha said, trying to sound reasonable. "We would need over a hundred people and they need 1920s clothes. It's going to cost—"

"Hell, we'll let the Montgomerys pay, or Frank can pay. Frank can buy some costume studio in L.A. and make a fortune off of it—as he always does. Don't worry about the money."

Looking down at her hands, then back up at them, she grimaced. The mention of Ornette made her feel a little queasy. "What about the band?"

"We'll ask Jubilee for the music."

She gave them a look of disbelief. "Jubilee is a hundred and one years old!"

"And bored out of his mind," Mike answered. "If we can get him away from his termagant daughter, I bet he'd love to help us."

Samantha wanted to say that the whole idea terrified her. It wasn't just the idea of singing in front of a lot of people that bothered her, although it did, nor was it the idea of trying to act in front of more than a hundred people. What bothered her was the outrage of that night. People had been killed that night; her mother had been murdered since then; her grandmother had spent a lifetime in hiding because of whatever happened on that night. She wasn't sure if she wanted to look into the face of that evil.

Mike saw her hesitation. Reaching across the table, he took her hand. "I think the idea of a show will appeal to Jubilee, and H.H. with that tattoo of his has got to be the biggest ham alive and maybe, if Maxie sees what everyone else is doing, she'll open up."

She looked at him. "And what about Doc?"

Mike took a while before he answered. "Doc is going to watch all of it."

At that Samantha laughed. "I can see the invitation now:

Miss Samantha Elliot and Troupe request the pleasure of your company at Jubilee's Place to recreate the worst night of your life."

Neither Mike nor Kane looked at each other, but Sam could feel them exchanging looks. "Mike," she said softly, "how are you going to get him there?"

"Let me worry about that," Mike said patronizingly.

But Kane didn't lie to her. Of course, he didn't have the motivation for lying that Mike did, for Mike was sure his life would be over if anything happened to Sam. Then, too, Mike knew Samantha's propensity for sticking her nose into places where it didn't belong.

"We're going to kidnap him," Kane said.

Samantha nodded, for it's what she'd thought when Mike had first said Doc was going to watch. "What has been done so far?" she asked, for she could tell that during the last days, while she had been grieving all over again for her mother, Michael had been very, very busy.

This time Mike and Kane did exchange looks, but it was a look of pride on Mike's part, as though he'd told his brother that Sam was the bravest person in the world and here was proof.

As they started talking, right away Samantha could see things that needed to be done, such as who was going to play Doc and what did Doc look like as a young man, and where were the headquarters for the many meetings that were going to be needed, and where were his parents staying, not, she hoped, in a hotel.

Kane sat back and drank a cup of coffee while he watched Sam and Mike argue over having his relatives move into Mike's town house for the duration. "They are perfectly happy in their various hotels. They have room service, maid service—and I have peace and quiet and privacy."

"All of New York is room service!" Samantha snapped at him. "And where is your brother staying? Your *twin* brother and his darling children?"

"Those brats are anything but darling!" Mike half shouted at her. "They've already eaten half my roses this morning and one of them dug a hole in my garden you could drop a car into. If I let them in my house, they'll destroy this place."

"Oh, is that it?" she asked, her mouth in a tight line. "It's *your* house, *your* relatives. Not any of it is mine, I guess, not even the upstairs. I should have understood that from the beginning, after all, I'm just your tenant and nothing else. I have no rights."

At that Mike took her in his arms. "Ah, baby, that's not what I meant. Of course you have rights. If you want all of them, cousins, whatever, here, then you can have them."

Looking over Mike's shoulder, Samantha winked at Kane. She may have played dirty in the fight, but she'd won, and wasn't that what counted? Kane raised his cup to her in silent salute.

31

After Samantha got over her initial qualms about the feasibility of trying to recreate a moment of the past, she went to work with a vengeance. The first thing she did was invite everyone who was to be involved in key roles to the house for dinner and a planning meeting.

"And I will cook," she said, to which Mike began to guffaw, saying that to her cooking probably meant punching the telephone buttons until her fingers were sore. Ignoring him, Sam gave Mike and Kane a very long grocery list that included such things as fresh cilantro, green chilies—"not those awful canned kind"—cumin, piñon nuts, and posole.

By the evening, when Mike's relatives arrived, the house was redolent with smells of chili, corn, and beef. Mike, Kane, and the twins had spent the day being ordered about by Sam as though they were in the army, as she gave them onions to chop, chilies to roast and peel, and, for the boys, bread to tear into pieces for bread pudding.

Everyone arrived hungry. While Mike poured margaritas they began to organize the recreation of the long-ago evening.

Jubilee with his mean-looking gray-haired granddaughter in tow came, but Jubilee sent her home after the first five minutes, leaving Ornette to stay with his great-grandfather.

It was as everyone was eating plates full of enchiladas, rellenos, posole, and pinto beans, exclaiming with every bite about how hot the food was and saying they couldn't eat it even as they reached for more, that Samantha began to believe that it was really going to work, because people were already talking of revealing secrets. Jubilee said that whoever was going to be directing Scalpini's men had better talk to him first. And H.H. (only the older children had been allowed to come and they were fascinated with H.H.'s tattooed hand) said he'd need to talk to Samantha/Maxie.

Halfway through the meal, when it was so noisy they could hardly hear each other, the front door opened and in came Blair, and she had Maxie on her bed, tubes connecting her to the machine rolling beside her.

"I tried to talk her out of it," Blair said, wearing her doctor face. "But she begged me. Well, is there any food left?"

For a moment, everyone gave Jubilee and Maxie some time alone as they held hands and looked into each other's eyes, sharing secrets that the others could only guess at. To the surprise of Mike and Sam, H.H. seemed to know Maxie very well. What's more, his respect for her seemed to be something that was usually reserved for overlords or, at the very least, great wizards.

"Who's going to play Doc?" Sam asked loudly, her hand on her grandmother's shoulder, wanting to break the somber mood the evening had taken, for Maxie looked weaker every day. "Of course it would help if we knew what Doc looked like in those days."

With those words Maxie became involved. All the way over in the ambulance that held Maxie's bed and machines, Blair had told her about what they planned, so Maxie knew what was needed.

Blair reported to Mike that the bloodstain on Maxie's dress was A positive, the most common type of blood. It could have been the blood of any number of people who were shot that night. It was not Michael Ransome's blood, which was O positive.

After Maxie arrived, Daphne entered with six of her friends. The sight of Daphne brought a hush over the crowd, for she was dressed as gaudily as a Texas tourist in Santa Fe, dripping sparkling fringe, with black and white feathers sprouting from her shoulders. After Samantha introduced her to Mike's family, Mike told them that Daphne and her friends were going to be the chorus and backup singers for Samantha. One of Mike's teenage cousins gaped at Daphne. When he recovered his powers of speech, he asked Vicky if they could measure Daphne and her friends for their costumes. Vicky rolled her eyes skyward, but one of Daphne's girls, looking at the clean-cut young men, said they'd not mind at all if the boys measured them—it would make them feel like schoolteachers.

When Samantha showed Maxie's clothes to everyone, Raine said, "Nice shoes," and they all laughed. Asking about the joke, Sam was told that Raine's mother loved shoes so much that she had a room full of them. Straight-faced, Sam asked, "What size?" which caused more laughter.

They ate bread pudding and bowls full of flan as they assigned roles and figured out how everyone was to rehearse. Some of them were to help the principles, such as Vicky, to make clothing, then later they were to be in the audience. Jilly was to be the resident historian, giving answers on any and all questions about what to wear, how to act, and what slang was to be used. Slang study was considered necessary after one of Mike's young cousins said he was sure the word *groovy* came from the twenties.

Only once did Samantha think of calling the whole thing off, and that was when Mike's dad, Ian, talked of arranging for machine gun practice. He saw Sam's face and told her the guns wouldn't be any more real than they were in the movies, but she remembered the death not too long ago of an actor who was playing with a pistol loaded with blanks.

It was late when everyone left, and there was lavish praise of Samantha's cooking.

"I haven't been in Santa Fe for years," Ian said as he stood at the front door, "but I remember it as being a rather sophisticated little town."

"I wouldn't say it's exactly unsophisticated," Samantha answered without a hint of smile, "but the brides there do register their china and silver at Wal-mart."

Ian chuckled all the way down the stoop while Pat and Samantha arranged for her and Ian to move into Mike's house the next day. When she left, she kissed Sam's cheek.

When everyone had left, Maxie with Blair back to the nursing home, Kane with the boys to the hotel to return in the morning with their clothes to move in, Samantha looked at Mike. And Mike looked at Samantha.

In the next minute they were on each other, making love on the foyer floor, then moving into the living room, then to the library, both of them feeling as though they hadn't seen each other in six months. In his exuberance, Mike began to bend Sam's body into unnatural shapes, but she was so limber from years of aerobics classes that she bent easily, her legs twisting about various parts of him with ease. They fell asleep on the floor of the breakfast room and woke in the wee hours, to feel bruised parts of each other's bodies. Mike, yawning, said they ought to go to bed, but Samantha said that she just had to have a bath—a nook and cranny bath. Grinning, Mike picked her up and carried her up to the bathroom.

Hell, Samantha thought, was rehearsing with Ornette Johnson. Never in her life had she met such a bigot, and when she called him that—after he'd told her for the fourth time in three hours that she was too white to sing the blues—a hush came over the room. According to Ornette, only white people could be bigots, and that idiocy sent Samantha into a rage.

When Mike entered the nursing home recreation room, he found Samantha standing on a chair shouting into Ornette's handsome face while he yelled back at her. Maxie and Jubilee sat to one side, looking on with expressions of adoration.

"So who's winning?" Mike asked, taking a seat next to Maxie.

"I'd say it was a draw, wouldn't you, Jube?"

"A draw, yes. I think Ornette's met his match."

Leaning forward, Mike quietly told them that he had arranged for a record producer to attend the night Ornette was going to play. "Who knows what will happen, but at least he'll be heard."

Smiling and nodding, Jubilee nudged Maxie to tell her that

Samantha had just called Ornette a racist and that they should watch the show the way the other residents of the nursing home were doing.

One morning, two days before the performance, Samantha threw up. "Nerves," she said as Mike handed her a washcloth. As he'd done before, Mike held her head while she heaved, then smiling mischievously, he suggested breakfast, which sent Sam back to the toilet.

By midmorning she felt better, ate some toast and juice, and took the vitamins Mike handed her. With a wicked grin, she said, "How's the dancing coming?" It had taken her four days of badgering to get Mike to tell her what he was doing to prepare for his role of Michael Ransome. When he'd at last told her, he'd had such a look of martyrdom on his face that she couldn't help laughing. Mike was taking lessons in ballroom dancing.

At eleven Mike went with Sam to Maxie's, then waited outside for what turned out to be three hours while Maxie told Samantha everything she knew about that night in 1928. When Samantha came out, she was white-faced and drawn looking.

"Find out?" Mike asked, taking her hand.

"Yes," she answered. "Most of it, but not all." Looking at Mike, her mouth was a hard line. "That corrupt old man," she said, and Mike knew she was referring to Doc. He also knew that Sam would have cursed, but there were no words to describe what she felt about the man.

Everything had gone so perfectly that there had to be something that went wrong, and it did. On the morning before the day of the performance, after Samantha had thrown up for the third time, Kane called and said that one of his sons was sick. He said it was nothing, but Samantha could hear the worry in his voice.

"Blair's with him and she says it's nothing to be concerned about, but I don't want to leave him. Could Mike get Dad or Frank to go with him to . . ."

"To get Doc?" Samantha finished for him.

"Yes," Kane said with a sigh, wishing Sam didn't know so much. "Dad will know what to do."

After Samantha hung up, she called Mike into the library and told him what Kane had said.

"Sure, I'll get Dad," Mike said as he moved toward the door, but Sam put her body in front of it.

"*I* am going with you."

"Ha, ha, ha, ha, ha," Mike's humorless voice said as he reached for the knob.

Samantha put her hand over it. "Mike, listen to me, it makes sense. I know what you and Frank have done, and don't even think of lying to me about it. Your brother thinks money can buy anything."

"For Frank it usually does."

"I know that this time his money bought the guards at Doc's place."

"It wasn't too difficult since they haven't been paid in weeks. Doc holds them off with promises of big money coming in from Europe, but I think he's broke. Frank could find out nothing about any money coming in from anywhere."

"Who did he ask? His Wall Street friends?"

"Money is money everywhere. Frank asked in places you don't want to know about."

"Simple little Sam, too dumb to hear all the facts."

"Dear little Sam whose life is in danger," Mike shot back at her.

Calming, Samantha looked at him. "How many of Doc's guards were you able to bribe?"

"Most of them. Okay, okay, eighty percent. There were three of them we couldn't get to and there's the house staff, such as it is. It's going to be dangerous getting in there." He leaned toward her. "Samantha, those guards carry guns."

She took a deep breath. "Mike, I'm small. I can go places you and your muscled brothers can't. I can climb fences and trees. What if you and your dad have to climb a fence? Who lifts whom? You can toss me over like a javelin if you need to."

"And land on your pretty head?"

"Don't you dare patronize me!" Putting her hand on his chest, her face softened. "Mike, you must take me. If there are any problems, Doc won't kill me and I can protect you."

"And what makes you think he'll stop at killing you? You know you're not his granddaughter."

"Because now I know what happened to Half Hand's money," she said softly. "And if Doc hurts either of us, he'll never see a penny of that money."

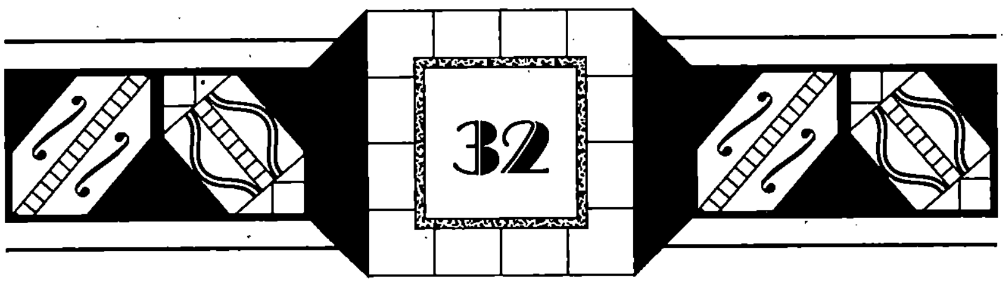

32

They had to go over the wall.

When they hid their vehicle in the trees, under cover of darkness, and went to the gate to find that it was locked, Samantha's first reaction was to turn around and go back to the city. According to Mike, Frank had bribed the men guarding the gate and it wasn't supposed to be locked.

"We don't have time for you to turn coward now," Mike said. He was afraid for her, true, but he'd had a lifetime of experience of living with his older brother: If Frank said the gate was going to be open, then it was—they were probably at the wrong gate.

At the far back of the walled property was a tree with a sturdy branch hanging over the tall brick wall. Climbing the tree first, Mike then helped Samantha up behind him. After throwing a few small packages of very fragrant meat onto the uncut lawn to ascertain whether the dogs were penned as they were supposed to be, he lowered Samantha to the ground. Lifting her hands above her head, lacing her fingers, she made a handle for her body, then Mike stretched out on the tree branch, slowly lowered her to the ground, then jumped down behind her.

"Run," he ordered and took off, Samantha on his heels.

As promised, the side door to the house was unlocked, and there were little night-lights on so they could see their way around furniture. Mike noticed that in a few places there were tables missing and places where chairs should have been.

When they sneaked past the kitchen, they heard voices, even though it was after midnight now and the house should have been asleep. Holding their breaths, they tiptoed past whoever was in the kitchen and went up the stairs.

One of the stairs creaked when Samantha stepped on it. Seconds later, a guard appeared, looking up the darkened stairs, but Mike's quick thinking saved them, for he practically threw her up the two remaining stairs where she crouched behind a sideboard, while Mike pressed himself into a doorway.

"You're getting nervous in your old age," they heard a man say.

"There's something going on tonight, I can feel it," answered another voice. "You think the old man's all right?"

"I think he'll outlive us all," was the answer, and the voice held no love for its employer.

When the men walked away, Samantha let out her pent-up breath and followed Mike when he motioned her to follow him. He seemed to have memorized the floor plan, because he knew where to go and which door to open.

Sitting up in bed, Doc was waiting for them. He wasn't sleeping, he wasn't reading, he was merely waiting. Fully dressed, on top of the covers, he didn't so much as blink in surprise when they entered.

"I heard you on the stairs," he said to Mike. "You would never have made a cat burglar."

"I leave thievery to you," Mike answered, then cocked his head at the man. "You're going with us."

"I had planned to. I want to see this party you have planned for me. It's been many years since anyone went to such trouble for my benefit, and I wouldn't miss it for the world."

"What do you know about us?" Samantha hissed at him.

When he turned to her, for a moment, Samantha's blood seemed to grow cold, for in this dim light, he didn't look like a pathetic, crippled old man but like a young, heartless gangster, a man who cared for no one and nothing.

"I did not live as long as I have by not knowing what goes on around me. I know that you have bribed most of my guards into leaving doors unlocked and penning up the dogs." He gave a nasty grin. "I relocked the front gate. I didn't want you to have it too easy, and in seven minutes I will have the dogs released."

At those words Samantha thought she and Mike should leave, and quickly, as she didn't want a wild run with snarling dogs nipping at their heels. This seemed to be Mike's idea too, but before he left the room, he scooped Doc's frail body into his arms, then took the stairs down two at a time, Samantha right behind him. By the time the two drowsy men in the kitchen looked up the stairs, the three of them were on their way out of the house.

Mike ran so fast Samantha could hardly keep up with him, but the idea of a pack of dogs coming after them, as well as a few men with guns, put wings on her feet. She had no idea where Mike was going, but she followed him as though her life depended on it—which it probably did.

When Mike stopped abruptly, she slammed into the back of him, but he didn't so much as waver on his feet. A narrow gate was in front of him. When Samantha, with a nervous backward glance, pulled on it, she found it latched with a lock with a big dial.

"What's the combination?" Mike asked the man in his arms.

Doc just grinned.

"If the dogs come, I'll throw you to them first."

"Young man," Doc said, sounding as though he were on a throne instead of being kidnapped, "you are the type who'd guard a man's life with his own."

Samantha thought that whatever else Doc was, he was an excellent judge of character, for she knew without a doubt that Mike was incapable of doing something as vile as throwing an ancient old man to a pack of dogs.

"What do we do?" Samantha whispered, scared half to death of what was coming.

For a moment, Mike looked at Doc, who was staring at them as though highly amused by all of this, then Mike turned to Sam. "Try 5–12–28," he said. It took Samantha a moment to realize that Mike had given her the date of the massacre, the date Maxie had run away.

With shaking hands, Samantha turned the round dial on the lock. When the combination didn't work, she looked at Mike in helpless terror.

"Try it again," he said, sounding as though they had all the time in the world.

The second time the lock opened, and they hurried through, with Sam taking a few seconds to relock the gate, hoping to hinder dogs and men who might pursue them.

They ran to the little truck that waited under the trees for them. Nearly a week ago Raine had called his older brother, Kit, and asked his advice about a very fast car, stipulating that the car had to have room for four people, one of them not well. According to all of the Montgomerys and the Taggerts, Kit was second only to his mother in knowing more about cars than anyone else in the world.

To the astonishment of them all, Kit drove down from Maine in a little black GMC truck called a Syclone. According to Kit, there had been only a very few of the trucks made in 1990 before the government took them off the market because they were much too fast (0 to 30 in 1.4 seconds). The only road-legal vehicles in the world faster than the Syclone were a Porsche 959 and a four-hundred-thousand-dollar Ferrari, both of which Kit owned, but they were two-passenger sports cars.

Kit had been intrigued by what was going on and had stayed to help. After outfitting his truck with a camper shell, he helped Blair equip it with an oxygen tank and the accoutrements of an ambulance.

Now, Blair was waiting for them inside the camper shell, ready to take Doc and see that he lived through what might turn out to be a very rough ride. As Mike put Doc inside the shell and strapped him to the bed, Samantha slipped behind the driver's seat. When Mike ran to the front of the vehicle, he told Sam to get over to the passenger side.

"I'm driving," she said.

"Like hell you are," Mike answered and started to push her into the other bucket seat, But Samantha was strapped inside her seat belt and didn't move so easily.

"Mike, I can drive! I drove in Santa Fe for four years and never had so much as a fender bender." She offered this explanation in the same tone that one would say, I won the Indianapolis 500 three years in a row, except that Samantha's words made no sense.

It was at that moment that the first shot rang out and Mike, disgusted, knew that he had no time to argue with Samantha. Jumping on the side of the truck, just inside her open door, he commanded her to drive.

And drive she did. There were three cars heading straight for them, big, heavy American cars, and Samantha maneuvered around them as though she were riding the dodge 'em cars at the state fair, passing them by quarter inches, but never so much as scraping the paint on Kit's precious, rare truck.

When she was past the three cars, she slammed on the brakes and ordered Mike to get inside. Without a word of protest, he rolled across the hood of the truck and dove into the passenger side, slamming the door after him and fastening his seat belt.

As Samantha started to drive again, he looked at her with new respect and not a little awe. For just a second, she turned her head and grinned at him. "If you think that was something, you should try a four-way stop in Sante Fe. No rules apply; it's whoever is the most macho goes first, and I learned to *never* give in."

For Mike it was a ride in hell. With the three cars pursuing them on the freeway back into the city, Samantha wove in and out of traffic as though she were an animated shuttle on a tapestry loom. The little truck was not only sickeningly fast, but it was also highly maneuverable, what's more it was four-wheel drive, *real* four-wheel in which all four wheels are independently driven, which meant that the truck could probably climb greased telephone poles. When Samantha saw an opening in the fence, she made a sharp right and ran up the very steep side of the embankment and suddenly changed freeways. Unfortunately, the truck had the road clearance of a BMW, which is to say that it had none at all, so they scraped bottom all the way up the hill, but when they'd made it to the top, they had lost their pursuers.

When they reached Maxie's nursing home, they had none of Doc's men behind them—but they did have three police cars.

Getting out of the truck, Mike found that he was shaking. Nothing he'd ever done in his life, not kidnapping a man and being nearly attacked by killer dogs or anything else, had frightened him as much as Samantha's driving. She, however, seemed perfectly calm as she ran up the stairs into the nursing home, leaving Blair and Mike to deal with the police, who would be shown the now-sleeping figure of Doc and told their drive through hell was a medical emergency.

As she ran into her grandmother's room, Samantha knew Maxie would be awake and waiting for her, for she'd known what Mike and Sam had planned to do tonight.

"It's done," Samantha said as she climbed into bed with her grandmother.

Maxie put her arms around Samantha. "Then he's here," she said softly.

"Yes," Samantha whispered, and in another minute she was asleep.

Here, Maxie thought. Doc was here under the same roof with her after all these years.

After spending the morning in the bathroom relieving herself of her dinner from the night before, Samantha spent the rest of the day of the performance with the other women in a brownstone hair salon in the East Eighties getting her hair set in a Marcel wave and a lesson in 1920s cosmetic application. Vicky had arranged everything. The women, who were to play gangsters' girlfriends, cigarette girls, and waitresses were happy and giggly and excited. Only Sam was subdued as she sat under a dryer and flipped through the latest issue of *New York Woman*.

Back at Mike's house there was no peace to be found, no quiet corner where she could sit and think about the approaching evening, for the house was the headquarters for everything that had to be done. It had come about naturally that Pat Taggert would become the crew boss, as she called herself. "*You* raise a dozen kids and see if you ever think anything else in life is difficult," she said to Sam.

One bedroom was a last-minute fitting room, another the makeup room, where Vicky had a couple of experts helping the women apply the cosmetics. Two other rooms were briefing rooms, one headed by Mike's father as he informed his players what they were to do. When Ian saw Sam standing in the doorway, without a smile, he shut the door in her face.

In the late afternoon, Samantha escaped to a corner of the garden to try to be by herself. She couldn't explain how she felt: calm but agitated, excited but tranquil. She wished Mike were with her, but he was away from the house, doing things he wouldn't tell her about.

When Kane's boys suddenly appeared before her, storybooks in their hands, she looked up and smiled at their father in gratitude. Pulling the heavy boys onto her lap, she began to read to them about Curious George.

It was evening when Vicky told her it was time to go to Jubilee's Place and get ready for the show. Kissing the boys goodnight, wishing she didn't have to leave them, Samantha went outside to the waiting car and started the drive north to Harlem.

In the previous weeks when everyone had been working, while Sam had been rehearsing with Ornette, no one had allowed her to see the renovation of Jubilee's club. Now, slipping in the back door of the stage entrance, she silently moved away from Vicky and walked to the front, where she stepped into a shadow, hidden from view so she could watch what was going on.

Jeanne had done a breathtaking job on the club. It looked like something straight out of the Art Deco period, which was the hottest, latest way of decorating in 1928. Everything was turquoise and silver, the dance floor in front of the band looking as though it had been appliqued with silver leaf. Behind the dance floor were tiny tables, what looked to be a hundred of them, each covered with long turquoise cloths and a little lamp in the center of each table.

On a dais was the band, with Ornette looking fiercely handsome in his tuxedo as he talked to his musicians, his beloved trumpet in his hand, and the sight of him made Sam smile. Under Ornette's façade of anger, he was a sweetheart, a perfectionist who loved music more than life, but a man who was afraid to show his soft inner parts. Now he was warming up his orchestra with a jazzy little number, and Sam knew he'd soon start on the blues. In 1928, during the very happy, rich time before the stock market crash, the country was wild for the blues, but after the crash, people only wanted cheerful songs, such as "Happy Days Are Here Again." As a result, singers such as Bessie Smith went out of favor.

As Samantha watched from her shadowy hiding place, she saw people begin to enter the club, laughing, the women beautifully, exquisitely dressed in long gowns. The 1920s fashions today might look shapeless, but there was so little to them that they showed off everything a woman had. When a woman walked, the draping fabrics swayed and clung to her in a very sexy way.

Two pretty young women came in together, their gangster men behind them, the men looking tough and complacent, smug even.

Watching them, Samantha moved farther back into the shadows so they wouldn't see her, for she was beginning to feel as though she were an anachronism in her slacks and casual blouse. Gradually, the club was beginning to fill up, and the more people who entered, the more Samantha felt as though she had stumbled into a time warp, for all the people and their surroundings were part of 1928.

When Mike entered the room, Sam pressed herself back against the wall as she watched him move about the club, obviously very familiar with it. Maybe she should have been jealous, for Mike flirted with every female in the place, but she wasn't, because this man didn't seem like *her* Mike; this man was Michael Ransome. This Mike walked differently in his beautifully cut tuxedo, and he used his good looks to advantage.

Samantha watched Mike go to one tootsie—the name perfectly suited the woman: too much makeup, movements too silly, a giggle that could be heard in Peoria, and, frankly, to Samantha's eye, too much breast—and ask her to dance. With a squeal of delight, the woman stood, actually, she wiggled into an upright stance, managing to make all the excessive parts of her jiggle. Before Mike took the hand she was offering to him, he looked to the man sitting across the little table for permission. The man had a fat belly that he'd encased in a spectacularly tasteless vest of black and yellow plaid. Looking over his belly, he gave a superior nod to Mike, as though he were a king granting a request to a subject. It always amazed Samantha that a person could feel superior because he or she was a criminal, as though the person had accomplished something that had meaning in life.

Escorting the woman to the silver dance floor, under lights so soft they would make the Wicked Witch look good, Mike took the woman in his arms and led her in a tango. Startled, for a moment Samantha held her breath, for she'd just discovered another of Mike's lies. He'd said he wasn't any good on a dance floor, at least not for anything except holding a girl tight and rubbing together, but as Sam watched him, she saw that he was a dream of a dancer. With as much muscle as he had at his disposal, he could lead a woman who was a less than perfect dancer in a dip; he could turn her when she was supposed to turn. Mike was even able to make the bimbo in his arms look as though she could dance.

When the tango was over, Mike led the floozy back to her gangster. After looking at him for permission, Mike kissed the back of the woman's hand.

"Hey, kid!" the gangster said as he imperiously motioned for Mike to come to him.

With no sign of what he must be feeling at such an autocratic command, Mike went to the man who then stuffed a ten-dollar bill in Mike's jacket pocket.

Samantha had to catch herself, for she was about to step forward into the light. How dare that two-bit nobody whose only claim to fame was that he'd engaged in illegal activities treat Mike like that!

"Are you ready?"

Startled, Samantha turned to see Vicky, who was wearing a lovely, slinky dress of blue satin, white feathers sticking up at the back of her head, a triple band of what Samantha had no doubt were real diamonds about her forehead. "Yes, I'm ready," Sam answered softly.

Following Vicky back to the dressing room, Samantha knew that with each passing minute, she was beginning to lose touch with reality. When Vicky opened the door, Sam was sure she was no longer in the nineties. Daphne and the other women were in various stages of undress; there were clothes strewn everywhere in front of a long, garishly lit, mirror-backed counter that held countless dirty bottles and pots of makeup.

"Lila?" Samantha whispered.

"Yeah, honey?" Daphne/Lila said, then turned to look Sam

up and down. "You better get ready. You're on in no time flat." Bending forward, Lila whispered. "Wouldn't want to disappoint Mike on the last night."

As though she'd been kicked in the stomach, Samantha drew in her breath. Lila wasn't supposed to know that this was Maxie's last night to sing in Jubilee's club.

Looking over her shoulder at the other girls, Lila whispered, "Don't worry, not one of them is going to tell."

Maxie—no, Samantha—nodded.

"Your dress," Vicky said, and when Sam turned, across Vicky's arms was Maxie's dress. It wasn't a reproduction as first planned, but the original dress. Mike had explained that it would have cost too much to reproduce the dress, so Jilly had contacted the Costume Society of America and through them had found a conservator who could clean the dress properly.

Samantha's hands were shaking as she took the dress from Vicky.

"The jewelry is on the table, and underwear is behind you."

"Break a leg," Lila called as she and the others trooped out of the dressing room, followed by Vicky.

Standing in the middle of the dressing room, the once-bloody red gown across her arms, alone in the long, narrow room, Samantha felt a chill go through her. Turning, she saw the couch, as always, covered with the discards of the women: torn hose, soiled blouses, heelless shoes. In the corner was another pile of clothes and Samantha knew without a doubt that buried under the heap was Maxie's little traveling purse that contained the life savings of both her and Mike, about five thousand dollars in hundred-dollar bills.

Still trembling, Samantha draped the dress over the back of a chair and began to take her clothes off, then put on Maxie's underwear. As before when she'd put on Maxie's clothes, she began to feel as though she were a different person. It was almost as though the clothes had magical properties that transformed the wearer into someone else. And no wonder, Samantha thought as she pulled the silk gown over her head. What the dress had witnessed that night was enough to leave an impression on fabric.

A few days ago her grandmother had told her what had actually happened that night that had changed so many people's lives. Maxie had told Sam everything up until she had walked out the stage door carrying her purse and Half Hand's bag.

Samantha had listened to her grandmother, had even felt some of what she was telling her, but sometimes it seemed to Sam as though she were almost numb. Just days before she heard Maxie's story she had been told that her mother had been tortured before she had been cold-bloodedly murdered. Wasn't there a limit to how much a person could feel? How much a person could even comprehend?

With the dress on, she sat down at the counter to check her makeup.

"Ten minutes, Maxie," came a man's voice from outside the door.

In ten minutes she was going to have to go in front of these people and sing for them; she was going to have to do what Maxie did that night.

Abruptly, she looked at the closed door of the dressing room. It was dirty looking, but there were no lacerations on it. No one had tried to claw her way out of *this* dressing room.

Making herself turn back around, Sam looked in the mirror. She had to remember that this was just a play; she was acting and she was trying to help Mike. He said he was going to have pictures taken to use in his book and he was—

Bowing her head, she put her head in her hands. Ornette was playing outside now, and she was having difficulty remembering that this was just an act. She was having a very hard time not thinking about her mother and her granddad Cal's loneliness after his wife had left him. Everything that she knew seemed to be screaming in her head, not being quiet as she usually managed to keep it.

It had all started on this night, everything that had happened began on this one long harrowing night: lives ruined, lives extinguished, hatreds kindled.

"I can't do this," Samantha whispered and started to get up, but then she saw a box of powder on the counter. It was an ordinary box, blue and white, with a big lambswool puff with a pink ribbon on top; the box was full of ordinary dusting powder.

Picking up the puff, she looked at it. Maybe it had started with the powder Maxie dumped over Michael Ransome's head. For a few moments Samantha put her head on her arms on the counter, releasing her mind to all that she had been told, not fighting it, but letting herself go, allowing herself to remember everything.

"You're on," Vicky said as she opened the door.

When Miss Samantha Elliot stood up, smoothing her blonde hair back in its perfect waves, she *was* Maxie, and she was ready.

34

Midwestern America 1921

Mary Abigail Dexter shot her fourth stepfather when she was fourteen years old, but by that time he'd been raping her since she was twelve. Her only regret was that she didn't kill him. She'd meant to, but she was crying and hurting and angry, and her aim was off. Rather stupidly, she had aimed for his very small head and not his enormous gut, so the bullet had grazed the top of his hairy shoulder instead of landing in his mouth that was once again laughing at her.

But the shot and the sight of his own blood had startled the bastard long enough for Abby to get out of the shack of a house and run, something she'd repeatedly tried to do in the past without success.

She walked for two days, going without food, but that was nothing unusual for Abby because her mother was usually too drunk or too busy with men to feed her only child. When she was far enough away from her "home" town (a place that fully believed in condemning the child for the parent's sins), she traded the gun for a one-way bus ticket to New York, a place where she hoped she could find anonymity.

When she got to New York, having spent as little as possible on food, she used what little money she had left on a cheap rayon dress, a pair of high heels, and a tube of lipstick, trying to make herself look as old as possible. Picking up a day-old newspaper from a park bench, she began to look for a job.

The only goal Abby had was to never live like her mother, who depended on the sexual desires of men for her livelihood. To men, Abby's mother seemed to be a good-hearted whore, someone who was always good for a laugh, who would do anything at all in bed with them. But Abby had seen her mother's desperation, for her mother had always dreamed of some man loving her and taking care of her forever. As Abby grew up, she learned that if a woman didn't take care of herself, no one else was going to do it for her. She vowed that she was not going to be forty-seven years old and living in the squalor her mother did.

There weren't many high-paying jobs for women listed in the New York paper and certainly none for an untrained, runaway fourteen-year-old. On her fourth day in New York, gathering her courage, Abby went to a bar in Greenwich Village and asked to see the owner to apply for a job as a cocktail waitress. The man took one look at her and said no, but Abby, by now nearly desperate, for she hadn't eaten in two days, had slept on park benches, and had raw and bloody feet from walking for miles in the cheap high heels, began to beg. Begging was something she'd never done before, not even with all that her mother's boyfriends and brief husbands—she often remarried but never bothered with a divorce—had done to her, but now Abby was begging.

"How old are you, kid?" the man asked, knowing that he had children older than this girl.

"Twenty-one," Abby answered quickly.

"Yeah and I'm Rudolph Valentino." Willie knew he was asking for trouble if he hired this kid who, if he guessed right, was in her early teens, but he could see under the hair that hadn't been washed in a long time and the cheap lipstick that was caking on her mouth that she had class—and she had brains. She didn't have that dull-eyed rabbit look of most of the girls who were cocktail waitresses at sixteen and would be at sixty if they hadn't died of some venereal disease before then.

"Okay, kid, you got the job," he said. "But if anybody complains, you're out."

The gratitude that was in her eyes made Willie shift nervously on his seat. Reaching into his pocket, he withdrew a twenty. "Here's an advance. Get yourself some decent clothes and get something to eat."

What Abby felt couldn't be expressed in words, so she just looked at the man and the bill in her hands.

"Go on, get out of here. Come back tomorrow night at seven."

When Abby returned the next day, Willie knew that he'd had the best of the deal, for the girl had taste. She was dressed as simply and elegantly as something out of a lady's magazine—and the moment Willie saw her he knew that his life was going to change.

Within two years, his business changed from being a two-bit bar/whorehouse to being a place where respectable ladies and gentlemen could come. Abby, who had been starving for respectability and responsibility, had been allowed to take over the place. She redecorated the bar, redressed the waitresses, made a code of conduct for all employees, and took over Willie's bookkeeping. By the end of three years, Willie was wearing custom-made suits with a three-carat diamond holding his tie in place.

It was in 1924, when Abby was seventeen years old, that she met the up-and-coming young gangster known simply as Doc. Right away, Abby recognized someone as ambitious as she was.

Doc was small and underdeveloped in a way that could only have been caused by malnutrition as a kid. There was a long scar across his neck that told of some old and life-threatening injury, and his eyes were never still. In fact, none of him was ever still, but always moving about, looking behind him, fidgeting with a bullet on a chain attached to his vest, and when he walked, one leg was a bit stiff.

Shadowing the little man was a tall, hulking, rather stupid-looking man with only half of a left hand called, appropriately enough, Half Hand Joe. Joe went everywhere that Doc went, to the restroom, wherever; he even tasted Doc's food before Doc took a bite.

After the first night that Doc came to the club, Abby took care of him herself, which she didn't usually do since she had become the hostess/manager, but there was something about Doc's halting walk and his nervous eyes that made Abby feel they were kindred souls. The two of them had been through a lot in their short lives, and somewhere along the way they had lost the ability to feel as other people seemed able to do.

For six months Doc came to the club and during that time he never spoke a word to Abby, but at the end of the six months, Half

Hand came to her and said that Doc wanted to speak to her in his car.

Abby took her time deciding whether to go or not, because she had an idea of what Doc wanted to ask her: He wanted her to be his mistress. On the one hand, Abby liked having the protection of a gangster. They usually gave their women expensive presents that Abby could cash in and use to someday buy her own place. Also, gangsters didn't seem to have very long life expectancies, which to her, when it came to men, was a good point. What she didn't like was the thought of sex with any man. Her mother's life and her mother's husbands had made her never want to have anything to do with sex again.

After a while, she decided to see what Doc had to say, so she went to the car, a long black limousine, and sat with him, only the ever-present Half Hand in the car with them. Abby had been surprised by Doc's request: He wanted her for his mistress, but he wanted her for show only. The rules were, no sex between the two of them and no other men for her. In return for her being his showpiece, he'd take care of her financially, even if she wanted to stop working at Willie's and do nothing all day but take care of her hair and nails. But Abby felt a great deal of loyalty to Willie, and even though he underpaid her and never said thanks for what she'd done for him, she wanted to stay with him; he needed her. Doc couldn't have cared less, and Abby breathed a sigh of relief, glad that he wasn't the demanding sort.

Sitting in the back of the limo, Abby agreed to Doc's terms and he presented her with the first of many presents: a diamond necklace. Over the next year Abby received a furnished apartment, the deed in her name, furs, jewels, and beautiful clothes. For her part, when she wasn't working she went with Doc wherever he felt he needed to go and she always looked her best, for that was what mattered most to Doc: He wanted to show the world that he could have the classiest of women on his arm.

It was in 1926, when Abby was nineteen years old, that she left Willie's. By that time, Abby had hired entertainment for the bar. One night the singer had strep throat and couldn't sing, so Abby was left with no one to entertain the customers. After spending hours trying to find a last-minute replacement, she decided to give singing a try herself.

From the moment she stepped on the stage, she knew she had come home. Everyone, including Doc and Willie, thought that Abby was a cool customer, that she was as cold inside as she appeared to be outside. No one had any idea of the passions that raged within her, for those passions came out only when she sang. Abby couldn't tell people what she felt, but she could sing what she felt. Every word of the blues songs she sang dripped with her misery.

Afterward, the audience came to its feet in thunderous applause, and hearing it, Abby knew what she wanted to do with her life.

The only person who didn't want her to sing was Willie, for he looked to the future and saw Abby leaving him and knew that he couldn't run his club without her, so he told Abby she was no good. With only his own needs in mind, Willie said that the applause had been for her looks, not her voice. With those words he lost Abby's loyalty. Abby had been willing to forgive him for not paying her well and for all the other slights, but she hated his lying.

She went to Doc and told him that she wanted to sing in a nice place, that she wanted to leave Willie's, so Doc installed her in Jubilee's Place in Harlem, a place where the women glittered with diamonds and the men were surrounded by auras of power. It was when she was signing a two-year contract with Jubilee that her name was changed to Maxie.

Maxie had trouble adjusting to the new place, for the other women didn't like her. At Willie's the women had been scared of their own shadows, and they had been in awe of Maxie. At Jubilee's, the girls in the chorus were also mistresses of gangsters, some of them working for Scalpini, who was a great deal more powerful than scrawny little Doc.

As though Maxie didn't have enough trouble, what with hours of rehearsals everyday, co-workers who were cool to her at best and hostile at worst, and the growing annoyance of always having to look utterly perfect for Doc, there was Michael Ransome. He had been hired by Jubilee to dance with the girlfriends of the gangsters who were too fat or too lazy or just plain too tired to dance with them themselves.

Michael Ransome was indeed a problem to Maxie, for all the girls were in love with him. It wasn't just that he was handsome, nor was it just that he had eyes that only opened halfway—bedroom eyes the girls called them. Nor was it his cleft chin and eyes the color of a stormy sea, somewhere between blue and gray, or his thick, wavy dark blond hair or his lips, full and sensual. No, what made all the girls love Michael Ransome was his manner, which was honey.

Hot honey. Hot, liquid, sweet honey. All Michael had to do was look at a woman and he could sense what she needed—then he gave it to her. He could be gentle and seductive or rough and demanding. He was whatever any woman had dreamed of in a man, and he had been known to seduce a woman without so much as uttering a word. All he had to do was look at her over a chilled glass of champagne with those slow, lazy eyes and women began to feel warm—so warm that they often felt the need to remove pieces of clothing. Sometimes the women whispered to each other that if a woman could somehow resist Mike's eyes she would never be able to resist his voice. It was deep and smooth and languid. He'd touch a woman's hand, lift it by her fingertips to his lips, all the while looking at her with that special, shaded gaze, then bring her palm to his lips, those full, sculptured lips, and he'd whisper, "I love you."

Never once had Michael failed with a woman. He got what he wanted from any woman and afterward she said, "Thank you."

But then Michael Ransome met Maxie.

The first time Mike came into the dressing room—what did it matter if he saw them without their clothes on since he'd been to bed with each of them—after Maxie started singing at the club, he gave her his second-best come-on. After all, why waste his energy when anyone who could sing with the lust that Maxie did had to be one hot number?

Instead of the easy conquest he expected, to his consternation, without uttering one word to him, Maxie dumped a full box of face powder over his head. At first neither Mike nor the girls could believe what had happened. Nobody turned Mike down. Going to bed with Mike was a sort of initiation to the club.

When they finally did realize what Maxie had done, it would be hard to decide who was more angry, the girls or Mike. For months after the powder-dumping incident, Maxie had to endure spiteful little things perpetrated by the women: makeup missing, one shoe not where she'd left it, a smudge on her dress. Maxie endured it all, never complained, never said anything to any of the women, but was always cordial and polite.

Harder to endure than the women's spitefulness were the snips that Michael Ransome took at her. He was truly angry that she'd turned him down and done it so publicly. After trying two more times to seduce her, he let the whole club know that she was frigid, calling her names like Ice Princess and telling people she thought she was too good to be in a nightclub. He harassed her without end.

It was Lila, the lead dancer, who told Mike to lay off and that she was getting sick of hearing his bellyaching and she was beginning to admire Maxie's fortitude and the way she carried herself. And it was Lila who first invited Maxie to go shopping with her and the girls, asking Maxie if she'd help them choose dresses that weren't so gaudy. Maxie was a little leery of what the women had planned for her, but she went and she had a wonderful time. When the women found out that Maxie wasn't so much aloof as she was shy, Lila guessed that the poor kid had never had a chance to learn how to make friends.

After that the women began to accept Maxie into their group, inviting her places and accepting Maxie's invitations.

But Mike kept badgering Maxie, still so angry at her that he intensified his efforts to get a reaction out of her—but he didn't succeed. When Lila told him to lay off and slammed the dressing room door in his face, Mike was angry enough to kill.

Then one night Michael's life changed forever. An hour after he left the club he realized he'd forgotten his wallet, having left it in his tux at the club. Annoyed with himself, he went back to the club to find it locked and dark. Knowing that a second-story bathroom window's lock was broken, he piled garbage cans on top of each other in a precarious stack and climbed in the window.

After he had his wallet, as he was leaving the club, he thought he heard something. Walking down a corridor, he saw a dim light shining from under the women's dressing room door. Silently pushing the door open, he looked in to see Maxie sitting at the table crying, but she was crying in that way that he and the other kids in the orphanage had cried: silently, as though, if they were discovered, they would be punished.

Without a conscious thought, he did what he'd always wished someone had done for him: He went to her, knelt beside her, and took her in his arms. After an initial moment of Maxie's fighting him, she calmed down and clung to him—and Mike clung to her. Had someone told him that the reason he bedded all the women was because he wanted to be close to them, that he wanted them to love him, he would have laughed, for he liked to think of himself as utterly independent, needing no one. He liked to think he was a love 'em and leave 'em guy, and he knew that's what the women thought of him. Not one of them was ever serious about a too-handsome dancer in a bar.

When Maxie couldn't seem to stop crying, Mike carried her to the beat-up old couch along one wall, moving a jumble of sequined and rhinestoned garments and torn netting, to sit with her and hold her.

It was the most natural thing in the world when they started kissing. Months of anger at each other quickly turned to passion as they began fumbling with each other's clothes, then tearing at them. They made love on the couch once, twice, three times, not talking to each other, afraid that words would break the spell, afraid that each would become what they didn't want. Mike was afraid Maxie would turn into all the other women, afraid she'd say, "That was swell, Mike, but I need to get back to my old man now." Maxie was afraid that she was just another one of Mike's girls.

It was nearly daylight when Maxie first spoke. Tired, sated, she lay in Mike's arms and knew she never wanted to leave this place where she felt safe for the first time in her life. "If Doc finds out, he'll kill both of us."

It took Mike a few minutes to calm his racing heart, for her words indicated that she intended to continue seeing him. "We will keep it a secret," he said, and Maxie nodded, for she sensed that he knew about secrets as well as she did.

Over the next months she and Mike met clandestinely in a cold-water flat that was a breeding pen for cockroaches and rats. They made love, yes, but they also talked, telling each other all about their lives, for the first time each having a friend to confide in.

At the club they did their best to keep their growing love for each other a secret. They said all the right things. Mike still called Maxie an icy bitch; he still sneered at her, and Maxie still stuck her nose in the air when he was around.

But they didn't fool the women. For one thing, Mike quit making passes at everything in skirts, even behaving himself on the dance floor. For another thing, there was that look in Mike's eyes. Where once he'd looked at Maxie with eyes that glittered with anger, they now glittered with love. Not lust, love.

Knowing that the women saw what was going on, one night Maxie tried her best to make them think that she and Mike still hated each other by tossing a glass of champagne in his face.

Mike ruined everything by grabbing Maxie's shoulders and kissing her hard on the mouth, and the girls recognized a familiar gesture when they saw one. When Mike walked out of the dressing room, there was silence until Lila said, "Honey, you oughta be real careful with a man like Doc."

Maxie could only nod.

35

12 May 1928

Maxie was sure she'd never been so happy in her life as she was tonight. Everything about Jubilee's club was especially beautiful, from the mirrored ball overhead that flickered flattering lights across people's faces to the people themselves. Tonight the club seemed to be full of Doc's men and even their crude manners couldn't dull Maxie's happiness.

It was difficult to sing the blues, difficult to sing about your man leaving you and no longer loving you when she knew that tonight she was leaving the city with Michael. Her bags were packed and ready, waiting for the last show to be over, then she and Mike were slipping away, going to the Midwest somewhere or to California, anywhere that was far enough away from Doc and his type.

As she sang, she saw Mike waltzing some woman with hair the color and texture of straw across the dance floor, her arm about his wide shoulders, her gum popping in his ear. As he passed Maxie, he winked at her, then rolled his eyes skyward. The song of misery that Maxie was singing became a caressing love song.

When at long last it came time for Maxie's break, with Lila and the girls coming on stage next, Maxie could hardly contain her excitement through the introductions.

As she was rushing toward the dressing room, in the darkened hallway, Jubilee stepped in front of her. "You oughtn't to give yourself away like that, kid," he said softly, and she knew he meant her singing and the way she had been smiling at Mike all through the evening.

Maxie was glad for the darkness to hide her blush. She felt bad for not telling Jubilee that she was leaving tonight, but she and Mike had agreed that their leaving had to be kept secret, and that meant telling no one, no good-byes to anyone.

Pretending she had no idea what Jubilee meant, Maxie went past him and headed for the dressing room, but Mike caught her in a shadow, pulling her into a dark doorway and kissing her as though his life depended on her.

"Mike," she said, trying to think, but his hands were all over her. "Mike, we can't be seen."

Tenderly, he put his hands on her cheeks and kissed her gently. "How's my kid?"

"Healthy," she answered. "Secure and happy, just as her mother is."

He kissed her again. "Just like his old man."

Quietly they laughed together over her calling the baby she carried "her" and Mike referring to it as a male.

Using what strength she had, Maxie pulled away from him. "Three more hours," she said. "In just three more hours we'll be off." Suddenly she was frightened, for it seemed that every person in her life had abandoned her. "Mike, you aren't—? I mean—"

Mike put his fingertips on her lips. "Am I playing with your affections? Have I impregnated you and now plan to abandon you to raise my kid on your own? The answer is yes, I want to spend the rest of my life waltzing brainless women around a floor, and I love spending my evenings with gangsters. Such stimulating conversation. 'Hey, Big Nose,' " he mocked. " 'How many you kill today? Only three? I got me four. You owe me ten bucks.' "

Maxie giggled. "Mike, you're awful. Now, go on and get out of here before someone sees us."

After another lingering kiss, he left her to go back to the dance floor while Maxie went into the empty communal dressing room to check her hair and makeup before she went on stage again.

A lipstick tube in her hand, she glanced into the mirror and at first didn't believe what she saw. A little boy about nine years old had silently pushed open the door and was standing there, tears slowly running down his cheeks.

Maxie turned to him. "What's wrong?" There was concern in her voice, true, but there was also fear; there was always fear about a place that was peopled with men like Doc.

"Somebody shot my daddy," he said softly.

Without another word, eyes wide, Maxie got up, went to the child, and offered him her hand. Taking it, the boy led her into Jubilee's office.

At first Maxie didn't see the man lying on the floor because he was partially hidden between the desk and a half-open closet door. It was Half Hand Joe, the man who followed Doc everywhere. At Maxie's first horrified glance he looked to be dead, for there was a bullet hole in the side of his head, an almost bloodless, neat hole at the edge of a forehead that already had several scars on it. But then Joe's eyelids fluttered.

Kneeling, Maxie went to him and gently pulled his head onto her lap.

"Joe," she whispered, stroking his hair back from his forehead. Already she could feel the blood from the wound on the back of his head seeping into her dress.

Opening his eyes, Joe glanced at her, but then his eyes went to his son standing at his feet and silently crying. Maxie hadn't thought of Joe as having children; in fact she hadn't thought much of Joe one way or the other, as he was just a shadow that followed Doc, never saying anything, seeming to be content to be near his master.

"Take . . . care of him . . . for me," Joe whispered, looking at his son.

"Be quiet," Maxie said. "I'll get a doctor."

"No!" Joe said, then closed his eyes and for a moment she thought he was dead, but he opened them again. "Listen . . ." he said. "Must tell."

"Yes," Maxie whispered, leaning forward. Even she knew that with a wound like his he wasn't going to need a doctor.

"Doc killed me."

This statement was beyond the belief of Maxie, for if there was anyone Doc cared about it was this man. "No, he couldn't have."

Weakly, Joe held up his mutilated hand. "Useless to him. Bad shot. Stupid."

Holding his head, feeling the warmth of his life's blood seeping onto her dress, Maxie still couldn't believe what he was saying. Joe started fumbling at his coat lapel and Maxie realized that he wanted something from his pocket. Reaching inside for him, she pulled out a zippered canvas bag, the kind the bank gives you to carry money.

"I knew . . ." Joe said. "I knew was coming. I took . . . money. Money marked. Don't spend."

Holding the bag, Maxie nodded. "No, of course I won't spend it."

"Help my boy." For a moment, Joe tried to lift himself, and his eyes were brilliant with their intensity. "Swear."

"Yes," Maxie said, and she could feel the tears running down her face. "I swear I'll take care of him."

Joe lay back down, his strength almost gone. "Doc doesn't know . . . about boy. Boy a secret. Money a secret."

"I'll keep your secrets," Maxie said. "All of them." In the next minute she knew that Joe was dead.

Tenderly, she lay him back on the floor, and turning to the little boy, she took him in her arms and held him for a moment while he cried, "I want my daddy."

By some instinct, Maxie knew that she didn't have time to comfort the child. Doc had said he wasn't coming to the club tonight, that he had other business to attend to and couldn't make it, and his absence was why she and Mike had chosen tonight to make their getaway. But now the hairs on the back of Maxie's neck were rising because she sensed that something horrible was going to happen. Something had made Doc lie to her and made him kill a man who had been his friend and bodyguard.

Abruptly, she pulled away from the child and stood. Time was at a premium now; she knew that as well as she'd ever known anything in her life. She had to take care of this child, then get to Mike and both of them had to get out of this club. If she and Mike were going to get away, they weren't going to be able to wait until after the last show, they were going to have to leave *now*.

Pulling the child behind her, Joe's canvas pouch in her hand, Maxie went back to the dressing room. There, secreted under what looked to be a pile of clothes, was her fat little traveling purse, filled with things she'd need for the coming journey, and hidden in the lining was an inch-thick stack of hundred-dollar bills, all the money she'd been able to save from years of waitressing and singing. She didn't hesitate as she took the money from the purse and wrapped it in one of Lila's rayon blouses that was hanging on the back of a chair.

"Who is your mother?" she asked the child, trying not to convey to him the sense of panic that was building within her, but not succeeding.

The child had no idea what she meant. His mother was his mother and no one else.

Maxie took the child's chin in her hands, maybe a little harder than she meant to. "Tell me the truth: Is your mother a good mother?" Maxie had had too much experience with bad mothers to trust a woman just because she had the near-holy title of "mother" attached to her.

Again, the child didn't understand her.

Exasperated, Maxie said, "Does she beat you? Is your house clean? Do a lot of men spend the night in bed with her?"

The boy's tears started again. "She doesn't hit me and she's always cleaning and only my dad sleeps in the bed with her."

Feeling guilty and wanting to comfort the boy, Maxie knew she couldn't. Like bile rising in her throat, she knew that time was running out and she had to get to Mike and get out of this club.

She thrust the bundle of money into the boy's hands. It was everything she and Mike had, and she had no idea what she and Mike were going to use to travel on or to set up housekeeping with, but she couldn't think of that now. Right now she knew that the most important thing in the world was to get her and Mike out of here alive.

"Give this to your mother," she ordered. "And tell her to get out of New York. Now run as fast as you can. Tell her she has to leave *tonight.*"

After a few red-eyed blinks at her, the boy scurried out of the dressing room and ran out the back door of the club. For a moment, just a tiny moment, Maxie stood and watched him leave before she turned back to the dressing room.

But she didn't enter the room, because Doc was standing there, and in his hand was a pistol with a very large opening in the end of the barrel. Without saying a word, he motioned her into the dressing room.

It would be difficult to describe Maxie's feelings at the time. She didn't feel terror as she would have thought, only a dull heaviness, because she knew that her life was over. A man like Doc wouldn't allow himself to be cuckolded without punishing the perpetrator, and she had no doubt that he knew about her and Michael. Maybe it's what she deserved, she thought, because she had agreed to his rules and she had broken them.

Silently, he stepped into the room behind her and locked the door with a big key that she hadn't known existed. Wanting to be brave, wanting to face death with her shoulders high, Maxie turned to him, her back to the long, garishly lit cosmetic counter and faced him as he took a seat across from her.

"How did you find out?"

With a little smile that made Maxie shiver, he shrugged, obviously not planning to enlighten her.

He's enjoying this, she thought, looking at him. My God! he's enjoying this! Nothing else in life gives him pleasure or excitement, not sex, not food, not people who love him, nothing pleases him but this, knowing that he is going to kill someone—having absolute, life-and-death control over another human being.

Knowing that now she had nothing more to lose, she said, "Why did you kill Joe?"

Again Doc shrugged. "He was too clumsy and he was of no more use to me."

"As I am of no more use to you?"

"Exactly."

Taking a deep breath, her hands behind her, she braced her body against the edge of the countertop and felt Joe's blood drying on the front of her dress, stiff and loathsome. "You'd better get it over with. The girls' act is almost finished and they'll be in here soon."

Doc's smile widened. "No they won't."

It was as though the blood suddenly drained from Maxie's body, and her first thought was of Michael. She didn't know what Doc had planned, but she knew it involved Mike.

Without thinking what she was doing, she lunged for Doc. He was little and scrawny, but he was strong, and with one backhand slap, he knocked her to the floor.

Slowly, painfully sitting up, blood coming from the corner of her mouth, she looked up at him. "Kill me," she whispered. "Do it now."

Still smiling, Doc said softly. "Not yet. You're going to die more than once tonight."

At first Maxie thought he meant he was going to torture her, but in the next moment she heard the first blasts of the machine guns and the accompanying screams. In terror, at first uncomprehending,

Maxie bolted for the door, meaning to go to Michael, but the door was locked. For a moment tearing at the knob, pulling frantically on it, she turned to Doc. "Give me the key," she screamed, barely able to hear herself over the sound of the machine guns and the screams of both men and women coming from the ballroom floor. "If you have any mercy in you, give me the key!"

But Doc just sat there with that enigmatic little smile, watching her, as though he were fascinated with her actions, as though he were a scientist observing a very interesting species of animal.

The machine guns seemed to go on and on, while Maxie clawed at the door until she had no fingernails left, then crying great sobs that came from her belly, she slid to the floor, leaning back against the locked door.

It was while she was crying, when she thought the pain in her would never be healed, that she saw what she at first thought was a mirage. On her right was Lila's big, overstuffed bag that she carried with her, full of clothes and shoes and heaven knew what else. Sticking out of the corner was a tiny pearl-handled pistol. Once, Lila had said that she carried her own bodyguard with her and when the girls had laughed, Lila had shown them the little two-shot derringer.

Maxie didn't think about what she was doing. With a movement as lithe as a snake's, she grabbed the derringer and, still sitting, spun around and fired. Years before, she'd made the mistake of aiming for a man's head, but this time she went for his belly, quickly firing two bullets into the exact center of him.

She wasn't a doctor and she couldn't be sure, but from the way Doc's legs collapsed under him, she thought she hit his spinal cord. While uttering a high-pitched scream, Doc slid from the chair, the .38 dropping from his hand to the floor.

Maxie had no thought for Doc's gun, for her only thought was to get to Michael. The guns had stopped now, but she still heard screams and moans of both pain and terror.

While Doc looked up at her from the floor with eyes that blazed with pain and hatred, she rummaged in his pockets until she found the door key, then with shaking hands, she unlocked the door.

Doc's voice made her pause at the doorway, her back to him. "Please," he whispered. "Please help me."

For a moment the humanity in her hesitated, but then she kept going, running toward the front of the club.

She was not prepared for what she saw: blood and more blood.

People with limbs missing. Lila was lying in a pool of her own blood, half of her face perfectly made up, the other half gone. Maxie saw three other girls, all three of them dead.

Already the place was filling up with hospital people and Maxie knew that in order to get here this fast they had to have been notified before the massacre. Doc's idea of compassion, she thought bitterly.

Stepping around the people, ignoring the way her shoes stuck to the floor, she searched for Mike—and when she saw him a white-gowned man was pulling a blood-soaked sheet over Michael's beloved face. Running toward him, the orderly caught her shoulders.

"He's dead and I don't think you should look at him. They blew the bottom half of him away."

Twisting hysterically, Maxie tried to get away from the man and go to Mike.

"Either you calm down or I give you something to knock you out," the man said. "We have enough to deal with here without the uninjured going crazy on us."

For a moment Maxie could only stare at him. Uninjured? she thought. She was far from uninjured.

"That's better," the man said when Maxie stopped struggling. "Why don't you go home?"

Go, she thought. That's what she should do, because if she stayed here she wouldn't be allowed to live another forty-eight hours. Right now she cared nothing for her own life, but she cared a great deal about Michael's child that was growing in her womb.

Mechanically, she turned away from the people writhing on the floor, looked away from all the blood and went back to the dressing room. Without so much as a glance at Doc lying on the floor, even though she could feel his eyes on her, she picked up her purse and the bag Half Hand Joe had given her. Somewhere inside her she knew that she should pick up Doc's gun and kill him, but she couldn't. She couldn't put him out of his misery as one would do for a beloved pet; she wanted him to stay alive and suffer as she was going to suffer.

Her eyes straight ahead, she walked out the back door of the club.

1991

Samantha awoke as though coming out of a hypnotic trance, and suddenly she was no longer Maxie but herself and it was no longer 1928 but 1991. She had thought Mike was going to train someone to play Doc, but he hadn't, for in front of her was the diminutive man himself—and he had that knowing little smile on his face. Everything had been played out as it had happened, nothing had changed with the passage of time.

On that night in 1928, Maxie had shot Doc and severed his spinal cord, yet for two years he'd managed to keep secret the fact that he was crippled before he told the world that he had been hurt in a car accident. Maxie had taken away his mobility and she'd taken away all the money Half Hand, acting under Doc's orders, had stolen from Scalpini. Doc, already eaten with hatred of Maxie for betraying him, made it his life's quest to kill her and anyone who knew anything about her. In 1964, when he'd seen the photo of Maxie with her granddaughter, apparently happy, he'd nearly gone berserk. His mistake had been in calling her to threaten her. By the time he sent a killer for her, she had already left Louisville.

By 1975, his days of power were on the wane so he'd sent a man to Louisville to find out if Maxie's family knew anything about Half Hand's missing money—his money.

Now, knowing all of this, Samantha found herself standing in front of the shrunken man sitting in his wheelchair—and there was a gun in her hand. At this range, whether the gun was loaded with blanks or live bullets, if she shot him, she'd kill him. Up until now she'd seen him as an old man, but now she saw the man who had mowed down a nightclub full of people to get to the man who'd impregnated "his" girl. She saw the man who, in order to gain control of illegal liquor sales, had killed his own men, blaming it on another mob boss.

"You killed a man who loved you more than he loved his own life," Samantha whispered, speaking of Half Hand. "You've murdered anyone who has ever tried to care about you. Has it been worth it? Now you sit here, an unloved old man, alone and lonely, and there isn't a person in the world who cares about you. You were crippled by your own greed. Has all the money been worth the pain?"

Doc laughed at her as though she were a simpleton. "You stupid child. You think everyone is like you. Yes, it's been worth it. I have never been bored a moment in my life. I've taken anything I wanted and I've won every game I've played. There is nothing more to life than that. I have won."

"My mother—" she whispered.

"She was nothing. Half Hand was nothing. Maxie was nothing except that she almost beat me. I had been told she'd taken a lover but I never knew she was pregnant until I heard from your muscle-bound boyfriend. I knew you weren't related to me and I never would have seen you if it hadn't been for the money."

It was difficult for Samantha to understand reasoning such as his. Maybe he was right and she did believe that everyone was just like her, but she'd always thought that everyone in the world wanted love and friendship. But if that's what all people wanted, there wouldn't be people like this man.

"I hate you," she whispered.

He smiled at her, a soft, smug little smile, as though he knew every thought that was in her head, and it was at that moment that Samantha knew he wanted her to kill him. Trying to look at him without hatred clouding her vision, she saw an old, frail man, and worst of all, she saw a poor man. Mike had said that, from what they could find out, Doc had no more money, that protecting his own life had taken everything. Who would take care of him if he had no money to buy caretakers? she wondered. Would he spend the rest of his life in a nursing home with overbearing nurses calling him Tony?

Looking again at him, she knew that if she shot him, he'd go to hell thinking he'd won the final round, for he'd made *her* go to prison for killing a murderer.

Moving her hand slightly to the right, she fired the pistol, all six rounds, into the wall behind him.

The next thing Samantha knew, Mike was holding a snifter of brandy to her lips. "Drink it," he ordered and she did, but Mike had to hold her hands as she was shaking too badly to hold the glass herself.

"How . . ." When her voice was trembling too hard to speak, she had to start again. "How did Michael Ransome survive?"

12 May 1928

When the orderly saw the body of Michael Ransome, he knew without a doubt that the man was dead; nobody could lose that much blood and live. There had to be at least twenty bullets in the bottom half of him; his legs looked like ground meat.

But when the orderly bent over him, the man opened his eyes, and instantly, the orderly yelled, "Hey, this one is still—"

With the little bit of strength he had left, Michael clutched at the man's arm and said, "If you have any kindness in you, don't let them know I'm alive."

The orderly was sure the man was going into shock and had no idea what he was saying. "You're bleeding to death."

"If they know I'm alive, I'll bleed more."

At that moment some man walked up, a big man with a bulge that could only be a gun under his coat and looked down at Mike's mutilated body. "How's this one?"

The orderly knew that this was a gang killing, but this time there were several women dead. In fact, all the women in the chorus had been mowed down. One uninjured man, who had seen everything, said that the women were the first to go, as though the men with the machine guns had been told to kill them first, as though they had a grudge against the women. The man had also said that three machine guns had aimed specially for this man under the sheet who should have been dead but wasn't, and for some odd reason, they'd shot him only below the belt.

The orderly covered Michael's face with the sheet. "He's dead." At that, the big man nodded and walked away, looking as though he were satisfied.

When the man was gone, the orderly leaned over Mike and whispered, "I'll do what I can to keep anyone from knowing you're alive." Later, he felt bad when he had to tell the woman that Mike was dead, but if he'd told her the truth, she would have given the secret away. The minute the orderly had a chance, he went backstage and tried to find her, but she was nowhere to be seen. In what was obviously the women's dressing room the orderly saw a pool of blood, but there was no body.

The orderly had to wait until all the people who were officially alive had been removed until he could get the man under the sheet to the hospital. At the hospital the doctor yelled at him for leaving a bleeding man for last and had even told the orderly it was no use trying to patch him up, that this man was beyond hope and he had others who needed him more. But the orderly had nearly begged and so, with a sigh, the doctor sent Mike to the operating room.

Two days later, it was the orderly who came to Mike's room and told him he had to get out. "They're checking the hospital and I think they're looking for you."

In a haze of drugs and pain, Mike asked the orderly to take him to a telephone, saying that he had to call someone.

Mike called his war buddy, Franklin Taggert, a man whose life he'd saved. Afterward, in the hospital, Frank had told Mike that if he ever needed anything at all, all he had to do was ask.

Now, Mike asked his friend for help.

Within two hours a barrage of police cars appeared and took Mike away to a waiting plane, and Mike was flown to Chandler, Colorado, to the home of his friend, where he was given the best of medical care. When he was well, his friend's family became his family.

During those years Mike wondered what had happened to Maxie; but he dared not make inquiries for fear of Doc's finding either one of them. Mike liked to think that Maxie and their child were safe somewhere, but it wasn't until 1964, when he saw the picture in the paper that he knew for sure that the woman he loved had not only survived but was happy, as he could see from the picture of her holding her pretty little granddaughter. *Our* granddaughter, Mike thought, glad that he was going to leave something of himself behind. It was after seeing the news photo that he began work on a book that was going to be titled *The Surgeon.*

1991

"I think you'd better come now," Blair said softly to Mike, her eyes telling him what he didn't want to hear.

"Sammy," he said softly.

Samantha took one look at him and knew. "I'm not fragile, Mike," she said, standing and smoothing Maxie's red dress. On the front of it was blood, not real blood, but the glycerine-based movie blood that stayed fresh and red forever. H.H. Walden had played Half Hand and it had been his father who had been the little boy hiding in the closet and seen Doc kill his father. It had been Maxie who had paid for H.H.'s education, as well as his siblings', and, after she had found them, had kept his family from starving over the years.

"My grandmother is dying, isn't she?" Samantha said, looking from Blair to Mike.

Mike wasn't going to lie to her, nor was Blair. "Yes," Blair said.

"Does she know?"

"Yes. She's asked to see you and Mike. She wants to talk to you."

"Yes," Samantha said, "I need to know about Granddad Cal." It suddenly seemed important to her to know that the man she'd loved so much had been loved by his wife, that Maxie hadn't just loved Michael Ransome.

Samantha didn't have to force herself to smile when she saw her grandmother lying on the bed covered with pretty pink sheets. Blair had had her moved to Jubilee's Place early in the day so she could watch everything, but after Samantha as Maxie had walked out the back door, Blair had moved her patient to a private room—the room that had once been Michael Ransome's dressing room.

As she always did, Samantha climbed in bed with her grandmother, but now Maxie was too weak to clutch her in return.

"Tell me what happened," Samantha said, smoothing Maxie's hair from her forehead, feeling that her body was already growing cooler. Both she and Mike had to lean forward to hear her.

"I walked out," Maxie whispered, her voice raspy. "I had no luggage, just what I had on, my purse, and the cloth bag Joe had given me. I went to the train station and bought a ticket, using all the money I had in my purse. I could go to Louisville, Kentucky, and no further. When I got to the depot in Louisville, I sat down on a bench. I was hungry—I hadn't eaten in two days—the man I loved was dead, I had wounded, possibly mortally, a man who would want revenge, I was three months' pregnant, and I had no home, nothing. All I thought I had was ten thousand dollars in a cloth bag, marked money, money that would cost me my life if I spent a penny of it, and some jewelry that could be traced if I pawned it."

As she took a breath, Sam and Mike waited for her to continue, knowing that she had to tell what she knew. "It was in Louisville, when I went to the restroom to try to wash the blood out of my dress, that I looked in the bag and saw a little pouch in the bottom of it. It was a pouch full of large diamonds, three million dollars' worth to be exact, all of Doc's take. Half Hand must have converted the money to diamonds to make it portable. After I saw those stones I knew for sure that if Doc or any of his men found me my life would be over. I went back to the waiting room to debate whether to end my life or not."

A smile came over Maxie's face. "A young man sat beside me and said, 'You look like I feel. You want to get something to eat and talk about it?' I looked into his kind brown eyes and said, 'Yes,' and that was how I met Calvin Elliot. He took me to a cafe, we drank coffee and ate, and I told him everything, while he listened completely, listened without judging me. When I'd finished he told me about himself. He'd just been discharged from the army and two years before both his parents had died of heart failure, and four months ago the girl he'd loved since elementary school had eloped with a man she'd known for six days. And three days ago the army had told him that a bout of mumps two years before had left him sterile."

For a moment Maxie had to fight for breath, while Samantha resisted the urge to tell her to rest, to be quiet, but both of them knew that now no amount of rest was going to save Maxie.

When she continued, Maxie's voice was just a whisper. "Cal and I sat there and looked at each other, neither of us knowing what to say next, when Cal said we ought to get married. He said it made sense, that he was never going to have kids of his own and it would be a shame if I had a child who had to grow up without a father. He said we didn't love each other now and we might never love each other, but we'd love the child and that would be enough."

"And you said yes," Samantha said, holding Maxie's rapidly weakening body.

"Not right away. I told him how dangerous it would be if Doc's men found me. But Cal said we'd create a new identity for me, and they'd never find me. I tried to talk him out of it. I told him there was nothing in it for him, but Cal laughed and said I hadn't looked in a mirror lately."

"So you married him."

"Three days later," Maxie said, closing her eyes for a moment. "And Doc didn't find me until he saw the photo in the paper, so I left, but even that didn't save your mother."

"And you did come to love him." Samantha's words were too loud as she changed the subject, as though her grandmother's closed eyes frightened her. She wanted to pray for God not to take her, but Samantha wasn't that selfish. Maxie had never said a word, but Sam knew that she was in constant pain that intensified daily; the doctor said that since Samantha had come into her life Maxie wouldn't take her pain pills because she didn't want to be groggy and miss a moment with her dear granddaughter.

"Yes," Maxie continued, her eyes fluttering open. "Loving Cal was very easy. He wasn't exciting like Michael, and he was never one for surprises, but he was always there when I needed him."

She looked up at her granddaughter with love in her eyes. "Cal always loved me, just as I loved him."

And that's how Maxie died, with a look of love on her face.

"I'm worried about her," Blair said to Kane. They were in Mike's town house, sitting beside each other on stools at the little counter in the kitchen, listening to the sounds coming from behind Samantha's apartment door. From inside they could hear Samantha crying—crying as Blair had never heard anyone cry before—and, what's more, it had been going on for hours. Maxie had died at about two in the morning. Afterward Mike had carried Sam from the room and taken her back to the town house, Blair and Kane following them. Mike's parents had taken Kane's boys and were spending the night at Blair's apartment.

As soon as the four of them had entered the house, Mike had taken Samantha upstairs. Through the door, Blair and Kane had heard Mike shouting, "Cry! Goddamn you, cry! Your grandmother is at least worth giving away some of those precious tears of yours!"

"Of all the—" Blair began and started for the stairs, horrified by the what she'd heard Mike say. How dare he treat someone like that after what Samantha had been through?

Stopping her, Kane looked hard into her eyes. As children Mike and Kane had been more than brothers, they were like clones of each other, and she doubted if either of them had ever considered keeping a secret from the other. She could tell from the look in Kane's eyes that there were things going on that she didn't know about but Kane did, and he was asking her to trust Mike.

There were more shouted words from Mike. Then suddenly, abruptly, they could hear Samantha crying, great, wrenching sobs of misery that seemed to echo through the house like a ghost that had died in agony.

Sitting downstairs, Blair and Kane listened in silence, neither of them speaking. What could they say while hearing the despondency and despair that was coming from Samantha?

After two hours, Blair said she couldn't stand it anymore, then opening her bag, she got out a hypodermic. "I'm going to give her something to make her sleep."

Kane put his hand on hers. "Samantha has years of tears inside her," was his cryptic answer.

Reluctantly, Blair put the hypodermic away and, instead, filled a pitcher with water. "She's going to be dehydrated," she said and went up the stairs. When she returned, Kane looked at her in question.

"Mike is holding her, and she's still crying as though she never intends to stop." Pouring herself another cup of coffee, Blair sat down with Kane to continue their silent vigil.

When they first heard Samantha's voice raised in anger, both Blair and Kane jumped and looked at each other. Samantha's voice became louder, then they heard her start to curse, curse so creatively that Kane raised his eyebrows in admiration.

When the first dish smashed overhead, Blair got up, as though to go upstairs and put a stop to this nonsense, but Kane put his hand over hers and halted her.

The shouting, the cursing, the sound of dishes crashing and shattering, and what had to be furniture being tossed about went on for over an hour. During that time they heard the words *father, Richard, sex* was mentioned often, *Doc,* and *Half Hand.*

Just when Blair was beginning to think that Samantha was

never going to stop, there was a sudden silence, and she and Kane looked upward, wondering what was happening now.

After a while Mike came down the stairs, and Blair had never seen him look so awful, but there was happiness behind the black circles underneath his eyes. "She's going to be all right now," he said, taking the stool vacated by his brother, who had his hand on Mike's shoulder. "She's sleeping."

Seeing the skepticism on Blair's face, Mike took her hand and squeezed it. "Really, she's okay. Pour me a brandy and a big glass of milk for Sam will you? I'm going to wake her up and tell her something."

At those words, he exchanged looks with his twin, neither of them needing words to know what Mike was going to tell Sam.

With the brandy and the milk on a tray, Mike went upstairs to Sam where she lay exhausted on her bed. The living room was a mess, and in the rest of the apartment she'd broken a great many things that had been chosen for her father, for at last she had been able to scream her rage at him for deserting her after her mother died and for practically forcing her to marry a man like her ex-husband.

Setting the tray on the bedside table, Mike woke her, took her in his arms, and told her that people die and people are born and that's what life is all about.

"Mike," Samantha said tiredly, "what are you taking about?"

"Babies," he said. "New life replacing the old." When she still looked puzzled, he placed his hands on her stomach. "You're carrying a new life, a life that will replace Maxie and your mother and your father and your granddad Cal."

Samantha was so tired that she could hardly understand him, but when she did, she put her hands over his on her stomach. "Do you think so?" she said, trying to sound calm.

"I'm sure of it." He wasn't fooled by her apparent tranquility, for her heart was pounding against his arm. "In my family I've had enough experience with morning sickness that I know when a woman's going to have a baby. I've held the heads of my pregnant sisters, cousins, aunts, even my mother when she was carrying Jilly. Samantha, my love, you've been having morning sickness for nearly a week now."

She was stroking her stomach and Mike's hand. "Do you think I might have twins?"

Mike kissed her ear. "Kane gave his wife twins on the first

try and I wouldn't want him to beat me, so I guess it has to be two of them, so drink your milk and make my kids healthy," he said, handing the glass to her.

"Michael, I lo—"

He put his fingertips over her lips. "I know." He didn't want to hear the words, words that were in every book, on TV, everywhere you looked until the words had become common—and meaningless.

"By the way," he said brightly, "are you planning to make my kids bastards?"

Smiling, she closed her eyes for a moment. "Mike, may I have a big wedding, a really very big, huge wedding?"

Mike was glad her eyes were closed so she couldn't see his grimace. "One of those weddings where they pray a lot and talk about 'uniting the love of these two fine young people'?"

Samantha opened her eyes, and the expression on her face matched his. "Heavens no! I want a cajun band and crawfish étouffé and enchiladas and lots of tequila and dancing that goes on for three days. I want lots of laughter and . . . and lots of children born nine months later."

Mike was looking down at her with shining eyes. "I knew the first moment I met you that I loved you, I just had no idea how much."

"Mike," she said as she licked away a milk mustache, "how long can we continue to, you know, before it hurts the babies?"

"In the delivery room," he said seriously as he ran his hand up her leg.

"Is that true?" Samantha asked, playing the ingenue.

He stretched out beside her. "Trust me, I know about these things."

"Wouldn't that, er, inconvenience the doctor?"

He was moving on top of her, running his hand down her side. "Naw, the doctor will be a relative, and they understand about my family."

"*Our* family. I'm going to adopt them."

"Sure, sweetheart, whatever you say." He was fumbling with her skirt. "Where's the goddamn button on this thing? Ahhh," he said at the sound of ripping cloth. "There's your button."

Epilogue

Samantha followed Mike out of the elevator, her stomach going ahead of her like a tugboat that she was moving in the wake of. Just this morning Blair's tests had shown that Samantha was indeed carrying twins, and while Sam sat on her chair, stunned, tears of happiness streaming down her face, Mike listened to the prenatal care that Blair proscribed for her.

Afterward, they went to F.A.O. Schwarz and bought toys, then bought maternity wear for Samantha. She wasn't big enough to need anything but loose garments yet, but she had insisted on wearing a maternity top out of the store.

"Show-off!" Mike had said, grinning with pride at her, wondering if in two weeks, when they were to be married in Colorado, in a reception with nearly five hundred guests, she'd wear a white maternity gown. Sam was so proud of being pregnant that he had no doubt that she would.

The only sour note in the day was that this morning an express letter had arrived from his brother Frank and in it was a key. Mike hadn't yet told Sam about the letter or the key, because the letter concerned Maxie's will, which she had given to Frank, naming him as her executor. Sam hadn't had enough time to recover from Maxie's death, and Mike knew that the death of Doc from what had apparently been a suicide had also affected her.

Maxie had left a letter telling that she had taken Half Hand Joe's diamonds with her when she left Louisville in 1964 and gone to Amsterdam and sold them. She'd also spent a little of the cash Half Hand had left her, but she was afraid to spend too much of it, afraid of being caught and leading a trail back to Cal and her family.

Frank, who, among other things, had a law degree, had made out the will for her and with his usual finesse had asked her what she'd done with the millions she must have received for the diamonds. Frank wrote Mike that Maxie had laughed and said she'd spent every penny of it. Mike could almost hear his brother's disdain for that remark, because Frank didn't believe in buying anything that wasn't going to triple in value.

One of the things Maxie had bought was an apartment in New York, where she'd lived in relative seclusion for many years after she left her husband and son, having decided to live in the city where she could keep an eye on what Doc was doing. Maxie told Frank that her biggest regret in life was the picture that had appeared in the newspaper after Samantha was born, for it had caused her to have to leave and, ultimately, it had caused the death of Allison Elliot. Doc had tired of searching for Maxie after he'd found her in Louisville only to have her disappear as she'd done after she'd crippled him in 1928. So, years later, he'd sent a man to find out if her family knew anything about where she'd gone. Unfortunately, Allison had been the one the man had caught.

In her will, Maxie left the apartment and the contents to Samantha, and that was where he was taking Sam now, having waited until she was in such good spirits that *nothing* would be able to bring her down.

Still glowing from Blair's report, Samantha floated into the apartment—and came up short at a picture of herself as a baby in a silver frame on a narrow table in the foyer.

"This is my grandmother's apartment," Samantha said softly to Mike, and he nodded.

With her hands on her belly that she dearly wished were

larger, she walked about the apartment. It was spacious, what the realtors called a classic six, a penthouse with three terraces. Samantha thought the apartment was decorated beautifully, not contrived as too many interior decorators made a place look. Maxie's apartment was the home of a beautiful woman to whom taste was as natural as breathing.

When Samantha walked back into the living room after exploring the other rooms, Mike was leaning against the mantlepiece, an odd expression on his face.

"What's wrong?"

"I think I know what Maxie bought with Half Hand's millions." When Samantha looked puzzled, he said, "Did you look at the pictures in this place?"

Like an English country house, the walls were covered with paintings, as were the tabletops and nearly every flat surface. "They're lovely," Sam said. "Don't you like them?"

Mike looked at a tiny watercolor on the mantel. "When I was in college I had to take an elective course in art so I chose something called Lost Art. It was a study of art that has disappeared over the centuries. A lot of architecture has been torn down, gold sculpture melted, jewelry broken up, that sort of thing, and many paintings have disappeared in the last one hundred years. The Russian Revolution, World War II, et cetera. I wasn't seriously interested in the course, but if my memory is right, I think I see three of those paintings on the wall behind you."

Pausing, he waited as Samantha turned to look at the oils—French Impressionists. "If my memory for paintings isn't good, I do remember numbers," Mike continued. "Sam, if these paintings *are* some of the lost art and if you can prove ownership, I think you may be a very rich young lady."

"*Very* rich?" she asked.

"Very, very, very rich." He quirked an eyebrow at her. "What do you plan to do with your newly found wealth?"

Smiling, Samantha answered instantly. "I am going to open some nursing homes," she said, as though she'd been thinking about what she'd do if she suddenly came into a great deal of money. "*Nice* nursing homes. Places where the people are treated with respect and the lights don't buzz. And I'm going to call them 'Maxie's.' " Then, with a soft smile of satisfaction, a smile that conveyed her feeling of irony, she said, "And the first one I'm going to open will be in Doc's Connecticut estate."

With a startled look, Samantha put her hand on her stomach. "Mike, do you think it's too early to feel the twins kick?"

"Yes," he said softly. "I think that was Maxie giving her approval for what you want to do. Come on," he said, holding out his arm for her, "let's go feed my babies." Pausing a moment, he looked at the late afternoon sun that touched her hair, turning it golden. "All three of my babies."

Thank You

I couldn't have written this book without all I've learned about New York over the last ten years, and I'd like to think that I couldn't have written it without the fulfillment of a dream: I bought my own apartment in my dear, beloved city.

I'd like to thank Paula Novick, realtor extraordinaire, of Douglas Elliman, for taking me to see town houses in New York and for finding my lovely apartment for me—and for becoming my friend along the way.

Nancy Miller of the Bank of New York (51st Street branch) helped me attain my dream and made me laugh while doing it. Thank you.

The people of Pocket Books readily wrote and rewrote letters of recommendation for me so that I could pass the co-op board:

Jack Romanos, who wrote about numbers, as well as said kind things about me.

Bill Grose, who went to the apartment with me and gave his approval and his advice.

Richard Snyder, who so graciously helped me with every aspect of my apartment.

Lily Alice's dad, a.k.a. Irwyn Applebaum, my publisher, who writes letters for me, cheers me up, gives me money, takes me to lunch, and makes me laugh until I can hardly stand up.

Thank you very, very much.

I'd like to thank Carrie Feron of Putnam-Berkley, for showing me some interesting parts of New York, such as the street fair and the antiques market on Second Avenue. Carrie was also one of the first readers of *Sweet Liar* and didn't mind telling me again and again that she liked the book.

I'd like to thank the people at the Santa Fe ComputerLand for selling me all nine of my computers, as well as eight printers—nearly all of which I still have. (I love the exasperating little dudes.)

My friend Judith McNaught taught me, by example, how to McNaughtize my book, then stayed up all night reading *Sweet Liar* and called me to tell me how much she liked it.

Special thanks go to the Pocket Books production staff, unsung heroes who make my books look so good. I pestered them a lot with this one. And, Sophie, we all miss you.

I would like to thank Lamont for climbing mountain after mountain with me while I plotted *Sweet Liar.* He was the best listener I ever had, never losing patience at hearing the same pieces of plot over and over as I worked them out. If he didn't have four feet, I'd marry him.

Most of all, I'd like to thank two very important people in my life: my secretary/friend, Gail; and my editor/friend, Linda. Thank you more than I can say.